THEIR

COLD

HEARTS

BOOKS BY CARLA KOVACH

DETECTIVE GINA HARTE SERIES

The Next Girl

Her Final Hour

Her Pretty Bones

The Liar's House

Her Dark Heart

Her Last Mistake

Their Silent Graves

The Broken Ones

One Left Behind

Her Dying Wish

One Girl Missing

Her Deadly Promise

What She Did

Find Me

The Houseshare

Meet Me at Marmaris Castle

Whispers Beneath the Pines

Flame

THEIR COLD HEARTS

CARLA KOVACH

bookouture

Published by Bookouture in 2023

An imprint of Storyfire Ltd.
Carmelite House
50 Victoria Embankment
London EC4Y 0DZ

www.bookouture.com

ISBN: 978-1-83790-238-5
eBook ISBN: 978-1-83790-237-8

This book is a work of fiction. Names, characters, businesses, organizations, places and events other than those clearly in the public domain, are either the product of the author's imagination or are used fictitiously. Any resemblance to actual persons, living or dead, events or locales is entirely coincidental.

I'd like to dedicate this book to everyone who is about to lose their home, has just lost their home, those who are sofa surfing, staying in a hostel or are on the streets. There's nothing worse than having nowhere safe to live.

PROLOGUE

Fifteen years ago

Shouting and laughter echoed through the building. She pulled her quilt right up to her neck, anything to keep the pinching cold out. The curtains didn't quite cover the window in length or width. Through the centre gap, she could see the moon at its fullest and she watched on, mesmerised as a cloud covered it, taking away her only bit of light.

From the bed next to hers, his gentle snores started again. Since he'd told the party to shut up about an hour ago, he'd fallen asleep with ease, not like her. She hadn't been close to sleep. He'd told her to try earplugs, like him, but she didn't like them one bit. She flinched as he snorted before continuing to snore.

The only thing separating them was an old divider. That piece of junk was the only thing that gave her any privacy in this dump. She missed her old room in her old house with its posters on the walls and her comfy bed. She missed her mum, but she couldn't think about her right now. It hurt too much.

A yell came from the end of the corridor, followed by a burst of laughter. She wondered what her best friend Meg would think of this place. It didn't matter though; she'd never bring Meg here. As far as Meg knew, she was staying with an aunt, not in a hovel in town. She'd been careful to come and go so that no one saw her. The embarrassment at school would get too much and she had already been picked on because of the damp smell that lingered on all her clothes. No one could ever know. She wished Meg would invite her to stay in her warm house. A few months ago, they were always having sleepovers. She pictured being in Meg's double bed with her super thick quilt and huge TV. Her friend always had the latest console and was able to watch Netflix, something she'd never had access to. Meg's mum was lovely too, always buying them a pizza and lots of goodies to eat. Instead, she shivered in the darkness.

The cold that felt like it was stiffening her bones never eased. She ran her fingers over her quilt, and it was as wet as the inside of the windowpanes.

The laughter on the landing stopped. She'd been told to keep away from the other residents, that they were trouble, but she liked to give people a chance. The other people on their floor were loud, they were drunk and maybe some of them were on drugs; but she felt sad for them. They had lost their homes too. She tried to remember to be kind if she saw any of them.

Bladder full, she began to wriggle in bed. She wasn't allowed to unlock the door and leave the room once they'd settled in for the night.

The gentle snores from the bed behind the divider continued. Maybe she could creep across the room, trying not to step on all their worldly belongings that seemed to be scattered all over the floor. She wouldn't need to turn any lights on so no one would know she was out there. She wouldn't even flush the chain. Either she went now, or she'd wet the bed and she'd never let that happen.

She poked her foot out of the bottom of the bed and it creaked as she moved. One foot out, then another. She stepped out and swiftly pulled the quilt back over the mattress, trying to preserve some of the warmth. If she could see, she knew there would be white vapour coming from her mouth every time she exhaled. Shivering, she took a few steps forward. Her bag of schoolbooks was just ahead. With her toes leading, she moved her foot trying to find them. The last thing she wanted to do was to crush her water bottle as she'd never get a replacement. *Slowly does it.*

She passed the other bed. Holding her breath, she waited for the snores to get louder before turning the lock.

Stepping into the corridor, she placed one foot in front of the other as she held on to the wall. There was a light ahead. A room door was open. Then she heard chattering and quiet laughter. Glasses clinked as the people swore and slurred. Thankfully, she didn't need to go as far as that room.

Running towards the toilet door, she opened it and locked herself in. She sat on the loo, panting with fear. Now, all she had to do was get back. Light still off, she unlocked the door and peered through the gap. One of the drinkers was on the landing.

Just open the door and run. Get back in your room and lock the door.

Taking a deep breath, she stepped out. A man stared at her as she swayed. The others shouted for the man to come back but his gaze stayed on her. Should she scream? Should she run? That would look silly. They were just a little drunk. 'Hi.' That was all she could say. She nervously tugged at the end of her pyjama top in the hope that he would stop staring and move out of the way.

A woman peered around the door and smiled warmly at her. 'Come join us. Have a drink.' The woman held a bottle out to her. She'd only ever tried cider once, that was when Meg's mum and dad had gone out. They shared a can and giggled all night.

She wasn't allowed to drink but she didn't want to upset the man. If she was nice, he'd be nice. They'd all be nice. She took the bottle as they led her into the room.

ONE

Saturday, 12 November

'Shut the door, arsehole,' the freak in the room on the bottom floor had shouted as Wesley had hurried up the stairs. He had shut the door, at least he thought he had. He didn't intend to wake anyone, and he had tried not to knock into the walls as he tripped up the stairs, but he was more than a little bit merry. It was hard trying to turn over a new leaf. He had so much to prove and yet, even with the effort he'd made to be considerate, he was still managing to annoy people.

'Sorry,' he called back, hoping that the man had heard him call all the way down the stairwell. He hiccupped as he pushed open his room door in the very eaves of the Cleevesford Cleaver Hostel. There were two rooms at the top. A single woman with a young child was staying in the one next door. He hated the way she looked at him when he was tipsy, the way she shielded her little girl as they passed. He'd never hurt a child, ever. Yes, he was unkempt but that didn't make him dangerous. He lifted his armpits up and sniffed. He did smell. Maybe that was it. Tomorrow, he'd try to talk to her and maybe say hello again. Clumsily feeling along the wall, he flicked the hallway light switch off.

He flung his door closed and it accidentally banged a couple of times before settling slightly ajar. This time, the weirdo on the bottom floor didn't come out to complain.

Wesley peered into the darkness of the landing. There was no lock on his door any more. He had to smash his way back in the other day when he lost the key, but who cared? He'd lived on the streets most of his adult life and there was no lock on his tent. If anyone came in, he'd do whatever it took to defend himself, although, given how much weird crap he'd poured down his neck that night, he wouldn't be able to do much.

The Cleevesford Cleaver was a dump, and everyone knew it, but it was his temporary home, for now. There was a stench that seemed to come from the walls and every time the wind picked up, the panes rattled like he was stuck in some Victorian horror film. People kept telling him that he should be grateful but why should he? Not one of them had really helped him. He sometimes got a room for a night, for a week or even a month but, inevitably, he always ended up back on the streets. Their help wasn't enough. The drink won every time and doctors, mental health experts; none of their assistance had worked on him. If it wasn't so cold, he'd prefer sleeping at the back of the graveyard where he didn't have hoity-toity idiots lecturing him on how to sort his life out when they had no understanding of why things were so bad. He still had his tent all folded up in the wardrobe, along with the sleeping bag that he'd had from the start and that made him shiver. All those cold nights spent battling the elements were enough to give anyone nightmares. As he swallowed, the pipes rattled like there were rats stuck in them.

Right now, the freeze that had given him a bad infection

had ensured that he got to spend a few nights here, at least until his lungs recovered. For that he was grateful, so he had to stop having these moaning thoughts. Some of his mates were still out there in the biting cold. It didn't matter about the smell or the pipes. He'd find a way of sorting his life out.

Earlier that evening after digesting his horrid encounter, he'd decided to meet up with the others at the Hangar. They'd pooled their drink collection, each one of them contributing something that would warm them all up. He'd stolen a bottle of this revolting liquor from the newsagent after leaving the pub, the only thing he could reach without going behind the counter and drawing attention to himself. He wouldn't get a caution this time if he got caught. He was sick to death of getting into trouble with shop security and the police. The others, they understood. They were just like him, lost and cold. Homeless support and housing officers never understood, the police just enjoyed throwing more stress his way, all of them stopping him from getting work or a place to live. No one knew what it was like to exist on the streets, to try and survive from day to day, and the worst thing, to feel invisible. His tribe never made him feel like that and they understood, not like his so-called best friend. He hiccupped while trying to remain upright then he shook his head. His tribe were family, but he had to break away. If he was to ever see his child again, he needed to stop drinking. He stared at the Alcoholics Anonymous phone number that he'd scrawled on the wall.

Tomorrow, he was going to call them, and he was going to change his life. He staggered across the room and held on to the bottom of the bed frame, not daring to move in case he fell. For a moment, he allowed himself to close his eyes for a second and imagined holding his little one close, taking in that sweet child smell and the unconditional love that children give back. AA had to work. Last chance and all that.

One minute he was staring at the peeling wallpaper behind

his bed with his mouth open as he began to nod off, the next, the light had gone out and he was plunged into darkness. The door to his room banged on its hinges. Wesley gasped. 'Who's there?' he whispered in a shaky voice through his warm alcohol breath. Eyes not yet adjusted; he still couldn't make out who the shadow of a person was. He went to stagger across the room but was interrupted by the single wooden chair that his clothes were sprawled over. 'Come any closer and I'll kill you.' He would, too. If that bully from downstairs thought he could scare Wesley Reid, he had another thing coming. Squinting, he tried to adjust his vision to the darkness, but his inebriated state had left him feeling like everything was swaying. He caught the outline of a face, but the features were blurred. Man? Woman? He couldn't tell.

Something wet splashed his face. Some of the drizzling liquid had reached his lips and slipped into his mouth. It was cider.

'Get back,' he called reaching out, but the stranger splashed him again, right in the eyes. He tried to rub the liquid from his aggravated eyes. Water, he needed to get to the sink in the side room. Staggering, he reached out with flailing arms, hoping to strike his aggressor but he had no chance. Blind and unable to stand, he was at a disadvantage. 'What do you want?' he yelled.

The stranger didn't reply. Panic rose in his chest and his stomach began to churn. He'd had his moments on the streets but nothing this weird had ever happened. Instead of running to the bathroom, he charged forwards, knocking everything every-where. He needed to get back onto the landing and knock on his neighbour's door for help. As he ran for the exit, his own door slammed into his face, knocking him violently onto the carpet. He fell to the floor, hoping to be able to grab anything that might make a useful weapon. He had a Swiss Army knife some-where. It was under the bed. Crawling in the dark, breathing heavily, he reached in the direction of the bed and felt underneath for the knife. As he went to grab it, the stranger crunched his fingers with a heavy boot, forcing him to miss the knife.

He wrestled with the foot and managed to get free. That's when he felt the white-hot pain in his neck, followed by a warm trickling down his back. He crawled a short way along the carpet then used the bed frame to heave himself up. All his years on the streets, all the fights and drunken accidents; he'd never felt pain like it. As he struggled for his last breaths, he flopped onto the bed and felt the stranger lift his legs up. He wanted to shout and scream. *Why? Why me? I'm no one.*

The stranger replied as if his thoughts had been heard. What he said sent a final shiver through Wesley Reid as he stopped fighting. All he could see in his mind's eye was his perfect little girl. How had he screwed up so badly? If only he could turn back time. His choking breaths filled the room as the stranger stood in the darkness.

As the life seeped out of him, he stared blurrily as the light of the moon caught the glint of metal in his attacker's hand.

No one would miss him. No one would care. That's when the stranger closed his eyelids. He couldn't fight it. The stranger leaned close to his ear and whispered, 'She's next.'

In his mind, Wesley was sobbing his heart out in a way he never imagined possible. The animal above him was going for his daughter and there wasn't a thing he could do about it.

TWO

Sunday, 13 November

Gina lay on the living room floor laughing as her and Gracie's den collapsed. Both still in their pyjamas, their toast half-eaten on the coffee table, she hadn't had so much fun in ages, and she had Gracie until Tuesday while her daughter Hannah was away with her partner, Greg.

'Nanny, can you help me build it again?' Her red-cheeked granddaughter smiled.

Gina reached out and tackled the little girl gently to the floor while grabbing her toy hippo and making ridiculous noises. 'Lettie is coming to get you,' Gina screamed as Gracie got to her feet and let out a joyous shriek as she ran into the kitchen. Gina's cat, Ebony, hissed and darted out of the cat flap, not liking their energetic guest at all.

Gina rubbed her aching back as she used the arm of the settee to pull herself up. She hurried into the kitchen, then she stopped and stared at her phone on the worktop. Briggs was calling.

'Nanny, come and get me.'

Gasping for breath, Gina leaned against the worktop, not wanting to answer his call. Speaking to Briggs was painful and too much talking would lead to more and that scared her. The intensity of what they had had complicated her life. Did she want that again, just because he was sorry? She swallowed as the phone rang and rang. He'd ended their secret relationship so he could be with Rosemary, then he'd discovered that the woman had cheated on him.

'Nanny,' Gracie said as she tugged the belt of her dressing gown. 'Let's go and fix the den.' The phone stopped ringing. She'd done the right thing. Focusing on herself and healing her broken heart had helped. She stared at the phone and sighed. He had left the hugest hole in her life. Her fingers itched to call him back.

'Gracie, can you give Nanny a minute?'

'But we're playing.'

Gina crouched and tucked Gracie's long light-brown hair behind her ears. 'I tell you what, while Nanny makes a phone call, can you go and hide, then I'll come and find you?'

Gracie bit her finger as if contemplating that idea over rebuilding a den, before nodding. 'Okay, Nanny. Count to one hundred, then come and get me.'

'Go,' Gina shouted, and the little girl giggled as she ran out of the room. Snatching her phone, Gina's stomach flipped as she pressed Briggs's number. He was calling while she had holiday booked, on a Sunday morning. He knew she had Gracie staying over, she'd told the team how much she was looking forward to spending quality time with her granddaughter. She hoped that whatever he had to say would be important.

'Gina.'

'I'm on holiday.'

'I know, and I'm sorry. I wouldn't call if it wasn't urgent. You can say no but I'll be honest, we need you on this case. As you know the department is stretched and quite frankly, there is no one else I'd rather ask to take the lead. It will take the whole team and your experience. I've never come across anything like it in my life.' He went quiet as he waited for her answer.

She exhaled. It wasn't a personal call, but it was an inconvenience. She had a child to care for and it wasn't like she could drop Gracie home. Hannah wasn't even in the country. 'I have my granddaughter.'

'Meet me at the scene, please. I'll look after Gracie for you. I'll do anything to have you on the case.'

She bit her bottom lip. Briggs had let her down, but he loved children and she trusted him to look after Gracie. She pictured her at the station with a stack of paper and some pens playing police make-believe. 'Where are you?'

'A man has been murdered at the Cleevesford Cleaver Hostel so I'm there, but I could really do with being back at the station. The press is already on my back. Forensics have just arrived. Jacob is at the airport, picking his mother up. Wyre and O'Connor are here. Thank you for saying yes. It's all a bit cryptic so we need the best brains on this one.'

'I haven't said yes. I asked where you were.'

She felt the weight of his pause.

'Gina, if this is about what happened, I am so sorry. I meant every word that day when I came to yours. I don't know what came over me. I craved that something I couldn't have but it was never Rosemary. It was a family and I realise now; I've left it all too late and being with someone else wouldn't work, but not having children has left a huge hole in my life. I can't explain how huge but it...' He paused and Gina could tell he was upset. 'Rosemary could never be you. I am the biggest fool in the world and I'm going to spend every day telling you that in the hope that you'll give me another chance. I literally hate myself and if I've lost you, it's nothing I didn't deserve.' He huffed out a breath.

Gina felt herself choking up, so she cleared her throat. She couldn't talk to him about this right now. 'Okay, yes, I'll head over. Tell me about the case.' She furrowed her brows as she listened to the details. Briggs was right. It was like nothing they'd ever come across before. 'Okay. I'm going to park at the end of the road. I want you to take Gracie away from the scene straight away. She isn't to see a thing. Okay.'

'Of course. See you soon.'

After ending the call, she ran her fingers through her unbrushed brown hair and sighed as she detangled a couple of knots. Nothing ever worked out as planned. She was meant to be enjoying a few days with Gracie but there was no way she was allowing the person who had committed such a brutal murder to stay on the streets a minute longer than needed. She huffed out a breath, annoyed that they were so underfunded and another one of her breaks had been interrupted. But she had to help. She couldn't leave her team struggling.

'Nanny, come and find me.'

She swallowed, knowing that she was going to let her granddaughter down. It was only for a few hours. She'd assess the crime scene and after that, she'd work on the leads from home. A message from Hannah flashed up on her phone.

Just checking in. How's Gracie this morning?

Gina replied.

We're just playing hide and seek. Don't worry about us, just enjoy yourself. See you in a few days.

Gina swallowed knowing that Hannah would be livid that

she'd taken Gracie to work with her, especially while working on a murder case.

Their victim was a husband and a father. Whoever killed him needed to be brought to justice. She pictured the dead man lying on a bed, stabbed in the neck. Clothes and sheets stinking of cider with a single pound coin left on his forehead, and the blood. The thought of that metallic smell made her stomach churn.

THREE

Gina pulled up just around the corner from the Cleevesford Cleaver Hostel, then sent a message to Briggs.

'Nanny, where am I going?'

'To the police station where you'll have lots of fun playing police. Nanny has a little bit of work to do.'

'I don't want to go to the police station. That's where bad people go.'

Gina turned around and glanced at Gracie on her booster seat, messy pigtails dangling down her shoulders. It had been hell trying to brush her hair in a hurry.

'You'll have so much fun, I promise.'

'Will I be able to make a den?'

Gina pressed her lips together wondering if Briggs really knew what he'd let himself in for. 'Yes, I bet Detective Chris and the others would love to make a den. They make them all the time.'

'Yay. Is that him?'

Her boss and ex-lover approached, his side-parted hair slightly flopping over his forehead. She swallowed. A part of her wanted to get out of the car, run her fingers through his hair and tell him that she understood, that she'd forgiven him. 'Yes.'

Gina opened her car door and let Gracie out of the back. She passed the booster seat to Briggs. 'Gracie, this is one of Nanny's friends and his name is Chris.'

Gracie didn't seem too bothered by him as she hugged her hippo. 'This is Lettie,' she said with a shy smile, a coil of white mist dancing as her warm breath met the freezing cold air.

Briggs bent over. 'She is adorable. Does Lettie want to play police today too?'

Gracie nodded. 'And make a den.'

'Right, chicken. Let's get you into the warm.' Gina popped Gracie into the back of Briggs's car and buckled the little girl up. Before closing the door, she leaned in and gave Gracie a kiss on the head.

'Sorry again,' Briggs said as he awkwardly stood and tucked his scarf into his thick coat. 'Oh, I have a proposition for you.'

Pressing her lips together, she waited for him to continue.

'Now, you can say no. I mentioned to O'Connor that Gracie was joining us at the station and a few minutes later, he said that Mrs O would love to look after Gracie if that was okay with you. Apparently, she's making a huge batch of cupcakes for a client's party this afternoon at the unit, and she said Gracie could go with her and make cakes for the day, then she could go back with her for tea and cakes. It's your call. Two hours of den making and a long afternoon of making cakes?' He raised his eyebrows and smiled.

Gina yanked the car door open again knowing that Gracie would have a lovely day with Detective Constable Harry O'Connor's wife, making cakes. 'Gracie, would you like to make cupcakes today? Nanny's other friend has a cake shop and she needs help, and you'd get some yummy cakes.'

'Yes, make cakes.'

'It looks like cakes are a goer. Please thank Mrs O for me.'

'Will do. Right, I'll get this little lady to the station and prepare the press release while making a den.'

'I best get this case cracked.'

He nodded and got into his car. As he drove away, Gina saw Gracie giggling at something he'd said. She went to wave goodbye, but Gracie didn't even glance her way. The stone like feeling in her gut told her that Hannah wasn't going to be happy when she found out that Gina had gone into work and left Gracie with her colleague. Gina wasn't happy but she wasn't about to leave a murderer running loose any longer than she had too. She cursed under her breath as she walked around the corner, taking in the scene. Bernard's van was parked the closest to the hostel and a shivering resident was trying to get PC Jhanvi Kapoor's attention as she filled out the crime scene log. Gina glanced up at the windows and saw Bernard walking past the top window in his forensics suit, his tall stature making him look like a giant next to his assistant. A couple of lights flashed as one of the crime scene investigators took photos.

An ambulance had pulled up on the opposite side of the road. Gina watched as a pale woman sat shaking in the back, while a little girl lay her head in the woman's lap.

Gina headed over and filled the log in. 'Morning.' Her fingers were numbing with the cold and her signature looked like spidery scrawl. 'Did Bernard say we could go up yet?'

'No.' Detective Constable Paula Wyre made her jump as she came up behind her. 'He said he'd come and speak to us in a short while. He's up there with Jennifer and a couple of CSIs. There's a communal lounge on the ground floor where we can speak to the other residents in turn. It's a lot warmer in there, guv. The woman in the ambulance lives in the room right next to the victim. She's in shock but the paramedics informed me that we should be able to speak to her soon.' The DC pulled her black woollen hat over her jet-black hair and began to blow warm breath into her hands. Her nose crimson from the cold stood out against her pale skin.

'Great, let's see what they know. Where's O'Connor?'

'He's just instructing the PCs on the door-to-doors. Should be back in five.'

'Right, fill me in with what you know.'

Wyre stepped from foot to foot as she spoke. 'Forty-year-old Wesley Reid is staying here temporarily. He's currently homeless. He either still is or was in a relationship and they have a daughter. That is literally all I have so far.'

'Has his partner been informed?'

'Not yet, but it should happen soon.'

'So, we don't want to release any personal details, not until the family has been informed. How about his parents?'

'We don't have their details yet. Sorry.'

A man stepped out of the main door. 'I want to speak to someone. I told the officer over there that it was urgent.' He pointed to PC Kapoor. She glanced back and raised her arched black eyebrows so that only Gina could see. 'Are you in charge?' He looked at Gina as he pulled his dressing gown tightly around his body.

'I'm Detective Inspector Harte and I'm leading the case. May we come into your room, or would you prefer to speak in the communal areas?'

The man ignored her question. 'There's something sick in this building, like evil in the walls. I heard it. I heard everything. I have to get out of here. You must tell the council to move me before me or my child gets hurt. Don't leave me here.'

FOUR

Wyre shuffled into the hallway and pushed the front door closed, trying to block out the bitter whistling wind that had picked up. Gina remembered when the Cleaver was a bed and breakfast but in recent weeks it had become a hostel for homeless people. She shivered as she allowed the building's past to get under her skin. Once it was a butcher's shop with living quarters above. If she inhaled deeply enough, she knew she'd smell the death of past and present.

'Can we speak in my room?' He opened the door wide to reveal a single bed and a made-up unfolded Z bed. A slight burnt aroma travelled up her nose. The set of green velvet curtains, wet from the condensation on the window made the air almost taste damp. Boxes were neatly stacked up against the back wall which quite possibly contained all the man's worldly possessions. Gina was saddened to see the child's toy pony on the pillow of the fold-up bed. A small worktop spanned across the length of the huge window and on it sat a toaster and a microwave. The humming of the mini fridge and tapping of the pipes was all Gina could hear for a few seconds until the man spoke.

'I'm scared, so scared. I heard some banging and shouting last night, and all I did was shout at him to shut up. I could have helped. I could have called the police, but I was angry with him. When he eventually shut up, I was grateful...' The man paused, knowing that what he really meant was that quietness had been restored so he thought no more of it.

'Angry?' Gina sat next to Wyre on one of the two wooden chairs in the kitchenette area.

'I hated the man. Last night, he woke my child up again, and I shouted something to him when he came in drunk. It wasn't the first time. It happened most nights.'

Wyre took out her pad and pen.

Gina glanced at the worktop. Had his anger boiled over? She scanned the area for a knife block, but there wasn't one. All that she could see was a butter-smeared, round-ended knife. 'Could I take your name please?'

'Gareth Alderman.'

'You said you are staying here with your child.'

'Yes, she's five. I took her to one of her friend's houses this morning, so she didn't have to be around all this. It's bad enough we must live here.' The man pursed his lips. 'My only crime was losing my job; I couldn't pay my mortgage after we lost her mother. Me and the little one ended up here. The council deem this place fit for children.' He smirked. 'You only have to look at it to know that no child should have to live in a place like this. I hate it. I hate everything.' The man ran his thickset fingers through his dirty blond hair. He appeared to stare into space for a few seconds, his attention on something that Gina couldn't see, then he scratched his stubbly chin.

Gina felt for the man. So many people ended up in hostels like the Cleaver, having to almost do their time before any precious social housing stock came up for rent. She glanced around again. Gareth was right, the Cleaver was no place for a child and the thought of a man being murdered two floors above made her skin crawl. She pictured the tiny girl in her mind, innocently hugging her stuffed pony while being awoken by the scary noises.

'Please tell me the council will move us.' His pleading stare cut right through Gina. 'This place gets under your skin after a while, it's like it starts to live and breathe in you. Can you feel it?'

Gina sighed. She couldn't feel anything but a cold damp building, but the stench of death was starting to permeate and it wouldn't be long before it overwhelmed them. She only hoped that Bernard and his team were working like the clappers up there. She returned his first question with a sympathetic smile. She doubted the council would listen to her even if she tried to put this man's case forward. Making false promises wasn't something she'd do. 'Mr Alderman—'

'Gaz, everyone calls me Gaz.'

'Gaz, could you please start from the beginning. Tell me about yesterday and when you first saw Mr Reid that day?'

'Mr Reid?'

'The victim. That was his name.'

'Sorry, I didn't know.' Gareth paused. 'He never made much noise during the day. It's like he slept while it was light and woke up when it was dark like some alcohol-drenched vampire. He always stank of booze. Cheap cider, I think.'

'When did you first hear him yesterday?'

'I think it was about five. Me and my kid were having dinner. We'd been to the chip shop, and we were sharing a bag while watching the telly. I heard the door slamming as he left. I knew it was him as I heard his boots thudding down the stairs and he was the only one in the building who slammed the door. Everyone else is a bit more respectful.'

'So, he went out about five yesterday evening, when did you see him next?' Gina watched Wyre catching up with the notes.

'I didn't see him as such. I just heard him. It was after

eleven, I don't know the exact time. Again, I heard his heavy feet thudding up the stairs and something alarmed me. I didn't hear the main door close which meant he'd done the second most annoying thing; he'd left it open to intrusion and the elements. I grabbed my dressing gown and went out there. I was right. The door was wide open and was swinging in the wind. The whole corridor was like an icicle, so I closed it. I remember being really annoyed as this old building is hard to heat and my daughter gets a lot of chest infections. She nearly died when she was a baby so I'm extra protective.'

'I'm sorry to hear that.' Gina could see the pain in the man's deep worry lines. She could see why he was so protective and maybe angry. 'What happened next?'

'I went back to bed. A few minutes later I heard a bit of banging, and I thought I heard shouting too. If I'm honest, I thought he'd fallen over drunk, or he was arguing with someone on his phone.'

'Did he argue on the phone a lot?'

Gareth brought his bottom lip over his top lip as he sat on his single bed. 'Yes, he'd pace the communal room with the door open while shouting.'

'Did he do that yesterday?'

'No, but he probably did it every day apart from yesterday. That's why I thought he was on his phone. It sounded like he was angry, but I couldn't catch the words. Sorry I can't help more.' He furrowed his brow. 'I didn't hear another person, though. Either he was on the phone, or the other person was really quiet.'

'Did you ever argue with Mr Reid, about the noise or anything?'

The man leaned back and clasped his hands together over his knees as he rocked slightly. 'Wait, you think I could have hurt him over a few slammed doors? He hasn't even lived in the building for long. Okay, I'm not his number one fan but I wouldn't wish any harm on the bloke. I get angry but I'm not vindictive.'

'We're just trying to establish Mr Reid's relationships and that includes those he has with the people in this building.'

'If you want to know the truth, I doubt anyone liked him. I only really speak to one of the others here in passing and that's Kayleigh. She's staying in the room next to him. She said he scared her daughter with his creepy looks. He was always plastered, and he had this glassy-eyed look about him. She said he'd been loud and sounded argumentative. Most of us in this hostel are here because we've hit hard times. We have children and people like him who are drunk or high, scare us. I know people have problems but people with his problems shouldn't be put with people like us. For heaven's sake, I wish the council would think of the kids when they place us. People like him need help but it's a different type of help to what we need.'

Gina knew that councils barely had a choice and that they were as badly funded as the police. Spare rooms were snapped up the moment someone dragged their luggage out the door. Councils were desperate for properties to become free, and the housing associations couldn't supply homes fast enough. The country was in a housing crisis when it came to the poorer people in society and Gina felt her anger simmering for him and everyone else that was stuck.

'It's true, I didn't like him, but I'd never hurt him. I'd never hurt anyone. I'm not a violent person. All I want is to leave this place and have a fresh start with my child.'

'Did Mr Reid have any visitors?'

'He only ever had one as far as I know. I saw him taking a man upstairs last week.' Gareth closed his eyes and clicked his fingers. 'It was Monday, the seventh. I remember that date as I'd just had a meeting with our homeless support officer. You don't forget meetings with homeless support officers as you go into them with this hope that they are going to magic up a flat for you. I've been here the longest, so I really thought it was my turn. It wasn't.' His shoulders slumped.

'What time was this?'

'Around five in the afternoon. It was quite dark outside, but I saw the man.'

'Tell me what they were doing?'

He scrunched his brow and stared ahead. 'I was looking out of the window, and they were standing under the streetlamp on the opposite side of the road. Hands were in the air like they were arguing. Mr Reid walked away but the man followed him into the building. I heard them running up the stairs. There was a bit of shouting, but I couldn't hear much once they reached his room. Minutes later, the man came storming down and left. That was it. I haven't seen his visitor since.'

It sounded like they had a suspect. 'Can you describe the visitor?'

'Vaguely. He looked about the same height as Mr Reid. I'd say between five nine and five eleven. He was smart-looking in his fitted coat. I remember his shoes had a shine as the light from the streetlamp bounced off them. I remember thinking that I wanted to smarten myself up and get a new job and it was on my mind that I needed to get some shoes. I'd guess that he was in his mid-thirties, clean shaven. Really smart, that's all I can think of. Brown hair, smart and nice clothes.'

'Did you hear anything at all when they were talking or arguing?'

'I wish I did. Wait, maybe I heard something on the lines of "Don't call me again."'

Gina leaned forward. 'Who said that? The visitor or Mr Reid?'

'The visitor. Oh, I did see him leave. He's a door slammer too. I looked out of the window and his hair was a bit mussed up. Maybe they'd been fighting about something.'

Gina pulled a card from her pocket and passed it to Gareth.

'If you remember anything else or you see this man again, please call me immediately.'

The man swallowed. 'I don't have any credit on my phone.'

She reached into her bag and pulled out a five-pound note, realising that some of the people in this building had nothing. 'I know it's not much, but it should help you make that call if you need to. Do not challenge him yourself, leave that to us. Who manages this place? Is it one of the homeless support officers?'

He shook his head. 'They come with updates and keep us informed but there is someone who lives on site who manages the day-to-day issues like the maintenance and cleaning of the communal areas. His name is Freddie. Don't know his surname. He lives in the annexe, but we barely see him. I normally just hear the vacuum going or the windows being wiped down. He seems nice enough.'

Gina waited for Wyre to finish noting the manager's name down. 'Thank you for your help. We may need to speak to you again.'

'Will you speak to housing for me? Get me out of here. Get Kayleigh out too. We can't stay here, not now.'

'I'll mention it to them, but I can't promise anything. I wish I could.' Gina wished she could take him away from this gloomy building. She glanced back at the stuffed pony on the bed and shuddered knowing a little girl was coming back to all this.

'Thank you. Speak to Kayleigh. She must have heard more than me with her being right up in the eaves. I know there's something on her mind, but she wouldn't say. She thought it was too silly to mention but given what's happened, it might not seem so silly. I wasn't joking when I said Mr Reid scared her little girl. I told you; this house is sick. It's evil. It does something to the people who live in it.'

Gina stood, wanting to bring the Amityville nonsense to a close. There was nothing sick in the building. In her line of work, it was people that were dangerous. 'Thank you again.

We'll see ourselves out.' Gina glanced out of the window as Wyre packed her things in her bag. As Wyre turned, she nearly placed her hand in a plate of ash. The tail end of an incense stick was left. The box next to it told Gina they were citrus scented. Gina inhaled but she could smell nothing but damp and maybe food, but that stick explained the burning smell.

The woman and her little girl were just getting out of the ambulance as a suited, middle-aged man walked across the road.

'Thank the Lord.' Gareth hurried to the door. 'That's one of the guys from housing. Maybe today's my day. It has to be.'

As Gina and Wyre left, Gareth let the man in. They stepped out into the cold morning where the frosty pavements had been replaced by a damp sheen. O'Connor hurried over. 'Door-to-doors are underway, guv.' He pulled a beanie hat from his pocket and pulled it over his shiny bald head.

'Excuse me, are you the police?' the woman called.

Gina hurried over. 'Yes, DI Harte. May I speak with you? Are you Kayleigh?'

'Yes, there's so much I need to tell you. Can we go in the warm?'

Gina nodded to Wyre. It sounded possible that Kayleigh was eager to tell them something that could crack the case.

FIVE

SASHA

'Hey, Trev. You know it's my day off?' Sasha pushed one socked foot out of the side of the quilt and shivered. It was going to be another chiller of a day and the last thing she would do was put the heating on. The price hikes would be the death of her.

'You're telling me. I'm meant to be leaving on a train to London later for my niece's wedding preparations so I'm in a hurry, too. My train is at five so all is good for a while. You're not going to believe it.' Her colleague's lips smacked, an annoying habit he had before he was about to reveal something big.

'Let me guess. Albie in admin has finally admitted that he and Esther have got it on. I've been saying for ages, the chemistry between those two is steaming hot. Never need to boil a kettle again. I'll just put my cold cuppa in the same room as that pair.' She chuckled as she stepped out of her bed and made a dash for her woollen dressing gown. 'Hang on.' She placed the phone down and slid her arms through the sleeves. 'That's better. Go on.'

'I wish it was, Sash. I'm over at the Cleaver. I'm technically on call until midday, but you manage this hostel, don't you?'

'Yes, what's happened?'

'Do you know a guy called Wesley Reid?'

'I know of the name. One of the local homeless charities referred him to me a few days ago. Apparently, he got admitted to hospital with a nasty chest infection and one of the charity workers went with him. He was only in for a day, but he needed somewhere to be discharged and a room came up at the Cleaver. I haven't met him personally as I was on another call when he came in, but I arranged his accommodation. You know how manic it can be this time of the year. I was due to see him tomorrow for the first time. What's happened?'

Trevor paused. 'So sorry, hun. He's been murdered. There are police everywhere. I thought you should know. I'm here now and I'm being pulled from pillar to post. Everyone wants to leave but I have nowhere for them to go. They're asking for you. I've been called useless, a muppet; you know, the usual. The people here aren't happy, and I get that they're scared. I would be if someone had been killed in the building I lived in, especially as it used to be a butcher's shop. I mean, the place is eerie.'

'Damn. I had plans today. My sister invited me over for lunch. I guess I could head over for a couple of hours, try to calm everyone down a bit and I'll be as quick as I can.' She bit her bottom lip as she flicked the kettle switch and threw a teabag into a cup. 'Do you know how it happened? Have they caught the person who did it?'

'Well, you know me. I've been hanging around trying to listen in. The lead detective is a woman called DI Harte. When I arrived, she'd already spoken to Mr Alderman in room one. I think she's about to speak to the woman who is staying in the other attic room as the DI is showing her into the communal sitting room as we speak. I did hear the two detectives talking and one said that Mr Reid was stabbed. I heard cider mentioned. Maybe it was a drunken row but that's only a guess.'

Sasha shivered. The very thought of someone she'd placed being stabbed gave her the chills. 'I know from his file that

Wesley had a drink problem and he'd had a bit of trouble on the streets. One of the team mentioned that he'd taken some pamphlets as he left with the key, and he said he wanted to get his life together. Give me a chance to get dressed and have a cuppa, and I'll be there soon. Are you okay to stay on site for a short while?'

"Course. I'll wait 'til you get here. But I can't miss my train, okay?'

'Okay. Just keep reassuring everyone. It was a one-off. No one is coming for them. Tell them that they're safe but to keep their doors locked. Can't be too careful. Right, the longer I chat away on the phone, the longer it will take. Have you spoken to the house manager?'

'No, he's not in. I think the police want to speak to him too.'

'Okay. Hopefully he'll be back soon. I'll catch up with you in a bit.' She ended the call and poured her tea. Glancing down at the car park from her upstairs flat window, she spotted the cracked eggs on the bonnet of her hatchback car. As if the constant damage to her car and the middle of the night phoning and hanging up wasn't enough. It was all too much. Slamming the cup down, she hurried to the bathroom and turned on the shower. She was sick of the unruly teens. One day she would catch them at it and then what? She pondered that question for a moment. What would she actually do to stick up for herself? The police weren't interested in their antics. She'd called them before.

A few minutes later, dressed and clean, her hurried footsteps echoed in the communal stairwell, until she reached the bottom. That's when she saw that her postbox was half open. That was odd. It was Sunday. There was never post on Sundays, not even flyers. She grabbed her key and the rusting box screeched as she opened it. Screaming, she almost slipped as she stumbled against the door of the downstairs flat. What she saw made her skin crawl. Her neighbour opened his door. 'Hello.' His dark messy hair fell over his eyes.

She'd never really spoken to him before. 'So sorry. I didn't knock. I accidentally bumped into your door.'

His gaze fell onto the slithering worm as it made its way to the edge of the box and fell to the rough carpet. 'How did that get there?'

Sasha huffed out a breath. 'Stupid kids. I seem to be their latest target. They keep messing with my car and now they've taken to this.' She snatched the piece of cardboard that was lodged in the letter box and unfolded it. It was blank. Merely a decoy to get her to check her postbox. She slammed it shut and locked it. 'Have they been bothering you?'

He shook his head. 'No.'

'I don't suppose you could let me know if you see anything untoward around here or anyone acting suspiciously in the hall-way?' She fished around in her pocket for her Post-it notepad and wrote her mobile number down, then passed it to him.

He took it and stuck it to his palm. 'Of course.' He smiled. 'Anyway, I best get going. Got to get to work.' He closed his door without so much as an introduction.

After tearing the piece of card in half, she used both sides to roll the worm onto it before opening the communal door and placing it on the grass. She might hate worms with a passion, but she didn't want to kill it. That went against all her princi-ples. Glancing up and down the damp car park, she tried to see if anyone was hiding and watching. Were the kids all standing against the wall around the corner, waiting to see her reaction to the eggs and the worm? She really hated those kids.

She flinched as a teen covered in an oversized black hoodie steamed past on an electric scooter. He spat gum out on the path by her feet. A couple of weeks ago, she'd lost her temper momentarily and shouted at him for scraping her car with the scooter. That was her one and only outburst. He shouldn't have been near her car anyway but in hindsight, she wished she'd left it because since that day, so many things had been happening. Were they scary things? Not really. More costly. The odd slashed tyre, eggs, or a fresh scratch on her car. Now the worm. She hated that it had gone this far. It's the first time the kid had come into the block of flats. Everyone must know that the trade button opened the door at all hours and that was something that made her feel less secure. The management company promised that someone would fix it but, as usual, they were useless. An uncomfortable churning began to take hold of her stomach. With the troublesome teen hanging around and knowing she was about to attend a site where a murder had taken place, the anticipation was sitting like a rock in her belly. The thought of having to deal with the aftermath of a bloody scene sent her heart racing. It wouldn't be the first time she'd needed to book a crime scene cleaner, but she'd need to do the initial inspection when police released the scene.

The teen was riding around in circles on the damn scooter. 'I've called the police.' Without seeming at all bothered, the teen boy pulled his hood even lower to the point she wondered if he could even see where he was going. 'Look, this has to stop,' she called, hoping he would pull over and talk to her in a civilised manner. She held her breath and listened to the pounding of blood pumping through her ears. Instead of stopping, he rode up close and put his middle finger up to her before speeding off. She released her breath, got into her car and locked the doors. All this angst and her day hadn't even started. All she could think was, what would he do next?

SIX

Gina and Wyre sat on the sofa opposite Kayleigh and her little girl. 'I know what happened must have been a huge shock.' Gina leaned forward, trying not to sink into the structureless seat. The wooden frame was broken, and the cushions were threatening to swallow her up.

'I, err...' Kayleigh swallowed and stood, holding her little girl's hand as she led her to a toybox at the other end of the room. 'Do you want to play with all the toys while Mummy talks to these nice people?'

The little girl giggled and knelt amongst the pile where she grabbed a box of jumbo plastic bricks.

'I don't want her to listen in on all this. Thankfully, I managed to shield her from the scene we were faced with this morning.' She wiped her sore-looking eyes and pressed her fingers into the brown skin on her face, then she scooped her straggly black hair into a ponytail. 'I've never seen a dead person before and the blood...' She took a deep breath. 'Sorry.'

'That's okay. You're in shock. Are you sure you're okay to talk? Do you need a drink?' Gina could see that Kayleigh was struggling from the raw bitten skin at the edge of her thumbnail.

'I want to talk, not that I can help you with much.'

'Did you see or hear Mr Reid yesterday?'

'Yes. I arrived back about five and he was just leaving. We passed on the stairs. I found him scary and so did my little girl, so I said hello. I hoped that he'd at least smile and put us at ease, but he didn't. Instead, he looked all clammy and jittery. I thought one wrong word or look would have him going for us. As he passed, he banged into the wall and swore under his breath. Whenever I've met him on the stairs or landing, my heart always does this thing where it speeds up. I get the urge to run. I think it's because it was just him and me up there and if he blocked my way down, I couldn't do a thing. He made me feel trapped.' She licked her dry bottom lip and winced as a sore opened up. 'A couple of days ago, I heard banging late at night. I prised the door open. It was nearly midnight, and I could see that he was trying to bash his door down. He turned and saw me watching. That's when he called me a nosy cow. I have no idea what I did to deserve that, especially as I was just seeing if he was okay.'

'Your neighbour, Gareth, said that Mr Reid had scared your daughter.'

Kayleigh nodded. 'Yes, it was on the day he moved in, about a week ago. The person who lived in that room before him was lovely. She was only about nineteen and liked to play with her, so I used to leave the door open. Anyway, my little one was playing on the landing with the stairgate up when he came stomping up the stairs. He swore and cast the stairgate aside instead of just opening it and walking through. As soon as I heard his voice, I ran out to bring her in. That's when I heard him saying that he had a daughter and that my little girl was so pretty, then he reached down and tried to pick her up. She instantly screamed and I don't know what it was about him, but it felt like we were in danger. I could smell the alcohol on him and for a moment, I thought he might fall on her or knock her down the stairs. I instinctively grabbed my daughter and told him to leave her alone. That's when he stood there, leaning against the wall while staring. It felt like forever, but I guess it was only a couple of minutes. I slammed the door closed and leaned against it for ages, listening. He didn't move. A short while later, I opened the door a smidge and I saw that he'd fallen asleep on the stairs. I needed to go out, but I didn't want to pass him. Instead, I cancelled my plans. It might not sound much but you can't imagine how scared I was.' She began to choke on her words as she stifled back a sob. 'We left her father because he was violent when he was drunk. Seeing him, like that, brought back a lot of bad memories. I was meant to get placed into a shelter but there are no places, which is why I'm here.'

Gina felt her body stiffen. She knew what it was like to live in fear of a partner that might hurt you at any time. She knew how it felt to hope that he might not come home drunk and do unthinkable things to you. 'I'm sorry to hear that you've been through so much. Do you feel like you might be in danger from your ex?'

Kayleigh shook her head. 'No. He doesn't live in Cleevesford and as far as I know, he has no idea where I live.'

'Does your daughter still go to the same nursery, or do you stick to the same routine as you did then?'

'Our old routine is gone. The only thing I do is see my friend who lives in Cleevesford. I haven't seen him around. I'm always on the lookout. My brother lives in Cleevesford and he's trying to help me rebuild my life.'

Gina shook away her own thoughts that were threatening to drown her. She wished she'd found the strength to escape from Terry instead of leaving him to die at the bottom of their stairs all those years ago. Maybe things would be different. She swallowed and shook that thought away. He never let her out of his sight, let alone allowed her to have any money. He alienated her from all her friends and her family. She had no one back then. His death had been her way out. Had he lived, he'd never have stopped looking for her. Gina swallowed as she thought of Briggs again. He was the only person in the world who knew everything about her past. Damn, she missed him. She shook her thoughts of him away and looked at the young woman in front of her. Kayleigh had made her escape and she deserved to feel safe. Gina only hoped that Kayleigh was safe. 'Going back to yesterday, did you hear Mr Reid return home last night?'

She nodded. 'Yes, and then there was a bit of shouting, but I placed my pillow over my ears. I prayed for it to stop. It sounded like he was talking to someone, but I couldn't hear anyone responding to anything he said. I thought he was talking to himself or that he was on the phone. As for the banging noises, I really thought it was just him clattering around. If I hadn't been so scared of him, maybe I'd have opened my door for a look but there was no way I'd risk our safety. After a while, everything went quiet, and I went back to sleep. Then this morning, I opened my door and was faced with carnage and that smell.' She shook her head and looked away, trying to hold back her emotions. 'I don't know if I'll ever be able to describe that smell. I feel as though it's in me now, every time I breathe.' Kayleigh held a hand across her mouth and closed her eyes for a second. Gina understood totally. There was nothing like the smell of a cadaver and she knew it would stay with Kayleigh for life.

'Are you okay?'

'Yes, it's just every time I think about it, I feel as though I might throw up. All that blood, his face...'

'I'm so sorry you had to experience that.' Gina paused, giving the woman a few seconds to compose herself. 'Is there anything else you remember?'

Kayleigh nodded. 'Yes, last night I could smell a weird herby smell, but not weed.'

'Herby?' Gina watched as Wyre finished writing that down

and furrowed her brows. 'When did you start noticing the smell?'

'Around midnight. I thought that maybe all had calmed down, or maybe it was some sort of essential oil. I'd seen him vaping too, so I also thought it might be scented vape juice. I didn't really give it a thought until you asked.' Gina wondered if it was the burnt down incense stick in Mr Alderman's room. Maybe the scent had travelled through the house. The man had told them he'd opened his door to deal with Wesley's return.

'Have you ever seen any visitors come to Mr Reid's door?'

'No.'

'Were you in last Monday evening?'

The woman shook her head. 'No, I met up with a couple of friends at the church. There was a fete and jumble sale, and I need very cheap things, so I went along.'

That would explain why Kayleigh didn't see Wesley's one and only visitor. Gina needed to find this man and fast.

'I saw a man sitting in his car this week. It was evening but I can't remember the day now. It looked like he was staring up at Mr Reid's window. He had dark hair and was wearing a thick coat. That's all I can remember. He may well have been waiting for someone else in the house, but it really did look like his eyes were on that window.'

'Did you recognise the man?'

'No. I've never seen him before.'

He could be the man they were looking for. 'What type of car was he sitting in?'

'I don't know. A saloon maybe.'

'Colour?'

The woman shrugged. 'A dark colour. That's all I can remember, sorry.'

'Was it earlier in the week or later?'

'Now I think of it, it was Thursday or Friday. Sorry I can't be more specific.'

'You've been really helpful, thank you.'

Her little girl ran over. 'Mummy, I'm hungry.' Kayleigh patted the girl's tight brown curls.

'Okay, lovely. We'll go and get you some lunch. I think we'll go out today.' She held her hands over her daughter's ears as she hugged her. 'I can't stay around here.'

'Do you have anyone to be with for a while?'

She nodded. 'Yes, I'm going to my friend's house for lunch.'

Someone knocked at the door. Wyre stood to open it.

'Hello, Trevor and Sasha,' the woman said, introducing them. 'Homeless support officers. Ms Blunt, can we have a word in a minute, when you're done?' she asked Kayleigh.

Gina stood and walked over to Wyre. She pulled a card from her pocket and gave it to Kayleigh. 'If you think of anything else, please call me.' They left the room, and Gina hoped that the homeless support officers could find some of the residents somewhere else to go.

'Ah, DI Harte.' Bernard Small, the Crime Scene Manager clumsily descended the stairs until he reached the bottom. He slightly loosened his crime scene suit and removed his face mask, releasing his unruly grey beard. 'You need to see this. You're going to need all your puzzle-solving skills for this one. Whoever did this has something to say. What they want to say is for you to work out.'

SEVEN

Gina and Wyre zipped up their protective crime scene suits as they followed Bernard up the creaky steps into the eaves. The officer at the midway point untied the crime scene cordon tape and allowed them through. A hint of mould caught the back of Gina's nostrils as she inhaled but it was the smell of the dead man that made her recoil. She could tell he'd died recently as she'd smelled much worse in the past, but she knew why Kayleigh had struggled. Nothing compared to the stench.

Bernard stopped at the top of the stairs, his head knocking the lampshade that hung down from the tall ceiling. He hunched his lanky figure forward to avoid any more crashes. 'The room is a bit cramped so please remain outside. You can see everything from where I'm standing. The occupant has very little in the way of belongings, so they've all been bagged, logged and placed in the evidence box outside the door. His phone seems to be out of charge and that's been bagged for you too. When we reach the top, please only step on the plates.' He waved his hand. 'I don't know why I'm telling you all this. It's not like you don't know.' He paused. 'For now, we've asked that the lady in the studio flat next to him stays away from here for the day. One of the crime scene assistants fetched her bag and their coats a short while back and she said that was all she needed for now. We'll be finished on the landing a bit later and she'll be able to come back up then.'

Gina heard the clicking of a camera and a flash lit up the dimmed top of the stairway. Although morning, the gloominess of the day had kept the skies dark. A few more steps and they reached the attic landing. She glanced into the very room that her own daughter had stayed in once when it was a bed and breakfast. It had been a dump of a place back then and nothing had changed. It still looked like it should be condemned. No wonder Gareth Alderman thought there was evil lurking in the walls. This place was enough to scare anyone. She inhaled, trying to pick up on whatever herby scent Kayleigh had described but there was nothing but damp and now to add to it all, the revolting smell of excrement coming from the cadaver that seemed to be masking everything else. Her gaze fell onto the corpse where it lay on the bed. The other crime scene officer nudged past with a jacket in an evidence bag.

'Man in his late thirties, early forties. Cause of death was the stab wound to his neck. He's bled out. There is no sign of the murder weapon, but the stab wound is around twenty millimetres in width. We'll know more when we've completed the post-mortem.'

Gina held her sleeve over her nose. Even with a face mask on the smell was intolerable. 'Can you estimate the time of death?' Wyre turned her head and heaved slightly.

'Rigor mortis has hit his top half and is working its way down. As an estimate, I'd say between eleven last night and one in the morning.'

Bernard's estimation of the time fit perfectly with the commotion described by Gareth Alderman and Kayleigh Blunt. She glanced at the CSI who was taking various photos of all angles of the room, including the phone number written on the wall and the words AA above it. The blood spatter told a story, one which she needed to question. 'There's blood on the carpet as well as the bed.'

'Yes. It looks like he died on the bed but from what we're able to decipher, he was stabbed while near the floor. You can see the blood trail soaked into the carpet, and we've left the Swiss Army knife in position for now. The blood on his hands and knees, along with the patchy trail tells us that he crawled towards the bed.'

'Maybe he was reaching for the knife.' She wondered if it had belonged to the perpetrator or Wesley. 'I'd like that to be fast tracked into forensics.' One set of prints might be all that was needed to bring the case to a close if the perp had accidentally dropped it and they happened to be on the system.

'We can confirm that none of the tools it contains were used to kill him but that's not to say the perp didn't bring it, so as requested, that will go top of the list. We can conclude that he was stabbed in the back of the neck. He crawled across the floor while bleeding, and he dragged the quilt with his bloody hand which means he may have been trying to pull himself up using the bed.'

'Anything so far that might help us identify the killer?'

'I hate to say this but there are so many different fingerprints in this room, it's going to take us an age to get through them and most are partial. There are hairs galore in the bathroom and in the carpet. From what we've seen, I doubt this dwelling has ever had a proper clean.'

Wyre stared at the man's face. 'That pound coin on his forehead, what could it mean?'

Gina took in the man's stubbly face, pallid with death and tinged blue on the lips. His head lay in the bloody mess that had dried to the quilt around the edges. One single coin had been placed in the centre of his forehead. She shook her head. She'd heard reasons as to why people placed coins over the eyes and mouths of the deceased but never the forehead. 'Symbolic, maybe? Something to do with payment for transportation to the afterlife. Or maybe it's simply there to make a point that all this is about money.'

Bernard cleared his throat and tucked a bit of escaped hair back into his beard cover. He stood up straight, his back making a slight cracking noise. 'He also smells of cider and we can confirm that he is doused in it. The bed is too.'

Gina scrunched her brow. 'Have you found any empty drink bottles or cans in the room?'

'No.'

'So, our perp either could have come in with the cider or took the rubbish out. Have the bins been checked yet?'

'We have a couple of assistants down there as we speak. There is one large communal bin which is making it difficult.'

'If they find any drink cans or bottles, or a knife, could you please let me know immediately?'

'Certainly will, and we'd obviously get them straight to the lab.'

'Did you smell anything else when you came in? Something like herbs?'

Bernard shook his head. 'I didn't but then again, I've just got over a stinker of a cold and I've been wearing a face mask. I haven't smelt much for a few days. Did any of you smell anything herbal?'

The two crime scene assistants shook their heads and the young man replied. 'I could only smell the cider and the body. It's not to say there wasn't a herbal smell in the air, the other smells may have overshadowed it.'

Bernard glanced across the room. 'The window was on the catch. It was cold when we came in. We had to close it, but we did take photos.'

Gina wondered if anyone would have smelled anything other than the smell of death. With the window being open, any vague scents may have dispersed. She scrunched her nose. The death smell never got any easier to tolerate, no matter how many crime scenes they attended. She glanced back at the landing where the assistant boxing the evidence was standing while filling in the log on his clipboard. 'I'm just going to have a look in the box. Did you say everything was in there?'

Bernard nodded. 'Sad really. All his worldly belongings in one box, except for the old sleeping bag and the pop-up tent next to it. They were found in the wardrobe. Most of his clothes had been draped over the wooden chair as you'll see from the crime scene photos. A few had been knocked off.'

'Is there anything else you can tell me right now?'

He scratched his forehead. 'Only that we'll need to take the body soon. Transportation is on its way. All the photos will be sent to you by lunchtime and if I do come across anything that might be of help, I will call you immediately. For now, we still have a lot of work to do.'

'Thank you.' Gina stepped back and gestured for Wyre to look at the evidence box with her. Each item from his room had been placed in individual bags, that had been marked up. She reached in and rifled through them, pulling out a picture drawn by a child. It looked like a crayoned man holding a child's hand, both with red smiles. Their victim, whatever his faults, had people in his life that meant something to him. He told Kayleigh that he had a daughter. That little girl would never see her father again.

'I suppose we need to find out where his family live and arrange to deliver the bad news.' Wyre exhaled.

'I need to do it. Finding more about his life might be the thing we need to catch the killer. A partner, even if they're now an ex, might be able to help, or maybe even his parents can. We need to get back to the station. We'll let forensics get on with their job and process everything and we'll send an officer up to get the phone over straight away where the digital forensics team can get it back up and running. Let's hope it just needs a charge.'

Gina glanced back at the dead man with the coin on his head and she shivered. Wesley Reid would never get the chance to turn his life around and become the parent that his daughter needed, and it was down to Gina and her team to make sure his killer was caught. She headed down the stairs and past the cordon leaving the pungent air behind. As she reached the front door and stepped out into the frosty morning, she pulled off her face mask and gasped in a few breaths of fresh air.

Wyre shook her head and leaned against the wall.

As she passed PC Kapoor, DS Jacob Driscoll and his fiancée, Jennifer Bailey from the crime scene crew, pulled over and stepped out of their car. Jennifer quickly tied up her dyed red hair and left Jacob to join the rest of her crime scene colleagues. Gina's whole team had now arrived, and O'Connor was ambling over.

Gina led them all to the kerb, just far enough away from the residents and members of the public that had begun to crowd the street. As she brought them up to date, she spotted a teen girl filming them. 'Hey, are you in charge? My followers would love to know what's going down here. I'm Macie Perrin of Macie Reportz Crime and Ghosts. Has someone died in this haunted house?'

Gina shook her head and ignored the girl in the black mac covered in huge white skull prints. It would be all over social media before she'd even dished out the next lot of instructions. Just as she was about to turn back to the house, Gina spotted a man stop dead in the middle of the road. The worried look on his face told her he was someone she had to speak to. He turned to walk away, back in the direction he came from. 'Stop, police.' Gina held up her identification. He wasn't going anywhere.

EIGHT

Gina broke away from the team and headed towards the man as he continued to walk away. 'Stop. Are you a resident of this hostel?' Now that was a smell she recognised. It smelled like he'd been smoking weed. Had he been trying to walk away because of that or was there another reason?

'No, I manage the place. What's happening?' His shoulders dropped in the thick donkey jacket he was wearing, and he stepped onto the pavement outside the house. He wiped his red nose with his gloved hand.

'Are you Freddie?'

He pointed at her. 'First of all, who exactly are you and why are all these people here?'

Gina didn't have time for games. Jacob walked up behind her. 'If you hadn't have walked away when I identified myself, you'd know I was police.' She held her identification up towards his nose. 'DI Harte and DS Driscoll.' Her colleague stood by her side and removed the moose hunting hat that he was wearing. His neat short back and sides stuck up from the static.

'Shit. Yes, I'm Freddie.'

'We need to speak to you. Where have you just come from?'

'Whoa, I haven't done anything.'

'I smell weed?'

'Well, I have no weed, as you can see. I don't take drugs.' He emptied his pockets out and there was nothing in them but a bank card. 'It's probably rubbed off someone I've been near. Why do you need to know where I've been?'

'Routine questioning. A very serious offence has taken place on the premises that you oversee. One of the residents was murdered last night.'

His mouth opened and he stared at the house. 'No way. You're kidding me, aren't you? No, that can't have happened. Everything is okay here. Everyone is happy.'

Gina sighed. From what she'd heard, no one was happy in that place but that wasn't necessarily his fault. 'We can either speak here or we can go to your quarters where it will be a bit more private.'

The man scrunched his nose.

'Or we could go to the station,' she said.

Gina turned around to watch the teen girl filming as she spoke to her phone. 'And something big is going down. I'll keep you all posted. Signing off from Britain's crime capital, Cleevesford.' Obviously another TikToker, YouTuber or podcaster. Everyone had taken to reporting everything lately. All in the name of social media popularity.

'Erm, yes. Follow me.' Freddie clearly wasn't enamoured with being filmed and having that shared with the world, and neither was Gina. She just knew that picking a battle with the girl would lead to nothing but holdups and more social media content for her. As they passed PC Kapoor, Gina left her with instructions to move as many people on as possible. They followed Freddie around the building to the annexe at the back. He shoulder-barged the door as he turned the key. 'Another job I need to sort. All the doors stick. It's the weather, I think. Come through.'

Gina stepped into the hallway and shivered. 'Do you live here alone?'

He nodded. 'I had a partner, but we split quite a while ago now. It's just me and the cat.' Jacob shuffled into the hallway beside her.

'Just give me a minute.' He made a psst noise and a cat darted towards him. He picked up the writhing creature and popped it on his bed. 'I'll feed you in a minute,' he called out as it began to meow. 'Come through.'

They entered the small lounge that was adorned with nothing more than a large television on a stand, an Xbox and a gaming chair. A couple of family-sized bags of crisps had been placed beside it. 'Who was it?'

'Wesley Reid, the man staying on the top floor. Can I take your full name?' Gina watched as Jacob took his notepad out and began marking it up.

'Frederick Bertram.'

'Did you book Mr Reid into the accommodation?'

He nodded. 'Yes, he was sent by one of the homeless support officers from the council after being referred by a charity worker.'

'Have you had any concerns or complaints about him?'

'Only that the woman in the next room to him found him a bit creepy. She hasn't complained, she just mentioned it in passing. I knew it wouldn't be easy on the others as Mr Reid has a bad drink problem. He was drunk when he turned up.'

'When did you last see Mr Reid?'

'Yesterday, well, last night.'

'What time?'

'It had to be around eleven, maybe eleven fifteen?'

Gina's heart rate picked up. This put Freddie at the scene just before Mr Reid was murdered. 'Were you coming or going?'

'I was just leaving. I came from around the back of the main house, the way we just walked, and I saw him staggering back.'

'Did he see you?'

'I doubt he was able to focus on much.'

'Did he go straight in?'

'No, he sat on the wall outside the house for a minute or two. He was slurring on his phone.'

Gina flinched as a small black cat nudged her leg.

'Come here.' The man leaned down and picked the cat up. 'I don't know. I walked off down the road and he was still on the phone. As I say, I didn't pass him. I came from around the back of the building. You know, I didn't think he would end up like this. Quite the opposite.' The man shook his head. 'I heard some of his conversation, well, a line at least.'

'Go on.'

'He shouted, "When I get hold of you, I'm going to kill you," down the phone. There might have been a name at the end of that, but I didn't hear it. Mr Reid was threatening someone. When I arrived home this morning and saw you lot, I thought he'd carried out that threat, that the person on the phone had come over and he'd hurt them. He sounded so angry.'

'Did you see anyone else at all while you were out there?'

Freddie shook his head. 'No, he was alone at the time I left, unless someone followed him in. I had my back turned as I was walking away. Actually, I just about heard him going in and a few seconds later there was some sort of argument, maybe with the man staying in the bottom room.' He clicked his fingers. 'Gareth Alderman, that's his name. That man has his moments.'

'In what way?'

'Don't get me started on the number of times he claims to have heard ghosts in the walls. The man's letting the fact that the place is a bit old and run-down get to him.'

Gina rubbed her cold hands together. Freddie's annexe seemed colder on the inside than it was outside. Beads of water ran down the inside of the window. 'Had there been any more altercations between Mr Reid and Mr Alderman?'

The man rubbed his black stubble and nodded. 'There are always complaints and altercations in a place like this. I'm mostly here to deal with check-ins and maintenance. I mean, I'm a carpenter by trade and I needed a job. This one came with a place, and I thought it would be a good idea. Some days, I feel more like a social worker. They get angry all the time when the homeless support officers are running late. I mean, it's a temporary hostel. It's one step away from being on the streets. As for those two, yes, Mr Alderman was angry that Mr Reid made so much noise. Every time I came in the building to do some work, he'd collar me and say that Mr Reid keeps making a racket, that he leaves the front door open, that's he's sometimes rude. Mr Alderman forgets that he can come across as rude too. He shouts at everyone for even breathing, saying that they're making too much noise. I think it's this place, it gets to people. It's certainly got to him.'

Gina furrowed her brow. 'When Mr Reid entered the building last night, did he shut the door properly?'

The man shrugged. 'I'm afraid I don't know. I didn't look back.'

'And where was it you went?'

'To see a friend.'

'Who is the friend?'

'Really?'

Gina nodded.

'I feel like I'm the accused here.'

'You're one of the last people to see Mr Reid alive. It's important that you tell us where you were.'

'I was with someone.'

'Okay, name?'

He shrugged and held his phone up. 'Killian. I met him on an app. He lives above the café on the high street. That's all I know.' He opened his messages up. 'Number 11A. I liked him. He's going to hate me when you turn up at his door talking about murder.'

'Did you walk or drive?'

'I walked. I'd had a beer earlier. I don't drive when I've had a drink.'

Jacob finished scribbling the notes and Gina passed him a card. 'Good to hear. Did you go straight to Killian's house?'

'Yep.'

'If you remember anything else, anything at all, call me straight away.'

He nodded and ran his hands over his shaved head. 'Can I go in the main house yet?'

Gina shook her head. 'It's best that you don't. The top half is cordoned off and the homeless support officers are talking to some of the residents. There are already too many people milling around, especially as it's a crime scene. The woman staying in the eaves, Kayleigh Blunt, she should be allowed back into her room later today.'

'Great. Will someone keep me updated? I have a few repairs to catch up on.'

Gina nodded. She saw that Jacob had made a note of the name and address of Freddie's hookup. Verifying when he arrived at Killian's would be a start. It would take him roughly fifteen minutes to walk there. By half eleven, he'd have arrived. She saw Jacob note that down too. They were both thinking the same thing.

'How was he killed? Wesley?' Frederick Bertram asked.

That was a strange thing to ask. The cat jumped onto the gaming chair and licked Gina's hand with its coarse tongue. 'We're not releasing that information yet.' She stroked the cat's head.

'Mr Reid said something strange the other day, but I don't think it's related.'

'What was that?'

'He muttered under his breath that he was out for his pound of flesh, that was after he'd been shouting down the phone. As I said, I'm surprised it's him who has been murdered when he was so threatening to the other person on the phone.'

The thought of the pound coin on the dead man's head gave Gina a chill. She gazed at Freddie. If he killed Wesley Reid and left that coin on the man's forehead, he was toying with them right now. The man picked his cat up and smiled.

'Wait, there is something else. The person Mr Reid was threatening on the phone. He was talking to someone called Neil, Nile, something like that. It began with an N. I also heard Mr Reid mention that he was going to the Angel Arms, here and there. Maybe he has friends there who may be able to help you.'

NINE

SASHA

She watched as Trevor left. Now she was alone with the problem of two temporarily housed residents who were screaming to be moved. She placed her tablet on the coffee table in the communal lounge while she stood there thinking. It didn't matter how many times she checked her accommodation availability, there was nothing. There were so many people still waiting for a room and had nowhere to go. People who were so cold right now, they'd take a room at the Cleaver despite what had happened. They literally had no housing stock available, so she had to disappoint them both. They either left and looked for their own accommodation or they stayed, it was as simple as that. It wasn't fair and she didn't like it but as her mother used to say, it was what it was.

Kayleigh came back in with her little girl, and she was closely followed by Gareth Alderman. The young woman stepped forward, tears springing from her eyes. 'Please don't make me stay in that room. I saw his body. I still have this revolting cloying taste at the back of my throat. I can taste death. Do you know what that's like?'

The little girl stared up at Sasha as she sucked her thumb. Sasha swallowed, wanting nothing more than to help the mother with the sweet little girl but she was powerless to do anything more than she was already doing.

'Don't make us stay here. I'm begging you. Look at her.' Her gaze trailed to her daughter. 'She doesn't deserve that.'

Gareth stepped further in. 'We can't stay here, either. You can't make us stay here. My little one already has nightmares.'

Sasha took a deep breath not quite knowing how to tackle Gareth. 'I really am sorry. I can't force you to stay here but I have nowhere else for you to go. Do either of you have any friends or relatives you can move in with for a while?'

Kayleigh clenched her fists. 'If I had anywhere to go, I wouldn't be here. I have a friend and I'm going over to hers for the rest of the day, but my brother is having problems too. He can't do anything for me right now. As for my friend, she has kids of her own and not enough rooms. She already sleeps on a pull-out bed in the lounge.'

'I really wish I could help you. We're struggling at the moment and so many people are in need of emergency accommodation.' This was a part of the job she hated. She could see the desperation in people and understand their frustrations. Turning people's requests down never got any easier. She'd quite often used her own credit card to book people cheap hotels in extreme situations. She wasn't meant to do that, but she was human. Seeing people with children who were scared and anxious wasn't something that sat well with her. Her training told her that she could only give people what she had available, that she couldn't solve everyone's problems and that she had to leave that baggage at the door when she finished work as it would slowly eat her up. But she couldn't. It was the people with children who really got to her. She allowed her fingers to feel for the credit card in her pocket. It was no good even thinking about it. The card was maxed out. She couldn't help them even if she wanted to and she didn't want to ask her dad to help her pay it off again.

'I've had it.' Gareth held his hands above his head. 'You can help us, but you won't.'

'I can assure you that's not true, Mr Alderman. If I could help you, I would.'

'This place is evil, and you want to leave us here so that we'll be next. You only have to look at the place to know it's the devil's house. A man was killed here. It's horrible. How will you be able to live with yourself if the next victim is me or Kayleigh? What if you come here and see one of us lying there in a bloody mess? Or worse, what if it's one of our children? You'd have that on your conscience. Do you have children?'

Sasha swallowed her upset down. 'No... I... there's really nothing I can do.'

'You can. Get on your phone and sort it,' he shouted, his face red and his stare, stark. 'You lot don't care. You just put us in shit places like this and tick a box. All done. Not your problem anymore.'

'That's not true, Mr Alderman. The housing department are working hard to find you somewhere to live.' That was the truth. Sasha loved nothing more than to hand someone in need a set of keys to their new home.

'That's what you all say but I'm still here, living in this dump with a murderer on the loose. I have to live in the same house as arseholes like the dead man. I can see why someone would want to kill him. People like him are scum.'

As he pointed, his finger almost jabbed her in the throat. Sasha stepped back straight into the police detective she'd seen earlier. 'I'm DI Harte, this is DS Driscoll. What's going on here?'

Sasha shuffled past everyone, taking a deep breath once

through the tight huddle. Kayleigh had walked her little girl back over to the toybox, away from the commotion.

Mr Alderman began to hyperventilate as he fell against a heavy sideboard, knocking a book onto the floor. 'I'm sorry, I don't know what came over me.' He puffed out a few bursts of breath and staggered over to the sofa, holding his chest.

Sasha furrowed her brows. 'We need an ambulance.'

The detective gestured to her colleague. 'It's okay, there's an ambulance still outside. We'll get a paramedic to come and check on you, Mr Alderman.'

Not knowing what to do, Sasha sat on the sofa, knowing she'd have to wait to see how he was. She glanced at her watch and knew she was going to be late for dinner at her sister's. Her phone pinged with a message from Trevor. The protests outside the new building they'd acquired had ramped up and the police had been called. Great! She'd message her sister in a moment and cancel their plans.

'I'm okay,' he said with a gasp. All the colour had drained from his face, leaving him looking a little clammy. 'I have anxiety. I don't need an ambulance.' He paused for a moment. 'That stuff I said.' He looked up at the detective. 'I didn't mean it. No one deserves to die like that, not even the arsehole.'

The detective wasn't giving anything away in her body language. She smiled at Kayleigh's daughter as her mother comforted her before making to leave. 'I have to get out of here and Gareth, how could you say all that in front of my child?' Kayleigh shook her head and stormed out.

Sasha furrowed her brows as she took in Mr Alderman's post-panic demeanour. She didn't know much but she did know that the detective was asking herself if the man in front of them could have killed Wesley Reid?

A paramedic walked in, and the detective moved out of the way. 'May we have a word, outside?'

Sasha was more than happy to escape the suffocating

lounge. She followed the detective out into the pinching cold air. A girl was videoing them as they left. The detective held a hand up and a uniformed officer asked her to step away from the cordon.

'Are you the homeless support officer in charge?'

Sasha nodded. 'I place people temporarily in this property. I don't know all the residents well, though. You wouldn't believe how many people I'm having to juggle now. We're having a bit of a staffing crisis over at Cleevesford Council.'

'I can well believe it. It's not much better at the police station.' DI Harte smiled warmly, instantly putting her at ease.

'Can I ask how well you knew the victim?'

'I didn't. I've never met him. I placed him here but one of my colleagues spoke to him while I was out of the office.' Sasha could tell that the detective hoped that she'd know more.

'How about his circumstances?'

'From his files, I know he has a drink problem. He's been living on the streets for a while following the breakdown of his relationship with his partner.'

'Do you have his partner's address?'

Glad to help, Sasha nodded. 'Yes.' She began searching for the information on her work tablet. 'Can I email it to you?' The detective nodded and gave Sasha her email address. Within seconds, Sasha had pinged the information over.

'That's really helpful, thank you.'

'Do you know much about the other tenant, Mr Alderman?'

Sasha dropped her shoulders. 'He's probably the most demanding person I have to deal with, calling almost on a daily basis. I mean, you heard him when you came into the lounge. He doesn't understand that I can't work miracles. I wish I could wave a magic wand and give everyone in there a house, but I can't. He also thinks the place is haunted. He claims that he hears things in the walls. I know we have a vermin problem here, but the pest controllers are getting on top of that. I've told him it's being sorted but he won't listen to logic, ever. One minute he can seem okay to talk to, another, he will go on about evil.'

'Is he okay with his daughter?'

'His daughter? There is no daughter. It's really sad but his wife died many years ago and his child was also killed tragically in a separate incident. I don't know the details. Mr Alderman is in some sort of denial. He had a recent breakdown too, so he's not been good. He's much better now. I just think that Mr Alderman has been allowing the house to get to him. It's a creepy house. Not only was it a butcher's shop at one point, it used to have abattoir facilities where the annexe is. If you go to the library, there are some interesting minutes from various meetings along with a record of all news articles published about the place. In the past, neighbours voiced their upset in these meetings, upset by the sound of the animals getting agitated when they joined the kill queue. The building's past does freak some of the residents out a little but for Mr Alderman, it seems to upset him more. He's sure he can smell the meat. He burns these horrible incense sticks that some of the other residents have complained about. It's not a pleasant smell but he claims it makes the place smell nicer. That's an overview on Mr Alderman.'

'Just to confirm, Mr Alderman doesn't live here with a child?'

'That's right. He is alone in his room. I'll put his move at the top of my list. It's obvious that being here and with what's happened isn't doing his mental health any good. Before this he was starting to talk more about his daughter's death, but he seems to have regressed. I know he's hard work, but I really feel for the man. No one should have to lose their child.'

'Thank you for all your help. Has anyone else reported any incidents here lately or maybe someone has reported any strangers hanging around?'

Sasha pulled out her tablet and searched the files for the Cleaver. She wished she could remember but there were so many reports, she struggled to know which one was from where and who reported it. She stopped. A colleague had made an update. 'A man has been seen watching the building on two occasions last week and he was staring up at the windows. It may be something, it may be nothing.'

'Who called this in?'

Biting her bottom lip, Sasha scrolled to that information. 'Wesley Reid. He made the report.' She inhaled deeply. If only she or her colleague had passed this information to the police at the time.

'Did he name this person?'

'No.'

'Is there a description?' The DI waited as Sasha continued to read the notes.

'Looks like a man wearing a dark coat and hat. That's all I have written here.' She shook her head. That description could be of anyone. Everyone was wearing winter hats and a lot of people had dark coats. She glanced up at the house, its crushing presence looking like it might eat her up. It looked like the killer had been watching the house.

'Thank you.'

Sasha checked her phone again as another message pinged over. 'I must get going. There's a protest going on at one of our other buildings. One of the protesters has got inside.'

The detective gave her a card. 'If you think of anything else, please call me. We may be in touch to speak to you again.' Sasha did the same in giving the detective one of her cards. The DI turned to face the crowd and the male detective headed over to the uniformed officers.

Kayleigh walked her daughter under the cordon and down the road. Mr Alderman peered through the front window from his room, his gaze on her. He grabbed a dark-coloured hat and pulled it over his head. Sasha shivered and it wasn't because of the cold. Maybe the man who was in denial that his daughter was dead had been trying to scare the man he hated. She broke eye contact with Mr Alderman feeling slightly sick from the weight of his stare. Maybe he'd even killed Wesley Reid?

TEN

Gina checked her phone after pulling up in the car park of the Angel Arms. She called Briggs. As she waited for him to answer, she couldn't get Gareth Alderman out of her mind. The poor man was battling with his ghosts, and he was losing. The thought that he was living in the past, believing that his child was still with him, gave her the chills.

'Gina, how's it going?'

'We've spoken to some of the residents and one interview has led us to the Angel Arms. Apparently, Mr Reid frequented the place. I'll be back soon for the briefing and hopefully with a wealth of information that will help the case. Just before I left, I tasked Wyre to make sure Mr Reid's phone reached the station. Could you please make sure it gets straight to digital forensics?'

'I'll look out for it. I've also prepared a press statement which I'm about to deliver. Annie in Corporate Communications has set up the room and we're expecting a few local reporters soon.'

'How's Gracie?' Gina pressed her lips together. This isn't how she planned her time with her granddaughter, but she had to work this case. She thought of Hannah and how she'd react when she told her what had happened. She wouldn't be at all happy, but Gina wasn't happy that there was a murderer on the loose. It wasn't her fault that they were funded on a shoestring and couldn't afford more staff.

'Gracie had a fantastic time here. We dressed her up in a police hat and a very oversized stab vest and got her to arrest one of the desk sergeants. I filmed it for you. Mrs O has just taken her to make cakes over at the unit. She was really excited to go so please don't worry. She's not missing you one bit. Sorry to say.'

Gina smiled, happy that her team had rallied around to help. 'It sounds like she won't want to come home with me later.' Gina paused. 'I best get on with it. The quicker I speak to everyone on my list, the quicker I get to relieve Mrs O.'

'Where are you?'

'I am outside the Angel Arms. Just waiting for Jacob before I knock. The victim was threatening someone on the phone, and he mentioned the Angel so we're checking it out. I've managed to find one photo of Mr Reid on his Facebook profile, one he hasn't posted on ever, but I saw the body and I can confirm it's him unless he has a twin brother.'

'I won't hold you up any longer, and Gina?'

'Yes.'

'Thank you for today and again, sorry to bring you in when you had a few days off. I hated having to do it. Maybe I can make it up to you, when this case is over.'

Gina cleared her throat. 'I best get going.' She ended the call. Not wanting to get hurt was her priority and Briggs had hurt her when she'd been going through some tough times. The menopause had been kicking her in all directions with the sweats, anxiety and palpitations but thankfully, although she still had bad days, things had improved with HRT. She no longer felt as though her life was a downhill train with no brakes. Her phone rang. Gina's heart rate instantly picked up as she saw Hannah's name. She had no choice but to ignore it and hope that Hannah just thought they were out, or she was driving. Throwing her phone in her bag felt like an awful thing to do but Gracie wasn't with her and answering would ruin Hannah's break.

Jacob pulled in and parked next to her. She stepped out of the car and wrapped her scarf around her neck. Time to speak to Elouise, the licensee, and see if she knew of Wesley Reid. Jacob led her to the main door. Gina could see through the leaded pub window. Elouise was kneeling while wearing the highest of heels in front of the open fireplace as she stoked the flames, in readiness for the pub opening soon. Her tight wiggle dress left her barely any room to manoeuvre. As Jacob knocked, her gaze met Gina's. She joined Jacob at the main door.

Elouise slid several locks across before opening the heavy oak door. 'We're not open yet but I guess you're not here for a drink.' She batted her fake eyelashes. 'I'm guessing you need to check the CCTV?'

It was all becoming a bit routine. Elouise knew the drill. With the Angel Arms being such a local's pub, everyone migrated there.

'Sorry to bother you,' Gina said as they stepped in. She undid her coat a little and enjoyed the heat from the fire. 'May we talk to you for a moment first?'

'Of course.' Elouise smiled and gestured for them to sit at the table nearest the fire. 'Brad,' she called.

A young man appeared from the back room. 'Yes?'

'Could you lock the main door, stop anyone from coming in early and is there any chance of a few coffees, love, for me and the detectives? I know you're busy.'

'Of course, Elle. I'll get the kettle on. Could do with a break. I've been working for a whole twenty minutes.' Bradley gave her a cheeky grin.

'He's a lovely lad. Right. What can I do for you? Ask away.' She twisted her dark hair into a knot and clipped it up.

Gina pulled her phone out and scrolled until she reached Wesley's Facebook photo. 'Do you know this man?'

She scrunched her nose and stared closely at his face. 'I've seen him in here occasionally. The reason I remember him is because we've had to throw him out a few times. I actually barred him from the premises last night. Wesley tends to go into pubs when drunk and tries to steal other peoples' drinks. When challenged, he can be a bit mouthy.'

'In what way?'

'Throwing names around, swearing. Things like that.'

'Why did you ban him last night?'

'For making threats and picking a fight. I've put up with a lot from him, but I can't be done with fighting in my pub. The odd stolen drink can be replaced. I know he hasn't been himself since the breakdown of his relationship. I hate to say it, but I've seen him out and about when he's sober. He's not a bad person. He's just going through a bad patch.'

'Who was he picking a fight with?'

'Another one of my customers, his name is Noel Logan. He dragged him outside into the car park and began pushing him around. Problem for Wesley was, Noel is a lot niftier than him. The man just kept dodging his blows. Anyway, I hurried out there and told Wesley he was banned. It was Wesley who started the arguing and dragged Noel outside. It wasn't Noel's fault.'

'Do you know what they were arguing about?'

'No. Their cross words were hushed to begin with. Wesley stormed in and within ten minutes he'd dragged Noel into the car park. It was as quick as that. I didn't call the police because Noel didn't seem worried, and Wesley left after being banned. No assault was committed except for Noel being dragged I suppose. A few moments later, Noel came back in, finished his drink and left. I asked if he was okay, and he just smiled and said yes. He said that Wesley used to be his friend and that he was just being a drunken jerk. I thought no more of it.'

'So, you heard nothing?'

'Just a collection of insults and one other thing. Wesley did say to Noel that he was going to get back what was his, even if it killed him. Maybe Noel owes him money.' She shrugged.

'Do you know where Noel lives?'

'He's a local lad. I say lad, he's probably in his mid-to-late thirties. I know he has a house on the new estate by the golf course because he boasts about being able to roll out of bed and have a game.'

'Is he in a relationship?'

'Not as far as I'm aware but I don't think he'd tell me if he was. I've never seen him with anyone. He's quite a catch so maybe he does have someone. Can I ask what the questions are for? Is one of them in trouble?'

'We found Wesley Reid's body this morning, over at the Cleevesford Cleaver. We're investigating his murder. Please don't say anything yet as we need to speak to his family.'

Elouise exhaled and held a hand to her chest. Bradley placed the coffees on the table and left. 'I wasn't expecting that. I can see where this is going now. Noel wouldn't do a thing like that. He's lovely and Wesley was threatening him. Noel didn't even fight back when Wesley was trying to punch him.'

Gina reached over the table and took one of the coffees, ignoring the milk and sugar as she drank it black. 'Would we be able to have a copy of the CCTV?'

'Yes, of course. Give me at least a couple of hours and I'll dump it on a hard drive for you.'

'Thank you. I'll get someone to collect it this afternoon.' She sent a quick message to PC Kapoor asking her to organise an officer to collect it.

Noel may not have fought back, and he may have looked

like the victim, but why was he hanging around in his car watching Wesley, then turning up at the hostel and arguing with him? She had a name, and she knew roughly where he lived. She sent a quick message to O'Connor, asking him to get an exact address for the man. There seemed to be two sides to Noel Logan and Gina was going to acquaint herself with both. But first, she had to break the news to Wesley's ex-partner before the press release.

ELEVEN

SASHA

'Trev, fancy seeing you again today,' Sasha said ironically as she met him by the gates to the empty building. It had been a heavy morning, but she intended to lighten it up a little and enjoy the rest of her day. She'd go in with Trevor and see if there was any damage to the building, then she was going to at least try to enjoy what was left of her weekend.

'If we're here too long, I may have to leave you to it. I have a train to catch remember and I still haven't finished packing my morning suit.' He raised his eyebrows, jokingly.

The crowd of about twenty people held up banners and a grey-haired woman shouted, 'We don't want any paedos here.'

She didn't have time to explain that it wasn't going to be a halfway house. It was going to be a hostel for people who needed emergency accommodation, but people had jumped to all sorts of conclusions. Another banner stated, 'Our children deserve better. Crack heads not welcome here!' A uniformed police officer came out of the building with a man in handcuffs. They'd caught the intruder and Sasha could see the spray can of black paint in an evidence bag. Great, the damage in question was graffiti. The renovation was already costing a fortune and she could do with the house up and running as soon as possible. She had an ever-growing list of people who needed rooms in a place like this and this building alone had fifteen much-needed bedrooms.

An icy blast of wind whistled past her ears as she stepped closer to the car park. A part of her never wanted to step inside again but it was her job and asking Trevor to go in alone wouldn't be fair. She shook her head and took a deep breath, the cold air a shock to her lungs.

She half-smiled and followed Trevor over towards the huge double-doored entrance to the building. Above her, the canopy rested on two imposingly thick pillars. They made her feel as though the walls were closing in. Her feet were twitching to step back into the car park. The painted rainbow had been left above the doorbell of what was previously a children's nursery. She was glad that it had been left. It was the only cheery thing about the building. It had double-glazed new windows, freshly plastered walls and lovely divided up housing units with fresh communal areas. She'd seen all the photos. They had made little difference to the old feel of the place. It was literally a bottomless money pit being such an old building.

This was the first time she'd seen it in the flesh since they'd bought the building and it sent a shiver running through her. She'd seen the plans and she'd seen the designs. Her job was making sure it opened and was swiftly filled up with the people on her list.

'Shall we go and review the damage?' Trevor pressed his lips together in a smile. He placed the huge steel key in the keyhole and turned it in the lock. The sound of metal clicking in metal sent her heart pounding. With a creak the main door allowed itself to be smoothly opened. They stepped in, leaving the commotion behind as they closed the door to the protest. She glanced through a side window and could see that some of the people were beginning to leave now that the police had come. They'd had a planning meeting a long time ago, and everyone had been notified. There had been objections but none serious enough to halt the project. What Sasha could see was a bunch of NIMBYs. *We want people off the streets, we want housing for all, but not in my backyard.*

'Yes. Let's check it out and get the hell out of here.' She followed him along the main downstairs corridor, their footsteps echoing in the empty building. The smell of damp plaster tickled her nostrils, and she listened out for the dripping sound coming from the side extension. She'd been told about the leak and as it had rained a short while ago, she was sure the large builder's bucket would be nearly full but there was someone booked to take care of it tomorrow.

'Are you alright, hun?' Trevor beamed a smile and nudged her. 'It's been a tough morning but we'll both be out of here before we know it. I'll be in London, and you'll be tucked up with your cocoa.'

She shook her head and felt her eyes welling up. 'I'm not alright. I just had to leave a mother and a child at the Cleaver. She's staying in the room next door to where the murder took place. She saw the body and all the blood. If only this place was ready now, I could have moved her here.' She pushed one of the downstairs bedroom doors open. Along one wall was a fitted wardrobe and along the other were two single beds. Just down a little further was the safe communal kitchen, ready to service four rooms and next to that a cosy lounge with new seating. It was nothing to look at from the outside but what they'd achieved with the layout was nothing short of a miracle. She barely recognised the place now. She swallowed and her dry throat protested, forcing her to quickly clear her throat. It may not be the same place now but to her it still had an atmosphere. Why did the council have to choose this building over every other suitable building in the area? She loosened her stiff shoulders and rolled them. If she wasn't careful, she'd be tarred with the same brush as Gareth Alderman. *It's just a building and all ghosts have been laid to rest.*

Trevor stepped into the lounge. 'Leaving people in places that aren't right is the hardest part of the job. I know exactly how you feel. But murder, that isn't run-of-the-mill. What happened is horrible. Do you want to talk about it?'

She shook her head. No, she didn't want to think about everything that was swimming in her thoughts for a second longer. As for Kayleigh, what was the point in dwelling when there was nothing she could do to help. She needed to banish all thoughts of Kayleigh's little dot of a girl and the fact that she'd be sleeping next door to a murder scene. 'I think I just need to check out the damage and get out of here. I've cancelled dinner with my sister, but you know what, if we hurry and make sure this place is secure, I think I may get there, albeit a touch late.'

'And I am not going to miss my train, so that's a deal.'

She spotted the smashed downstairs window. Scattered glass reached the furthest parts of the room.

Trevor scrunched his nose. 'So, we need to get an emergency glazier out.' He stepped out of the room and began tapping out a message on his tablet. 'I think dinner with your sister is just what you need. Spend some time with that lovely niece of yours.' As they trawled through all the downstairs rooms no more damage had been spotted. Maybe the police had got here just in time to prevent the man using the spray can.

'I think I will.' It wouldn't make all her problems go away, though. She still had the troublesome teen to contend with. After finding the smashed eggs on her car, the worm in her letter box and the night-time calling and hanging up, she shuddered at what else might happen. The worst thing was, she couldn't prove it was him so the police probably wouldn't be able to do a thing. She pulled out her phone and sent a message to her sister. She needed some normality and, if she was honest with herself, she didn't want to go straight back to her flat. It was cold and miserable; her sister's house was warm and full of joy, and she loved her little niece so much. Maybe a cuddle would lift her mood.

'Right, we best go upstairs. Maybe it's our lucky day and no damage has been done. We could be out of here in the next hour.' His tablet lit up. 'Glazier is on his way so that's sorted.'

Sasha followed him up the dark stairs. The electricity to this part of the house hadn't been connected so they were in darkness until light seeped from the first-floor landing. 'Damn.' Each room they passed had one sentence sprayed on each wall. 'Paedos die!' But it was the room on the left, just past the bathroom that almost made her choke on the air that she'd inhaled. 'The spray can the police officer had bagged up was a black spray paint. Every bit of graffiti is black. This is red spray.'

Trevor updated his diary as they entered. Sasha stepped closer and stared as she read it again.

'You okay?'

She nodded, but she wasn't okay. Trevor continued tapping away on his device, oblivious to the worry lines forming on her face as she stared at the writing. The message was loud and clear; she had a feeling it was for her. I WILL MAKE YOU PAY.

TWELVE

Gina watched Jacob park in a space opposite the wide block of flats that overlooked a football pitch and playing field. She blew on her chilly fingertips as she waited for him to finish sending a message and do his coat up. Sheltered in the overhanging porchway she pressed the buzzer for number ten. The intercom crackled and a woman spoke in a quiet voice. 'Hello.'

'Mrs Lydia Gill?'

'Who is this?' The sound of a child yelling in the background caught Gina's attention. She knew Reid had a daughter.

'I'm DI Harte and I'm here with my colleague, DS Driscoll. May we come in? We need to speak to you.'

'What's this about? If it's Wes, I don't want to know. I'm sick of all his problems.'

'I'd rather not speak through the intercom. There's been an incident and we really need to speak to you in person.' As Gina waited for the woman's response, Jacob folded his arms together to keep his body heat in.

She released the door. They stepped into a warm communal area and proceeded to follow the number signposts until they reached the second floor. Before Gina had a chance to knock, the woman opened the door and peered through the gap. 'What's he done now?' Her forehead creased with a worried look. She opened the door wide and let them in. Gina and Jacob followed her along the dark hallway with its closed doors to a small lounge with a Juliet balcony at the far end. The little girl who looked to be about Gracie's age had a collection of plastic ponies out on the carpet. She grabbed the green-haired one and began brushing its synthetic mane.

'Would you mind if my colleague played ponies with your daughter for a few minutes while we speak?' Gina didn't want to upset the child and she knew Jacob was good with children.

The woman nodded and drew Gina towards the small dining table at the end of the narrow lounge. She grabbed the remote control and turned the volume up on the music channel. 'Yes, whatever it is, I don't want her hearing it. Whatever he's done, it's nothing to do with me anymore. We've split up. He thinks we might get back together but I've given him so many chances. No more. I've moved on.'

Gina watched as Jacob picked up a pony and began talking to the girl. She laughed and passed him a comb. Lydia sat and gestured for Gina to do the same. She zipped her purple onesie up to the neck and began twisting the ends of her long straight mousy hair. She looked young, a lot younger than Wesley, maybe mid-twenties. Gina saw the trail of acne scars running along the woman's forehead where skin met her hairline. 'I'm really sorry to have to tell you this but Wesley Reid was found dead at the hostel he was staying at.'

The woman stared at Gina, her lips slightly apart. 'What?'

'I'm also really sorry to have to tell you that he was murdered, and we really need your help. First, is there anyone I can call to be with you? I know this must be a shock.' Gina exhaled. This was a job she hated more than any other. Lydia and Wesley may have split up, but that man was still father to her child. They still had history and had shared moments together.

'No... you're serious?'

'Sorry. Is there anyone I can call for you?'

'I don't have anyone. My parents disowned me when I took up with Wes at seventeen. It's just me.'

'I'm really sorry to hear that.'

'Me too.' Lydia blew out a puff of breath and rubbed her eyes. 'I don't... I can't... Who? How?'

'We haven't arrested anyone yet and forensics are working the scene at the moment. I should have more information later.' Gina wanted to wait until the press release before any further information about the murder was shared. So far, no one had been told about the coin. That was only for them to know.

A stream of tears began to trickle down Lydia's puffy cheeks. She wiped them away with the back of her hand. Her daughter shrieked with laughter as Jacob pretended that the pony had jumped over her toy car. 'For all his faults, Molly loves him to bits. She's going to be devastated. I had hoped that he would stop the drinking and after that he would have been able to have her, to do things with her. He promised he'd go to AA and sort himself out. There was no hope for us, but I did hope that he and Molly could have a father-daughter relationship.' She grabbed her hair in her hand, elbows on the wooden table. 'What am I going to do?'

Gina didn't have the answer, she tilted her head. 'Can I make you a drink, maybe a sweet cup of tea?'

The woman shook her head.

'Can we talk about Wesley?'

She nodded. 'I want whoever did this found.'

'Can I ask you a few questions?'

'Yes.' Lydia sniffed.

Gina pulled out a notepad from her bag and headed it up.

Jacob was too busy looking after the child to join her. 'When did you and Wesley split up?'

'It was at the end of September. I gave him loads of chances to get help. I dealt with so many drunken nights and hungover days and it wasn't just that, it was the money. I work and he'd barely been able to hold a job down for the past year as he got worse. This cycle has been going on since we met. I had this idealistic idea that I could help him, that he'd get better, and we'd be a happy family, but I realised I couldn't help him. He had to want to help himself and I realised that he didn't want to. I also realised that I didn't love him. I wanted more for me and my daughter than an unpredictable drunken person living with us.'

'So, you split up at the end of September? Where did Wesley go then?'

'I don't know. He grabbed a bag of clothes and some other items, and he left.'

'What other items?'

'Toiletries, some cash that we kept in a tin in the food cupboard and an old Swiss Army knife that used to be his father's. I asked where he was going but he ignored me. I saw him on the high street in Cleevesford, sitting alongside the entrance to the supermarket asking passers-by for coins. I tried to talk to him, but he refused to listen to me. He said he didn't want my help and it was my fault because I'd kicked him out. I told him we should go to the council, see if they had any temporary place where he could stay but he walked off. I hated myself for days. After that, I got in touch with a local charity and asked them if they could help. They help the homeless and someone there promised that they'd talk to him.'

'What charity was that?'

'Safe Night. They operate out of a room in the community centre. A woman called me back a few days ago and told me that they were helping him, and they'd found him a place at a hostel. I begged them to help him with his addiction too and they said they'd do what they could.'

'Do you know the name of the woman you spoke to?'

'No. She did introduce herself, but I can't remember. I thought he'd be safe when he got a roof over his head. It's my fault, I shouldn't have interfered.' The woman stifled a sob.

'Lydia, it's not your fault. You did your best for him, but we need to find his killer. Do you know of anyone who would want to hurt him?' The woman looked so young, almost childlike as she hiccupped a couple of sobs.

'He used to hang out with some right unsavoury people. I told him they were trouble. That was something else we argued about.'

Gina perked up slightly at hearing that. 'Who were these people?'

'There's an old park, not too far from the Cleaver. If you take the path down the back, you get to what is left of it. There's nothing more than a wooden frame of what was once a playhouse with a slide. It's surrounded by a ring of unruly bushes and trees, and he called it the Hangar.'

'And who used to meet him at the Hangar?' Gina scribbled a few notes. She knew of the old park. It had been like that for years, the structure almost reclaimed by nature.

'A group of drinkers with nowhere to go. They hang around there. He used to join them. Sometimes when we had no money at all, he'd go there and scrounge a bit of their drink. That place was the cause of so many of our rows.'

'Did you ever go there?'

'Only once. I followed him there. I wanted to know where he was going all day and how he was coming home drunk. I knew it wouldn't be the pub because we were short of money. He got caught shoplifting a few times. He'd been trying to take vodka and cider from the supermarket. When you turned up today, I thought that's what had happened.'

Gina cleared her throat. 'What happened when you followed him?'

'We reached the Hangar. I kept back so he couldn't see me and watched as he greeted the others. There were three others, all men and one of them instantly handed him a bottle to swig from. One man shouted something in a joking way, along the lines of Wes needing to bring something to the party next time. They all looked a bit down and out. Some had sleeping bags, and another had a pop-up tent. It looked like these people lived at the Hangar. It both broke my heart and angered me at the same time. I didn't confront Wes that day. I went home and seethed for hours. That's when I knew I had to put myself and my daughter first, so I told him to leave.'

Reading over her notes, Gina was happy with what she'd jotted down. They would follow up on the Hangar, see if Wesley Reid had been there on the day he was murdered and find out if he'd fallen out with any one of the others. She thought of the pound coin and wondered, if it was relating to some sort of debt, maybe Wesley didn't fulfil his end of the bargain and take a bottle for the others to share. Maybe he took off them and never gave and having so little, made one of them angry enough to hurt him. Her thoughts went back to Noel Logan, the man who Gina suspected had been lurking around the hostel and had been arguing with Wesley on the night of his murder. 'Do you know a man called Noel Logan?'

Lydia stiffened and sat up straight. 'Yes, but he has nothing to do with all this.'

'Do you have an address for Noel?'

'Yes, he lives at twenty-five, The Greenway.'

'We need to speak to him. He was seen with Wesley on the day of his murder.'

'It wasn't Noel.'

'How can you be so sure?'

'He's a lovely man. Noel and Wes used to be best friends.

He'd do anything for Wes and like me, he tried to get him help to kick the drinking habit. They'd been friends for years.'

'Why would Noel have gone to see Wesley at the hostel?'

Lydia ignored Gina and began picking her nails and shaking her head.

'Lydia, is there something we should know?'

She began to cry, her bottom lip trembling. 'He had something to tell him, something that could only be said in person.'

'And what was that, Lydia?'

Lydia shook her head.

'Lydia, please.'

'I'm pregnant.'

'Let me get this right. Noel Logan, Wesley's friend, went to the hostel to tell him that you are pregnant with his child?'

'Yes. I didn't want Wes to know but it's getting harder to hide now that I'm five months. It's not Wes's baby. Wes and I were together then, but I love Noel. Noel treats me right. He wants to be with me, and he said we could all be a family. Me, Noel, Molly and the baby. We knew it would be tough to tell Wes, but Noel had known him longer than me. We decided it would be best coming from him. Noel had even finished with a woman he was seeing casually. He is serious about me. I'm not some fling.'

That's why Wesley had been trying to fight with Noel in the pub. Gina pictured Wesley leaving, maybe going to the Hangar or hanging around the streets after. Finally, he went back to the hostel at gone eleven. Had Noel been waiting for him to return? Wesley's voice had been raised. He'd have been upset and angry. She pictured the other man in the room pulling out the knife and plunging it into their victim's neck before scarpering away.

'Have you spoken to Mr Logan over this past day?'

'No, he was meant to call me back after he met Wes at the pub last night and he hasn't. He's not answering his phone and

I've been worried.' She began to cry, this time she wasn't trying to hold back or stifle her emotions.

'Mummy,' the little girl ran over and hugged the woman.

'I'm okay, baby girl. Everything will be okay.' She gripped her little one closely and Gina swallowed down her emotion as she thought of Gracie. She didn't know how Lydia was going to cope with telling her child that she'd never see her father again. Gina had never had to have that conversation with Hannah about Terry. Hannah had been a baby at the time, and she'd grown up not having Terry in her life.

Unless Noel Logan could prove where he was at the time of Wesley's murder, he was their prime suspect. The fact that he couldn't be contacted by the woman he supposedly loved had just made everything worse. They needed to find him now.

THIRTEEN

As Gina and Jacob reached the car park, she pulled out her ringing phone. 'Sir,' she said as she waited for Briggs to update her. He continued speaking, giving her the information that she needed for now. Jacob quietly stood next to her, eagerly waiting to hear what was being said. She in turn gave Briggs an update on her visit to the Angel and her interview with Lydia before ending the call. She relayed everything to Jacob. 'Briefing now, back at the station. PC Smith and a team are staying at the Cleaver and continuing with the door-to-doors, but the rest of the team are heading back now. They've widened the search to public areas and neighbours' bins. It looks like the dog team has been dispatched. Hopefully they'll be able to sniff out the murder weapon or something that can help us to identify Wesley Reid's killer.'

Several minutes later they were back at the station and Gina was seated at the top end of the table by the boards that Briggs had prepared in their absence. He'd marked it up with the scene details and the crime scene photos that Bernard had sent through. A list of witnesses and their person of interest, Noel Logan, had been written on the next board. She grabbed the coffee pot that O'Connor had just placed on the table and poured a mug for herself, before grabbing a flapjack and biting into the chewy oats. Wyre zipped up her jacket and PC Kapoor turned on the fan heater. Jacob passed her a folder in which all their notes to date had been collated but not yet put on the system.

Briggs strode in, brushing his hair flat against his head with his palm. Gina could tell that he'd been running his fingers through it from the front to the back, which sometimes left a little sticking up out of place. He loosened his tie.

Why had he messed up the good thing they had? She shook those thoughts away. Her headspace should be focused on finding their suspect, not on what she once had with Briggs. It would be a long time before she could trust again. 'Has uniform tried Noel Logan's house yet?'

Briggs nodded. 'Yes. As soon as we spoke, I got someone down there immediately. No answer. We checked to see if he has a car, and he does but it wasn't on the drive or parked up nearby. All units have been alerted and hopefully he will show up on ANPR and we can bring him in.' He clapped to calm the hum of the room down. 'Thanks for getting back so fast. We have a lot to cover and it's going to be a busy day so let's not waste any time. As you can see by the boards, everything I've had fed back in real time has been added. Wyre. Your writing is by far the neatest.' Briggs passed Wyre the pen and she stood at the board. 'Gina?'

'Yes, sir.' Gina knew that Automatic Number Plate Recognition would pick Noel Logan's car up if he travelled on any of the main roads that they had covered by the system.

'You're Senior Investigating Officer on this case.'

'Okay, thanks, sir.' A part of her wondered if she could handle running the case with having Gracie to look after, then she gazed around at her team. They depended on her. She had to do this. Her heart began to hum. Mrs O had Gracie for the day. What was she going to do tomorrow? A thought flashed through her mind, and she shooed it away. No way would she ask her dead husband's mother to look after Gracie, even though Gracie knew her well and had stayed there on many occasions. She couldn't face the woman who deep down knew she had something to do with Terry's death and threats to his brother. There were things in Gina and Briggs's past that they could never speak of again and threatening to frame Terry's brother Stephen for a crime in order to get him to leave Gina alone, was one of them. The woman had even blamed Gina for Stephen being in prison for another crime, one he really did commit but domestic violence ran rife in their family. Asking Hetty was not an option and never would be.

'Gina.' She flinched as Briggs said her name, taking her away from her thoughts.

'Yes.'

'We're all up to date with the scene of the murder. Can you quickly summarise what you found out this morning?'

Gina stood beside the board and Wyre remained poised to note everything down in the right places. 'Jacob and I have visited the Angel Arms and the victim's ex-partner this morning. Her name is Lydia Gill. We have a name and address of a suspect called Noel Logan. It has been reported that a man has been hanging around the Cleaver and it has also been reported that Noel was arguing with our victim at the Angel Arms on the night of his murder. So far, we haven't been able to locate Mr Logan, so we need to speak to him. We do know that Lydia Gill has been in a relationship with Noel Logan for at least five months as she's five months pregnant with Noel's child. We also know that Lydia Gill asked Wesley to leave at the end of September, which is only five or six weeks ago at most, so while she and Noel were having an affair. She said Noel was going to tell Wesley yesterday and that may have been the cause of the argument and tussle at the Angel Arms. We don't know what was said or what happened after that but I'm guessing that Wesley didn't take the news well. Wesley tried to hit Mr Logan but missed. It could be that Noel Logan still saw Wesley as a threat to his new life. Lydia Gill seemed to still have a lot of sympathy towards Reid, even intervening and trying to get him help from a charity. She wanted him to remain in their daughter's life. Maybe that didn't fit with Noel Logan's plans giving him a motive. Of course, all these are theories. What we really need to do is speak to Noel himself. All units are on alert. Kapoor?'

Kapoor nodded and smiled.

'Can you organise for an officer to remain outside Mr Logan's house at all times? If we don't catch him on ANPR, we will pick him up when he comes home. We know he drives a blue Volvo, and we have his registration. Also, it would be good to ask Elouise at the Angel to keep an eye out for him. The Angel seems to be his local. He might just turn up there.'

'Will do, guv.' The young officer took her police hat off and scratched her head.

'Did you get the CCTV from the Angel?'

She nodded.

'Great. O'Connor, could you go through it. I'm going to update the system as soon as this briefing is over. I want you to please make sure that what was said tallies with what actually happened. Elouise is normally great at remembering things but we're all only human, things can be missed. I need exact times.'

'Will do, guv.' O'Connor swigged his coffee down in one and poured himself another.

'This is what we have so far. The Cleaver. At the scene we have a witness who found the body. A young woman called Kayleigh who has a little girl. There is also a man who lives on the bottom floor, his name is Gareth Alderman. We need to treat him with care as I don't want to exacerbate his mental health issues. Tread gently.' She paused before continuing. 'He spoke a lot about his daughter and when Wyre and I went into his room we saw the child's bed made up. We found out later that his child was no longer alive. He thinks the house is haunted from what I'm gathering, and he shouted at our victim on the night of his murder. Wyre, would you be able to delve more deeply into Gareth Alderman? Like I said, tread gently. He has suffered a breakdown and he had an anxiety attack while we were there, but I can't ignore the fact that he didn't like our victim and was angry with him.'

'Could you tell us about the scene?' Briggs asked.

'Yes, Wesley was stabbed in his room, not too far from his bed. He then crawled towards the bed, using the quilt to pull himself up. It looked like he had been positioned on his back where he continued to bleed out. There was a Swiss Army knife under the bed. Since speaking to his ex-partner, Lydia, we can confirm that the knife belonged to Wesley. We also know that it wasn't the weapon used to stab him. His sheets and clothes smelled of cider, but we have yet to locate any empty cans or bottles in his room. Any updates on the bin search? We don't know if the murderer brought the alcohol with them, or if the cans or bottles were already in his room.'

Kapoor nodded. 'I was there when they were going through the bins, guv. There are a lot of empty cans of cider all in one bag, along with general waste like crisp wrappers. There is also a letter from housing with Wesley Reid's address on so we can conclude that we found one of his rubbish bags. The whole bag has been booked into evidence so it will all be checked.'

Gina clasped her hands together. 'That's great. The one thing that was striking was a one-pound coin that had been placed in the centre of his forehead. We have no idea what this means but bear in mind that it's probably symbolic in nature. It won't be made public. If anything comes to mind while we're investigating, mention it straight away. It also suggests that Wesley was chosen for a reason. It's personal. As for our assailant, the scene would suggest that they'd have been lucky to not have any blood on their clothing or even spatter on their face. The dogs are out. Maybe, just maybe, they'll pick something up. Jacob and I will fully update the system as soon as we're finished here, and you can go through it thoroughly. Have digital forensics managed to start up Wesley's phone? I know it was sent from the scene and booked into evidence here.'

Wyre held her pen up. 'I checked on that, guv. Tech will get the message and call log reports emailed over very soon. They're working on it as we speak.'

'There is one other person who needs looking into and that's the house manager, Frederick Bertram. He was the last person to see Wesley Reid alive. Jacob and I will go and check his alibi out. If you find out anything about him we should know, call me straight away.' Gina glanced at Wyre and O'Connor, knowing that one of them would do that as soon as they had a moment. 'Oh, and yet another job to add to the list, can someone find a contact we can visit at the Safe Night charity. We know that they helped Wesley Reid, and this help was instigated by Lydia Gill. Sir, what time will the press release be aired?'

'Within the next half an hour. No names will be released yet but I've appealed for witnesses. At the time I gave it, we hadn't spoken to Lydia Gill.'

'Hopefully we might get some witnesses come forward. Right, let's not waste a moment. We all know what we're doing next. Thank you, all, and keep me updated.'

Wyre hurriedly updated all the notes on the board. Gina glanced at the map with its one pin stabbed where the Cleevesford Cleaver was. She grabbed a handful of pins and popped a few more in, showing all the places they'd been and marking them up.

'Guv.'

She turned around and smiled at O'Connor.

'Wesley's phone report is ready to view. We've just had an email.' O'Connor hurried over to a computer and logged on. With a few clicks of the mouse, he was in the system and opening the messages that were on Wesley's phone from Noel.

I need to speak to you. Meet me at the Angel at seven.

Then there were others from Mr Logan, sent after.

You're nothing but a loser, stay away from Lydia. She's never loved you. Go near her and I'll kill you!

Wesley hadn't replied to any of the messages. The last message sent a chill across Gina's shoulders. It had been sent only an hour before the other residents in the house had heard Wesley come back. She stared at the gun emoji at the end of the message. It was clear now. Noel Logan was on the run, that's why no one had heard from him, and he wasn't home.

You're a dead man, Wes!

FOURTEEN

SASHA

Sasha turned into the country road and, from her car window, took in the welcoming orange glow of her sister's lounge. Full of love and warmth, she couldn't wait to get in and unfreeze her toes. Their two black-and-white cats sat on the window ledge and her niece was twirling with a ribbon on a stick. As hard as she tried, she could not forget those words on the wall. They couldn't be personal, surely? It was simply some vandal that had gained access to the building, not the kids that had been terrorising her. She swallowed. Paranoid was now her second name. Trevor had stared at the writing for a moment, then simply rolled his eyes before arranging for a decorator to come along and paint over the mess. The protester had been arrested for the graffiti and that was the end of it, but those words had lingered in her thoughts.

Her gorgeous brown-eyed niece ran to the window and waved frantically. The cats scarpered. Sasha held a hand up, grabbed the large packet of chocolate buttons and the bottle of white wine that she'd picked up from the petrol station and exited the car. The frost had melted after being hit with a light rain shower. She ran to the door and waited as Yasmin flung the door open and charged at Sasha, hugging her. 'Aunty Sasha, come and see the cat house I made.' Leaving the gifts on the console table, she removed her shoes. She smiled as she allowed this perfect little nine-year-old being to lead her to the lounge where she began to tell her about the cardboard box that she'd drawn castle features on.

Her sister was clattering pans in the kitchen. 'I'll be with you in five. Just getting the broccoli on. Dad's running late too.'

Sasha kneeled on the rug, trying hard to forget the horrible morning she'd had and immerse herself in family, just for a few hours. 'You are such a fabulous cat house maker, Yasmin. I love it. Have the cats tried it out yet?'

'No.' Yasmin scrunched up her nose and laughed. 'I haven't finished. I still have to colour in the other side.'

Her flustered sister walked in, wiping her hands on her stripy apron. 'Dinner will be done in five and Dad's just pulled up. Can you let him in?' Tanya rushed back out to the kitchen. Her sister, although two years Sasha's junior at thirty-seven, didn't look much over thirty. Their blonde hair, freckled noses and curvy figures were where the similarities ended. Being wealthier had kept Tanya looking fresh with all her spa days, honeyed highlights and nail bar trips. Her home was always warm, and she ate the best of food, not like Sasha who mainly ate microwave food. Granted, Tanya was widowed at an early age which paid off her mortgage. Sasha never resented having less, she loved her sister with all her heart and appreciated how hard she'd had it.

Sasha left her niece and hurried to open the door. Her dad removed his cap and wiped his feet before stepping into the hall. 'I'm so glad I have my girls together today. I thought you weren't coming.' He took off his coat, throwing it over the newel post at the bottom of the stairs and gave her a hug. 'You've made your old dad's day. Haven't seen you in ages, Sash. Where've you been?'

'Sorry, Dad. Work has just been so busy. Tanya held dinner off a bit as I got called out to one of the buildings I look after.'

'It's the Cleaver, isn't it?'

She furrowed her brows. 'How did you know that?'

'I just saw the press release on the local news. Man murdered. You know, love, I think dealing with things like that is beyond your job description.'

Sasha shrugged. 'I had scared residents. I couldn't just ignore what had happened.'

'Well don't go putting yourself in any danger.' He stood and assessed her, his wrinkled blue eyes meeting hers. 'Are you okay?'

He could tell that something wasn't right. He always had that ability, but she wasn't going to burden her dear old dad with stories of graffiti and her car being egged. He was too much of a worrier. 'I'm all better now I'm here and that chicken is making me drool. I'm so hungry. Shall we go and help?'

'You go ahead. I'm going to catch up with the bestest grand-daughter in the whole world,' he shouted as Yasmin ran over to him, delighted that she had someone else to show her cat house to.

Sasha ambled through the farmhouse kitchen where her sister was pulling a pan off the Aga ready to drain the vegetables.

'You may have pulled the wool over Dad's eyes about all being okay, but I can tell when my sister is holding back. What is it?' Tanya started plating up chunks of roast chicken and potatoes as she spoke.

Not saying a word, Sasha took a swivel seat at the breakfast bar and sat with her head in her hands, slumped over the worktop. 'I don't want to ruin dinner.'

Tanya wiped her hands on her apron and walked over, placing a warm arm around Sasha. 'We're family. We have each other and I don't care about dinner. I heard Dad mention the murder. Is that what's upset you?'

'Partly. I had to tell a mother with a little girl that I couldn't get a room anywhere else. She is staying in a room next to where the man was murdered. Not only that, she found the body. I can't begin to imagine how horrific that was. When I came in and saw Yasmin... I can't get her little girl out of my mind.' She sniffed and wiped her dampening eyes. 'Sometimes this job stinks.'

'I don't know how you do it.'

Tears began to fall. Feeling her sister's warmth was bringing out emotions she'd been suppressing all day. 'And some kid threw eggs at my car and posted a worm through my letter box.' Her chin began to wobble as she sobbed in her sister's arms.

'Aww, sis, have you called the police?'

Sasha pulled away slightly, grabbed a piece of kitchen roll and wiped her eyes. 'No. I haven't actually caught him doing anything. He just whizzes past on those bloody illegal electric scooters and the police don't give a stuff. I guess with murders happening in the town, they have bigger things to deal with.' She sat up straight and took a deep breath. Her sister was being so kind, but Sasha really was spoiling dinner now. 'It's no big deal, really. The murder has got to me, that's all. That stupid kid did nothing. He'll get fed up. I'll ask a few neighbours if they've had any problems with him and maybe we can all keep a look out on each other's cars.'

'Do you want to stay here for a bit? You're always welcome to take the sofa in my home office. I don't think you'd want to sleep in Yasmin's cabin bed.'

However, much as Sasha loved her sister, she didn't want to move in, even temporarily. It got chilly but she loved her own space and her flat. She loved that when she had a bout of insomnia, she could get up and put the telly on. She wouldn't feel comfortable at all in someone else's house. She remembered back to when they were teens, and they shared a room. Their hormones made sure the arguments they had were explosive. 'I'm honestly okay. I'll be fine. It's just been a bad day at the office.'

'Right.' Tanya threw an apron at Sasha. 'Can you take the crumble that I've made in that bowl and put it on the apple in the dish, then pop it in the oven?'

Sasha smiled and did as she was told. 'Now you can tell me all about the new man in your life and when do we get to meet him?' An update on her sister's new relationship might just take her mind off her horrible day.

Dinner was most welcome, and the crumble was to die for. Much tastier than anything she'd eaten since the last time she came for Sunday dinner at her sister's. As they all sat in the lounge, the log burner blazing away, Sasha felt her eyes drooping as she sat back in the chair and dozed to *The Little Mermaid*. Her dad had fallen asleep at least an hour ago and her sister was taping away on her iPad. Afternoon would soon turn to evening, and she'd have to head home. Her phone buzzed in her pocket. She yawned and pulled it out. She read the message from the neighbour she'd spoken to that morning.

Hi neighbour. I thought you should know; I just saw a figure dart by and a second later, I heard a window smash. When I went out, I saw it was your window. Sorry to be the bearer of bad news and sorry I was in such a hurry this morning.

She jerked up and grabbed her bag. 'I have to go.'

'Already,' Tanya replied. 'I thought we were going to play a game in a bit.'

'Work stuff.' She wasn't going to tell Tanya what was in her message but the thought of her window being smashed was making her stomach sick. It was no good, she had to start keeping a log and then when she had enough, she'd call the police. She was clearly being targeted and this kid wasn't going to stop.

FIFTEEN

Gina and Jacob had rushed to input everything into the system and then she'd taken up Jacob's offer of driving them to their next destination. Afternoon was soon becoming evening and darkness had crept upon them. She needed to get a move on. Gracie would wonder where she was. Her phone buzzed. She opened the photo of Hannah and Greg at the top of the Eiffel Tower, her daughter's blonde hair flying in the breeze as they stood in front of the mesh at the top. She read the message underneath.

Tried to call earlier but you didn't answer. Is everything okay? Has something happened?

She pressed out a quick reply with shaky hands. Lying to her daughter wasn't an easy thing to do but she didn't want to upset Hannah.

Sorry, I should have called you back, but we've been out and about. I was driving at the time. Gracie has fallen asleep but she's good. Love you loads and have a lovely time. Don't worry about us.

A sick feeling whirred around in Gina's stomach.

Jacob steered the car into the supermarket car park opposite the high street and put the handbrake on. 'Everything okay?'

She nodded and forced a smile. They stepped out and Gina glanced at the café. She could see the door next to it and it was marked up in black paint as 11A. After failing to locate a bell, Gina rapped on the wooden door and waited. She glanced up. A light was on so someone was in. Jacob placed his ear to the door. 'There's someone coming.'

After a struggle, the man wrenched the door open. His peacock kimono blew in the breeze revealing his bare feet as he stared at them. 'Can I help you?'

Gina held her identification up. 'I'm DI Harte, this is DS Driscoll. May we come in?'

He scrunched his brow and scratched his ice-blond buzz cut hair. 'I guess.' He went first and Gina followed as Jacob closed the bottom door. The stairway opened up to a large living room that was painted in a deep grey and surrounded by bookshelves. A large lamp with a flamingo base sat on the beautifully carved occasional table. 'Take a seat.'

Gina moved a couple of plump cushions aside. The young man picked up a carafe and poured a drink into a diamond cut glass.

'Do you want a brandy? I find it warms up these cold nights.' His smile seemed to reach across his face and for a change Gina felt they were welcomed.

'That's very kind of you, but we're on duty.'

'So, we move on to how I can help you. I trust I'm not in any trouble as I haven't done anything wrong.'

Gina smiled. 'We're investigating a very serious crime and we need to check someone's alibi.'

Jacob fidgeted on the sofa as he struggled to know where to throw the cushions. After a few seconds, he pulled out his pad and pen.

'Ooh, an alibi. Let me guess, it has to be for Freddie. I'm guessing at him as I've not really seen another soul for a couple of weeks, unless we're going further back that is.'

'It is. Frederick Bertram said you were with him last night.'

'That's correct. He stayed with me and left this morning. Is that all you needed to know. He left early as it was still dark. I was half asleep, so I didn't check the time. All I heard was his struggling to pull the door closed.' The man sipped the amber liquid in his glass. 'Has this got anything to do with the murder that was mentioned on the news earlier? I know Freddie works at the Cleaver. When I saw the report, I thought of him.'

'Sadly, it does. Could you please confirm the time he arrived at yours last night?'

Killian's eyes sparkled in the lamplight. 'It had to be about twelve thirty, maybe a touch later. No, it was twelve thirty. I almost gave up on him coming but then he knocked.'

'How did he seem?' Gina felt her heart rate picking up. Frederick Bertram should have arrived at Killian's by eleven thirty-five at the latest. He hadn't told them the truth which put him on the suspect list. Gina didn't know what his motive might be, but he'd lied to them.

'He seemed chilled.'

'How well do you know him?' Gina knew Frederick's side of the story, she needed to check Killian's side. Maybe they'd spoken on the phone or had lengthy talks in the night. The more she could get to know about the man, the better.

'I don't know him, but I really enjoyed his company. Last night was the first time I met him, and we've only messaged once on an app. He was local, we had a few things in common, so I thought why not? I've been single for a long time and right now, I'm ready to let someone into my life. I thought Freddie seemed nice.'

'What happened when he arrived?'

'We had a drink and then, erm... I guess I don't need to go into detail. Fill in the blanks. After we lay in bed and talked for a couple of hours. He's a funny guy. He told me about his upbringing and his previous relationship. We spoke about how we came out and how my dad freaked.' Killian let out a small laugh. 'I told him that I was a writer and that I was looking for more than just a fling. We seemed in tune. He was happy and so was I. That's what happened. We eventually fell asleep, and you know the rest. He did promise that he'd come back tonight. If you're thinking that Freddie could hurt that man, you really are barking up the wrong tree. He's as gentle as they come.'

Killian had painted a lovely little story of loves first meeting but she still had Frederick's lie to contend with. From what the man in front of her was saying, Frederick couldn't hurt a fly but then again, Killian had only met him in person the previous night. They had to question him again. Getting him into the station was the only way.

'Thank you for your time. If you can think of anything else, please call me.' She placed her card next to the flamingo lamp base and stood, not wanting to get off the comfortable settee and go back out into the cold.

'I will. Please see yourselves out if you don't mind. I'd like to get back to my film.'

Gina pressed her lips and nodded to Jacob as she started walking to the stairs. Killian picked up a pound coin from the arm of the velvet chair he was sitting in, and he began to twiddle it between his knuckles, but he dropped it and shook his head.

'You're learning to do coin tricks?' Gina asked, the pound coin piquing her interest.

Killian laughed. 'Freddie was trying to teach me how to run a coin along my knuckles. He's really good at it. He left this next to the bed and said I needed the practice. See, I said he was a fun guy.'

As soon as they got outside, Gina spoke. 'We need to get word to the station. Frederick Bertram has a lot of explaining to do. Will you call them. Ask uniform to bring him in for a statement? If he refuses, we'll have to make it formal.'

SIXTEEN

UNKNOWN

There were people everywhere this morning and it's all down to me. Police, medical staff, kids recording everything on their phones – they were all out. As soon as the detectives in plain clothes arrived at the scene, I kept a low profile.

The nosy people with their phones and the YouTuber were most welcome. I wanted them to record what was happening and I wanted *her* to be here. I need her, she just doesn't know it yet.

My heart bangs in my chest as I replay what happened, second by second. The fear in Wesley's eyes brought a level of joy that I could never have imagined I'd ever feel. He's scum. He did nothing but make those around him unhappy.

Up until last night, I'd been unsure as to how far I would go but it was simple beyond belief. Before that, I'd only imagined how it would feel to end him. A part of me thought that when the time came, I'd crumble. Or maybe he'd put up a harder fight, but he had no strength in him. He was so tanked up and swaying all over the place, a child could have taken him down. After I plunged that knife into his neck, the level of jubilation I felt was incomparable to anything.

I feel amazing still, like I'm riding on some weird high. I run my fingers through the pocket of pound coins that I've collected and know that my plan is being played out as it should be. I need another fix, and I know who's next. Wesley was just the start.

Reaching into my rucksack, I feel for the blade. It is exactly where it should be and is begging to revel in the blood of the guilty.

Glancing up at Lydia Gill's flat, I watch as she pulls the curtains closed, blocking out the night. She is finally free from him, and I know deep down, she's thankful. Her poor daughter didn't need a daddy like that in her life. She'll have a new daddy soon and she'll forget that Wesley ever existed. I know everything about her. My research has been thorough. I know all I need to know about everyone.

As I swallow, I feel a lump in my throat and for a second the world sways a little. I need to hold on to the swing post in the park while I get a grip. Another wave of reality hits me. I killed him. That actually happened. Maybe I'll sit for just a moment to process that thought. I press my feet into the hard ground. The metal frame creaks as I swing back and forth.

I seriously didn't think I'd have it in me, but I'd been pushed over the edge. When a certain piece of news had been announced, all those memories came flooding back and I knew I couldn't ignore them. Then came that video on YouTube. It really meant a lot and I knew it was time to act. It was my calling.

At first, I couldn't sleep or eat. The crazy nightmares had me questioning what was real, but I fought my way out of the fog. I haven't seen with such clarity for years. All that angst that I'd turned inwards until it felt like poison bubbling within me, burning through my gut from the inside out, was now neutralised by my mission. Yes, my mission. My purpose. My reason for existing. For years I've felt dead inside but now, that spark of returning life is an erupting volcano.

I pull my phone from my pocket and watch back the recording I made this morning. In the clip, the crowd of people milling around seem unsure as to what was going on, but it is that certain female who claims my attention. She doesn't know it yet, but she is the chosen one. Very soon, the world is going to know who she is, and she'll have me to thank.

What I've tasted so far is sweet and the only way I can satiate my appetite is to greedily consume more. This is only the beginning. I go online and stare at the face in the photo.

You're next!

SEVENTEEN

MACIE

'Welcome back. I'm Macie Perrin of Macie Perrin Reportz Crime and Ghosts! Have I got something for you all tonight? A murder! Yes, you heard me right, a murder has taken place at the Cleevesford Cleaver. Now a hostel for the homeless, it was once a butcher's back in its day. If you want to know more about the Cleaver and its history, check out my Cleaver vid. The link is in the deets.' Macie paused knowing she was going to cut at this point. She would show some of the footage she took of the ambulance staff and police entering the building and then she'd flash up the name of her Cleevesford Cleaver video. That would lead to more clicks. 'Kerching,' she whispered under her breath.

'Macie?' her father yelled up the stairs. She turned off her ring light, hurried to her bedroom door and opened it.

'What? I'm trying to record up here, Dad. It would help if you didn't shout.'

He ran up the stairs. 'I don't care what you're doing. This...' – he pointed at the pile of wrappers and plates on her chest of drawers – 'has to be sorted. It stinks in this room and I'm sick of clearing up after you. You're eighteen but sometimes I feel as though I'm living with a twelve-year-old.' He sighed. 'I had a call from the school earlier. You didn't attend any lessons last week and they wondered if you were okay.'

She wasn't expecting that. How dare the school call her dad. She was an adult now. She'd been eighteen for a whole two weeks. Surely, they had to call her if they had any problems. Besides, she didn't know if she wanted to finish her A levels. 'I'm going in tomorrow. It's just—'

'What? You're ruining your future?'

'No, this is my future, Dad.' She pointed to her desk and ring light. 'Last week, I had seventy thousand hits, and my subscriber numbers are going berserk.'

He walked over to her desk and slammed a hand on it. 'This won't pay your bills. This won't give you a future and it's no substitute for getting all the qualifications you need to become a journalist. Don't blow it all for a bit of social media popularity.'

She felt her insides twisting. He knew nothing. TikTok and YouTube were the future. No one cared about the news on TV or even read a physical copy of a newspaper any more. They checked out TikTok, watched YouTube and listened to podcasts. He was out of touch, and she was the future. He just couldn't see it. 'I'm onto something big, Dad, but I don't expect you to understand.'

'What the hell? You sound like a child. You are throwing your future down the pan and if your mother could see you now, she'd be turning in her grave, rest her soul.'

'Dad, I'm not. I want to show you something. Look.' She grabbed her tablet, swiped a couple of screens and passed it to him.

He scrunched his brow. 'What is this?'

'It's my YouTube account, what they pay me.'

He slowly stumbled back until he was sitting on her ruffled bedding. 'You... you earn this?'

She nodded slowly and took the tablet from him. 'Yes, and for every video I post, I get more. Don't you see, Dad. This is the future.'

Very soon, she'd be up to one thousand pounds per month and the sky was the limit with all the new subscribers that were coming her way. She was happily chasing stories about spooky buildings and local crimes at any given moment. Going to school was paying her stuff all. Now was her time and if she didn't capitalise on it, she would be stuck in a dead-end job working for someone else for the rest of her life. She'd be told when lunch break was, when she could go to the toilet and how many weeks of holiday she could take in a year. No way. That wasn't what she wanted. She'd had enough of that at Cleevesford High.

'The future it might be but you're going to school tomorrow. You can do this in your free time, but I won't have you blowing your education. Whatever you might think, there is no substitute for proper qualifications.'

She swallowed. 'Okay, deal.'

'I'll be calling in and checking that you're there.'

'Dad, I'm an adult.' She threw her tablet to the bed.

'Then start acting like one and clear that rubbish up. I'm sick of the house smelling like the local tip and did you have to get that nose ring?'

'Yep.' She grabbed a pile of plates and nudged past him. If he kept on at her, she would take her earnings and rent a room somewhere. She didn't need his lectures any more.

'And, Macie?'

She sighed and turned to him on the landing flashing a scowl his way.

'I love you, okay. All I want is what's best for you.'

She shrugged and continued down the stairs, not wanting to continue their conversation any longer. She had a report to film and edit, and now she would have to go to school in the morning. As she finished loading the last plate in the dishwasher, her phone buzzed. She pulled it out of her pocket and opened the private message on her TikTok account.

You are the chosen one.

EIGHTEEN

As Gina hurried into her office, her phone beeped. It was Hannah again.

Thanks so much for having her, Mum. This trip was just what we needed. I really do appreciate you helping me with her. What have you both been up to?

Her fingers hovered over the keys as she swallowed down her guilt. Maybe she should come clean and tell Hannah what had happened. No doubt Gracie would once Hannah arrived home and collected her. Gina pressed her lips together. If Hannah had one sniff of what was happening, she'd probably get on a plane immediately. Instead, she replied.

I forgot to say in my last message. Gracie made cupcakes today. I'll send you a photo in a bit. X

Aww, I'd love that. Give her a kiss for me and when she wakes up, tell her that Mummy loves her. X

Gina hoped that Mrs O would send Gracie back with a few cakes so that she could take a photo of them. She hated keeping everything from her daughter, but she had no choice. Gracie was safe. She'd had a lovely day and Gina would be taking her back home soon. Her stomach began to churn. She had no idea how she was going to deal with tomorrow, let alone Tuesday when Gracie had to be back for school after a teacher training day. Maybe she'd have to drive to Hannah's that morning, drop Gracie off and drive straight back to Cleevesford. She'd cross that bridge when she got to it, but at least she had a plan of sorts. Her brain ached with all the problems she was trying to work through.

'Ah, guv. I was just about to call you but then I saw Jacob and he said you were in your office. Gracie is on her way back,' O'Connor said. 'They'll be about half an hour.'

'Thank you so much. Is Frederick Bertram here yet?'

'That's another thing. No. Uniform went to his annexe, and he wasn't there. They asked a few of the residents and no one has seen him this afternoon. One of them went out earlier and saw him leaving.'

'Any luck with calling him?'

'No answer.'

'Great. I guess as soon as Gracie gets here, I'll head home. If any of you need me, I'll be working after I've put her to bed.'

He sidled in a little further. 'Mrs O said she'd have Gracie again tomorrow if you need her to. She really enjoyed having that little gem with her today and tomorrow she has a day off.'

Gina felt her heartbeat ramping up. Hannah wouldn't be happy, but Gina had no choice. Her team needed her on the case. Gracie was going to spend the day with someone who loved children and who'd cherish every moment with her. She knew that Mrs O would look after Gracie like she was the most precious person on Earth.

O'Connor smiled. 'I'll rephrase that. Mrs O said please

could she look after Gracie again tomorrow? I told her how huge the case was, and she would really love to take Gracie to the nature reserve in Birmingham to see the wallabies.'

Gina smiled. 'Of course. Gracie would love that, and I really am grateful. I owe you and Mrs O a big one.'

'Nonsense. It's all her pleasure. Thank you too. My wife will be so happy.' He smiled and hurried out of her office. With no time to waste, she headed straight to the incident room for a quick catch up before Gracie returned. Without Frederick Bertram being brought in, she was ready to leave as soon as possible. As she entered, Wyre had just finished updating the system and O'Connor was standing next to the board with Jacob.

Briggs came over and gestured for her to follow him into her office. 'O'Connor said that Gracie is on her way back, so I assume you'll be heading off soon. I just wanted to thank you for coming in today. All the statements you've collated have been really helpful—'

'Sir, I'll be back tomorrow and working from home tonight. I'm not letting this killer walk the streets for longer than needed and the more brains on this, the better.'

'Okay. Thank you, again.'

'Mrs O has kindly offered to take Gracie out to see some wallabies tomorrow so we're okay. Tuesday is a problem for me, though. I was meant to go and stop at Hannah's tomorrow evening as Gracie is back at school on Tuesday. Tomorrow is a teacher training day, so all is good but come Tuesday, there is no one else.'

'Are you sure you can be here tomorrow? I know your time with her is precious.'

'I'm already invested, and I want to interview Bertram. Besides, I've been informed that Mrs O is really excited about tomorrow and I know Gracie will love going out with her.' Gina began scooping a pile of files into her bag, ready for later. As soon as Gracie had gone to bed, she'd get them out and continue where she left off. She'd look through O'Connor's notes on the CCTV and maybe go through it again herself. She'd see if Bernard had any further information and she'd be waiting to hear any updates on whether Logan or Bertram had been found.

'Great. If you're working later, can I come over and join you? With work, that is. I could bring a takeaway while we go through all the statements again.'

'I err...' She looked up at him, wondering if work was really the only thing on his mind. 'Probably best not. I need to spend some time with Gracie, but...' She paused before she said any more.

'But what?' Hope lit up in his eyes.

She threw her bag over her shoulder and ushered him out as she turned her office light off. 'Call me.' She hurried away from him wondering if she'd just said the right thing. Her head was crying 'no,' but her heart was steering her right back towards him.

'Nanny.' Gracie ran down the corridor and flung her arms around Gina just at the right time. 'I made blue cakes with flowers on them. Can we send Mummy a photo?'

Gina nodded. 'Of course we can, chicken. As soon as we're home, we'll do that.' She swallowed, hoping Hannah wouldn't call after she sent the message. Lying by omission was still lying and she had lied to her daughter.

O'Connor hurried behind her. 'I'm just off, guv. Mrs O has gone to collect a takeaway, so I thought I'd deliver this little one to you. Here are the cakes that Gracie made for you.' He passed Gina a cardboard box.

'Thank you. I can't wait to eat one of these.' She kneeled down to Gracie's level, opened the box and took in the lovely buttery smell of the cupcakes. 'These are beautiful.'

Gracie chuckled.

'Guv.' Wyre hurried towards her. 'The dogs have found something.'

'Gracie, love. Could you wait with Harry for a second?' She mouthed the word sorry, but O'Connor smiled and began giving Gracie huge praise for her cakes and asking her about the nature park.

'What do you have?'

Wyre waited for O'Connor to get a little further away then she spoke. 'The dogs picked up a scent and it led to a blood-stained towel. It's gone to the lab but it's likely that the blood will match Wesley Reid's.'

'Where was it found?'

'You know the old nursery where the protests have been taking place?'

'Yes.'

'It was found in the garden area around the back.'

Gina took a deep breath. 'I want the building area cordoned off. Has the building been checked?'

'Earlier today, police were called as one of the protester's got in and began spray painting some of the upstairs rooms. The homeless support officers came to check the place over and a glazier and decorator have since visited the building.'

'Has the work been done?'

'The broken window has been boarded up and the perimeter of the grounds has been secured. The decorator hasn't painted yet. Also, the protester got in through one of the windows which had been smashed. He claims that it had already been broken and that he simply climbed in.'

Gina scrunched her brow. 'Hmm, who broke the window and why? Is he still here?'

'No, he was bailed earlier. After questioning, we know he was at work the previous night. He's a night security officer and finished his shift at six that morning. It was a twelve-hour shift and we've confirmed with his employer the times he was there.'

'So, he couldn't possibly be the person to have left the cloth on the grounds. He would have been at work at the time of the murder.'

Wyre bit her bottom lip and continued. 'It's not looking likely unless he left it there this morning and someone else gave it to him. Given the protests, there have been a lot of people milling around. One of them may have seen someone or something suspicious. There is something else.'

'What's that?'

'A handful of the protesters were threatening to go back there tomorrow.'

'So, we can interview them. Great. Can you please be there first thing, Paula? Maybe see if either PC Kapoor or PC Smith will assist. I'll be there a little later to look around the building. Could you arrange for a keyholder to be there?'

She nodded.

'And can you contact the security officer who was arrested? Bring him in. I'd like you to interview him. He might have details of the other protesters who might not be there tomorrow. Someone must have seen something, and he might be key to finding our killer. If Bertram or Logan turn up in the meantime, call me immediately. I can't leave Gracie, but I want to be a part of everything that is going on.'

NINETEEN

SASHA

Sasha stared at her broken kitchen window. The jagged stone had come through and chinked the edge of her fake marble worktop. She shivered as a chilly breeze howled through the open window. She grabbed her dressing gown and pulled it on over the two jumpers she was already wearing. Her flat felt cold and unhomely, a bit like the old nursery that she'd been in earlier that day. Those words, 'I will make you pay', swirled around her thoughts. It was ridiculous to think that they were aimed at her. She hadn't done anything or hurt anyone, at least not intentionally. Maybe not at all. Her mind was in overdrive. She needed to chill the hell out.

She stared at the mess, trying not to touch anything until the police arrived. The kettle was calling. A warm cup of tea would make all the difference, but she didn't want to contaminate the scene. She didn't want the police to simply issue her with a crime number and be on their way. It had taken everything she had to insist that someone came out. A crime number would be no good anyway, she didn't even have any insurance to claim on.

She leaned against the door frame and wished she could have stayed at her sister's for longer. Right now, she'd be sitting in front of a cosy fire after playing games with the family. Since losing their mum many years ago, her sister had worked so hard to keep them all close by cooking meals, organising family days out in the summer and bringing them all together at Christmases. Her niece would now be snuggled up in bed, and she'd probably be sipping a hot chocolate with marshmallows on top while her grandad read her a story.

The sound of the buzzer made her flinch. She hurried to the intercom. 'Hello.'

'Police. May we come up?'

She pressed the button and waited with her door open. The two uniformed officers soon reached the top of the stairs. She recognised one from earlier, at the renovation.

'You're the homeless support officer?' the male PC said.

She opened the door allowing them into the living room. 'Yes, it seems there is a lot of window smashing going on today. I know who did this.' She pointed to her kitchen. 'There's a kid, it's him. He threw eggs at my car too. He's burst my tyre in the past and he's scratched my car. He should be easy to spot. He rides around here illegally, all over the pavements, on an electric scooter. They're not even legal, are they?' Sasha knew that some towns rented the scooters out, but not Cleevesford.

'They are not,' the shorter officer said. They both sat and spent a short while listening and taking her statement. She knew her statement hadn't helped. She didn't know who the teen was, where he'd come from and the description she provided of him was loose at best. She hadn't seen him for long enough to go into more detail and she'd never actually caught him in the act, which made her statement carry less weight. The male officer finished noting down everything she'd said before closing his notebook. It was all over in a matter of a few minutes.

'Do you want the stone? It might have fingerprints on it. I haven't touched anything in the kitchen.'

The officer headed through with an evidence bag and removed some gloves from his pocket. Just like that, the stone was taken. She didn't hold out much hope. 'Do you have CCTV?'

'No, I wish I did but I can't afford such luxuries.' Keeping her flat and car on one average salary didn't buy her much and she doubted she'd be up for a pay rise from the council. Not to mention that her credit card repayments took a chunk too.

'I hate to say this but there's probably not much we can do at this time. I can offer you an emergency number of a glazier. They will be able to board your window up.' She knew that would happen. They'd dealt with a lot of properties where minor vandalisms had taken place and the police hardly ever did a thing. It was always insurance or the council repair pot that picked up the tab. She knew that would be the end of it.

She sighed and shook her head. 'I've already called someone. He'll be here when you've gone. I didn't want to disturb the crime scene which is why I waited. What will you do about that kid? It's all getting too much.'

'If he comes back, call us straight away.'

'But he doesn't stick around. He'd be gone by the time you arrived. Can't you put a patrol on around here?'

'I can't guarantee it, but I will put in a request when I get back to the station.'

A few minutes later, the officers had gone. It was a waste of time calling them. All it had done was delayed her getting her window boarded up. She glanced out of the window as she put the kettle on. The police drove away, and the car park was left in silence. She poured her tea and gripped the hot cup, allowing the feeling to come back to her fingers. As she glanced back, her stare met that of the youth and her hands began to shake with anger. He stood by her car, arms folded in front of his oversized sweatshirt, his mouth covered in a thick scarf that had been wrapped around his neck and lower face.

Rage rose within her. How dare he cause her all these problems then rub her nose in it. Slamming her cup down, she ran out of her flat, down the stairs, put the catch on the main door and flung it open. 'Why are you doing this to me?' she yelled as she charged towards him. He grabbed his scooter that was leaning against her car, and he stepped on it, but she chased him. She was going to grab the hood, and she would yank him off that damn scooter. Enough was enough. She wasn't going to spend her life being intimidated by a stupid kid and she no longer cared if he got hurt in the process. The faster she ran, the further away he got. She'd been stupid to think she would get anywhere near him. With her many jumpers and her dressing gown flapping behind her, she was no match for the youth. 'I hate you!' she called out, tears drizzling down her face.

The youth brought the scooter to a stop at the end of a row of houses. He stepped off and turned to face her. His frame just evaded the glow from the lamplight above, but she could see his outline. She could see him raising his finger as he pointed at her and in his tinny voice, he said slowly and clearly, 'I will make you pay.'

Those words written on the wall at the old nursery, they were for her. It was the kid. He was doing all this, but why? Pay for what? What did he know that she didn't? She went to speak but no words came out. She wanted to shout at him, call him a few names, swear loudly or go over and shake him until he explained himself, but he was taller and stockier than her, and they were alone. What had she done? With all she had, she turned and ran back to her flat, locking her door behind her. With a jolt, she felt a hand on her arm. 'Ms Kennedy?'

She screamed as loud as she could.

'Sorry, so sorry.' He held his hands up and stepped back. 'I've come to board up your window. Your door was open. I thought you were in, so I called. Then, I thought you were in... err... danger,' he said in an accent she couldn't identify. He held his phone up. 'I was just about to call police.'

She took a few deep breaths until her heart rate returned to normal. It was just the window man.

'Are you okay. Shall I call police? You look upset. Are you hurt?'

She shook her head and wiped her eyes. 'No, I'm okay, thank you. I just need the window boarded up.' She showed him through to the kitchen, silently wanting to kick herself for leaving her home and the whole block open while she chased the youth. Anyone could have got in. She left the window fitter in the kitchen, and she ran straight to her bedroom and closed the door. All her emotions came pouring out. Her chest tightened and she gasped for breath.

For that youth to have left the same message on the wall of the development, he had to have known she would have been called out to attend. He had to know what her job was. He had to know where she was all the time and he had to know her.

She couldn't stop shaking. This wasn't some juvenile prank; it was a personal attack. She scurried over to her bedroom window in the dark, wanting to see out. The police said to call if she saw him but once again, it was too late. The youth had already gone. Next time, she'd use her phone and try to take a photo. Everything always happens too fast, but she needed to anticipate it. When she left the building, she needed to already be recording. Maybe then the police would do more.

There was no sign of anyone in the verges or by the trees. The more she stared, the more the shadows danced. Leaves fell from the trees as the breeze caught them. Was it the breeze? Were the shadows those of branches or were they limbs? Her vision tracked every movement, attempting to seek out any sign of the youth.

He was watching her every move. There was no other explanation. A shiver ran across the nape of her neck. He was out there.

TWENTY

JUDITH

Monday, 14 November

Judith Morgan hurries up her driveway and watches as her cat scarpers towards the front door. By going out to buy milk before work, she'd already clocked up three thousand steps and soon she'd clock up more. For the past week, she'd been walking to work. Not using her car had made her fitter and saved her money so it was an all-round win. Smiling and talking to her cat like the baby that he is, she fishes in her bag for her keys. He's hungry as usual, but that's nothing new. He's always hungry. He weaves in and out of her legs, no doubt leaving strands of his glossy black fur all over her favourite work trousers. She turns the key in the lock and steps in. As always, she removes her shoes and nudges them against the wall with her toes before sinking into her thick warm carpet. The sound of the heating humming is music to her ears and all she wants now is her muesli.

'Come on then, Buster. Mummy has a treat for you.' The

black-and-white cat darts in and heads straight to the cupboard, the one he knows contains all the treats. She follows him along into the narrow kitchen and pulls out the little bag of meaty biscuits and hand feeds him a couple. That's when she spots the wet patch of mud next to the washing machine. 'Who's been bringing the garden in?' She pulls a few sheets of kitchen roll from the dispenser that is attached to her wall and wipes the mess up, leaving a smear.

She shivers. The kitchen is the coldest part of the house but still, it's not too bad. She's one of the lucky ones. She inherited some money from the grandma she'd barely ever spoken to, and it had bought her this Victorian semi on a nice street and left her some cash in the bank. At forty, she's sorted and the part-time library job she does gives her enough to live on as long as she doesn't go mad. She checks her watch. It's only early but she's excited to try her dress on again, in readiness for her second date with Luther. Those butterflies are flapping. Breakfast can wait. After placing the milk in the fridge, she takes a deep breath and keeps telling herself that everything is going to be fine. He likes her, she likes him, and tonight was going to be the night. He was coming over and she had promised him something he'd never forget and if the messages they'd exchanged were anything to go by, he was more than eager.

She pulls the lacy bra and knickers from the shopping bag on the worktop. These beauties are going to sit perfectly under the tight red dress that she's laid out on her bed. She wore it on her last date, but she didn't like him. Something about the way he acted, the way he hid his phone told her he was probably married or seeing someone else. After telling him she wasn't interested, he'd sent a barrage of mean messages, telling her she was ugly and that no one else would shag her – his words. Totally uncalled for. Her instincts about him had been right. Luther was different. His messages had been sweet, and she felt he was genuine.

She leaves her cat licking his paws next to the cat flap. 'Don't you go out again and come back in covered in mud.' She laughs, knowing that he doesn't understand and even if he did, he wouldn't take any notice.

She places her phone on the console table and runs up the stairs. An upstairs door crashes, stopping her at the halfway mark. Heart beating, she calls out. 'Hello.' That's when she hears wind whistling through the spare room. Maybe she left the window open. She was in there ironing her shirt earlier and she always gets hot when she irons. She creeps up the last few stairs and places her ear to the door and she hears the banging again. She did leave a window open. Hurrying into the room, she can see that she's being ridiculous. There is no one in her house, just an open window that didn't settle on the catch. The kid that has been causing a bit of nuisance would have no way in anyway. She needed to report him to the police. She slammed the window closed and walked across the landing into her own bedroom, where she stared out of the window. The kid often comes up and down this road on that damn scooter, sticking his finger up at her if he sees her looking. She knows it's him who burst her tyre. She knows it was him who posted a parcel of dog muck through her letter box.

Anyway, she has more pressing things to think about and that thing is Luther, pressing against her on her bed. She smiles and feels an electrical-like flutter shooting through her body. It's okay, she has half an hour to spare before she needs to leave for work. Just enough time to try on her dress again. She pulls the door to her en suite closed and then she shuts the curtains. She slips out of her trousers, then she removes her sports bra and pants, letting her comfy undies drop to the floor. Tonight, wasn't about being comfortable, it was about netting her catch and this new bra and pants set was going to do the trick. She slips the pants on, past her newly waxed legs and then she tugs the bra into place. Turning from side to side, hips jutting out in a pose, she admires the curves that are going to drive Luther wild. She unclips her long black locks and allows them to fall over her shoulders. That's exactly what she wants him to see when he peels her dress off in this very spot.

She reaches down to her bed to grab the dress but all she feels is the shiny blanket on top of her quilt. Maybe she left it on the hanger in the wardrobe. She scrunches her eyebrows and gazes around the room. It's not draped over the chaise longue in front of the bay window either. She slides the fitted wardrobe door open and reaches for the red dress but it's not there.

Heart pounding, she can't help but feel that something isn't right. She inhales and there's a strange smell, like herbs, like Christmas dinner, and it's coming from her en suite. Smoke billows out through the gap underneath the door. There's a fire in her bathroom. What could have started it? She grabs the door and is faced by a puff of white smoke which makes her cough. That's when the figure emerges, and she stumbles back onto her bed.

She has no time to think. Just as she tries to focus on the figure a splash of liquid hits her face and forces her eyes closed. She panics and waves her hands in front of her. She's heard about women being attacked with acid and she wonders what she's done and who's after her. Letting out the loudest scream she can muster, she knows it's pointless. Her neighbours work in the day, and she is alone. Her feet reach her attacker's leg. She needs to aim for the groin, but everything is blurred. Reaching for her face, she can feel that there are no burns. Her skin is fine. The liquid's scent reaches her nostrils, some of it slips over her tongue as she goes to scream again. Her attacker has poured cider over her. She yells but this time she sees a scrunched-up blob of red coming down on her face. It's her dress. She fights her attacker with all she has but this person is strong, and now they have her hands pinned down.

'No, please.' He's going to rape her. In her mind, she begs

him to stop but he can't hear her. That's when she feels the sharp pain in her neck. He whispers in her ear. 'I said I was going to make you pay.'

Tears gush from her face as she feels blood spilling onto the bed underneath her. The boy on the scooter, he said those exact words and she told him to get lost. Pay for what? She hadn't done anything wrong. Was this something to do with him?

Her silent cries go unheard as her world begins to fade. She feels her cat brushing his tail over her feet and she knows he can't help her.

Just as her world goes black, the attacker whispers in her ear again and it's like a light has been turned on. She knows why she's been hurt, and she wants to plead with her attacker, but she can't. She can't think, she can't see, and she is losing her sense of touch as death pulls her ever closer and she breathes her last.

TWENTY-ONE

Gina's head was thick with lack of sleep. She'd spent the whole evening going over everything again and gained absolutely nothing more from the process. Then there was Briggs. He had called her, and they'd talked and laughed. It was like back then, before Rosemary, and she had come close to telling him to come over.

Gracie had slept until about one in the morning, then she had crept into her bed. With the little girl's gentle breaths tickling her neck, Gina ended up leaving Gracie alone to sleep in the spare room where Ebony the cat kneaded her most of the night. At five in the morning, Gracie had woken her, asking when it was time to go and see the animals.

Now at the station, she yawned and took a long swig of black strong coffee in the incident room. Her phone beeped and it was a message from Mrs O. She looked down and saw a photo of Gracie strapped into her car seat looking thrilled. She swallowed, wondering how long she could keep what was happening from Hannah.

'Morning, guv. No sign of Noel Logan or Frederick Bertram.

We also had an officer check to see if Bertram went back to Killian Foster's flat, but he didn't.' O'Connor bit into a bacon sandwich. 'Sorry, guv. I should have called in to see if anyone wanted me to get them a butty from the snack bar, but I thought everyone was out.'

She smiled. 'It's okay. I'm not that hungry yet. I ate too many of Gracie's cupcakes last night and went to bed feeling a bit sick. That was after stopping at McDonald's on the way home.'

He sniggered and filled his mouth with doorstop bread. 'Yes, that buttercream is a bit rich.'

'I'm going to head to the old nursery to see how Wyre is going with the protesters. Jacob is heading straight there too. I had an email. The post-mortem is taking place late morning. When it's over, can you give me an update?'

''Course.' He finished the last of his sandwich and licked red sauce off his thick fingers. Gina had no idea how he could even think about eating a greasy sandwich when he was about to see the victim's organs removed and weighed, but he seemed okay.

Briggs walked in, his shirt looking a little crumpled and his eyes looking dark underneath with tiredness. His hair had grown a little untidily around his ears now that Rosemary wasn't trimming his hair every five minutes. He'd opened up on the phone, telling her that he didn't miss Rosemary, but he did miss her little boy. He'd admitted that the reason he'd wanted to try and make things work with Rosemary was because he craved having a family. That had broken Gina. It wasn't love he thought he had; it was the fairy tale. She glanced his way for a few seconds too long and he caught her gaze. She cleared her throat and walked over to the coat stand. She slipped her arms through her thick winter coat and began doing up the buttons. He gave her a knowing smile.

He walked over to a computer and began clicking. YouTube

came up. 'I spotted this on social media last night and I've watched a few of her videos.' He pressed play.

Gina and O'Connor walked over and watched as the video began. Ominous music played with a few sounds that reminded Gina of nails scraping a blackboard, they were then accompanied by flash images of bloodied knives and ghostly images.

'This is Macie Perrin Reportz Crime and Ghosts. She's on TikTok and YouTube and seems to have a load of followers and a slight obsession with the Cleevesford Cleaver. Did you see her there yesterday when you attended the scene?'

Gina nodded as she took in the pasty-looking girl on the screen wearing a nose ring and thick, black-rimmed glasses. 'Yes, she was also wearing a mac covered in skulls. She's hard to forget.' Her dark hair piled up on her head with straggly bits sharply framing her face. Eyes smudged with smoky make-up and lips a deep burgundy. 'Yes, we hoped that uniform would be able to send her on her way, but she remained for a while amongst the crowd.' The short video continued playing and Gina watched herself on it, approaching the Cleaver with Wyre. The girl talked to the camera, saying that she was reporting from the Cleaver and that something big had gone down.

Briggs pressed stop as the end music played. 'That was it. It's a teaser for something bigger that she's working on. I want to make sure that she doesn't jeopardise the case. It's clear that while she was filming earlier, she had no idea what had happened at the Cleaver but then look at the end scene.' He pressed play again. Lettering filled the screen as the images fade to black. 'Has the Cleaver's butcher struck? Have the ghosts in the walls come out to play? Only I have the full scoop! See it here first.' The blank screen was then replaced by a huge ice cream filled cornet and a tub of soft scoop ice cream. 'Subscribe and Like.'

Her ghostly face pops up. 'I am the chosen one.'

'What the hell was all that about, sir.' Gina slumped on a chair.

'Clickbait.' They watched as her likes, and subscribers began to climb rapidly. Comments came thick and fast.

Love you, Mace!

You legend.

Love your alternative newz. Those who don't believe will never know the truth.

Liked and shared. Hurry with main vid.

Can't wait. It's the Cleaver butcher. That house is sick. Love it.

Gina began reading the video description.

Where dark goings on culminate in death. The Cleevesford Cleaver has a past that is sinister, where the occult has been practised and now the ghosts have been awoken. Of course, a murder has been committed but who did it? Was it nothing more than an argument that got out of hand after too much drink, or was it the evil emanating from the walls? Had the victim's ghosts finally come to take him? You will only get your answers here. Macie Perrins Reportz and you will get the truth here first!

Gina shook her head. Her phone rang. 'Wyre.'

'We're here at the old nursery on Salbei Avenue, guv. There aren't many protesters, and they don't seem to have much to say. We did however catch a girl trying to film through a couple of the windows. She breached the cordon from around the side of the building.'

Gina sighed. 'Has she got dark hair and a nose ring?'

'Yes, it's the same girl who was outside the Cleaver yesterday. How did you know?'

'I'll explain when I get there. Keep her with you. I'm on my way.' Gina ended the call. 'Macie Perrins slipped the cordon and has been filming at the old nursery. What would have led her there? How is she seeing the connection? We haven't yet released that the bloodied towel was found there.'

'Maybe it's just a separate story for her.' O'Connor scrunched his brow.

'I don't buy that at all. She seems to be ahead of us, and I want to know what she's releasing in her video later and how she has managed to link the two buildings. She's interested in ghosts and murder by the looks of it and prefers to combine the two.'

'The old nursery is quite creepy. It could be coincidence. I mean, she has a story with the protesters being there. It could all be separate.' Briggs clicked out of her YouTube channel.

'Let's hope so. There's a chance our killer might be following the gossip on social media and YouTube. We need to tell digital forensics to keep an eye on everything and track any regular likers or commenters, or anything concerning.'

O'Connor nodded. 'I'll let them know before I leave for the post-mortem.'

'Right, got to go.' She hurried off down the corridor and out past the main desk before stepping out into the misty morning. She got into her car and turned the fan onto full to clear her windscreen. While she waited, she searched for Macie Perrin's Instagram. The girl was pulling a sad face while pointing directly at the viewer. The caption underneath read, 'Police caught me snooping while I was seeking the truth. But, lucky for you, I don't give up easily. #ChosenOne.'

'For heaven's sake.' Gina threw her phone onto the passenger seat and started driving. The girl was telling everyone that ghosts were behind everything and that she was the chosen one. Gina didn't feel the need to worry too much. Most sane people might think it's all a bit silly and might just enjoy getting caught up in a bit of supernatural storytelling, but Macie Perrin had now stepped onto a crime scene. That was unforgivable. Gina swallowed. However hard she tried, knowing that a YouTuber might be on their level when it came to linking the old nursery and the Cleaver wasn't sitting well. In fact, her stomach was dancing to a nauseating tune.

TWENTY-TWO

Gina pulled up behind Jacob on the main road. She could see the sulky-looking girl sitting in the back of PC Kapoor's police car. She stepped out and joined Jacob and Wyre outside the old nursery, careful not to trip on any of the uneven slabs. Although the building looked like it had received a bit of a freshen up with new windows and painted brickwork, the exterior with its half-pulled down trailing ivy and scattered shale still looked tatty. To top it off, a police cordon had been tied to a tree at the far end and Gina knew it would cover the whole perimeter of the back garden, all the way around. It would have been obvious to the girl that she shouldn't have crossed it.

'The girl is in the car. Kapoor arrested her for disorderly conduct but in all likeliness, she'll be dismissed with a caution later,' Wyre said.

'I saw her. We'll deal with her in a bit. I was hoping to get inside the building. Where exactly was the bloodied towel found?'

Wyre fiddled with the end of her woollen gloves. 'Around the back of the building at the far end of the garden. Keith and Jennifer have been working the scene. They were over the other end when the girl ran through. They called us, we caught her and they're continuing around the back. Someone from the council was meant to meet us here fifteen minutes ago but she still hasn't turned up. I called and they said she was running slightly late.'

'Great. I guess we just have to wait for now. I could speak to the girl first, but I'll let her stew for a short while. Entering a crime scene and sneaking under our cordon is not on. How did it go with the security guy who broke in here yesterday? Did he manage to provide any more information?'

Wyre shook her head. 'Not really. He repeated that someone had broken in already when he got here. He said he didn't smash the window, and that when he arrived, he knocked out the last of the glass and climbed in. He also said he wasn't responsible for all the graffiti and was eager to point out that he only had black spray paint. He said that there was more, but it was in red. In his statement, he claimed that when he scouted the place out earlier in the morning, he saw someone climbing out of the broken window but when he got close, they scarpered.'

'Did he provide a description?'

'No, he said it was too dark. He only saw the outline of a person. He couldn't say how tall they were, anything about their build, or their clothing. He said he wasn't that bothered as he thought it might just be another person who was angry about the up-and-coming hostel. He seemed quite regretful of his actions and said he got carried away. Some of the locals had told him that it was going to be used to house paedophiles.'

Gina exhaled and rubbed her cold hands together. 'Is it?'

'No, guv. Just run-of-the-mill people who have nowhere to go, from families who have lost their homes to people who are sleeping rough.'

'Hi.' A woman interrupted them and jangled a few keys as she stood next to the heavy front door. She stamped the mud off her feet and took shelter from the drizzle under the pillared outdoor porch. Yawning, she rubbed her eyes.

Gina recognised her straight away. 'Sorry that we've met again so soon. It's...' Had the homeless support officer told Gina her name? If she had, it had slipped her mind.

'Sasha Kennedy. Homeless support officer for Cleevesford Council. Is there any news on what happened over at the Cleaver? I woke up to a million emails, all requests from people staying there to be moved.' She unlocked the door and pushed it open, her voice turning to an echo as she stepped into the vacuous space.

'We're still investigating, and a police appeal has gone out.' Gina didn't want to divulge too much at this stage.

'I wasn't told why I've been asked to come here today. Is it about the break-in yesterday?'

'Partly. We've found some evidence that relates to the incident at the Cleaver on the grounds here, which is why we want to look inside. It's kind of you to come back and show us around.'

'So, you only care about the vandalism because it ties in with a bigger case? Police don't give a stuff when a no one gets their window broken.'

Gina scrunched her brows as she wondered what Sasha was going on about. 'Excuse me?'

The woman made a tut noise with her tongue. 'I'm sorry.' She shook her head. 'Just call it a bad day. A kid threw a stone through my window last night. The police weren't going to come and when I insisted, they did, but nothing was done. Now I'm out of pocket because I had to pay to get my window boarded up and I still need to get a new window fitted. They drive around on these illegal scooters and you lot do nothing about that either.' Sasha stopped in the corridor and swallowed. 'Sorry, again. I know it's not your fault and I shouldn't moan so much, especially when someone was murdered yesterday.'

'No, we're sorry. I can understand how frustrated you are.' She pressed her lips together and gave the woman a sympathetic smile. She could tell that Sasha wasn't convinced.

'Right, follow me.' Sasha led them to the room at the far end where the window had been boarded up. 'This is how the protester got in. He must have smashed the window. Has he been charged?'

'Yes, there is a bit more to it. I'll get someone to call your office with an update on the broken window and the vandalism. I'm sorry that I don't have more information for you but we're investigating the murder.'

'Do you think the protestor might be the murderer?' The woman folded her arms on top of her ample chest as she leaned on the door frame.

'We are investigating a lot of avenues at the moment; this is just one of them. We haven't arrested him for murder.' Gina smiled. She also knew that the security guard had claimed to have climbed in, sprayed a few walls with black spray paint and left. That was all he'd admitted to doing and no other spray cans had been found on him or in the vicinity. He also had an alibi. 'Could you please show me the graffiti?'

'Yep.' She expelled a full breath of air and led the way back down the corridor. 'He graffitied all the rooms upstairs. It's going to take ages to sort out.' She hurried up, leading the way.

Gina inhaled the scent of fresh paint that was now tarnished by the words 'Paedos die.' She left the homeless support officer behind, snapped on a pair of latex gloves and kept pushing doors open. Each wall sporting the same words. Their vandal had admitted doing this. The last room had only the word 'Paedo' sprayed on it and the trail of paint told her that he got interrupted at this point. She pushed the door closed and headed through into the room near a shared bathroom. As she pushed the door open, a loud creak broke the silence. Wyre stepped closer to her. 'I will make you pay,' Gina said, reading the words on the wall aloud.

Sasha stepped into the room and stared at the graffiti. As Gina cleared her throat, the woman flinched. 'I, err, do you mind if I wait outside?'

Wyre tilted her head. 'Are you okay?'

The woman fanned her face with her hand. 'Yes, I'm just a bit hot, that's all. I'm not feeling too good this morning.' Sasha turned and strode down the corridor until Gina could no longer hear her footsteps.

Gina stepped closer to the graffiti. 'A bloodied towel was found out the back and our graffitist is claiming to have seen someone in the building around five in the morning. It's too early to say that this could have been our killer, it could have just been another protester. What we do know is that after Wesley Reid was murdered, a bloodied towel led the dogs to this place. Our killer walked with that towel from the Cleaver to here.' Gina pulled her phone out and took a photo of the writing. 'We don't know the exact time when Frederick Bertram left Killian's flat, and we don't as yet know anything about Noel Logan's whereabouts since the night of the murder.' Gina glanced out of the window at the road below and spotted Jacob standing on the pavement with PC Kapoor. No protesters were in sight and the road seemed quiet. The girl in the back of Kapoor's car slowly turned her head and her gaze met Gina's.

Gina stepped back, moving out of the girl's line of sight. The last thing she needed was to appear in her next Instagram story.

The room was bare except for a chest of drawers that had been pushed against the wall. She walked over and slid the drawers open, one by one. She stopped and stared at the contents of the last drawer.

'What is it, guv?'

'A pound coin. Let forensics know that they need to go

through this room next and I want some of the officers searching the rest of the building. We have reason to believe that the murderer has been here. The place is almost empty so it shouldn't take too long.'

Wyre walked over and stared into the drawer. 'Damn.' She pulled out her phone and began making the call.

Maybe it was just a random pound coin or maybe the killer was toying with them. The more she stared at it, the more she knew that the killer had planted it. She couldn't prove it yet. Her mind conjured up the image of Killian feeding the coin through his fingers, a trick that Frederick Bertram had taught him. They needed Frederick and they needed him now.

TWENTY-THREE

Gina stepped outside and hurried to PC Kapoor's car. The closer she got, the more she could hear the girl's protests. 'You can't keep me here. Just caution me and let me go.'

Gina bent over and peered through the car window. 'Macie Perrin.'

'Who are you?' The girl grinned. 'Oh, you're a police detective. I saw you yesterday at the Cleaver. Can you shed any more light on the case so far?' She held her phone up in Gina's face.

Gina placed her hand over the phone and lowered it. 'Macie Perrin, please stop recording so that we can talk.'

The girl pressed her lips together and stared at Gina for what felt like ages before ending the recording. 'I haven't done anything wrong. I'm just trying to report news.'

Gina stepped back and opened the door. 'Would you step out of the car for a moment?' She didn't want to be cramped up in a car with the girl while she asked her a few questions.

Reluctantly, Macie stepped out and brushed her mac down. 'Glad to. This car stinks of piss.'

Gina ignored her. 'Officers tell me that you climbed under the cordon while the patrolling officer and the forensics team were at the other side of the house, and you began recording. You stepped onto a crime scene, one which we are trying to preserve and that is disorderly conduct which is why you've been arrested.'

'But I only wanted to film some of the inside. I didn't touch anything.'

Gina exhaled. Although brash, she could see that the girl was quite immature. 'How old are you?'

'Eighteen.'

'In a short while, you'll be taken to the station but first, I want to ask what you were doing here?'

Macie shrugged and looked away. 'Like I said. It's for my YouTube channel. I'm a crime reporter.'

That was stretching the truth. Gina wondered how Macie ever thought she'd be taken seriously as a crime reporter when she was hunting ghosts half the time and not adhering to police procedures when turning up at a crime scene. She almost wanted to laugh but Macie was young. She realised that Macie still had a lot to learn and mocking her wouldn't get her anywhere. 'What led you here?'

'Nothing—' The girl went to speak but then stopped. 'It's just a creepy building, innit?'

'So, you came here because it was creepy?'

She bit her bottom lip and her burgundy lipstick scraped off onto her front teeth. 'Yep.'

'And you were at the Cleevesford Cleaver yesterday. I saw your video.'

She shrugged. 'I hope you liked and subscribed.'

'This building has been here for years. You could have come at any time. Why did you decide to come this morning?'

'I've got nothing more to say. In fact, I don't have to speak at all. I know my rights.'

'You do and I'm glad you do. Macie, may I call you Macie?'

She shook her head. 'It's Perrin. I don't believe in the word

Miss. It's stupid that women have to be a Miss or a Mrs or even a Ms. Irrelevant. So, Perrin.'

Who was Gina to argue with her? She had a point. 'Okay. Perrin, as you know a man was murdered at the Cleevesford Cleaver and I was hoping that you could help us in telling us why you're really here today?'

Macie tapped her chunky trainer-clad feet on the tarmac and folded her arms in front of her chest. 'I told you. Creepy building and all that. I'm sorry about your cordon. I didn't realise that I wasn't allowed to go under it. I didn't mean to interfere with a crime scene. I'm trying to help.' Her tough exterior was beginning to crack.

'I'm sure you are but you've now contaminated the scene.'

'Why is this place cordoned off? Maybe I could ask you a question every time you ask me one.'

Gina tilted her head and smiled. 'Perrin, it doesn't work like that. You've been caught breaking onto a crime scene.'

Macie cleared her throat. 'I tell you what, Perrin sounds weird. Can you call me Macie? I'd like us to work together. Can we work together? Can you give me information from your side, for my videos, and I'll help you investigate? I really want to be involved.' That was it, Gina had made a breakthrough. The budding reporter was almost pleading for a story now.

'I don't have anything I can share with you right now, but we do have regular press updates which you should keep an eye on.'

'How long will I have to stay at the station for?'

Gina shrugged. 'I can't say. It depends on how long it will take to process and question you.' Gina didn't imagine it would take too long and the girl would probably leave with a caution, but Macie was worried, she could tell that much. 'Have you ever been cautioned or arrested before?'

'No.'

'It's best not to be. You can make your videos and find out

the things you want without breaking the law. Criminal records don't go down well. I'm not saying all this to scare you, I don't want to see someone with all your potential go down the wrong path. You seem bright and from what I can tell, people love your videos, but gather your information legally.' Gina watched the girl scrunching her dark brows as she thought.

'Someone sent me an anonymous message, telling me to come here so I followed up on it. I'm sorry, okay. I should have said something, but they'll stop giving me more information if they know I told you. I don't know why I'm here.' She removed her glasses and began cleaning them with the end of her jumper.

'We need to take a formal statement down at the station and you need to tell us everything.' Gina felt her heart race. If the murderer had chosen Macie to be the bearer of his or her news, then she could be in a dangerous position. How would anyone else be able to link the two places? Gina could see the slightest glint of fear in Macie's face, the way she swallowed and the quickening of her breath. She reminded her slightly of Hannah when she was about the same age. Defiant but underneath the exterior was a worried young person who was trying to navigate being a new adult.

'Okay.' The girl nodded and got back into the car. Gina knew that Macie Perrin hadn't just wandered down on a whim. She closed the car door and hurried back over to PC Kapoor. The young officer was talking to Wyre. 'Jhanvi, can you get Macie Perrin back to the station immediately. I know she's crossed a line, literally, but we need her to be treated like a witness. She claims that someone sent her a message telling her to come here. It's possible that the murderer has chosen her to convey information through. I wondered why she was hash tagging "the chosen one" on her social media, now I know why. We need to find out how they messaged her and see if we can get a trace on the number or an IP address if it was an email.'

She glanced at her watch. Time was running away, and she wanted to visit the charity, Safe Night, who had helped get Wesley Reid a room at the Cleaver.

Gina stared up and down the road. Had the murderer been watching them? Had they been and gone? Were they watching from one of the houses that surrounded the old nursery? Gina glanced up into the grey skies and along the line of upstairs windows. All she could see were reflections. Then, she took in the eighteen-year-old who was nervously chewing her nails in the back seat of a police car. It was their job to keep her safe. Gina only hoped that Macie would allow them to.

A message beeped on Gina's phone.

I thought you were looking after Gracie! I bet Hannah would like to know where you are right now. You messed up my sons' lives, now I'm going to mess you up.

She swallowed as she took in the name at the top of the text. It was Hetty, her ex mother-in-law. One son was dead and the other was in prison, and Hetty blamed Gina for both. The woman who hated her most in the world. A woman who would enjoy telling Hannah everything. Gina glanced across at the people milling around and saw the hunched woman holding a banner saying 'No Paedos' on it. The woman's smug smile turned into laughter as she broke from the crowd and hurried into a bungalow at the end of the road. Hetty could literally ruin everything.

TWENTY-FOUR

Gina stood on the road outside Cleevesford Community Centre waiting for Jacob to arrive and staring at her phone. Hannah could call at any time and her nerves were reminding her of that. She watched as a young man with a stringy brown beard left, a cigarette dangling from his mouth. Another man went in. As the door opened, she could hear the hustle and bustle of people, the clanking of plates and cutlery. She read the sign outside telling the homeless community that they could turn up for breakfast between eight and ten thirty.

Jacob turned his car into the road and pulled up behind hers. She smiled and waved as he hurried over. She put her phone away and hoped with all she had that Hetty wouldn't tell Hannah.

'Right, let's see if Safe Night can help in some way. Maybe there's something we're missing. I know he was helped by the charity but maybe he's been coming here since his girlfriend ended their relationship. Maybe he opened up to someone. Maybe some of the others who hang around at the Hangar come here.' Gina pulled her bag over her shoulder and pushed the door open. She and Jacob stepped into the large hall with the canteen at the far end, the smell of bacon and disinfectant hitting her nostrils. Gina recognised the woman serving break-fast immediately. It was the local vicar, Sally Stevens.

Sally held a hand up to Gina and smiled. Her black, knee-length smock dress was only broken up by her white dog collar. Her deep red hair had been twisted in a bun on the top of her head. 'I guess you haven't come for breakfast?' she called out. 'Be with you in a mo.' She piled hot beans onto a slice of toast and passed it to a mature-looking man who was hunched over the counter. He scurried off, taking one of the plastic seats at a table full of other men. Everyone eating in the room was male, except for one younger woman who was wearing fingerless gloves and a large quilted coat.

Gina stood against the radiator, enjoying its warmth. Seeing so many people without a home made her heart sink.

'Do you both want to come through to the kitchen?' Sally came out from behind the counter.

'Yes, thank you.' Gina felt slightly guilty at not calling Sally. She did a couple of times, but their potential friendship had fizzled out. Gina had long decided she'd be a bad friend, always working, not really that sociable and not one to talk about herself.

Gina and Jacob followed her along a corridor until they reached a brightly lit room with stainless steel worktops. Light bounced off every surface. Several large empty oven trays were piled up next to a huge sink, ready for washing.

'We've all heard the sad news. Poor Wesley. Have you caught the person who killed him?'

Gina shook her head. 'We haven't. That's why we're here. Can you tell us anything about him, about how he seemed or if he mentioned any problems with anyone?' Gina realised that she'd blurted out too many questions. She took a breath. 'What was he like?'

Sally leaned her lithe figure against a cupboard. 'I didn't really know him well, but he started coming here about the end of September, I think. He'd had a relationship breakdown. He seemed pleasant when sober, but he had a real drink problem. We try so hard here to feed people and find them temporary accommodation but it's not easy. I could see that Wes, as he liked to be called, had been struggling more than the others. He really had nowhere else to go. He'd been sleeping in a tent at an old park they all call the Hangar. One of the other guys found him half-frozen one morning and brought him here. He had a severe chest infection. Took us about an hour to get any sense out of him, which is why I went mad at the council to find him a room, at least until he was better. It was just his luck that on that day a room in a hostel had become free. I sent him to the council to speak to a homeless support officer called Sasha Kennedy. That was the last I heard of him until I saw the news last night. I couldn't believe it.'

'Did he ever talk to you?'

Sally frowned in thought. 'Only a couple of times. He seemed quite private, but he did speak about his little girl. He wanted so much to get better for her, but I could see his struggle. He'd come here in the morning, have breakfast and say he hadn't touched a drop but a couple of days later, I could tell by looking at him that he'd slipped. I'd try to ask him how he was, but he'd close himself off from me and the other volunteers.'

Jacob took a few notes and Gina paused until he stopped writing. 'Did he mention his relationship?'

'Yes. He said his girlfriend had told him to leave. He said she'd been distant for weeks and blamed his drinking.' Sally paused. 'I can see it from her point of view too. I can't imagine that it was easy for her. I just wish there were safety nets for people like Wesley and indeed, every one of the people who come through our doors for help. We could all be in their position one day. What is it they say? Most people are only a couple of paydays away from homelessness.'

Gina had to agree. Like Sally, she saw how bad things were. They saw things that those with security and love had never contemplated. 'Did Wesley ever mention any friends, or anyone he may have had any issues with?'

'Oh yes. A guy called Noel. His best friend. He couldn't understand why Noel wouldn't help him or let him temporarily sleep on his couch while he got back on his feet. He said he'd helped Noel a lot in the past. He'd landscaped his garden. He'd fixed his garage roof. He'd always welcomed Noel into his home, and they'd been best friends for years. He told everyone that he'd even begged Noel to let him sleep in his garage, but Noel had said no. As far as Wes was concerned, Noel's name was muck.'

'Do you know if he met up with Noel?'

'I don't.'

'How about here, did he have any other friends, maybe friends from the Hangar?'

'I don't know of any in particular. Really sorry.'

Gina still didn't know where Wesley had gone between arguing with Noel and returning to the Cleevesford Cleaver on the night of his murder. 'This is a long shot but did you by any chance see Wesley on the evening of Saturday the twelfth?'

She shook her head. 'I was all tucked up with my hot chocolate this Saturday night watching *Strictly*, and I only went out to take the dog for a walk around the church grounds so that he could pee.' She paused. 'Wes wasn't everyone's cup of tea, but I liked him. I truly believe that he wanted to beat his addiction, that he wanted to be a good father and that he needed a chance. All those people in that canteen, they deserve a chance. Is someone targeting our homeless community? If so, I need to warn them. They might feel like they're on their own out there, but I care. I care about each one of them.' Sally swallowed and raised her eyebrows.

'I know you do. I'm sorry for your loss, I truly am.'

'Sometimes I feel like I'm banging my head against a brick wall. We're firefighting. I'm scared for them.' She bit the inside of her mouth. 'I'm going to open the church up in the evenings for a couple of hours every night – do tea, cake and keep people warm.' She picked up a ladle and dropped it into a sink full of murky water. 'We do what we can.'

'Is there anything else you think might help us?'

She shook her head. 'I still have your number. If I remember anything or I hear anything, I'll call you straight away. I want whoever killed Wes to be found fast.'

'Thank you, again.' Gina started to leave.

'If you fancy a drink one night, let me know. We've still got to put the world to rights.'

'That sounds like a plan.'

As Gina followed Jacob back through to the canteen, she noticed that it seemed quieter now. There was no hum of people, only the man who was eating beans on toast and the woman with the fingerless gloves.

'Are you police?' the woman called.

Gina turned to face her and Jacob weaved between two tables, heading her way. 'We are,' he said.

'It's about Wes, isn't it?'

Gina stepped closer. 'Did you know him?'

'He was an alright bloke. We heard the news, we all heard. Sad days.' She shook her head. 'I know where he was on the night he was murdered.'

Gina and Jacob stood around her table. 'Do you mind if we sit?' Gina asked.

'Go ahead.'

'Where was he?'

'He was at the Hangar. It's not a place I normally frequent

but I went there Saturday. Thought I'd give it a go, but it wasn't my thing. I'm trying to get clean but that place, it just makes you want to use and drink. I spoke to Wes, and he wasn't happy at all. He was livid and he said he was going to kill Noel and that the bastard had taken everything from him. In his words, Wes was going to make him pay.'

TWENTY-FIVE

SASHA

Sasha locked her car and zipped her coat up as she hurried towards the warmth of the supermarket. She checked her watch. In half an hour, she needed to be back at the office. Several appointments filled her afternoon, and it was going to be a long one. She shuddered as she thought of the writing on the wall at the old nursery. In her mind, all she could see was the youth pointing at her, saying those exact words.

As the electric door closed behind her, she almost jumped back. The whirring of the doors sounded a lot like the youth's scooter. She held one hand over her beating heart. If someone was trying hard to scare her, it was working. She snatched a basket from the pile and tried to focus on the nondescript piped Christmas music. Christmas was still a while away but that didn't stop shops from playing everything with jingly bells in the tune. The front of the shop had already been stacked with racks of mince pies and huge tubs of chocolates.

Hurrying past the fruit and veg aisle, she stopped at the yellow sticker fridge and quickly grabbed the food at the front. A sausage roll and a bag of limp salad for dinner it was. She never decided what to eat, the God of reductions chose for her.

She rummaged past the celery and saw a crème caramel for ten pence. She threw that in the basket too. Glancing around, she wondered if her sister was in the shop or one of her colleagues and her face flushed. If her sister could see how she was managing, she'd insist on helping her out. Then she'd have to explain how things had got so bad. She'd have to tell her sister that she spent her money on helping people and her sister would go ballistic, insisting that she had to look after herself first. It all seemed okay giving people a bit of money or paying for the odd night in a cheap hotel to get them into a safe place. She didn't use to worry. She simply put it on her card. Now and again, she had a blowout which involved getting takeaways and wine to fill her lonely nights. But her limit had been reached and the repayments were too much. She missed a couple and the charges piled up. She eventually got a loan to cover one of her cards but all she ended up with was more monthly payments. Then the fridge packed up and that was soon followed by the second-hand washing machine. On the card they went. Everything had happened at once. She felt her hands clenching as she thought of that line politicians always spouted. Help for hard-working families. Where was the help for single person households who were struggling with only one wage coming in? Not that families didn't need help. She didn't begrudge them getting help. Times were tough for all, but she wanted help too.

She felt a tear drizzling down her cheek as she reached for a yellow-stickered jam doughnut next to the fridge. Surely there had to be something better than struggling like this. Throwing the doughnut back on the shelf, she continued. She didn't want to be cold in her home and have to exist on food she hadn't chosen. She craved vegetables and a roasted traybake of some description but the cost of using her oven was becoming a joke. She'd watch her smart meter whirring away, like it was shouting at her.

Her thoughts turned to Wesley, the man she'd only ever met

on paper, and she hated herself. She had a home, and she had some food. How dare she feel sorry for herself when he'd struggled on the streets and now, he'd been murdered.

She was about to approach the Christmas aisle and her better self was telling her not to go there. It would only upset her. She'd love some new decorations, something to brighten up her flat. It was the smallest of things that brought happiness.

The old nursery began to creep into her thoughts. 'I will make you pay.' The youth had also taunted her with that line. Amongst the glistening fake candlelight, she spotted a grey hoodie. The wearer turned into the Christmas aisle. It had to be him. He was following her and not only that, he'd now know how truly pathetic she was. She used the back of her coat sleeve to wipe her damp eyes. The bravado she showed last night when she ran out of her flat to confront him had long gone. Now she knew his attacks on her property were personal, and that the police weren't interested in what he'd done. The trembling in her knees had travelled to her upper body. The metal handle of the shopping basket jangled against the house key ring that dangled down the side of her bag, telling him that she was scared. Was he standing around the corner, listening and laughing?

A hefty older woman crashed into her as she came out of the pet section. 'For heaven's sake. Why do people stand like morons in the aisles?' The look of anger in her eyes was all that was wrong with the world. Everyone was in a rush. They were so full of anger, and they had such little regard for what others were going through. The woman didn't apologise. Sasha rubbed her arm which would no doubt bruise. The woman turned into the Christmas aisle and vanished.

Again, she wondered if the youth was there and if that had been his hoodie. She glanced all the way down the shiny floor of the shop, right to the tills. She should go now. Pay and leave as fast as she could, but she'd never know. She was in a supermarket. If it was the youth, what could he do to her here? She was as safe as she could be.

She tried to prise her feet off the floor, but it was as if they were stuck. *Come on, Sasha.* She took a deep breath and tried again. This time, she stepped slowly and turned the corner into the Christmas aisle. There was no one there. It was just her and stacks of Santa and Rudolph decorations. She smiled, then a slight laugh escaped her lips. How silly she'd been. The youth hadn't been walking down the Christmas aisle or anywhere in the shop. Her mind was playing on her worries.

I'm safe.

No one can harm me in here.

She kept repeating those word in her head as she brushed rows of luxurious tinsel. Yes, she had no money, but nothing could take away the joy of shaking a snow globe or the smell of gingerbread that came from the edible tree decorations, and the shiny Christmassy letters that would usually spell out something like merry Christmas on a fireplace. She stopped and placed a hand over her mouth.

Those words again were spelled out in Christmas letters and leaned up against stacked up chocolates. I WILL MAKE YOU PAY. The holly décor in the corner of each one did nothing to quell the nausea that was toiling in her gut. She dropped the basket. The strip lights felt as though they were falling from the ceiling and melding with the fake candlelight. She stumbled into the snow globes, sending a couple smashing across the hard floor.

'Excuse me, are you okay?' a shop assistant called.

She went to speak but nothing came out. Her tongue felt too big for her mouth as she garbled a word or two out. She had to get away before she fainted. Sobbing, she darted like she was drunk out of the shop and into the cold air. Without even looking around the car park, she pressed her central locking and jumped into her car. The only sound she could hear as she engaged the reverse gear was that of her thumping heart as it fired blood around her body. As she jerked backwards, she saw the youth through her rear-view mirror and pressed her brake pedal so hard, the car forced her back then forward as it rocked, her forehead hitting the top of the steering wheel. The shop assistant ran out and opened the car door.

'I think she's hurt,' he called to a colleague.

Sasha reached out and grabbed the handle. 'I'm okay. Leave me alone,' she yelled as she yanked the door shut. She turned her aching head to check for the youth but there was no one there. Without a second thought, she pulled off and sped out of the car park. She was losing her mind. That moment, that feeling of being overwhelmed, it was like nothing she'd ever experienced in her life. If someone was out to make her pay, it was working. She was now terrified. Something else told her that this was just the start of worse things to come.

TWENTY-SIX

Gina held on to the rusty old rail that led down the Hangar steps. Wisps of fog drifted through the naked trees below. As she reached the halfway point, her phone rang. It was Hannah. Now was the worst time ever. She was at work and Gracie was with Mrs O.

'You going to take that, guv?' Jacob passed her on the steps, trying hard not to slip on the clumps of damp moss that had gathered at the edges.

'I don't want to, but I have to.' With shaking hands, she stared at the ringing phone before answering. 'Hannah, how are you, love?'

'Don't love me, Mum. Where's my daughter?'

'I guess Hetty messaged you.'

'She called me, and I know, Mum, I know you're at work. How could you when you promised that you'd take care of her?'

'Gracie is at an animal farm, with Mrs O. You know my colleague, Harry? His wife the cake maker? She was going today and asked if she could take Gracie. Gracie is having an amazing time. I'll send you some photos in a minute.'

Hannah went silent. 'I don't want photos. I wanted you to look after Gracie, not farm her out.'

Gina sighed. 'Sorry, love. A case came in and I really needed to be on it. Gracie is fine with Mrs O, she's loving her day out. I promise you.'

'You're telling me you've left her in the care of a stranger?'

'Mrs O is not a stranger.'

'She is to me, Mum. You know what, nothing's changed. This is just like when I was little. You left me with anyone who would have me and I never knew when you would finish a shift. You were never on time picking me up. You missed every milestone that was important to me. I don't want that for Gracie.'

Gina swallowed her upset down. She'd actually been really cautious about who she'd left Hannah with, and it was never just anybody. 'I'm so sorry.'

'No, you're not sorry. I'm calling Nanny Hetty and you are going to take Gracie there when she gets home from whichever animal farm she's gone to with Mrs O. Nanny Hetty is far from perfect, but I know she won't let me down, like you have.'

'Please, Hannah—'

'No, Mum. I'm not having her passed from pillar to post. She's precious to me, not like I was to you.'

'That is not true.' Gina's hands trembled that much, she thought she might drop the phone. Gina had brought Hannah up as a single mother and a widow. From the start, life had been hard, but not once had she put Hannah in danger. In fact, Gina had made sure that danger had died when she left Terry to breathe his last at the bottom of her stairs. She had done everything in her power so that her little girl had grown up safe from her monster of a father. She wanted to shout all that at her ungrateful grown-up daughter, but instead she ended the call. The last thing she needed was to say something she'd regret. Instead, she sent a message.

Hannah, please don't make me take her to Hetty's. I'm doing my best. Gracie is safe. She's happy and I love her being with me and we'll go to yours tonight as planned. Please. X

She only hoped that her daughter would see sense. Gina was now sure that she had everything worked out and Hannah needed to see that. The thought of facing Hetty again made Gina recoil in disgust as she took a step down towards the Hangar. The woman hated her, and Gina had no time for Hetty either.

She glanced at a message from Hetty that had come through while she'd been talking to Hannah.

Always were a shit mother, always will be. Now you get to be a shit grandmother too.

'Guv, you coming?'

She wanted to throw her phone to the ground and stamp on it in a temper but instead, she put her phone away. There was nothing she could do right now to improve her situation, but she did need to do her best for Wesley Reid. 'Yes. Is there anyone down there?'

'A couple of guys seem to be living in the old wooden house.'

As she reached the muddy bottom, she followed Jacob through the tangled branches and stood in the overgrown clearing. She could see why they'd chosen to bed down here. There really was only one safe way in and one safe way out – if she could call the crumbling steps that she'd just walked down safe. The density of the trees and shrubs wouldn't allow anyone through, not without them being badly injured. The old wooden house still had its roof which provided a bit of shelter from the rain. Branches were entwined around what was left of the walls and steps, acting like a wind break, but nature had reclaimed most of it.

She stepped onto the trodden mud patch and looked at the two men taking shelter. In the house, the one man was nailing the edge of a tent to the back of the structure, to shelter them better. The other man perched at the front dangling his soiled trainers over the edge. 'What brings you here?' He swung his legs back and forth.

'I'm DI Harte, this is DS Driscoll. We need to speak to you about Wesley Reid.'

The man shook his head and began to play with his brown beard. 'We don't speak to the likes of you.' He folded his arms and stared at each of them in turn.

'Someone killed your friend.'

'Who says he was a friend of mine?'

'Was he?' Gina could do without the run around.

'Not saying another word.'

The man finished nailing the tent and put the hammer down.

The other man stared right at Gina, then Jacob. 'The moment I talk, you try to pin it all on me. I'm homeless and yes, I spend most of my life out of my tree, but I don't hurt anyone, and I mean anyone. We all argue around here, it's the way things are.'

'Did you argue with Wesley?'

'No, I'm just sayin', it's the way things are. We get blamed for things we didn't do.'

Gina sighed. 'I can assure you; we only want to find out who killed Wesley and we were hoping that you could help us.'

He stared a little longer and twiddled his fingers in thought. His shoulders dropped. 'I want you to find who killed Wes, so I'll make an exception and answer your questions, but you start falsely trying to pin anythin' on me, you won't see me for dust. I don't hurt people, okay?' He pulled a roll-up from behind his ear and began to press it between his thumb and yellowed forefinger.

Gina half-smiled. 'Thank you. That would really help us. We want to catch his murderer too.' She trod carefully, knowing that stepping into the Hangar was like her stepping into their home. She had to treat it with respect and wait to be invited. She needed information from them and if they were willing to help, that was better all round.

'I'd say take a seat and ask if you'd like a cuppa but as you can see, no kettle, no settee, so I guess you'll have to stand.'

The other man put the rock he was using as a hammer down and joined the sitting man. He grabbed a body warmer that was hung on a nail and slipped it on before also sitting.

'What are your names?'

'Sid Payne and James Caid.'

'We've been told that Wesley Reid—'

'Wes. Call him Wes, for heaven's sake. He'd hate being called Wesley,' Sid replied.

Gina cleared her throat as Jacob began noting their names down. 'We've been told that Wes was here on Saturday night, that's Saturday the twelfth. Can you confirm that?'

'There were a few of us here. It's a regular meeting place, especially on a Saturday night. The Hangar comes to life. We have to find pleasure where we can.'

Stepping forward, Gina nodded. 'I can understand that. What do you normally do on a Saturday night?'

'We just have a laugh, well as much as we can. Everyone brings a bottle, and we share. We're like that.' James shrugged.

'Did Wes say where he'd come from?'

Sid nodded. 'The Angel Arms. He looked angry. He was stomping around with clenched fists, and he was bleating on about some mate who'd upset him. Said he was going to kill the man, so maybe that's where you should be looking. That man was Wes's friend, and he wouldn't even let him stay for a few weeks while he sorted his life out. A few days before, he said that the same bloke had turned up at his hostel and had been hanging around outside.'

'Did he mention a name?' Gina knew they were on about Noel, but it would be good to hear it from them.

'Noel. He said that this Noel bloke had just told him that he'd been having it away with his girlfriend and it was because of them he was now homeless, and he couldn't see his kid. It was all this Noel's fault. He said Noel had asked him to meet him at the pub and that Noel had hit him. That Noel sounds like a right, violent thug. You need to catch him and lock him up.'

If only they could. Noel hadn't been back to his house since they'd started looking for him. 'What time did Wes arrive at the Hangar on Saturday?'

Sid scrunched his brow. 'Err, it was about nine on the night, wasn't it, James?'

'Yea, maybe a bit after or before. We wondered why he was back when he had somewhere warm to be, but we guessed something 'ad upset him.'

Gina thought back to that night. Wesley would have been at the Angel until about eight thirty where, after he fought with Noel outside, he would have gone straight to the Hangar. That all fit into the timeline. 'When did he leave here?'

'I think it was between half ten and eleven. I can't be too sure.' Sid wrinkled his nose. 'Sorry, I was wasted. We both stayed here, though, didn't we, Jammy?'

'Yeah, we didn't leave at all,' James replied.

'Did anyone leave with him?'

Sid looked to the side and began fiddling with the hem of his coat. 'I don't know. I wish I knew more but I don't. Sorry. I was wasted, like I said.'

'Did Wes mention anyone else? Do you know if he had any known enemies?'

'Oh yeah.' Sid smiled. 'That geezer in the bottom room at the hostel used to freak Wes out. He used to talk to a kid that didn't exist and shout like mad if he even made the slightest of noises when he walked past. I don't know his name, but the man sounds like a nutter.'

Gina shuddered at the use of the word nutter. They had no idea what that man had been through or was going through but Gareth Alderman had cropped up again and she needed to find out if they had anything on him, past or present. She checked her watch. Time was once again running away from her, and Macie Perrin was at the station. Gina had hoped to see if more had come out of her interview or if tech had garnered anything about her messenger. 'Thank you for your help. I'll leave you with my card so that you have my number. If you hear or find out anything that can help, please call me.' Without waiting for the man to tell her had no money, she pulled a ten-pound note from her pocket. 'Just in case you need some money to make the call.'

'Will do, police lady.'

'Detective Inspector,' she corrected him. She'd worked hard for her position.

'A DI.' He popped the card in his pocket.

'Wes said something that I thought was odd,' James said.

'What was that?'

Jacob stood next to Gina.

'He said someone had been in his room when he was out.'

'How did he know?' Gina's heart began to beat a little faster.

'Someone had left a pound coin on his pillow, twice, and his room stank of something weird, but he didn't say in what way. That's all he said. It was starting to freak him out. He also said that the lounge in the house had a dodgy window. He lost his keys one night and found a way in through it. He'd also broken the lock on his door to get in on that same night, so anyone could've got into the house and his room. You might want to tell whoever runs the place.'

'Thanks, James. That's really helpful.'

The smell that Kayleigh Blunt had described had reared its head again. There was a link and Gina needed to work out what it was. A weird smell and pound coins. However hard she tried to rattle her brains; she couldn't figure out what it meant. She thought of the incense sticks in Gareth Alderman's room. The smell could have easily made its way around the building.

A message pinged up on her phone. A part of her didn't want to look after receiving that vile message from Hetty. It had cut her to her core. She hoped it was Hannah, telling her that everything was okay with her keeping Gracie, but it was Wyre.

There's been a sighting of Frederick Bertram. We're heading to the Cleaver and hope to pick him up.

TWENTY-SEVEN

Gina rushed back and hurried into the station and straight to the incident room. 'Do we have Bertram?'

Wyre smiled. 'We certainly do. He came back and the officer watching the place stopped him from leaving and arrested him on suspicion of being involved in a murder. He's in interview room two and he hasn't requested a solicitor.'

Jacob entered and pulled his coat off his shoulders and went to sit.

'Don't get comfortable. We have Frederick Bertram. I want to know why he lied to us. We know he didn't go straight to Killian Foster's flat. He has a lot of explaining to do.'

Jacob pushed his chair back under the main table and smiled. 'Let's do this then.'

As they walked to the interview room, Gina checked her phone. There still no further news from Hannah. The waiting was killing her inside. Briggs came down from the other end and smiled at her.

She entered first. Frederick Bertram gripped the Styrofoam cup of coffee and held it to his chest. His puffy black jacket was done up to the top of his neck and a thick grey hat covered his shaved head. His nose twitched and he lifted one of his hands and used a finger to scratch it. He sniffed hard and twitched again. 'I didn't do anything.'

Gina took a seat and Jacob joined her. 'You can tell us everything in a minute.'

Jacob turned on the tape and introduced everyone in the room, finishing with the time. 'It is now thirteen hundred hours.' They went through the formalities, confirming his name and date of birth.

Gina cleared her throat. 'Right, you understand that you have been arrested on suspicion of being involved in the murder of Wesley Reid, and you'll be asked a series of questions about the night of the twelfth of November?'

Nodding, he bowed his head. He picked at the sides of the now empty cup and began piling up the white material onto the table. 'Yes,' he murmured.

Gina had no time to waste. 'In your initial statement, you claim to have seen the victim, Wesley Reid on Saturday the twelfth of November at around eleven fifteen on that evening. We know you arrived at Killian Foster's flat at twelve thirty. You should have arrived at Mr Foster's place by eleven thirty, maybe eleven forty at the latest. Where were you for the missing hour?'

'I left the Cleaver, like I told you. I was nowhere near the place when Wesley got murdered.'

'Where were you?'

No answer.

'Mr Bertram, answer my question.'

He shrugged. 'I was walking and thinking, you know how it is.'

Gina sighed. 'Let me get this straight. You were eager to meet up with Killian Foster at his flat. You left to be with him, yet you went for a very long walk first?'

'That's right.'

'Did anyone see you when you were out walking?'

He shook his head.

'Killian told us that you showed him a coin trick.'

Frederick Bertram scrunched his nose again. 'I picked a coin up from his side table and ran it through my fingers if that's what you mean. It isn't really a trick. Is that what this is all about?'

'So, you got the coin at Mr Foster's flat?'

'Yes. I mean, a lot of people know how to run a coin across their knuckles. I don't know what this has to do with anything.'

Gina watched the man for a moment. He leaned forward, placed what was left of the torn cup next to the pile of bits. However much she felt he could be guilty, he seemed to think it was odd that she was asking him about the coin. 'The next morning, when did you leave Mr Foster's flat?'

'I don't know. It was still dark. Maybe five, six.'

'When I saw you arrive back at the Cleevesford Cleaver, where you live and work, it was light.'

'I walked to the garage for a coffee on Caldwell Street. We had a bit to drink, and I needed a strong hit of caffeine. My head was all muzzy and my throat was like sandpaper. I also like the caramel lattes that they serve in their machine.'

'The one by the old nursery?'

He scrunched his brows. 'I don't know any nursery. Don't have any kids, or is it plants?'

'How long did you stay at the garage for?'

'I dunno. I knew I needed to get back to the Cleaver. There's always someone who needs something fixing or cleaning up. While I was there, I sat on one of the stools by the large window that faces out on the road for a bit. I read the paper that was on the side, drank my coffee and then left.'

Gina watched as Jacob made a note. They'd be able to check his alibi with the garage and check their CCTV. If Frederick Bertram had time to go snooping around the old nursery and leave the bloodied towel there, he'd have even more explaining to do but getting hold of the CCTV would be the first step. Again, his reaction to her mentioning the old nursery gave nothing away. It really did look like he'd never heard of the place, but Gina had seen some great acting when it came to interviewing suspects. 'Going back to the night of Wesley's murder, you say you were walking. I need to know exactly where you were walking. I need road names and times.'

'Err.' He scratched his face. 'I walked along the high street in Cleevesford.'

'For close to an hour?' Gina paused, giving him time to take in what he was saying. 'Several businesses have CCTV along that road. If we pull their CCTV, we should see you on it. That will confirm what you're saying.'

'Shit.' He exhaled and rubbed his head with his shaky hands.

'Mr Bertram, where were you really?'

He huffed out a quick sigh and shook his head.

Gina had no motive for Freddie murdering Wesley, but he was clearly hiding something big. 'Frederick Bertram, did you murder Wesley Reid?' The man remained silent. He had lied to them. He was lying about his whereabouts and had a clear opportunity to kill their victim.

'I want to see a solicitor.' He stood. 'I want to see someone now.'

'And that is your right. Do you want us to call someone specific or is it the duty solicitor?'

'Duty.'

'We will need the keys to your annexe and your phone.'

'You can't go in my home.'

'You've been arrested on suspicion of murder. It would be better for us if you gave us the keys to enter or we'd have to break the lock. We want to do the least damage possible.'

He wrenched the single door key from his pocket and threw

it onto the table. Then he reached into his other pocket and placed his phone down with a little more care.

Someone knocked at the door and Jacob spoke to the tape. As soon as he finished, Gina stood and opened it, leaving Jacob to explain to Frederick Bertram what would happen next. Wyre beckoned her out.

'Any progress.'

Wyre nodded. 'Our YouTuber has had another message but this time from a different number. I've spoken to digital forensics, and they can't trace where the last message came from, and the phone number is no longer in use. And the number used to send the latest message, it's already dead. Whoever's behind this is using the number once and disposing of the SIM card. They're using burner phones.'

'When was the message sent?'

'A good hour ago. Tech had downloaded everything from her phone and then they left it on the side, not noticing that the new message had come through.'

Gina glanced through the window. Frederick hadn't been with them that long. He would have had time to send that message and destroy a SIM or a burner phone. She wasn't ruling out the option that he could also be working with someone else. Her mind flashed to Noel Logan; another person of interest who was nowhere to be seen. It was a bit of a coincidence that both men had been missing at the same time. She needed his solicitor to hurry so that they could continue with the questioning. She still needed to know where he'd been and if he knew Noel Logan. 'What did the message to Macie say?'

'It said, "I got my pound of flesh but a pound is more than just a pound. What is it? Ask the police to explain." We have no doubt it came from our murderer. And there—'

Gina interrupted. 'He's talking about the pound left at the crime scene.' She felt a cold shiver run across her neck. The murderer or murderers had chosen to communicate with them through Macie Perrin. This was a game to them, and Gina and the department had no option but to play along.

'I was going to say, there's more.'

'What?'

'The message continued with, "Two down and she's next."'

'Two, who's the other one? Is it Macie? Make sure we don't leave Macie alone.' Gina's heart began to pound. 'Who is the she?'

'I don't know, guv. We haven't had any reports of bodies being found.'

'There's another one out there and we need to work out who's next before they die too. Watch Macie, she has been chosen for a reason so that puts her in danger. Get a team together, we need to search Frederick Bertram's annexe now. We don't have much time.'

TWENTY-EIGHT

Gina followed Wyre to the incident room, joining O'Connor. Jacob wasn't far behind. 'Duty solicitor won't be here for at least an hour and a half, but Frederick Bertram isn't going anywhere for now.'

Gina stepped further into the room and grabbed her coat. 'Well, we best go and search his annexe under a section eighteen. We are looking for the murder weapon, something that smells musty or herby which might put him at the scene but that one will be more difficult as he looks after the house. I know this is outside of Bertram's annexe, but I want to check the lounge window. One of the men down at the Hangar said that Wesley Reid claimed that the window was broken, and someone had been in his room. Either the murderer followed him in through the main door, had a key, or entered through that window. We have three possibilities. Any news on Logan?'

O'Connor popped a cup on the table after finishing its contents. 'PC Smith has headed over with a small team and they're speaking to the neighbours. Hopefully one of them may know something. Even a place of work would be a start.'

'That's great. Let's hope they lead us to him. It's odd that he still hasn't come home.'

'There is something in his past, guv.' O'Connor shuffled a few sheets of paper and held one up to read. 'He was caught carrying a knife fifteen years ago. No one was assaulted as far as we know but it was a random stop and search outside a night-club in Birmingham. Another man saw it sticking out of his pocket. When questioned he claimed that he had to walk back on his own as he didn't have enough money for a taxi and needed it for self-defence. He claimed he was jumped and had his phone stolen a couple of weeks before.'

Gina scrunched her brow. 'He felt justified in carrying a weapon, more specifically a knife.' She scratched her forehead. If only they had him here. 'How about Gareth Alderman?'

Again, O'Connor shuffled through some more notes. 'Sorry, guv. I was just about to update the system. Nothing helpful. He's had two spells in a psychiatric hospital for breakdowns. Once after losing his wife and then after losing his child. Unless believing in ghosts and an afterlife is a problem, he's all okay now.'

Gina shook her head. 'The poor man thinks his daughter is still with him, but I guess cuts to mental health services have ensured that he's been let down too.'

Wyre did her zip up. 'We still need to consider him, though. He hated Wesley Reid. He had opportunity and he could have snapped.'

Gina nodded. 'Keep Logan and Bertram on the main list for now, pop Gareth Alderman underneath them.' She watched as Wyre grabbed a pen and updated the board. 'Are we all ready?' A hum of yesses filled the room. 'One last thing, any further updates on our chosen one?'

Wyre smiled. 'Macie is being very cooperative and seeing all this as an adventure. However, we are concerned for her safety after that last message even if she doesn't seem worried.'

'The murderer has chosen to contact her, and we don't want them to know that she's involved us. The perpetrator has already claimed to have killed a second time and that they are going to kill again, and that the next victim is female. Stay with Macie. I propose that a couple of officers go home with her and stay there, ready and on hand for any incoming information. I want her phone line and every other means of communication monitored by tech, and I want her to continue with what she'd normally do in a routine way.'

'I think she'll be more than up for that. She's staying here for now and sitting with Garth in digital forensics. We'll organise her going home when we get back from the search,' Wyre replied.

'Right, I'm leaving, meet me at Frederick Bertram's. Let's get this search underway.'

TWENTY-NINE

Gina stepped out of her car opposite the Cleevesford Cleaver and checked her phone again. There was still nothing from Hannah and her insides were squirming away. The wait was killing her.

Gareth Alderman parted his curtains and peered out. The uniformed officer standing at the main door smiled and held a hand up, waving at Gina. Gina smiled back before watching as Kayleigh walked past the officer to enter the building.

'I'm just walking down the side of the building to check the windows,' she called to the officer. Following the tight path, she placed her arm in front of her face to try and shield her eyes from sprawling branches until she reached the window that led to the communal lounge. After a wiggle and lift, the sash window slid up. Warm air and a musty smell seeped out of the deserted room. She fiddled with the catch, and it wobbled. It was indeed broken. James at the Hangar had been right in what he'd heard. Anyone could have got into the building. Gina hurried back to the front and mentioned it to the officer.

Jacob pulled up in one car and O'Connor and Wyre came together in another. They all hurried out and followed Gina to the back of the building, ready to search Frederick Bertram's annexe. As she turned into the back drive, she stood and stared. His front door was wide open. She swallowed and entered his annexe, not knowing who she was going to find. All she knew was that they were in there given the sound of the living room door slamming. She held her finger to her lips and whispered, 'We're going in.'

Gina gestured for the others to follow. They crept into Frederick Bertram's hallway. She placed her hand on the door handle knowing that as soon as she pushed it open, she'd be confronted by whoever was in there. Slamming through, she shouted, 'Police.' That's when she saw the large living room window flapping in the wind. The games console and all Bertram's games were strewn everywhere. His wastepaper bin had been turned upside down. She peered through the open kitchen door and saw that his cupboards had been messed up too. All the tins and packets had been scattered on the floor, leaving pasta and rice everywhere. Someone had beaten them to the search.

Running across the lounge and jumping over the toppled gaming chair, Gina leaned out of the window and held her hand up, gesturing for everyone to stay silent. She heard a rustling in next door's garden. Without a second thought, Gina clumsily forced her body through the window that wasn't quite big enough. After a moment of straining, she almost stumbled onto a patch of weeds. Then, she heard the creaking of a fence. 'They're running in that direction.' Wyre followed her and they darted around the first garden that led to an overgrown passageway that serviced all the gardens. She ran, pushing twigs away, crunching on all sorts of debris. Jumping over a pile of bricks, she stopped again and heard a woman shouting for someone to get out of her garden. 'Three doors down.' The end of the path led to a huge housing estate. If he reached it before they did they'd lose the intruder to the rabbit warren of houses and roads. There's no way they'd find him then when there were so many possible turns to take.

It was no good, the intruder had darted off into the direction she didn't want them to go. As they reached the end of the pathway, there was no one in sight. 'We've lost him.'

'Damn.' Wyre exhaled and hit the fence. Gina shook her head and panted heavily as she got her breath back.

Gina walked a little way down and listened from behind the gate as a woman told a man that someone had climbed over her fence. Gina reached for the catch, but the gate was locked. 'Police, can you open your back gate?'

Footsteps clonked up the garden path and the woman slid the lock across. 'Where were you a few seconds ago? Some man was in my garden, nearly scared me half to death.'

'We were chasing him. There's been a break in at the Cleaver.'

'That place is nothing but bloody trouble since it became a hostel. There're always weirdos hanging about, shouting, drunks peeing in my front garden. I'm sick of it. No wonder everyone's protesting at the old nursery. I hate it here now. And now one of them has broken my fence.' The woman pointed to the fallen fence panel that was touching the grass in her neighbour's garden. 'To top it all off, someone was murdered. I'm never going to sell my house.' She roared in frustration and turned back to the man.

'Look, Lacey. It's not their fault.'

She dismissed him with her hand. 'I know, I know. I'm just sick of it, that's all. So, you lost him?'

Gina nodded. 'Sorry to say, but yes. Can you tell us what he looked like?'

'I literally saw a dark mass of clothing making off over my fence. I know I've been calling this person he, but I have no idea if it was a man. The bulk and frame looked more manly, I'd say. Maybe he was slightly broad shouldered. Or, it could have been a teenager. I can't tell how tall he was, it all happened too fast. He was wearing a dark-hooded top, dark tracksuit bottoms and black trainers.'

Gina looked down at the earth the intruder had trodden. There were deep footprints in the mud and that mud had been trodden over the fence panel. 'I'm going to need forensics here,' she said to Wyre. Gina turned back to the woman. 'Can I ask that you go in your house and don't disturb anything.'

'Do what you need,' she replied. 'If it catches him then that's a good thing.' She paused. 'My heart is racing. I just thought, could he have had something to do with the murder?' She placed her hand over her chest.

Gina needed to reassure the woman. Whoever had murdered Wesley Reid was not after her, but she didn't know if the man who was running away had something to do with it. Had Bertram managed to tell someone that he'd been taken to the police station? Had he sent someone over to destroy evidence? She had to consider that as a possibility. 'A uniformed police officer will be staying outside the Cleaver tonight and a team will be in your garden soon.' She passed the woman one of her cards. 'If you get worried about anything at all, however small, please feel free to call the station or call me straight away.'

'Thank you.' The woman took the card and headed back into her house.

'Stay in. A couple of forensics people will arrive shortly, and a police officer will accompany them.'

The woman nodded. Gina turned to Wyre. 'We need to know what the intruder was after, that's unless they found whatever they wanted and took it. Let's get back to the others.'

Jacob waved from Bertram's living room. 'Did you catch him, guv?'

'No, he got away.'

'O'Connor and I have been searching the place and you won't believe what we've found.'

Gina peered through the window. 'Don't hold back.'

'It's possible that the intruder was looking for this.' He held up a shoebox-sized wooden box and opened the lid. Little bags of powder, scales and unused baggies were scattered in the box. 'It looks like he's been dealing. There's just a bit too much for personal use. We found this hidden under loose floorboards in the bedroom. It appears that the intruder hadn't got to that room yet.'

Gina felt something push against her ankle. His cat. She leaned down and picked up the slight animal and it began to panic and claw. As she let it go, it jumped through the window and meowed. 'Great work. Any sign of a knife?'

'Sorry, no.' Jacob pressed his lips together.

'So, we found ourselves a drug dealer but failed to link him to the murder and find that knife. Have you looked everywhere?'

'Not yet but we'll keep looking.'

'Can you call forensics? We have some great footprints on a fence panel. Whoever was here hadn't really thought out their escape too well. Forensics need to go through number twelve's garden.'

Jacob nodded and began making the call. Wyre began to walk back around to the front and Gina followed. There was no way she'd climb back in the way she left. As she reached the front door, her phone began to ring. She flinched. It had to be Hannah demanding that she take Gracie to Hetty's. She exhaled when she saw Briggs's name flashing. 'Sir.'

Briggs cleared his throat. 'We have another body. Woman's friend and neighbour found her. Bernard is on his way.'

Gina shivered. It was starting to get darker now and the temperature was dropping. 'Any link to the last one?'

'Afraid so. She has a pound coin placed on her forehead. The victim's friend who reported the murder said that the house also smelt of sage. You need to get over there now. Can you do that?'

She swallowed. 'The second victim.' Mrs O still had Gracie and Hannah hadn't messaged so she needed to act with speed. 'I'm on my way.'

THIRTY

When she arrived at the second victim's house Gina messaged Mrs O to see if Gracie was okay. It warmed her heart to hear that Mrs O had taken her to a soft play centre where she met up with her sister and nieces. Gracie was fine and she didn't need to be sent to Hetty's. She checked her last message to Hannah and still her daughter hadn't replied. If only Hannah could be happy that Gracie was having so much fun. A message popped up. It was Hetty again.

> *When's my lovely little great-granddaughter coming over? I won't dump her on everyone like you do. She'll grow up and see you for what you are, Gina. I will make sure of it.*

She was tempted to call the woman right there and then, tell her where to go but instead, she took a deep breath and put her phone away. She wasn't going to let Hetty get to her. Hurrying across the road to the Victorian semi, she smiled at the uniformed officer as he gave her the form and pen. She signed the log. 'Is Bernard in there?' The upstairs lights cast moving shadows over the dark drive, and she spotted Bernard through a window as he walked across the bedroom.

'Yes, he's with three crime scene assistants. He asked if no one could go in and said he'd be down in a short while.'

'Thank you.'

'The woman who found the victim, Ms Allinson, is waiting in her house next door,' the uniformed officer said.

'I'll wait for my colleague, then I'll speak to her. How is she taking it?' She noted that an ambulance was parked further down.

'It was a shock for her but she's okay. She told the paramedic she was fine, but I could see from her trembling that finding the body had taken it out of her.'

'Thank you,' Gina replied. Jacob pulled up and ran over. 'Right, we'll go and speak to the neighbour. If Bernard comes out, could you ask someone to let me know, please?' She watched on as another officer stood by the outer cordon, trying to distract passers-by and curious neighbours.

'Will do, guv.'

'Jacob, we'll go next door first. Bernard can't speak to us yet.'

He nodded and followed her to the adjoining semi. Gina opened the tiny gate and walked up the short path to the front door, where she knocked. A female officer opened it and let them in. 'Ms Allinson is in the kitchen. I've just made her a cup of tea. She said her teenage daughter is due home soon. She's obviously worried about her coming home to all this.'

'I'll try to be as fast as I can. We'll ask her to come down the station or speak to another officer later to give a formal statement.' Gina entered the hallway. She glanced into the spacious lounge with the period fireplace as she passed. The fire wasn't lit, and the house was as cold as the situation. She continued to the compact kitchen, passing a lit-up fish tank to her right. The shoal of neon tetras darted to the back of the tank. Then she saw the woman hunched over a breakfast bar, sipping tea and staring at the Aga on the back wall. 'Ms Allinson,' Gina said as she stepped towards her.

'You must be the detectives.'

'Yes. DI Harte and DS Driscoll.' Jacob went over to the other side of the breakfast bar, leaning his notebook on the wooden surface. 'We need to ask you a few questions, are you okay to answer them now?'

The woman with the ash-blonde bun nodded and placed her cup on the worktop. 'Yes.'

'Can you walk us through your afternoon, from when you arrived home?'

She nodded and gasped. 'It was such a shock.'

'Can I call someone to be with you?'

'No, I don't want anyone here. Are we safe, my daughter and me? I mean, this happened in broad daylight in what I've always felt is a safe neighbourhood. Nothing like this has ever happened around here.'

'An officer will be posted next door for a short while. I hope that makes you feel safer.'

She shrugged. 'I saw my friend covered in blood, on her bed. I don't think I'll ever feel safe again.'

'I'm so sorry. I can't begin to imagine what you're going through.' Gina paused for a moment until the woman turned to face her, eyebrows raised. 'Can you tell me what happened?'

The woman nodded and began playing with a loose strand of hair, twirling it between her fingers as she stared at her tea. 'I'll try. Everything feels a bit fuzzy.' She swallowed before continuing. 'I got home about three. I work until two thirty every day at Millington's on the industrial estate. I do admin part-time. As usual, I got in my car, popped to the shop to grab a bit of shopping and headed straight home. When I got back, I noticed that my daughter had left a parcel on the side for Judith. It must have arrived before she left for college this morning.'

'What time does your daughter start college?'

'On Mondays, it's...' She reached over and used her finger to find today's date on the calendar that hung on the wall. 'Ten thirty. She probably left around nine thirty as she has to get the bus to Redditch.'

Gina watched as Jacob made a note. 'And after that?'

'I went to take the parcel to Judith. I knocked at her front door but there was no answer. I thought it was strange as her car was on her drive and I knew she'd be finished at the library but then again, she does walk sometimes but not often. She too works part-time and some afternoons we sit in each other's houses, go for walks or drink coffee. We're good friends... were. Anyway, I knew where she kept her spare key in the garden so thought I'd just check to see if she was okay.'

'So, you were concerned?'

'Yes, because she's diabetic and I went over once, and she'd slipped into a diabetic coma. I guess I got worried that something like that had happened again.'

'Where was her key?'

'It was under a loose block-paving tile.'

'So, you retrieved the key and let yourself in through the back door.'

The woman shook her head. 'No, I should have known something was wrong. The key was already in the back door, so I just went in.'

'Was the door closed at this point?'

'Yes. I went into the kitchen, took off my boots and left them by a muddy smear on the kitchen floor, then I called for her. When she didn't answer, I was really worried. Then, I darted up the stairs and I heard her cat meowing in the main bathroom. He'd been shut in. I let him out and he went downstairs and out of the cat flap. Then, I opened the door to the spare room where she does her ironing. Nothing looked odd.' The woman paused and dabbed the corners of her eyes. 'I pushed open her bedroom door. That's when I saw her laid out on the bed. There was blood everywhere and a coin on her head. I freaked and ran back down the stairs and out of the front door. Then, I called nine-nine-nine.'

'You mentioned a smell when you called in.'

'Yes, it was sage which is also odd as when I make a roast, Judith sometimes comes over and has dinner with us. She hates sage and onion stuffing because she can't stand sage. She would never have that in her house.' Ms Allinson let out a teary laugh. 'She called it an evil weed. That and coriander.'

Gina waited for Jacob to catch up. 'How close were you and Judith?'

Ms Allinson wiped her streaming eyes with the sleeve of her chunky blue jumper. 'We were so close. We went out together. To the pub, the theatre, wherever took our fancy. She'd tell me about all her dates, and she was so funny, the way she'd go on about what catastrophes they were. Wait...' Ms Allinson pulled out her phone and read one of her messages. 'She messaged me last night. She had a date today with someone she went out with the other night, a man called Luther. He was meant to be coming to hers for dinner.'

'Did she say anything else?'

'Only that she was really excited to see him again. She told me the other day that they'd clicked. She really liked him and was looking forward to seeing how this one blossomed. She thought he might be the one.'

'Do you know anything else about Luther? A surname, maybe?'

'She showed me a photo of him that was on her phone.'

'Can you describe him?'

'Handsome. Square jaw. Light brown skin. Brown eyes. Short, shaved black hair. Thin-framed glasses. She said he worked out but I only saw a portrait photo so I can't comment on his build or height.'

'That's a really good description, thank you.' Gina waited

for Jacob to catch up. She needed to speak to Luther. He was meant to be coming to Judith's house and now she'd been found murdered. Gina pressed her lips together as she let her mind run with that. From what she'd been told, the crime scene was identical to the one at the Cleevesford Cleaver. Unless Luther had anything to do with Wesley Reid, she'd struggle to see the link but without knowing more about the man, he could be the exact link they were looking for. He could have arrived at her house earlier, killed her and left.

'Have you seen anyone suspicious hanging around lately?' Someone must have seen Judith's house being watched. The killer would have had to watch her to know her working hours. They'd know when she was due home, and they'd know where she kept her spare key. There was a chance that this person had been watching her for a long time.

'Now that you come to think about it, there is a boy that Judith was getting fed up with.'

'A boy?'

'Some teenage kid on an electric scooter. The kids are a pain around here. I know Judith had one of her tyres slashed and someone posted dog muck through her letter box a short while ago. It was just after Halloween. She'd told a group of trick-or-treaters to go away as they were scaring her cat. She wasn't sure whether it was them or the kid on the scooter who posted the muck or slashed her tyre.'

Gina made a note to pass this information to uniform about the amount of illegally driven electric scooters in the area. Those vehicles were becoming a menace and it seemed the kids were too. 'Have you seen the boy?'

The woman shook her head. 'No. I only know what Judith told me.'

The sound of a key in the front door stopped them all.

'Mum, what's going on out here? There are police at Judith's. Is she okay?'

'These are detectives, love.' Ms Allinson ran to the girl and hugged her. 'Judith has been murdered.' She burst into tears.

'No way. How?'

Gina moved away from the worktop, allowing the girl to lead her distraught mother over to a stool.

'I'll fill you in in a bit. I found her body.' Tears streaming, the girl passed Ms Allinson a box of tissues as she hugged her mother.

'Have you got who did it?' The girl looked to Jacob for answers. He shook his head.

Gina interjected the moment. 'Have you seen a youth on a scooter hanging around?'

'Oh, that prick. Yes.'

'Why do you say that?'

'I was walking home a few nights ago and it was quite late. I'd been out with my college friends. Judith had just pulled onto her drive. The kid was standing by her door. He kicked her car bonnet and quickly rode off on his scooter. I asked her about it, and she said she was going to report him to the police. I guess she never did. Was it him?'

'That's what we're trying to find out.' Gina left a card on the side. 'If you remember anything else that might help with the investigation, or if the boy turns up again, please call me straight away or tell the officers by the cordon. Can I take your name?'

'It's Fiona,' the girl replied.

There was another knock at the door. Jacob left the kitchen to answer. 'Guv, Bernard is waiting to speak to you. He's on the drive next door.'

She nodded and went to leave the mother and daughter to it. They all went silent as loud meows came from behind the kitchen door. The girl opened it and in ran a glossy cat. The girl picked it up and hugged it. 'I guess you can stay with us. Can we keep him, Mum? Judith wouldn't want him to have to go to a pet rescue centre. I'll look after him.'

Ms Allinson nodded. 'Yes, Judith would want that.'

'Oh, that night I saw the youth kicking Judith's bonnet,' the girl continued, 'Judith shouted to him as he rode off. She said, "If you ever touch my cat again, I'll kill you." I don't know what he did to the cat, but I don't think he's a nice person. He stopped the scooter and began staring her out like some psycho, until he rode off. It has to be him. You must find him.' The girl hugged the cat and kissed its head.

'What was he wearing?'

'Dark hoodie, dark trackies and dark trainers.'

'You said you saw him staring. What did he look like?'

'All I saw was a glint of light in his eyes. He had his hood up. I really didn't see him in any detail.'

Dark clothes, exactly the same get up that the intruder at Bertram's annexe had been wearing and they had been unable to catch him.

Ms Allinson exhaled. 'She had a date with a man a few weeks ago and he was horrible.'

'In what way?' Gina paused and waited for her to answer.

'He messaged some mean things to her after she refused to let him come back to her place. He was a bit of a sex pest on all accounts, kept trying to persuade her to take him to hers but she didn't like him and said no. He messaged her saying she was ugly and that no man would want her anyway, things like that. Really horrible words.'

'Did she tell you his name?'

Ms Allinson nodded. 'Yes, it was Noel.'

THIRTY-ONE

SASHA

Sasha pulled her curtains closed. No one could see her. She'd made sure of it when she sat in her flat with all the lights off. Too scared to even look out of the window, she'd remained huddled on the settee under a snuggle blanket since hurrying home. What must the staff at the supermarket think of her? She'd run out like a deranged thing, driving up a kerb as she skidded out of the car park. If they were going through what she was, they'd feel the same intense fear. She'd sprinted out of her car on returning home, almost tripping on the straps of her handbag as it dropped to the ground. She'd bashed into her downstairs neighbour and ran into her flat, sliding the chain across.

Sneaking into her dark kitchen, she felt safe with the window still boarded up. She knew she needed a cup of tea, or maybe something stronger. Something to take away the shake in her hands and the quiver in her breaths. Maybe she should go to her sister's house. It would be safe there. No, she knew her sister would worry and then she'd tell their father and that would get him even more worried. She poured her tea and took a sip.

She pulled out her phone and called Trevor. 'Hi.'

'Sasha, I've made a few calls from London much to my sister's anger while she's trying to prepare for the wedding, but she'll get over it.' He let out a chuckle. 'I've managed to find Kayleigh and her daughter a small temporary flatlet. It's much more suitable for her needs. She moves in tomorrow. I have told her, and she's thrilled to bits. Considering what happened in the room next to her, we put a priority on moving her.'

She held her hand to her chest. 'That is the best news. She and her little girl shouldn't have to stay there but I thought we had nothing else. How did you wangle that?'

'I think I made about a million calls. Nearly lost my voice.'

'Thank you so much, Trevor. That's a weight off my mind. I just wish that I'd been there to see her face when she was told.'

He paused. 'I did try to call you earlier, but your phone was off. Are you okay, by the way? I called the office which is when they said you weren't in.'

The last thing she wanted to do was talk to Trevor about her episode in the shop or the youth that was giving her grief, or the writing on the wall at the old nursery. It was all getting too much. 'I'm fine. I think I have a bug. My stomach is all over the place.' That wasn't a lie but it was more because of nerves than a bug.

'There's so much of it going around. I wish I could offer to cover for you, but uncle duties are calling. I'm currently wrapping up the bridesmaids' gifts. I think I'd prefer to be at work.'

'I'll be fine tomorrow. Don't worry about me. Just enjoy all the wedding plans and the wedding. Take care, Trev.'

Her intercom rang.

'Someone at your door?'

'I have no idea who that could be. It's probably a delivery for someone else in the block. I'm always getting other people's parcels.' A cold draft drifted past her neckline as the wooden board rattled in the breeze. She couldn't even look out of the window to see who was outside because it covered the whole window. 'Sod it. I'm not answering.'

'I best let you get some rest. Get well soon. I'll bring you some wedding cake back.'

She listened. Behind the boarded window, she could hear a voice. Maybe the person ringing was calling about something more important than a parcel. 'I best go. Not feeling so good.'

'Bye.' He ended the call.

Her intercom buzzed again. Holding her breath, she walked through her windowless hallway and listened to the heavy foot-steps that were tramping up the communal stairs. They stopped outside her door. She needed to breathe but if she did, they'd hear her. She gasped, unable to remain silent any longer. The figure didn't move. It remained at the other side of the door, no doubt enjoying the fact that she was terrified. She could open the door and burst out, try and hit them, but her feet were rooted to the spot. What if he hit her? Or it could be worse. What if he had a knife? Chasing the youth had been stupid the other night. She wasn't going to put herself in that much danger again. She felt the door creak as the figure leaned against the wood. Clasping a hand over her mouth, she trembled. *Please go away. Please*, she kept thinking.

It was as if he read her mind. She heard the dainty thud of something dropping on her doormat. The heavy-footed person went back the way they came. As soon as she heard the main door slam, she fell against the wall, giving in to her jellied legs. Breathing rapidly, she almost felt herself toppling as giddiness took over.

Gently, she slid the lock and opened the door. On the mat, there was nothing but a single pound coin. She leaned over and examined it, like it was a clue or a sign. She slammed the door and ran back to the sofa, wrapping herself back up as she gripped the coin. What did it mean? What were they trying to tell her? How was she going to pay?

THIRTY-TWO

Gina lifted the cordon for herself and Jacob before heading over to meet Bernard on their victim's drive. 'We need Noel. He'd argued with Wesley and now he was harassing Judith. Both of them, murdered.'

'Pop these on and you can both come in.' Gina and Jacob took forensic suits, gloves, shoe covers and masks from Bernard. He adjusted his beard cover a little. 'As usual, stay on the stepping plates and stick to the edge of the stairs.'

Gina finished putting all the protective clothing on and Jacob finally pulled his face mask from under his chin to over his mouth, ready to enter the crime scene.

'We'll start with downstairs.' Bernard held his arm out, gesturing for them to proceed. 'The lounge. We haven't found anything in this room so far. This door was closed when we arrived.' The sound of their footwear echoed in the high-ceilinged hallway as they all stepped on the metal plates, walking in a line.

Gina cast her gaze over the lounge which a mirror image of Ms Allinson's. Judith had a plump settee that faced the fireplace and a chair at the back of the room. Both had been covered in colourful throws and cushions. The footstool had a box of chocolates and a magazine resting on it. 'The neighbour said she came in through the back door, the one that leads to the kitchen. She said the key was already in the lock of the back door when she arrived.'

Bernard led them both to the galley kitchen that was a lot smaller than the one belonging to Ms Allinson. 'The key has been dusted and placed into an evidence bag. We've taken partial prints from the gate latch and the back door.'

Gina glanced at the kitchen. A trail of cat paw marks left a curved line on the worktop. 'Was there a muddy smear by the back door?'

Bernard shook his head. 'Yes. We have been through the bin and it contained a few sheets of muddy kitchen roll.'

Gina furrowed her brow. 'Just thinking this through. The intruder comes in through the unlocked back gate. He or she knows where Judith keeps her spare key. They use it to enter the house but leave it in the back door. When they step in, they deposit a bit of mud on the floor. They either tried to clean it up or Judith saw it when she came home, and she wiped it.'

'The kitchen roll will be entered into evidence. We've found trace evidence on less likely things.' Bernard stepped back and stood in the kitchen doorway, giving them a chance to spread out a little and breathe as they took the scene in.

Jacob made a sniffing noise. 'I can slightly smell sage, even with a mask on.'

Bernard cleared his throat. 'I was going to come onto that next. We found a burnt sage stick in the en suite bath. There is about an inch left of it. The whole room smelled of the stuff.'

'A sage stick? Like incense?' Gina's mind flitted back to Gareth Alderman and his smelly sticks.

'No. They're thicker. It's more like a wad of dried sage bound with string. They look a bit like cigars in their unburned state.'

Gina exhaled. 'Sage, like bless-this-house type sage. I'm with you. One of the residents said that she smelled something herby on the night of Wesley Reid's murder. I wonder if a sage stick was burned there but the killer took it away with them. I wonder if they slipped up this time, accidentally leaving this one behind.'

Jacob adjusted the hood on his crime scene suit. 'It's all sounding a bit weird now what with sage burning and the pound coins. It's sounding a bit occult-like. What the hell is going on?'

Bernard stepped back into the hall. 'Shall we go upstairs?'

Gina nodded. 'Yes.' She needed to see for herself how Judith Morgan had been placed by the killer.

Jacob turned out of the kitchen first, following Bernard along the plates and up the stairs. Gina stayed close behind them. As she got nearer to the body, her heart missed a beat. A person should feel safe in their home, but their victim had been anything but. She peered into the second bedroom which was mostly full of clothes rails and an ironing board. Jacob stopped and stared in the main room. He looked away for a few seconds before stepping back to let Gina shuffle in. She stood at the far end, sticking to the plates.

Bernard stepped over to the other side of the bed. A crime scene assistant was changing the camera settings before heading back into the en suite. Jacob waved at the other CSI. Gina could see that it was his fiancée, Jennifer. She began filling out the details on the front of the evidence bag in her hand.

Bernard began to speak. 'The victim was stabbed halfway down the bed as you can see from the spatter around that area. The stab is to the front right of her neck. She then moved into this position, her head on the pillow, legs placed neat and closed at the bottom of the bed. We have left the coin in place for you to see. There is something else. Can you see it?'

Gina bit her bottom lip as she scrutinised the scene. 'Her clothes don't have much blood on them.'

Bernard nodded. 'She was changed into this dress after being stabbed. Most of the blood had pooled midway down before she was moved. You can see how drenched the middle of the bed is around her. She literally bled out there.'

'The killer watched her die and then changed her clothes.' Gina stared at the blood-red dress. 'Have you found what she would have originally been wearing?'

He shook his head. 'That's odd too. We've looked everywhere. They're not in this house or the garden or the shed. There are no other bloodied clothes anywhere.'

'The murderer took them. Keepsake? Maybe something happened. The murderer could have sustained an injury if Judith fought back. Maybe some of their DNA was left on her clothes during the attack, which is why they took them.'

Bernard continued. 'Maybe, we have taken so many samples. You never know what will come back. As you can see, the carpet is also splashed with blood.' Gina glanced past the yellow evidence marker, taking in the spray of blood. 'The victim is covered in cider, and it too has sunk through the quilt. If you move closer to her and inhale, you can smell it, amongst other things. As before, there are no empty cider cans or bottles on the premises or in her bin.'

'Exactly like the last crime scene. Have you found her phone?'

'Yes, but it's password protected.'

'We need to get that to the station urgently, see if we can learn more about the man she was dating. One of our suspects had also been on a date with Judith. I want to see exactly what he sent to our victim.' Gina glanced at the woman. Blood soaked through her thick mane of hair and her dead dark-eyed stare made Gina shiver. She inhaled through the mask, and she too could smell sage, albeit only slightly and she could smell cider.

She turned away from the body, not liking the metallic waft of blood layered with urine. 'Any sign of sexual assault?'

Bernard shook his head. 'Not that we could tell.'

'Time of death?'

'Given her temperature and the environment, I'd say sometime this morning. From nine onwards but I can't be exact.'

'Is there anything else you can tell us right now that will help with the investigation?'

'No. I need to get all this sent to the lab for processing. We've got swabs and prints galore. There are a couple of footprints on the grass, and we will be taking a mould. Keith has also called me. He's attended the last scene you were at. The house near the Cleaver. Again, all results will be collated at the lab.'

Gina took one more look at Judith and turned away. 'If the footsteps match in any way or you can identify who any of the fingerprints belong to, call me.'

'We certainly will. Also, the post-mortem is likely to be later tomorrow.'

'Guv.' The officer guarding the door called her.

'Thank you,' she said to Bernard as she swiftly left. Jacob followed. The officer was waiting on the step outside the house.

'A man has just turned up to see the victim. Says his name is Luther.'

Just the person she wanted to speak to. Right now, Gina knew their prime suspect was Noel Logan, but she couldn't rule out Judith's latest date, Luther. Returning to the scene and pleading surprise could definitely be a killer move.

THIRTY-THREE

Gina glanced into the crowd that had formed. People huddled and some even gripped travel mugs as they drank and gossiped. She recognised Luther straight away from the description that Ms Allinson had given her. He stood on the opposite side of the road, a bunch of red roses in one hand and a box of chocolates in the other.

Gina whipped off her forensics gear and popped it in the bin by the front door. Her phone beeped. She reached for it in her pocket, almost dropping it as she fumbled amongst the rest of the rubbish. She had two messages. She opened the one from Hannah first.

I've told Hetty you'll deliver Gracie to her this evening. Don't worry. I won't ask you to look after her again. I'll text you her new address.

That was it. A blunt message. Gina's heart began to thump. She had no choice but to face the woman who hated her. She swallowed. Maybe she should have left this case to everyone else and looked after her granddaughter. She hated that she'd upset Hannah so much. It broke her heart, but it was too late for regrets now. Another text from Hannah followed. Gina swallowed. That bungalow that Gina had seen Hetty walking into by the old nursery was hers. The thought of having to leave Gracie there turned her stomach. She opened the other message. It was from Wyre.

> *I'm going back to Macie Perrin's house with her in a while. We need to be there in case the killer makes contact again. PC Smith is also going to be keeping an eye on the property as we're worried for her safety. Paula.*

Gina sent a brief message updating Wyre with what they had discovered and Noel Logan's link to the latest murder. Bertram couldn't be their killer unless he was working with someone else. They needed Noel Logan.

> *Would you please ask O'Connor to interview Frederick Bertram about the drugs we found on his premises? I'd also like to know who was at his annexe when we arrived. Any sign of Noel Logan?*

Wyre quickly messaged back.

> *No, but one of his neighbours said that he works away a lot. We're waiting to speak to his place of work. Someone is meant to be calling me back. O'Connor and I went to the unit after finishing up at Bertram's annexe, but there was a sign on the door with a number as there was no one on the premises. As soon as I have any news, I'll message you.*

Deflated, Gina popped her phone back into her pocket and pressed her lips together.

'Shall we go and see what Luther knows?' Jacob asked.

She nodded, following him back under the cordon. They pushed through the huddle of neighbours and crossed the road.

'Luther?' Gina called.

The man nodded. 'What's happened? I'm meeting Judith here. This is the address she gave me. The policeman at her door wouldn't tell me anything. He told me to wait for you.'

Gina stepped onto the path. 'We need to ask you a few questions.' She could see the confusion in the man's face. 'I'm sorry to have to tell you, Miss Morgan was found dead in her home.'

The flowers he was holding up took a dive as his arm dropped, a couple of the roses slipping out of the wrapping. 'I, err, no, that can't be right. I messaged her this morning. She was fine. Was it her diabetes?'

Gina smiled sympathetically. 'I'm really sorry to have to tell you this. Miss Morgan has been murdered. How well did you know her?'

He stared at Gina blankly for a few seconds while he took the news in. 'We went on a date. It was Friday night. Throughout the week we called each other a lot and sent messages.'

'Can I see those messages?'

Without hesitation, Luther handed his phone over. 'There's no password and the messages are on WhatsApp.'

Gina scrolled through his phone.

'I didn't hurt her. I would never hurt her, I mean, I really liked her.' His Adam's apple began to bob as he swallowed down his emotion.

Gina found the messages. There were some tender messages, each of them telling the other how much they enjoyed their date. She read the most recent messages, they were more sexual in nature suggesting that she and Luther were planning a big night at her house. The last message was sent from Judith at seven thirty in the morning. She spoke of the red dress and the special underwear. Gina passed it to Jacob so that he could see. She thought of the woman lying stabbed to death on her bed, wearing the exact dress and probably the underwear she was describing in the messages. Judith was a normal woman, enjoying a normal happy life until someone came along and ruined it for her. She thought of the sage and the coin. It had to mean something. The killer was throwing clues out, but Gina couldn't read them. 'I'm sorry to have to ask you this but where were you all morning? From eight to midday.'

He sniffed a little and Gina could see that his eyes had welled up. 'I was at work. I'm the finance manager at Greydon Electronics in Bromsgrove. I was in meetings all morning and I clocked in around seven fifteen as I knew I had to prepare. I only left about forty-five minutes ago so I've been there all day. I stopped to get these flowers and chocolates and came straight here. I've never been in her house. I only met up with her the once, that was at a pub, but you know when you meet someone, and they make such an impact.' He wiped a tear away.

Gina glanced at the man. His paisley tie stuck out over the top button of his overcoat. She'd request that an officer verified his whereabouts. 'Did Miss Morgan mention anything or anyone who might be worrying her?'

'She mentioned a kid on an electric scooter when we were out on Friday. She caught him messing with her car on her drive. The cat went up to him and she said...' he paused, '... she said he kicked her cat out of the way. She was extremely upset and was going to call the police. He was watching her house. She said she caught him looking through her windows. I offered to help but she said she had it under control. You need to catch him before he hurts someone else.'

Gina spotted PC Kapoor speaking to one of the neighbours. She must have just arrived. Gina waved, calling her over. 'We'll need a formal statement off you.'

He exhaled. 'Of course.'

Gina explained the situation to PC Kapoor and left the officer to take his statement. 'Jacob, can you call Greydon Electronics now and speak to someone in authority who can confirm Luther's alibi.'

'Yep.' He stood to the side and began looking for their number.

Gina glanced up and down the road, seeing if she could spot the boy on the scooter. She spotted a group of teens milling around in the curve of the cul-de-sac. They were about to walk away from the scene, down a path between two houses. 'Stop,' she called as she ran as fast as she could. 'Police.'

The girl at the back turned and stared as she applied a layer of lip gloss to her bottom lip. The two boys and the other girl stood behind her. 'What? We haven't done anything.'

'I never said you had. Sorry, I'm DI Harte. I just want to ask you a couple of questions.'

The girl glanced back at the others and after a few looks between them, they relaxed a little. 'What do you need to know?'

'Have you seen a boy on an electric scooter over the past couple of weeks?'

One of the boys piped up. 'We didn't buy any drugs off him. We don't take drugs.' Gina guessed that they looked about fourteen, maybe fifteen.

'Has he been trying to sell drugs to you?'

The girl nodded.

'Can you describe him?'

She bit her glossy lips and looked at the others. 'He isn't a boy. He's a man. He just dresses like us.'

'Can you tell how old he might be?'

She shook her head. 'Maybe twenties or thirties.'

'What does he look like?'

'He's always wearing a hood, but he had stubble the one time. He was also wearing thick black gloves.'

'He's approached you more than once?'

They all nodded.

'We need to call your parents or guardians. You're not in any trouble at all. I will need them to come with you down to the station to help us with an investigation.' She called Kapoor over again, explaining what needed to be done. She hoped the parents would be fine to escort their children to the station and happy for them to be interviewed. Her phone beeped again. It was O'Connor.

> *Gracie is at the station waiting for you. Briggs is keeping an eye on her. She's had a lovely day again and she's also been to a burger joint for dinner.*

He finished his message with a smiling emoji. Whether she liked it or not, she had to tell Gracie what was happening. It was going to hurt, leaving her granddaughter with Hetty. Not only was the woman in total denial over how abusive Terry was towards her, but she also knew that Gina had some involvement with his death and the woman blamed Gina. In the past, she'd tried to plead with her, from one abused woman to another, but Hetty was still in denial about her own abuse. It was going to break her heart to hand Gracie over to that awful woman on that street, but she knew there was no point pleading with Hannah. Her daughter had made up her mind.

Gina glanced at the scene, hoping by some miracle that she'd see a man on a scooter, but she knew he wouldn't hang around while there were police everywhere. It was worrisome that a man was hanging around trying to push drugs onto kids and pretending to be one of them. A man that was possibly capable of committing murder. Bernard would have mentioned if his team had found any drugs at Judith Morgan's house. Did she suspect he was dealing and threaten to report him? She was planning on calling the police. Had he also tried to sell to

Wesley Reid? Maybe Wesley had something on him or maybe he too had threatened to report him for hanging around. Frederick Bertram had something to do with this case. He had a large quantity of drugs and had been charged with supplying. Had he alerted the scooter menace to clear his annexe out? Gina was getting more confused by the minute, and she couldn't get Noel out of her mind. Was it him? Was the man leading a double life, selling drugs and stalking women who had turned him down? Nothing surprised Gina any more.

THIRTY-FOUR

SASHA

After making a mad dash to her car, Sasha had driven straight to her sister's house. She knocked at the door. On her way over, she'd come up with what she was going to tell her. *Her window had been damaged and it had been boarded up. She just wanted somewhere to stay for the night until she got a new one. No, it had nothing to do with the job she did or the murder at the Cleaver.* She rang the bell and waited.

She'd be protected from the youth here. In the country, in the middle of nowhere, it felt safe. There were a lot of places an electric scooter could take a person, but this wasn't one of them. She danced from foot to foot, trying to keep warm as she waited for her sister to answer. After banging on the door again, she called Tanya's name through the letter box.

'Coming.' That wasn't Tanya's voice. What was her dad doing here?

He opened the door. 'Alright, love. I was just helping Yasmin get her pyjamas on.'

She stepped in and threw her damp coat onto the stair post. 'Where's Tanya?'

'She had to pop out so she asked if I could watch Yasmin.

She shouldn't be long. Shall we put the kettle on and wait for her to get back? You look like you could do with a hot drink and a warm-up.'

Sasha nodded. She had really hoped that her sister would be in. The last thing she wanted was to worry her dad, but she didn't want to stay in her flat. Not tonight. She wanted to feel safe and to sleep well and deeply without the worry that someone might come to her flat again. Reaching into her jeans pocket, she felt the pound coin and that reminded her of how scared she'd been. Heart humming away, she followed him through and sat at the large farmhouse table. Her dad flicked the kettle switch.

'Grandad, I can't make my film work,' Yasmin called from the top of the stairs.

'I'll just be five minutes.' He smiled at Sasha. 'You can make the tea. Yours is better than mine anyway.' He left the room. She checked her phone and saw that she had a message.

Did you like my gift?

Gift? Was the messenger referring to the pound coin? With trembling hands, she dropped her phone next to the kettle and stared at the message. The messenger had a withheld number. Was it really the youth and how would he have her phone number? Why would he leave a pound coin on her doormat, send her a message or break her window? The window sounded plausible but not the coin. All she was doing was accumulating questions but coming up with no answers.

Another message came through almost immediately and all it contained was a link to a YouTube channel. She held her finger over it, wondering if she should select it. She'd heard of people getting viruses on their tech by doing that. Was someone trying to get her to install a virus that would lead them to hacking her bank account and all her personal data? She didn't bank on her phone. That was something to alleviate the worry, and it wasn't her work phone so nothing confidential could be extracted.

She clicked into the link and the page slowly loaded up. A video began to play and the words, 'Macie Perrin Reportz Crime and Ghosts,' came up on the screen. Title of the video – Murder at the Cleaver. It had to have something to do with Wesley Reid. Sasha turned the volume up a little as she listened to the girl talking about Wesley. The girl went on about the house, about the ghosts of the past, the crying animals as they'd historically been slaughtered in the annexe. She claimed there were spirits trapped in the walls and that Wesley had been an unfortunate victim of a sick house that just drew death in. A photo of Wesley flashed up.

As her dad walked in, Sasha almost crashed backwards into the boiling kettle. She stopped the video on Wesley's face and stared. Up until now, he had just been a name. She recognised him but she couldn't recollect where from. She knew Wesley and the person who had sent her the message, knew that she knew Wesley. Where from? That was a question she couldn't answer. Day in, day out, she saw so many people, too many people. Maybe the person who was behind all this was someone who was angry at her. In her position, she was always being abused and sworn at. Angry and scared people were a part of the job and she had spent many a time feeling threatened and worried.

'You look like you've just seen a ghost. Your old man can tell when something's not right.' He led her back to the table and popped her phone next to her. 'What's happened, love?'

She burst into tears and turned her phone off. 'Someone smashed my kitchen window, and the kids are horrible where I live. This boy damaged my car, and the police won't do anything. He goes around on this scooter and...' She saw the worry on her dad's face. The coin was too much to mention.

She liked living in a flat because there was an extra barrier for people to get through but with the broken trade button constantly letting people in, she no longer felt safe. She was a target. The police had come, and they hadn't been that interested. She was nothing more than a number, just another person being terrorised by teens in their area like millions of other people up and down the country. The police were as short-staffed as her department was. She understood that it was hard for them to investigate everything, but still, she couldn't help but clench her fists. All this had something to do with Wesley and her knowing him.

Her dad wrapped his bulky arms around her, drawing her into one of the bear hugs she'd always loved as a child. He patted the back of her head. 'You've had a bad night, love, but you've come to the right place. I have cake.'

She let out a slight laugh. Her dad always thought that cake fixed everything, just like her mum had. It was sweet but cake wasn't going to help in the slightest. Although, she was nervy, she felt sick with hunger. Her stomach growled. 'Thanks, Dad. I knew I could rely on you to make it all better.'

As her dad went back to the kitchen and threw a tea bag in a pot, she turned her phone on again and stared at Wesley Reid's face. Where did she know him from? His eyes, they looked so familiar but the rest of him, there was no recognition. His face was quite plump, and his lips were fairly thin. Then there was the message, the constantly reinforced message that she kept seeing and hearing everywhere. What did she have to pay for? It wasn't her who had hurt Wesley or killed him. A flurry of notifications flashed up and she clicked on the one that took her to the 'What's up Cleevesford' Facebook group where a woman had posted a photo of a murder victim who had been named as Judith Morgan, underneath an RIP message. Sasha stared at the photo of the woman; brows furrowed. Again, there was a hint of recognition, but she couldn't remember where from. Another message popped up.

You didn't lock your car. Anyone could break in and steal this picture of your precious niece. She is a treasure.

Her heart felt as though it had stopped beating. The locket she kept dangling over her rear-view mirror contained a photo of Yasmin. He had to have been in her car. She ran to the stairs and grabbed her car keys from her coat pocket. Through the living room window, she stared at her wing mirrors which automatically tucked in when she locked it. They were both sticking out. She hadn't locked her car. She wasn't safe here. Not knowing who she was dealing with, she didn't know if staying here would put her dad, sister or niece in danger. She needed to get as far away from them as possible and call the police again. No, she was going to drive directly to the police station and show them the message. Her life was in danger. They had to help her this time.

'Got to go, Dad. The window repairman has just called. He's on his way.'

'Shall I put your cake in a box?'

'No, I'm fine. I'll call Tanya later. Love you.' She garbled out a few more mixed-up words, telling him not to tell Tanya. With that, she snatched her wet coat from the stairs and ran straight to her car. How did the messenger know she was here? She looked at her phone. Had it been hacked? Were they using her location? No, the messenger had known that her car was unlocked. They were here. Gazing up and down the dark road, she swallowed. He had to be watching her right now. She switched her phone off and threw it on the passenger seat. That's when she saw another pound coin.

Shaking, she locked herself in the car and checked the back seat before looking through her rear-view mirror. There was no one around. As she backed out, she glanced up and down the country road but there were no lights on the road at all. The trees that lined the opposite side of the road were a front for the dense woodland that went back for acres. Her heart almost stopped when the full beam lights came on from a passing place just up the road, almost blinding her.

She pressed her foot hard on the accelerator and wound the car up to its limits, leaving the stationary car behind. Her mind was awhirl with the coins, the youth, the messages and Wesley Reid's face. It was all to do with him, but how? She didn't kill him. She had nothing to do with his murder. Maybe someone was after revenge, thinking that it was her fault as she had placed him at the Cleaver. Had he asked her for help in the past and had she turned him down because she couldn't help him?

Was the killer chasing her or was it someone who blamed her for his death? The vandalism on her car had started before Wesley's murder. The youth was one problem, the murder was another. She shook her head and swerved the car back onto the right side of the road. The two were connected. Those words, 'I'm going to make you pay.' She'd seen them at the old nursery. The youth had arranged the Christmas letters to say that, and he'd said those words to her.

A car horn woke her from her hypnotic state and the lights were startling as they bounced off her rear-view mirror. She swerved so sharply, the car hit the grass verge and she screamed as it rolled sharply into the ditch. He had her right where he wanted her and now, he was going to kill her, just like he had Wesley.

THIRTY-FIVE

'Nanny, I want to stay with you,' Gracie whined from her seat in the back of Gina's car. Her granddaughter clutched the stuffed lamb that Mrs O had bought her from the nature reserve. As she drove past the old nursery, she shivered. Police tape fluttered in the breeze. An officer was meant to be driving by every hour to check on the building.

'I'm so sorry, chicken. Mummy thought it was best that you stayed with Nanny Hetty as I have so much work to do.'

'Not fair. I wanted to finish making our den.'

Gina looked at her through the rear-view mirror. Gracie folded her arms and brought her bottom lip over the top one in a sulk. 'I know it's not fair. It's my fault and I am sorry.'

'But I want to go out with Mrs O again. I said I wanted to show her how to make a den like the one we made. She said she would love to play dens with me.'

'And you will be able to play dens again soon, just not this week.' Gina pulled a face in the mirror and saw Gracie looking. The little girl's grumpy expression turned into a laugh as Gina gurned. She pulled over on the road. 'Right, we're here.'

Gina stepped out of the car and opened the rear door,

unclipping Gracie and grabbing her bag. They walked up the short path and Gracie rang the doorbell. The hunched over woman she dreaded being near the most opened the door. Her grey shoulder-length hair blew back as the breeze hit it. 'Gracie my love. It's wonderful to see you. I have lots of fun things planned, and it starts with ordering a pizza and eating cake. Go through.'

Gina crouched and hugged Gracie. 'Love you, chicken. Have a great time with Nanny Hetty and I'll see you again soon.' As she swallowed, a lump in her throat formed. Gina had to believe the sacrifice was worth it, that she'd catch the killer who had struck twice. Her underfunded and understaffed department needed her.

The little girl gripped her tightly. 'Love you, Nanny. We'll finish the den next time.'

'Come on then, Gracie.' Hetty tried to prise Gracie away, but Gracie held on to Gina. Slowly her grip weakened, and Gracie stepped into Hetty's warm hallway.

'Why don't you go and sit by the log burner in the living room. There's a surprise in there. I've got a puppy and his name is Benji.'

'A puppy, yay.' With that news, Gracie was gone.

Hetty shook her head and tutted.

'Just say what you mean to say, Hetty.'

The woman smiled. 'Thank you.'

Gina furrowed her brows. The woman had never thanked Gina for anything in her life.

'Thank you for going into work instead of looking after her when you were meant to, because I actually want her here.' With that Hetty slammed the door. Gina felt her fingernails digging into her palms and her neck aching with tension. She wanted to kick that woman's front door, but she'd never stoop that low or upset Gracie. Instead, she turned around, got into her car and slammed her fists onto her steering wheel until they hurt. She turned back to the bungalow and all she could see glowing in the lamplight of Hetty's living room window was Hetty's victorious grin.

She sent Hannah a message.

I've just left Gracie with Hetty. I'm sorry. X

She doubted that Hannah would reply but she had to say something. O'Connor was calling. She answered. 'Hello.'

'Guv, the officer watching Noel Logan's house has just called. A woman has turned up for him.'

'Who is she?'

'Someone he's seeing.'

'Is it Lydia Gill?' She wondered if Wesley's pregnant ex was struggling as much as they were to contact her baby's father.

'No, it's another woman.'

THIRTY-SIX

Gina paused in her car. Leaving Gracie with Hetty was knocking her sick. Yes, the woman would look after her, but she'd fill the little girl's head with how wonderful her dead granddad, Terry, was. A flashback of Gina trying to hold him back from shaking their crying baby jolted her back into reality. There was no doubt in her mind she'd done the right thing in letting him die.

Hetty would always be Gracie's great-grandma. Not even death would rid Gina of Terry. She'd be tied to this mixed-up family forever if she wanted to be a part of Gracie and Hannah's life. She swallowed. That's if Hannah would want her to be a part of their lives after this. The police car drove past, and an officer pulled over. He got out, shone a torch on the old nursery and got back into his car before driving off.

She checked her phone to see if there were any updates and she called Briggs. The rest of the team were tied up. 'Hi. How's it going back at the station?'

'It's been busy. O'Connor and uniform have been conducting everything here. The kids from the Judith Morgan murder scene have all turned up at the station with their parents and are in the process of giving statements. Bernard and his team are still at the victim's house. Wyre has gone with Macie Perrin to her house and the girl has already uploaded a quickly produced video, just to make everything seem normal, and Frederick Bertram has also been arrested on drugs charges, but he wouldn't speak of the intruder at his home. O'Connor couldn't get anything out of him. On his solicitor's advice, he didn't say much but the evidence spoke for itself.'

She thought back to the statements taken after the murder at the Cleaver. 'Two people were spotted watching the Cleaver in the run up to Wesley Reid's murder. One that fits the description of Noel Logan and another. Maybe this hooded man who was trying to pass himself off as a teen was the other. He has some connection to Frederick Bertram. We need to find out what that is. I'm thinking he's another dealer as he was trying to sell drugs to the kids. Or, given what we now know, Logan could be the hooded drug dealer.'

'How are you? It must have been painful dropping Gracie off at that woman's house?'

'I've just left and yes it was. She's grinning at me like a Cheshire cat out of her window right now.' Phone on hands-free, Gina drove off, needing to get to Noel Logan's house to speak to this woman.

'Ouch, I don't envy you.'

'Was Gracie on her best behaviour when Mrs O dropped her off?'

'Yes, we've all loved her being around. She's a wonderful little girl and she definitely brightened the department up.'

Gina felt her eyes welling with tears. 'I know she is, and I've let her down again.'

'You haven't. You can't think like that. We've all pulled together, and she's created fabulous memories over the past couple of days. She's made cakes, been to an animal farm, talked about the fabulous den you made with her, and she's arrested half of the staff in the building. I've never seen a child laugh so much. We all told her that her nanny is a hero too and she said she was going to tell her friends when she went back to school.'

'I know and I love our police family. Hannah won't see it like that. She thinks I abandoned her.'

'Working parents feel like that all the time. From all that I've heard, guilt comes with the territory. You've mentioned that Hannah leaves Gracie with friends and she's left her at kids' clubs when she's had to work. It's no different.'

'Hannah doesn't really know you all and Mrs O like I do. She knows her friends. I can see it from her side. Anyway, there's nothing I can do about that now and I need to get in the right mindset for questioning this woman about Logan. Maybe we'll finally get to the bottom of where he is.'

'Gina?'

'What?'

'I know my apologies won't ever be enough, but I love you. I just wanted to say that.'

Now was not the time for this conversation, but it had to be had. She waited at a red light and listened to the engine humming for a few seconds. 'You lied to me. Then I accepted that you'd found someone new. I understood that you wanted something I couldn't give you but when I told you I saw Rosemary with another man, you made out that I was some jealous, lying witch. That hurt more than everything else. You spoke to me in a way I can't get over.' She paused. 'I also know that you'd go to the ends of the earth to protect me, and I can trust you with my life. You know a side to me that no one else will ever or has ever known but I'm worth more than the way you treated me. After Terry...' A couple of tears sprang from her eyes. She cleared her throat.

'Gina, I really am so sorry. All I can think about is you and us. I miss being close to you. I miss our chats, our takeaways, our shop talk, lying next to you in bed, stroking your hair. I just want you back and I'll do anything.'

'I'm just about to pull up at Noel Logan's house.' She pulled the handbrake on. 'I'll see you back at the station later tonight.'

'Gina...'

She ended the call and wiped her damp eyes. The uniformed officer walked over. She stepped out. 'I got the call that someone had turned up for Noel Logan. Where is she?'

'In her car. Just there.'

Gina glanced at the woman sitting in the driver's seat of a blue Jaguar. The woman glanced back, her blonde hair flowing over her shoulders. 'What's her name?'

'Tanya Kennedy-Williams.'

There was something hugely familiar about the woman's face. The shape, her feline eyes and her buxom chest. Kennedy, she had come across that name. The woman in the car looked a lot like Sasha Kennedy, the homeless support officer she'd met at the Cleaver and the old nursery. How had she too ended up being a part of the murder case?

THIRTY-SEVEN

MACIE

Her dad's key turned in the lock. 'Macie, what the hell is going on? A policeman just stopped me at my own door to ask me who I was.'

She ran across the landing, leaving DS Wyre sitting on her bed, monitoring her comments with some guy from the police tech department called Garth. Garth with a strange ponytail, wearing a battered old leather jacket. For a young guy, he dressed oddly. She hoped her dad wouldn't moan about the smell of cigarettes that came from him. 'Sorry, Dad. I tried to call you.'

'I've been in meetings all day. Why didn't you leave me a message?'

'I thought I should actually talk to you.'

'That's a first. Why is there a police officer outside our door? What's going on?' He walked up the stairs and his gaze fixed on DS Wyre. She smiled. 'What's all this?' He pointed at her bedroom and sniffed a couple of times. 'Have you been smoking?'

'Sorry, that's me,' Garth said.

Macie hung back behind her dad as he took the scene in. A

table had been set up next to her workstation and Garth had plugged in a load of his equipment to hers. She had no idea how it all worked but he was staring at his laptop too. There were cables everywhere. 'You know the murder at the Cleaver?'

'I heard it mentioned on the radio.' He paused and his mouth parted slightly. 'Macie, what have you got mixed up in?'

DS Wyre stood up. 'Macie is helping us to investigate. Unfortunately, we suspect that the killer has chosen her to communicate through, so we need to monitor everything. The police officer at the door is for both of your protection. Macie let us into her room and allowed us to set up here.'

'Shit.' He ran his hands through his salt-and-pepper brown hair.

'When we arrived with Macie, a pound coin had been left on your doormat,' DS Wyre said.

'A pound coin? What has that got to do with anything? I probably dropped it when I left for work this morning.' He furrowed his brows.

Macie took a seat at her workstation and swivelled in her chair until she faced DS Wyre. She was finally a part of a full-on police investigation and it felt good. She had information that other people didn't have and that excited her. At the end of all this, she'd have the most amazing story to share, and she was going to sell it for all it was worth. She could tell her dad didn't feel as enthusiastic about this upturn in her career. She wondered if she'd have to wait until after the court cases. Murder trials took ages. Anyway, the longer she sat on the story, the more it could be worth. She could write the book while she was waiting.

'This information hasn't been released to the public and it can't be, or the case will be jeopardised. As your daughter is involved and it is your house, I'm going to fill you in on how the pound coin is relevant.' The detective sat a bit further on the bed. 'A pound coin was found at the murder scene at the Cleaver and at another murder scene today.'

'Are you saying the murderer knows where we live?' Macie watched as her father nervously scratched his fine stubble.

'It's too much of a coincidence so we're saying yes.'

'How would this person know where we live? Macie, you haven't put our address online, have you?'

His accusation bored through her, and the intensity of his stare made her feel like squirming on her chair. She was really in trouble now. 'I did a video review of my ring light when I bought it. I know it's not crime or ghosts, but people click on that stuff, and I get paid when people watch. Garth went through my videos, and he showed me how the killer could have got our address. I left the label on the box when I was filming.' She hunched over slightly, knowing it was her fault and there was no way she could dress up the fact that she'd posted a video revealing their address.

'So, all these murder-obsessed crazies know where we live? No!' He began to pace, and he clenched his fists.

For the first time that day, Macie felt a pang of regret. She had put them in danger from all types of weirdos. She'd been so stupid. What an amateur. Only idiots leave their address on show for all to see when making videos.

'Mr Perrin, I know this situation is difficult, but it would help if we all stayed calm,' the detective said as she stood.

'Calm. Some psycho murderer knows where we live, and you want me to stay calm. What shall I do, take a bubble bath, watch a bit of telly while sipping a hot chocolate and pretend that our lives aren't in danger? This maniac not only knows where we live, he's been to our house and left my daughter confirmation that he's the murderer and you want me to stay calm. Macie, how could you be so stupid?'

'I'm sorry, Dad.' She rubbed her watery eyes. She'd been so caught up with her rapidly growing online popularity and earning money, she'd let her personal security take a back seat. 'It'll never happen again.'

'Too right it won't. This idiocy has to stop. You need to spend more time concentrating on school and becoming a proper journalist, not turn out stuff that will be the death of us both.'

'It was one mistake.'

'One mistake,' he repeated, shaking his head. 'When your mother was dying, I made her a promise that I would do my absolute best for you and look where we are now. Police at the door. Everything being monitored because a double murderer is communicating through my only daughter. This stuff happens in films not to normal families on normal estates.' He raked his fingers through his thin hair and blew out a breath.

'Mr Perrin.' Macie was glad of the detective's interruption. 'I know all this is a shock but what we need to do is catch this person. Once we've caught whoever is behind all this, you'll both be safe again and we are not going to leave you alone until you are. Macie is helping us, and we fully appreciate her help and your cooperation. Would you like a drink and maybe we can talk some more?'

He huffed and roared in frustration. 'Would I like a drink in my own home?' He shrugged. 'I suppose I have no choice.' He stormed out of the bedroom and the detective followed him. Macie was super grateful that the detective hadn't mentioned her snooping at the old nursery, but things had moved on since then. She'd been reclassified as a witness instead of a criminal. The kitchen door slammed. She guessed her father wanted to talk to the detective about them being here.

Garth flicked between screens and pinched the bridge of his nose. He pulled his glasses off and blinked hard a couple of times before putting them back on. 'It's been a long day.'

'Anything?' Macie asked.

'Nothing helpful. I know back at the station they're going

through all your previous communications. There are literally tens of thousands.'

'Yes, I don't even get to read them all myself. My channel has taken off big time.'

The man began to shift between screens, then he checked her phone and his phone. He scrolled through her tablet and then checked her YouTube comments. She peered over his shoulder. She recognised some of the commenters. They were her regular supporters, and this story was certainly whetting their appetites. Her subscribers had gone up by another two and a half thousand since last checking and notifications were pinging up everywhere. Everyone was looking to her for updates. She loved her dad and he had done his best for her but even with the danger, there was no way she'd give up what she had. Was she nervous? Terribly. Was she excited? Definitely. Adrenaline pumped through her body as comment upon comment filled her feeds and Garth shook his head.

He swiped to her TikTok account again and began checking all the new comments and messages that had flooded her inbox. 'Can I use your loo?'

Macie nodded. 'Door at the top of the stairs.'

'Don't touch a thing while I'm gone.'

'Okay.' She sat on the bed, watching the lightning pace at which the comments and shares were flashing up in her notifications. Then a comment popped up on TikTok from someone claiming to be the Grim Reaper.

A pound is not just a pound and a herb is not just a herb. I know the police are there and here's me thinking we had an understanding. Macie, you have let me down.

'Garth,' she shouted. The man ran back in. 'It's him. He knows you're here.'

THIRTY-EIGHT

Gina tapped on Tanya's car window. The woman buzzed it down. 'I'm DI Harte. May I speak with you?'

She nodded. 'I've left my dad looking after my daughter and I promised him that I wouldn't be long.'

'I'll try to be quick.' She smiled, hoping to reassure the woman.

'Can we sit in my car? It's warm in here.'

Gina walked over to the passenger side and sat in the passenger seat. She pulled a notebook and pen from her bag. 'We are looking for Mr Logan in connection to a case we're investigating, and I was hoping that you could help us. Can I just confirm your full name?'

'Tanya Kennedy-Williams.'

'Are you related to Sasha Kennedy? Only you look so alike.'

'She's my sister.'

'That explains the similarity between you both.'

'How do you know Sasha?'

'We've spoken to her with regards to a case.'

Tanya tilted her head. 'Yes, the murder at the Cleaver. She didn't say much about it to me. My dad just called. He said some scumbag had thrown a stone through her kitchen window. Anyway, how can I help?'

'How well do you know Noel Logan?'

'We've been seeing each other for a few months, only casually up until recently.'

Gina wondered if Tanya knew anything about Noel also being in a relationship with their first victim's ex-girlfriend, Lydia Gill, or that he'd been harassing Judith. 'Do you know where he is?'

She shrugged. 'He works away a lot, something to do with sales. I think he has to head the trade shows, so he travels regularly. He told me that he was travelling to Paris last Friday for a few days and he was meant to be back today. I haven't heard from him so thought I'd pop by, see if everything was okay.'

'Have you spoken to him since then?'

'No, not since late Friday night when he called me. I didn't recognise his number at first. He said he had his phone stolen while walking under the Arc de Triomphe, so he'd bought an emergency phone and SIM there.' Gina knew that Noel Logan had been seen on Saturday at the Angel Arms. He'd obviously been lying to Tanya and had not picked up any calls from Lydia.

She had to tell the woman what she knew. Maybe it would open the conversation a little more. 'Noel Logan was in the Angel Arms and at the Cleevesford Cleaver on Saturday night.'

She stared at Gina for a few seconds, brows furrowed as she processed what Gina had said. Tanya went to talk and then closed her mouth. 'You mean he's been lying to me?'

'Yes. How long have you been seeing each other?'

'Around six months. We meet up mostly at weekends or when my daughter stays with one of my friends or my dad. I haven't introduced him to my family yet. As I said, we haven't been that serious until recently.' She paused. 'My husband died a couple of years ago. I'm ultra-careful about introducing my daughter to anyone and I needed to be sure. I thought I was sure about Noel. We'd just started talking about him meeting my daughter and us moving in together...' She sniffed and turned away. 'But not now I know he lied to me.'

Gina needed to start digging a little deeper. 'Did Noel ever mention the name Wesley Reid?'

'Yes, they were good friends up until the end of September. He told me they'd fallen out because of Wes's drink problem. Only a week before that, we'd been out for a meal with him and Lydia. Lydia is Wes's partner, well his ex-partner. They split up and I can see why. The poor woman had had enough. Noel got really angry about the way Wes was speaking to her. Wes was beating on about how she wasn't supporting him enough. He moaned about what she was wearing and even told her she was fat. He was so nasty, and I know it was the drink talking. I remember wishing that Noel hadn't organised the meal. I've never felt so uncomfortable and out of place.'

'Have you watched any news over the past couple of days?'

'No, have I missed something?'

Tanya really didn't have a clue. 'Wesley Reid was murdered on Saturday night at the Cleevesford Cleaver.'

'Shit, I had no idea. My sister came to dinner on Sunday, and she'd come from the Cleaver. She never mentioned Wes by name, but she wouldn't have known that I knew him. I told her that I'd been seeing someone, but there's no way she could have known it was Noel's friend.'

'Did Noel speak about his relationship with Wesley?'

She puffed out a breath. 'They'd had a falling out after the meal and Noel said that he wasn't speaking to him. When I asked him what had happened he said he didn't want to talk about it. That's when I started to doubt him.'

'Doubt him?'

'He wouldn't tell me why they fell out. It's ridiculous. We'd been speaking about taking our relationship to the next level, but he couldn't even tell me why he'd fallen out with his friend. I said that I should call Lydia, see if she was okay but he said not to and he wouldn't give me her number. He said he wanted nothing more to do with them. To be honest, things have been a bit weird since, but I had my hopes on this relationship working, so I continued to make an effort.'

'In what way had things been weird?'

'He's been distant. I thought it was because commitment scared him, so I came here tonight to give him an ultimatum. Either he stops treating me like an idiot and tells me what's changed or we're over. I can do without the drama. It's a shame as we got on so well before. Now I know he's lied about being in Paris, I can't even be bothered to be here now. Has the falling out got something to do with Wes's murder?'

'We don't have any information as yet, but we do need to speak to Noel Logan. If you see him or if he contacts you, please call me straight away.'

'Should I be scared? I have a young daughter and I live alone with her?'

'I will speak to uniform and organise for an officer to regularly drive by your house. If you see him in the meantime, please call me straight away and an officer will be dispatched immediately. We will need you to head to the station and make a formal statement. Would you be able to do that now?'

Tanya nodded and sighed. 'Yes, I'll give my dad a call. Let him know what's going on. There is something else that's been playing on my thoughts.' She furrowed her brows. 'On the night we went out for that meal, Wes kept looking at me in a weird way and he started drinking more heavily, which annoyed Lydia. I don't know what was going on between them or why he was being weird with me, but it's like the air became thick. It was like he recognised me from somewhere, but I know I've never met him before. At times, I felt the weight of his stare on me as he knocked back the shots. When he and Lydia went up to the bar, I told Noel I wanted to leave, and Noel was happy to oblige. Lydia also did this thing where she kept looking away from us, like she couldn't wait for the evening to end. I thought it was because of Wes's behaviour but I think there was more going on.'

Gina knew that Lydia and Noel were having a relationship. She'd have been pregnant, and Noel would have known. Did Wesley suspect something? Why would he be making Tanya feel so uncomfortable when he didn't know her? So many questions still needed to be answered and the only person who could answer them was Noel. 'Has Noel ever mentioned places he likes to go or family he might stay with?'

'He likes camping, he goes Bear Grylls style, back to nature stuff. He would have told me if he'd gone camping.' She bit her bottom lip. 'Well, I thought he would have told me. I'm not so sure now.'

Gina wondered if their prime suspect knew they were after him and if he was holed up somewhere in a tent in the Warwickshire countryside. She made a note, maybe she needed to convince Briggs to put out a missing person for him, claim that people are worried as they've been unable to contact him. He had been missing since late Saturday night. It might just encourage a rambler that may have seen him to come forward. 'Did he have any favourite camping spots?'

'The Lake District.'

'Can I take the number that he called you on?'

'He's not answering.'

'It would still help.'

'Do you think he might be hurt? I know he's lied to me but if he's at the bottom of a hill, injured and freezing cold, I still hope he'd get help.' The expression changed on the woman's face. A moment ago, she looked scared but now, she looked concerned.

'We hope not but we might contact the media and get them

to report him as a missing person on the radio and local news. Another thing, did he ever mention the name Judith Morgan?'

'No, I don't recognise that name at all.' Tanya's phone rang. 'It's him.' She swiped to accept the call and placed it on loudspeaker. 'Noel, where are you?'

'Hello, this isn't Noel. I just found this phone while walking my dog and you were the last person called. I'm just trying to return it.' The reception hissed and the man's wavering voice could barely be heard.

Gina cleared her throat. 'Hello, I'm DI Harte from Cleevesford Police. We're looking for the owner of this phone, Noel Logan. Where are you?'

'By the car park at the back end of the countryside centre's lake in Cleevesford. I'm walking across the Rectory Avenue car park.' The man paused. 'I can also see a backpack floating in the water. Do you need me to wait here?'

'That would be really helpful. I'll get an officer over immediately. Is there a blue Volvo parked up?'

'No.'

Gina would have to ask the team to check the other car parks or parking places on arrival. Noel may have parked up on one of the surrounding fields or behind a hedge along one of the country roads. She took the man's details and ended the call.

Stepping out of Tanya's car, Gina reported back straight away. Her heart began to bang, and she hoped that their prime suspect wasn't their third victim. Rectory Avenue was also close enough for Noel Logan to have stayed local throughout.

She spotted a message from Wyre that had come through on her phone while she'd been driving before speaking to Tanya. The killer had contacted Macie again. She had to go now.

'Is he dead?' Tanya began to weep as she alighted her car. 'You have to let me know what you find. I need to know if he's okay.'

'Of course. I'll leave you with the police officer and he'll let the station know that you're on your way to make a statement.'

Logan's car hadn't been flagged up on the roads, maybe he was travelling around on an electric scooter, weaving illegally and quietly through the streets, avoiding all the ANPR points. Maybe he'd dumped his phone to get them off his back. It was time to find out.

THIRTY-NINE

SASHA

Sasha pressed various points on her head with her jittery fingers and shook herself awake. What happened? There had been lights in her rear-view mirror, and she'd been dazzled. She'd panicked and driven off the road. 'Help,' she called in a gruff voice as she tried to open her car door. It was jammed and the road was silent. She wiped the warm trail that was slipping down the side of her face and she flinched. There was a cut on her head.

It was all coming back. The message – he'd been watching her and when she came out of her sister's house she'd been followed.

She tried to roll her wrist, but a flash of pain stopped her. She tried again and she managed a bit more movement. Loosening up, she tried to reach for her phone in her pocket. It wasn't there. It had been there.

Where was her phone? Her attacker must have come into the car when she was unconscious. He'd taken her phone. She turned her stiff neck, shaking as she half-expected him to be there staring at her but all she could see was the moonlit grass behind her and a stone wall in front of her. A wave of lightheadedness struck, and she took a deep breath to quell the nausea. Had there not been a ditch she'd have driven head on into that wall. She tried to rotate her ankle and then the other one. Both were stiff but they were working. She hadn't broken anything.

A flash of light passed as a car sped by. She knew the driver wouldn't see her from the road. Maybe her phone slipped out of her pocket when she crashed. She fumbled around, flinching with every movement. Trying to reach down was impossible. The ache in her shoulder told her to stop trying otherwise she might snap something. She gazed around again at the surrounding darkness and shivered. Teeth chattering, she felt for the ignition. If she could turn the engine on, she could turn the lights on and blast the horn. She'd have heating and she could keep warm. She felt for the key, but it wasn't there. He'd forced her into a ditch and taken her key, leaving her to die on the quietest country road she'd ever known.

How long would it take for hypothermia to set in? Panic filled her lungs and she let it out with a scream. She grabbed the door handle again, but it wouldn't open. She felt along the inside of the door. It had crunched inward.

'Help,' she yelled as tears filled her eyes. 'Help.' She needed her phone.

Pressing the seat belt release button, she screamed again as she threw the top half of her body onto the passenger seat, knocking the locket with her head. Every movement sent a deep thud of pain through her body. Teeth chattering, she reached for the door handle on the passenger side, and it opened.

She almost cried as she heard her phone beep, but she couldn't see it. The noise came from above the brow of the ditch. Her only option was to drag her body out of the car and up that verge. Like a snake, she wriggled until her middle was past the gearstick. Her shoulder was loosening up. Getting to her knees, she trembled as she crawled over the passenger seat until she fell out of the car, rolling into the icy wet mud that had pooled at the base of the ditch. She clawed at the mud, grabbed a root and managed to pull herself up the hill and onto the roadside. That's when she spotted her phone on the kerb. She reached down to grab it, but the world began to spin as she tripped into the road. Just as she landed with a thud a car skidded to a halt right in front of her. She rolled into a ball and braced herself for impact.

The man stepped out and she sobbed. She was safe. All was going to be okay. Through fuzzy vision, she could make out his dark clothes. 'My phone,' she muttered. 'Call the police.'

He bent down, picked it up and placed it in his pocket, then a sharp blow left a searing pain in her head. Her attacker had finally come to make her pay and the next thing she felt was the final blow that left her sinking into unconsciousness. She fought and fought to stay alert, but it was a battle she was losing as her vision speckled.

She thought of her niece and her lovely sister. She cried for her dad because she knew she'd never see her lovely family again. Like an ignited spark, it finally came to her. She knew exactly where she'd met Wesley Reid and Judith Morgan. The image of them in her mind was so blurry but she was now so sure. What scared her most was that she was now the only one left. All the clues had been there. *He was making her pay.* Sinking further, that last spark of a thought left her and made way for the nothingness that was death.

FORTY

The emergency lights that flashed in the darkness were Gina's guide when it came to finding exactly where the scene was. Two police divers stepped out of a van, carrying equipment towards the lakeside. She pulled up and got out of her car, heading to the officer keeping a log at the outer cordon. Jacob had beaten her to it. He waved and she hurried over to him. 'Have they got the rucksack? Is it his?'

Jacob nodded. 'A couple of divers are just heading out with an officer on a boat. It seems to be caught on something, but we can't tell what. It's a bit deep to wade out.' A floodlight lit up the edge of the lake. 'Ah, we have light. They said they won't be going in until daylight, but they are checking the area out. Obviously if Noel Logan needs rescuing, they're there to help. It's not looking likely though.'

Several more portable lights flashed on and lit up the ripples on the lake's surface. The sound of the breeze and the humming of the generators filled the night air.

'While we wait for them to get the rucksack, we should speak to the man who spotted the phone. Have you checked the phone?' Gina asked.

'Yes. There is absolutely nothing on it except two calls. One on Friday night and the last one was made by the man who found it, to the same number. It's a burner phone so isn't registered to him or anyone.'

'Noel Logan bought this phone, hid out and remained undetected for days and now, who knows where he is.' She glanced at the lake as the dinghy took off. 'Right, let's see if our witness saw anything else.'

Jacob followed her towards the stone bench that was set back by the trees. A man sat there patting his Great Dane. The huge dog nestled its chin in the man's lap as he fed it a treat.

'Hello, I'm DI Harte.'

'I'm glad you've arrived. It's getting ever so cold.'

Gina could see that the man must be in his seventies. 'Do we have a blanket?'

Jacob nodded and hurried back towards the car park.

'I only found a phone; I didn't see anyone drop it. Are they looking for a body?' He pointed at the divers in the dinghy and the officer who was trying to retrieve the bag.

'Can I ask what your name is?'

'Malcolm Bird. Call me Malcolm.' Jacob sprinted back, a checked blanket over his arm. He placed it over the man's shoulders. 'Thank you.'

'Do you live close by?'

He nodded. 'Yes, just behind these trees there is a long path, and it leads to two cottages. I live in one of those. That's why I bring my dog here for his walks. It's normally peaceful at night, especially at this end of the lake. It's not like the other end where there's a park and the kids sometimes hang about, or the other side where the boat shed is.'

'Have you seen anything unusual out here recently?'

As he exhaled, white mist coiled into the crisp air. 'Not really.' He grimaced and used the side of his finger to dab his nose.

'The past couple of nights, I've felt as though someone else has been out here.'

'In what way?'

Jacob scribbled a few notes as Gina spoke to the witness.

'The snapping of a twig or a rustle of the leaves. It's the small sounds that give away a person's presence. I've lived here over forty years. I know how the lake and the trees that surround it sound. I can tell if a footstep is that of a fox or a badger. If you get close, a fox will scarper. A bird hops. The sounds I heard didn't belong to the creatures I expect to hear at this time of the night. They were heavier, more calculated. My dog was alert as well. I called out and flashed my torch last night and I was sure I saw the sleeve of a dark jacket escaping behind a tree. The last thing I wanted to do was hang around as it was gone midnight, so thinking it was a potential burglar, I hurried home and made sure the house was locked up. I wasn't worried as I have an alarm and so does my neighbour. Plus Prince here, of course!'

'Did you call the police?'

'What? About someone else walking around at night that didn't burgle me in the end? No, I just went home to bed and didn't worry too much. I wasn't scared, I just thought it was strange. It's not like they jumped out and ran at me.'

'Is there anything else you've noticed?'

'No, sorry. Do you think that whoever was out there threw himself into the lake? If he did, that's really sad. Maybe I should have called out to see if he was okay.'

'We certainly hope that hasn't happened and that could be anyone's bag. We're just being precautionary.' One of the divers grabbed the rucksack and passed it to the officer. 'I'm going to have a word with the officer over there and get someone to walk back home with you.'

The man smiled sympathetically. 'Thank you. That's really kind.'

She headed over, leaving Jacob with the man. A few seconds later, she was back with a uniformed officer so that Jacob could join her. The man and his dog were on their way back home. The officer would take the rest of his details should they need to speak to him again. The boat was being driven back to shore. She ran to the pebbled beach area and waited. 'What did you see under there?'

The diver stood and stepped off the boat. 'We couldn't see anyone out there but we'll come back tomorrow and take a look under the surface.'

'If you find anything at all in the morning, please call me straight away.'

The diver nodded. She turned her attention to the officer with the bag and she slipped on a pair of latex gloves before taking it from him. She placed it on the tarpaulin that had been laid out and Jacob took a photo of it. He started filming. Slowly, she unzipped it and removed a pair of track bottoms. 'There's something in the pocket.' She reached in and pulled out a card. Holding it to the light, she could see it was a golf club membership card. 'It's Noel Logan's card.' She removed a soaking wet black hoodie and socks. She placed those down and then she pulled out a tightly wrapped carrier bag containing a dirty white towel. 'That looks like the remnants of a bloodstain.' She laid it out and the reddish-brown smears were smudged over the material. Reaching in again, she pulled out an empty cider can and what looked like a burnt down sage stick. 'He's been dumping evidence. I want a dog team out and I want all the surrounding land searched.'

Gina glanced at the trees surrounding the lake. Had Logan been watching them? Was he still there or had he long gone? Right now, she had no idea if she was staring into the eyes of a double murderer who was lurking in the darkness, one she couldn't see. She shivered as she placed the cider can down on the plastic sheet. 'We need to get all that to the lab. If that blood belongs to Wesley Reid or Judith Morgan, we are closer to proving it's him.' She listened above the sounds of the scene for that heavy-footed snap of a branch, but she couldn't hear anything. Her phone rang. She grabbed it. 'Sir.'

'We need a briefing now. It's about the man on the scooter, Frederick Bertram has decided it is in his best interest to give us some details. You need to come back quick.'

FORTY-ONE

Gina rushed into the incident room. Bags of chips wrapped in paper were piled in the middle of the table as the team took their seats. Only Wyre was still missing. O'Connor tugged at a bag and opened it out, releasing the smell of vinegar and oil. Gina's stomach began to growl so she swiftly joined him in opening a bag of chips as she stood at the head of the table. A message pinged on her phone. It was Hetty again. She opened the attached photo showing Gracie smiling and cuddling a Labrador puppy.

She's not missing you one bit and Hannah thinks you're a useless waste of space too.

Briggs entered. 'Frederick Bertram is with his solicitor in interview room one. We'll be able to speak to him in about ten minutes. That gives us a few moments to catch up. Did you find anything at the lake?'

Gina swallowed a hot chip and it almost lodged in her throat. She closed the message. She pushed the hot food aside, not wanting any more. 'Yes, Noel Logan's rucksack. It contained a bagged up bloodied towel, an empty can of cider and a burnt down sage stick. The dog team had just arrived as I was leaving so we're keeping everything crossed that they manage to track him. That's unless he's in the lake. The dive team couldn't find him but they hadn't covered much of the area so that could still happen.'

Briggs pinched one of her chips. 'Noel Logan's girlfriend came in to make a statement. She didn't add anything to what we already now know.'

Gina watched as Jacob cracked open a can of cola and he reached over to take one of O'Connor's chips. 'Oi, get your own,' O'Connor said jokingly.

Jacob took another and grinned. 'What's been happening at Macie Perrin's house?'

Briggs pointed to the board under Macie Perrin's name. 'This is what the message said. "A pound is not just a pound and a herb is not just a herb. I know the police are there and here's me thinking we had an understanding. Macie, you have let me down."' Briggs exhaled and wiped his greasy fingers on a tissue. 'He's using the name, the Grim Reaper. That's original.'

Gina threw the chip she was about to eat back into the packet. She'd managed to gobble a fair few in the couple of minutes she'd been eating, and heartburn was beginning to creep in. 'We have a drug dealer going around on an electric scooter who wears a dark hood. We have Logan as a suspect and he could be the scooter rider. The kids claim that this same person is an adult which really puts him in the picture. They claimed that the man on the scooter looked to be in his twenties or thirties.' She stared at the message. '"A pound is not a pound." It's a riddle of sorts. What else is a pound?'

Jacob piped up. 'A measurement of weight. One hundred pennies.' PC Kapoor nodded as she sat next to PC Smith.

'Yes.' Gina pointed at him and smiled. 'We have the pound of flesh reference. That's from Shakespeare's *The Merchant of*

Venice, where Shylock wanted his pound of flesh. Did Judith and Wesley owe their murderer something? Did the killer feel entitled to take their lives in return for what they owed, or what they took? The messenger is telling us that the pound is symbolic. They want us to know why they're doing this, and that it means something to them. How about the sage?'

Jacob shrugged. '"A herb is not just a herb." The killer is telling us that this specific herb has been burnt for a reason. Do they believe they're banishing evil?'

'It's possible.' Gina nodded. 'They might think they're cleansing the souls of their victims or the buildings they live in. But I don't think that is what's happening. The herb is a clue but to what? Let's consider locations. We have the Cleaver which has a bit of a creepy past and is the source of a few urban legends, and we have the old nursery. Until recently, it has been used as a childcare centre. The common factor between them is that one is being used to house homeless people and the other was being fitted out to accommodate homeless people. Have we got any results back on that bloodied towel found at the back of the old nursery?'

O'Connor nodded. 'Yes, guv. Just before you got back the lab called to confirm that the blood on the towel found at the old nursery matched Wesley Reid's.'

'Great. Why would Logan leave a bloodied towel near the nursery and take another one with him? Any more information on Gareth Alderman, the man in the bottom room at the Cleaver?'

O'Connor flicked through his notes. 'I was just about to update the system with this but no. He has nothing in his past that involves violence. We've really dug deep and he's as clean as a whistle. He has a social worker and is apparently being looked after by the mental health team. They both confirm what we know. I flagged up our concerns, that he thought his dead child was still living with him and he was hearing things in the walls, and they said they're going to pay him a visit to see how he's doing.'

'Do we know of any connections at all between Judith Morgan and Wesley Reid, apart from Noel Logan?'

Jacob flicked through his notepad. 'A general search has been done for basic information on both of our victims, but we need to delve a lot deeper, go into past addresses and medical records. We know Wesley had a drink problem and his relationship had just broken down, but we don't know much about Judith. She worked part-time in a library and inherited a bit of money a few years ago which she spent on her house. She has no criminal record and no close family.'

'So, the only thing we have is Noel wasn't happy with either of them. He was angry that Judith turned him down and he was mad at Wesley as he thought Lydia might still go back to him.' Gina spoke to the room. 'Have we found a next of kin for Judith?'

O'Connor shook his head. 'She doesn't seem to have anyone. Parents are dead. No siblings, partner, ex-husband or children. It was just her and her cat.'

'Was she close to anyone at her workplace?'

'Not that we know of.'

Gina pressed her lips together and swallowed. No one except her friend and neighbour would miss the woman and that saddened Gina. 'Thank you for that update. Finally, any more results back from forensics or Wesley Reid's post-mortem?' She glanced at O'Connor again as he'd attended that one.

'I've updated the system with the dimensions of the knife and wound. Nothing else stood out. There were a lot of finger-prints, mostly partials, but they could belong to previous occu-pants. Either that or our killer has never had their prints taken before. Some could even belong to Noel Logan.'

She puffed out a breath and stood up straight as she glanced at the board again, not wanting to miss anything. 'Right, we need Noel, so keep on it. Don't flag. Oh, did digital forensics manage to get into Judith's phone?'

O'Connor nodded. 'Yes. As mentioned by Ms Allinson, there were several insulting texts. One claiming she'd be too ugly to find someone else. Several telling her that she'd missed a real good time when he'd turned her down. A photo of his genitals and a final message saying that no one else would touch her with a bargepole. These were sent over the last month with the latest one sent last Thursday. Judith ignored all of them.'

A uniformed officer peered around the door. 'Frederick Bertram is waiting to be interviewed.'

Gina glanced at him. 'Thank you. Right, while Jacob and I speak to him, please look over everything again. Check with Garth and Wyre, see if he's managed to get any info on the bloody Grim Reaper. Also, I want to go into Judith's house and see if there's anything else that might help us find her killer.' She turned to PC Kapoor, who had been there earlier that evening. 'Could you please call Bernard and see if we can go in yet?' Kapoor nodded and the rest of the team began talking around the table while eating chips as Gina and Jacob left the room.

As they reached interview room one, Gina glanced through the little window and saw Frederick Bertram and his solicitor staring at the wall opposite, not saying a word to each other. She opened the door and took a seat. Jacob sat beside her.

'My client wants to help you and he wants you to take into consideration that he's been cooperative with a murder investigation.'

Gina nodded and Jacob started the tape rolling. He introduced the room and Gina sat back. 'Who was in your annexe when we arrived to search it?' First and foremost, they needed to apprehend the intruder.

'I need to start at the beginning.' Freddie's nose twitched

and he scratched it. 'First of all, I'm an addict and I'm so sorry. I'm ashamed of what I've got myself into and I say all this because I want to change. If I wasn't an addict, I wouldn't have got embroiled in all this, you have to believe me.' He coughed and scratched his nose again.

Gina wanted to jump in and shout at him, reminding him that he was working with some of society's most vulnerable people, but she held her frame still and waited for him to continue. She had to remind herself that he too had his own problems, and she knew what drugs did to people. He was speaking and they needed him to continue.

'On the night of Wesley's murder, you are right. I did not go walking along the high street in Cleevesford. I met up with my dealer and bought some coke and dope.'

'Please describe your dealer.'

'He's about my height, so five eleven. He wears a hoodie and dark trackies and trainers. He also gets around on an electric scooter.'

'How old does he look?'

'I can't tell. He's always well covered, scarf around his mouth, things like that and it makes his speech quite muffled. His hood hangs low, almost covering his eyes. I don't ask him anything and he doesn't tell me anything.'

'Was he there when you left the Cleevesford Cleaver on the night of Saturday the twelfth?'

'I didn't see him. I was on foot so he could have easily been at the Cleaver and still made our rendezvous if he was on his scooter.'

'Did you tell him to go to your annexe and clear out the drugs?'

'No, but I didn't pay him on Saturday, and I promised I'd meet him the next day to give him the money and I didn't, so I think he'd come for what I owed him. You turning up when you did was nothing more than a coincidence.'

'Where did you meet him to buy drugs?'

'By the Hangar.'

'The Hangar?' Gina didn't expect him to say that.

'Yes. At the top of the steps. I didn't like meeting him around.' He swallowed. 'When Wesley moved into the Cleaver, I recognised him from the Hangar, but he didn't recognise me. Probably because I don't hang out there. I normally just meet the dealer at the top of the steps. Anyway, on Saturday night, the dealer took ages to get there so I waited. He rolled up on his scooter and I begged him for a wrap of coke.'

'How did you communicate with him?'

'I don't. I meet him at the same time every Saturday night. Always outside the Hangar but I never go inside. I saw him dealing one day so I approached him and asked him for some stuff but that was months ago. I've been meeting him there every week since.'

'You already had drugs in your annexe. Why did you meet him for more?' He wasn't telling her everything.

'They'd been cut, and I wanted something purer. That stuff you've found, there's barely any coke in it. Besides, I've already confessed to dealing. The drugs at the annexe were to sell. I only said I'd do it to pay my debts to the dealer. It was all getting too much.'

'So, he gave you the wrap of coke, what next?'

The man's head dipped. 'He gave it me on credit. I promised him he could have his cheap gear back as I couldn't sell it and he got mad. I told him I'd find another way of getting him his money. A legal way. I've never been so scared. I thought he was going to kill me, but he just jabbed me in the kidney. He said we had an arrangement and that I was now working for him and that if I didn't sell the gear, my head would be on a block.' Bertram paused. 'I don't think he's high up in any chain. He mostly sells his own stuff and I think he was trying to get me to do his dirty work. I haven't actually sold any of those drugs he passed to me so I'm not sure if I've really been dealing. I told him I would, and he dangled coke in front of my face. But I couldn't do it. I don't want to be a drug dealer. I don't know what to do. I just want to make it all stop. I stuffed up. I think he came looking for me to intimidate me. He knew where I lived. I've seen him hanging around the hostel.'

'When?'

'I don't know.' The man placed his head in his hands and began to claw at his head and he let out a cry. 'I need help.'

'Mr Bertram, can you give me any more information about this man?'

'Only that I heard someone calling him when I'd left the Hangar area. It was dark and, to be honest, I was trying to get away from him as fast as I could to get to Killian's flat, but something made me stop. I wanted to listen to what was being said.'

'What did you hear?'

'The man who called him said, "Alright, Jam-my-man." I have no idea what that meant.' Bertram began to shake and break down. 'I don't feel well.'

The solicitor cleared his throat. 'My client has said all he set out to say and more. As you can see, he's not well and he too is a victim in all this.'

Gina only had Frederick Bertram's word for it that he'd never dealt but the evidence would be looked at during his case, if it even went to court. She almost wanted to smile as realisation set in. 'Thank you.' She knew who Jam-my-man was, it had to be James Cain, also known as Jammy, from the Hangar. Now Jammy had a lot of explaining to do. They wound up the interview and Gina stepped outside. Jacob gathered up his file and hurried after her. Noel might not be the man on the scooter, but he might be the one pulling all the strings.

She smiled. 'We need to get to the Hangar. Gather up all the help we can get. We're going to need it.'

FORTY-TWO

MACIE

Macie sat at the back of her bedroom on a beanbag, feeling like a spare part. Since the message had come through, they'd kept her away from the screen. Garth tapped away on his keyboard while the detective drank the coffee that she'd brought upstairs with her. She listened for her dad, but she couldn't hear him. So far, she hadn't spoken to him alone. He'd come home from work to all this chaos, and it was her who had caused it. He had to know that there was a bigger picture in all this. His nightmare was her big break. She'd gained the trust of a real-life killer. How many people could say they'd managed that?

She stared at her phone, the one she wasn't allowed to touch any more. She wanted to check her socials and see if any of her friends had messaged her. It was getting late, surely they'd wind it all up soon and she'd get her phone back. 'Can I use my phone?'

Garth leaned back in Macie's chair and glanced over his shoulder. 'Sorry. It's all hooked up to the system and we need to monitor all incoming communications. Who called you this morning? There are five numbers but no names?'

'Oh, it was just the school and my English teacher. The

other is my friend who has a new phone. I should save their names, but I haven't got around to it. I got another ticking off for not turning up to class.'

When all this was over, she had to try again. Make an effort with school. Her dad was wrong. She didn't need all those qualifications to be successful, but it wouldn't hurt to get something under her belt to make her look more credible. Then her thoughts veered to how big this story was going to be. When all this was over, she'd be naming her price. She was really going to have it all. She visualised the true-crime show she'd have on Netflix. YouTube phenomenon, Macie Perrin, brings you real-life crime. That's the image she needed to keep in her mind. She didn't want to work for a local paper reporting on how the knitting circle was getting on. No, laser-sharp focus on the prize is what she needed, and that prize was fame in her field. While all her friends had been trying to get into pubs and hung around smoking weed, she'd worked hard on her channel. That sacrifice hadn't been made for nothing and when she got big, her dad would be proud. She twiddled her fingers.

'One of these numbers is no longer in use. Who did you say called you again?' Garth scrutinised what was on his screen.

'That's my friend, Becky. She found her phone. You can see she called me just after.'

'Hm, yes.' The man went back to staring at her life on his laptop.

'Can I go downstairs and sit with my dad?' She really wished things were better with Becky. When all this was over, she was going to let her hair down, go to the clubs with her. Her eighteenth had passed in a flash, and she'd been a naff friend.

The detective stretched and turned around, stifling a yawn. 'Of course, if we need you, I'll pop down and let you know.'

Macie forced a smile out. This wasn't as exciting as she hoped. In fact, it was boring her socks off. She checked her watch, the one she'd taken to wearing again since they took her phone. 'Thanks.' She left her room and crept down the stairs. Her dad was talking on the home phone. She placed her ear against the closed door. He said that she'd brought trouble to the door with her stupid channel. No doubt he was talking to her aunty. The pull almost dragged her into the room as he snatched open the door. 'Thought I heard you. Can you empty the dishwasher and take the full bin out?'

She nodded and he closed the door again. Glancing back, she could see the outline of the uniformed officer behind the glass of the front door. They really were worried about the messages, but she wasn't worried at all. Sometimes people had a story to tell, and this murderer wanted her to tell his. He wanted the world to know what he'd done and why. She too wanted the answers first, and she was going to get them.

Tying the bin bag handles, she unlocked the back door. She checked the time again and took a deep breath. There was a damp chill in the air. She inhaled, enjoying filling her lungs, and feeling refreshed after being stuck in her stifling house. Was he out the back, watching her every move? She listened for the noises of the night. A fox visited regularly, she knew because she'd fed it and seen it. She couldn't hear it sniffing around, not tonight. She glanced up at her room from the middle of the garden and she saw the outlines of Garth and the detective behind her light curtains, and she grinned. They thought they knew her; they couldn't be more wrong.

Her footsteps echoed as she stepped on the crazy paving until she reached the end of the garden. She popped the bag in the wheelie bin and placed her fingers on the slide lock. Slowly, she dragged it across. She pressed the latch and opened the gate, flinching as it creaked. Glancing up at her bedroom window, she hoped that the police hadn't heard.

Heart thumping, she remained still for a minute until she realised that they hadn't heard a thing. She was about to meet him. The man had killed two people. She'd heard them talking about the other one, Judith Morgan, but she hadn't managed to do any research without access to her gadgets. Was she making a big mistake?

The police hadn't yet checked that it was Becky who called her on the number that was no longer in use and for that she was grateful. They had believed every word she told them.

She swallowed down her nerves. Success came with risk. She took a step out onto the uneven concrete path that ran along the back of the terrace. A figure stepped out of the darkness, one covered in a hooded black coat. From his pocket he pulled out a phone and he passed it to her. 'You did what you were told. Good girl.'

The shaking in her legs was obvious. She didn't think she'd be this scared of him, but he was right. She had done what he asked, and she knew he'd respect her for it. She went to the police and told them that she was his chosen one. He was going to make her famous. He promised her exclusivity to the whole story, and she trusted him.

She glanced at the dumb phone and checked the contacts. Not a single number was listed. He passed her a charger which she coiled up and put in her pocket.

'Who are you?' she whispered, her voice a quiver.

'You're going to be famous.'

A cluttering sound came from the kitchen. She stepped back to see what was happening. It was her dad unloading the dishwasher. 'I have to go.' She turned back, but he'd gone. She tucked the phone in her pocket, along with the charger and stepped back into the garden.

'Macie, Macie,' her dad called.

'Coming.'

'What are you doing out here? It's dangerous.' Her dad ran out. She knew he'd been angry about what she'd been up to, but the concern on his face overrode that. He placed an arm around her shoulders and led her back into the house. 'It's not safe out here.'

'It's okay, Dad. I was just feeding some scraps to the fox. There's no one out there.'

He looked at her for far too long. She knew he didn't trust her. Fixing her grip on the phone in her pocket, adrenaline began to course through her. Head throbbing as blood pumped around her body sent her legs to jelly. She'd just taken a phone from the murderer. He could contact her at any time now. She should be terrified but she wasn't, not any more. That was a thrill like no other. He trusted her. She trusted him, and she wasn't going to blow her chance at the big time. She was Macie Perrin and soon everyone would know her name, like he promised.

FORTY-THREE

It was close to midnight and Gina followed Jacob and a uniformed officer down the steps towards the Hangar. 'Stop.' They all halted. 'I just want to listen first. We don't know what we're walking into here or how many people are down there.' With so many officers being taken up at Judith Morgan's house and the lake, they were too short-staffed for a task like this. She and Jacob had two officers, that was all, so to apprehend their suspect, they were going to have to strike at the right time. She edged past Jacob and the uniformed officer and took another couple of steps.

'You're just an arsehole. Take, take, take, that's all you do.' Gina recognised the voice as Sid Payne's. Was he talking to Jammy?

There was a loud roar, and something made a thwack sound. A man yelled. 'Let's go.' She hurried down the steps, stab vest in place and she charged at Sid, just as he was about to whip the man again with the huge twig he was holding. Jacob held a torch up while she snatched the spindly weapon from the man's hands and dropped it to the ground.

'Let go of me. He robbed me. You should arrest him. He stole my jumper. I want it back, you tosser,' Sid shouted, slurring at the other man.

The drunken man in the little house staggered around before falling onto the wooden floor. 'I didn't nick your jumper, mate. Don't want fleas, do I.'

'Where's Jammy?' she called out.

Sid sat on the edge of the house and wiped spit from his chin. 'Jammy, cops are 'ere for you.' Sid paused and waited. 'Jammy?' He stood and walked over to the edge of the bushes. 'I thought he was kipping in here.' Sid lifted the side of a tent that hadn't been there on their last visit. 'Looks like he went out with that posh mate of his again.'

'Posh mate?'

'Yeah, a guy seems to give him money and lets him use a fancy scooter to get around on. Personally, I think Jammy is selling his arse but that's no business of mine.'

'When did you see him last?' Jacob asked.

Sid scrunched up his nose and shrugged. 'I don't know. I really don't know.'

The other man piped up holding a scruffy grey jumper. 'Here it is, Sid. Told you I didn't take it.' He threw it at Sid.

'Have you seen Jammy?' Gina asked the other man.

'Nah. I only got here half hour ago. Thought I could cadge a spliff but there is no Jammy as you can see.'

Gina scrunched her brow. 'And Jammy deals drugs?'

The man huffed out a laugh. 'I'm not talking to you, or you, or yous.' He pointed to Gina, Jacob and then the two officers.

Gina held her hand out. 'Shh.' She latched onto a distant sound. It was the whooshing of an electric scooter. Jacob's gaze met hers, telling her that he'd heard it too. She ran back up the steps, gazing into the darkness. From the other side of the road, she watched as their suspect slowed down and stared in her direction. 'James Caid. Stop, police.' She held her identification up as she walked towards him.

With that, he turned and headed down a narrow alleyway. Gina ran as fast as she could, through the maze of streets as she followed the sound of the scooter. Her sides were aching like mad, and she could barely breathe after a few minutes of sprinting. There was no way they could chase the scooter with a car, not down all the paths at the back of houses. Jacob passed her. 'Don't lose him.' The two officers were on his tail.

She grabbed her phone and called it in. 'Send backup. James Caid, aka Jammy, is giving us the run around. We're by the Hangar. He was last spotted going down the alleyway alongside Meadow Road. Two officers and DS Driscoll are still chasing him but he's on a scooter.' She ended the call in the hope that backup would arrive. As she headed back to her car on the main road, the scooter came from nowhere and crashed her to the ground. She roared with frustration as she tried to grab the frame and missed. All she could do was watch as James Caid drove off into the darkness, while her colleagues were nowhere to be seen. They knew the streets well, but Caid lived and breathed them. She could now add assaulting her to his list of charges if only they could catch him.

Her phone went. She lay on the path, half in a cold puddle and snatched her phone from her pocket. Jacob emerged from the alleyway. 'Guv, you okay?'

She nodded. 'We lost him.' She swiped to answer Briggs. 'Yes.'

'Firstly, backup is on its way. I'll get some officers out searching the area. The Judith Morgan scene has been freed up, so we have more people available. Forensics are just finishing up there. Do you want the good news?'

'You mean there's good news?' She couldn't help but laugh as the water seeped through to her underpants. Was it that she was now free to search Judith's house?

'Logan flagged up on an ANPR camera, but he gave chase. We set up a stinger and we have him. He should be with us soon.'

FORTY-FOUR

Tuesday, 15 November

Gina checked her phone. She hadn't received a reply from Hannah at all. Maybe her daughter was totally ignoring her or maybe she was going to make angry contact in the afternoon, once she returned from Paris. She yawned and stared at the last message from Hetty, once again. She bit her bottom lip and fought back the rage inside. She was trying so hard to have it all. She wanted to be the best nan to Gracie. She wanted to be the best DI and the best mother, but it wasn't happening. The rage passed and a sadness washed through her. Who knows what would happen when the case was resolved, and Hannah returned home? Maybe she'd lost Gracie and Hannah forever.

It had been ages since she'd had any rest and with Noel Logan still to interview, it wasn't looking likely that she'd go home soon. She glanced at Jacob as he placed his coat on the back of a chair. He looked like he needed a good sleep too. They were all in the same exhausted condition.

O'Connor rubbed his eyes as he passed her a cup of strong-looking black coffee. 'Thought it might help with the interview. Given what we found at the lake, amongst other things, Logan's been arrested on suspicion of being involved in Wesley Reid's and Judith Morgan's murder. He's also been arrested for perverting the course of justice in relation to disposing of evidence. We now have twenty-four hours to bring charges, or we'll have to let him go. He also turned down a solicitor, for now.'

'Thank you. You and Kapoor should head off. I hope Wyre is heading home from Macie's soon. Garth has said he can manage on his own and the officer is remaining in place outside their door. As for tomorrow, we're meeting up at Judith Morgan's first thing to search her house. Seven a.m., sharp. We should have a few officers available to assist by then. The whole day has been full on, and tomorrow is going to be the same.'

'Thanks, guv. See you there.'

She followed Jacob to the interview room. Her usually smart colleague was looking dishevelled from the chase and Gina was uncomfortably wriggling to prise her damp under-pants from once again coldly sticking to her bottom. She wanted nothing more than to head home and have a steaming hot shower to warm up. She blew out a breath. 'Let's get this done. Mr Logan, take a seat.' The man was standing in the corner of the room in a standard-issue sweater and jogging bottom set. He stared at Gina as she and Jacob sat opposite him.

Jacob introduced them all for the tape. She took a sip of the coffee O'Connor made hoping it would lubricate her scratchy throat. All that calling after Jammy had done her vocal cords no favours. 'We found your phone at Cleevesford Countryside Centre. We also pulled a backpack from the lake. It contained a bloodied towel, a burnt-out sage stick and an empty can of cider, amongst other things. We also found your identification in the same bag. These items are at the lab as we speak. The items in your bag put you at the scene of Wesley Reid's room at the time of his murder. What do you have to say about that?'

The man shrugged.

'Where were you on the night of Saturday the twelfth of November?'

He shrugged again.

'Where were you on the morning of Monday the fourteenth between seven in the morning and midday?'

He ignored her.

People had described Noel Logan as smart and wealthy looking but all Gina could see was a man who'd been roughing it for a couple of days. His stubble had grown awry and dirt smudges struck his face. 'Let's talk about Wesley. He found out about you and Lydia's affair. He knew about the baby. You'd already taken everything from him, why did you take his life?'

'I didn't,' he yelled as he kicked the leg of the table. 'Why the hell do you think I haven't asked for a solicitor even though you lot have arrested me for murder? Wes was my friend.'

Gina wondered if he knew the meaning of the word friend. 'Yet you turned him down when he asked you if he could stay with you, leaving him with no option but to live on the streets.'

'You don't understand. He was an alcoholic. I was helping Lydia and things happened. They shouldn't have happened, but they did, and she loves me, and I don't know what the hell to do. Wes could get angry, throw a few things. He was a scary guy to be around. I didn't want him in my house, and I knew he'd soon find out about Lydia and that would make our living arrangement worse. I needed him to just find a place to live. I thought if he was on the streets, the council would help him and then he'd get a flat. If I had him at mine, he'd have been there forever. They don't prioritise people with a couch to sleep on, especially single people. We all know how the system works. I was doing him a favour.'

'You had an affair with his girlfriend and got her pregnant.'

'Like I said, it just happened. I was comforting her one night after she and Wes had a really bad argument.'

Gina had heard it all before. 'And then you ditched evidence from the murder scene into the lake. You can see how it looks.'

Jacob opened the file and pushed the photos of the rucksack, bloodied towel, cider can and burned-down sage stick, all next to Logan's golf club membership card.

'I didn't know what to do.' He clenched his fists and teeth, then he roared in frustration.

'What happened that night, Noel? You were seen arguing with Wesley at the Angel Arms earlier that night. You went outside with him—'

'And he went for me. He tried to punch me, and I dodged him. That's all that happened. I wasn't trying to hurt him.'

'How do you know Judith Morgan?' Gina said that sentence as fast as she could in order to gage his immediate reaction.

'I went on a date with her.'

Gina pulled out the transcripts from Judith's messages and waited while he read them. She spoke for the tape. 'I'm handing Mr Logan a copy of the messages and photo that he sent to Judith Morgan.'

'Shit. I can see how it looks. I never saw her again after our date.' He threw the transcript back on the table. 'Those messages were stupid, but I didn't kill her. I was nowhere near her house yesterday morning.'

'Where were you?'

'Sitting in my car by the lake wondering what the hell to do.'

'Did anyone see you?'

He shrugged. 'Maybe, I don't know.'

'Why did you go to Wesley's room at the Cleevesford Cleaver on the night of his murder after you'd argued with him at the pub?'

Noel shook his head and pressed his lips together.

'What were you arguing about?'

Noel slammed his fist on the table. 'Lydia.' He slunk back in the chair and began tapping his fingers nervously. 'I knew I had to be the one to tell him.'

'Tell him what?'

'That Lydia was pregnant. That's why we were arguing. It was only a matter of time before she'd start showing and he'd know it wasn't his. They hadn't had sex for months. It was going to be obvious. She's not the bloody Virgin Mary.'

'Let me get this right. That was the first Wesley Reid had heard about Lydia's pregnancy?'

'Yes.'

'Tell me about the rest of your evening?'

He huffed a couple of times and sat up straight. 'I needed to speak to him. I worried that he might go to hers and upset her, so I waited by the Cleaver a little way down the road in my car. I thought I could explain, maybe placate him a little. Anyway, I fell asleep. When I woke up, it was around one in the morning, and I knew he had to be back, so I thought I'd try my luck. I was going to ring his room bell, but I didn't want to wake everyone. Wesley had mentioned a broken window in the lounge, so I walked around the building, found it and climbed in. When I got to the top floor, I pushed his door open and turned on the light as I whispered his name. That's when I saw him lying on the bed. I grabbed a towel off his chair and ran over to him to try to stem the blood, that's when I realised it was too late. There was an empty can of cider on the bed. I picked it up. I saw that weird twig on the floor and in my shocked state, I picked that up too.'

'Why didn't you call the police?'

'He was dead, and I panicked. I grabbed the towel, the can and the twig thing, then with my sleeve I half-wiped the light switch after turning it back off. I was terrified that his murder would be pinned on me. People had seen us arguing that night in the pub. They might have seen my car parked up close by. I'd been hanging around the area, walking by the lake, trying to pluck up the courage to tell him about the baby. Anyway, I ran out of the main door. I took the things I touched, and I knew that very soon I wouldn't be able to go home, use my phone or my car. I hoped that by the time you caught up with me, you'd have caught the murderer and I'd be okay.' He paused and stared at his hands. 'I went to a garage, bought a cheap phone and SIM and I don't know where, but I lost my phone. I went to go back to my house later the next day, but I saw police there, so I've been sleeping in my car by the lake. It was parked in a bush right around the far end.'

'Why did you go to the old nursery early that next morning?' Even if Noel Logan didn't kill Wesley Reid or Judith Morgan, he would end up being charged with perverting the course of justice after taking evidence from a murder scene.

'The old nursery? The one on Salbei Avenue,' she asked again.

'I don't even know of Salbei Avenue.'

Gina stared at the notes and gasped as he repeated the name of that road to her. A tingle running through her body sent alert signals and she was buzzing. She'd cracked it. Why could she not have seen what was right in front of them? The answers to the murderer's riddle had been there all the time. 'When is a pound not a pound?'

'What?'

'When is a herb not a herb?'

'This is crazy. I think I need a solicitor if you're going to throw weird riddles at me. I know I'm an idiot. In my shock, I accidentally picked some things up and took some items from a murder scene and then I panicked, but I am not a murderer. I sent some awful texts to Judith, and I feel bad but I didn't kill her.'

Maybe he wasn't but it was too early to rule him out as

James Caid's posh friend, the one who gave him the scooter to use. He fit that description well. She glanced at Noel Logan again who looked as confused as anything.

'Do you own an electric scooter?'

He scrunched his nose up. 'No.'

'Do you know James Caid or Jammy?'

'I have no idea what you're on about. No. I want my solicitor. I'm not answering another question until I've spoken to my legal representative.'

Gina wrote her discovery on the notes and Jacob's eyes widened as he read her words. The bone-heavy tiredness she'd felt had subsided with their revelation. 'Interview terminated at one twenty-nine on Tuesday the fifteenth of November.' They hurried out of the room, leaving Noel Logan alone and waiting to be told what was happening next. 'The killer's clue. We solved it! We need to head there now.'

FORTY-FIVE

MACIE

Macie lay uncomfortably on the settee. She had nodded off, but the detective woke her up when she heard her saying goodbye to the uniformed officer on sentry duty. Then, the tech guy had come down and made yet another coffee. Her dad had left her to it at around midnight.

She missed the comments and messages from her fans. That was why she did what she did. The reactions of the viewers and her ever-increasing subscriber numbers gave her a thrill that was unmatched by anything else, except for the secret phone.

Rubbing her eyes, she lay on her back in the dark, staring at the shadows cast from the tree in their front garden which was lit up like a halo by the streetlamp behind it. The dappled orangey glow danced through the unlined curtains. A car growled as it passed, then the officer walked down the path, then back up, like he had been doing all night. No doubt he was trying to keep warm.

She pulled the phone from under the cushion and stared at it. Still, she hadn't had a message. How long was it going to take for him to make contact? Biting her nails in anticipation, she thought back to the moment he gave her the phone behind the back gate. He'd merely been a dark shape emerging from pitch blackness. She thought back to the scene at the Cleaver. Had he been there watching? Maybe he'd been standing at the back of the crowd, hanging out with the other nosy neighbours. He'd blend in like the rest of them. She thought back to her footage. She might have even taken footage of him. No doubt, Garth and the detective had gone through it all frame by frame. They'd been looking at it earlier. The detective had been making notes while he'd been navigating the footage. They'd been doing that while they read her comments, messages and fan mail.

She threw the phone onto the carpet. The waiting was killing her.

She blew out a breath and sat up. There was no way she would get any sleep now. Her mind raced and her muscles were itching for her to get up. He'd chosen her because she had reach, she had influence, and she was a rising star. He knew she wouldn't let him down. Maybe he'd got cold feet, or saw something that had compromised his trust in her. It must have been weird for him, coming to the back of her house, knowing that the police were there. As arranged, he turned up on time. The call he made to her earlier had prepped her for his arrival. All day, she'd been sick with nerves, hoping that the police would let her out of the station in time, and they had. She'd banked on being given a caution but not on them coming back home with her and camping outside the door and in her bedroom. That pound had been his sign, so she knew they were still on for their meeting at her back gate. The police were never meant to see it or know what it meant. None of that mattered now. Macie had managed to do everything she set out to do, regardless.

Her phone flashed. Snatching it, she opened the message.

I need to know that I can trust you before we take the next step, Macie. This is a test. Creep out of your house around the

back, waking no one. When you leave your garden, turn right.
Go to the end of the path and wait for further instructions.

Her heart began to bang in her chest. Was she really ready
for the next step? No guts, no glory. Like hell she was. He
wouldn't hurt her, he needed her to spread the word and now
she was going to get the words to spread, just like he promised
her.

FORTY-SIX

UNKNOWN

The more I think of her, the more I hate her. To me, she is everything that is wrong with the world. For a few seconds, I try to get her disgusting face out of my head. It's the last thing I need in there, along with the others. I do fear they will haunt me forever, though, and that's something I must accept.

I drive past 97 to 104 Salbei Avenue, the old nursery, and I know the police will have clicked by now. Maybe they are as incompetent as I think they are, and they haven't clicked that Salbei is the German word for sage. They should have seen the sage sticks. There are a hundred pennies in a pound. 100 Sage Avenue, that's what I want them to investigate. The answers are under their noses. If they haven't clicked, they must be totally stupid. I couldn't have made things clearer. I told them a pound was not a pound and a herb is not just a herb. It's so easy when you have the answers.

I remain hidden which I'm grateful for as there are still things I need to do. Killing is never easy, that's what I used to think. I've changed my mind.

The police don't see me. I blend in. Being ordinary has that effect. At the Cleaver, with the crowd bustling around, I blended in there. At the old nursery protest, I faded into the background, then after, I watched from beyond. I really am a nobody. I was a loved one and I gave so much love, but now I'm empty with only my mission to complete. I don't care what happens after. When a person loses everything, it becomes irrelevant. People need more in life. No one should be invisible, and I am going to make them see.

I was an empty vessel with no destination, but the news of the old nursery development sparked a fire within me. The video that Macie shared about the old nursery in one of her ghost videos sent shivers running through me. That spark is now ravaging my insides and reaching out to burn everything down with it. It's a destroyer and there is no way back. To think only a short while ago, I was living a normal life as I tried to forget the past.

I flick the miniature teddy bear that dangles from my rearview mirror and smile.

As I take a turn onto the dark lane, I get out of my car. I take the long road towards the back of the estate, then I peer through a gap in the trees. That's when I see little Macie. She thinks she's so grown up but, in my eyes, she's a child.

I need to know she's alone, so I send her another message.

Cross the road, take a right and sit on the swing.

If she so much as looks back or hesitates, I'll abandon the mission. I don't want to, though.

My phone flashes with a call. I have to take it. As I listen to the voice droning on the other end of the call, I watch her and deliver my next set of instructions.

I need Macie. She is the one. She is my route to freedom. 'Do as you're told. Come to Daddy.'

FORTY-SEVEN

MACIE

Swinging back and forth, all Macie could hear was the creaky metal frame. It was as if no child had used the cold metal swings for ages. She pressed her feet into the strip of mud to stop the swing. She was doing exactly what he told her to but where was he? She glanced around, taking in the houses at the other end of the small playing field. Every house was in darkness as their occupants slept without a care in the world.

Her heart almost leaped out of her mouth as a startled cat darted from between two trees, mewling like it had been attacked. She stared into the dark void, hands shaking while she waited for him to come forth. 'Hello,' she called, pushing her glasses up her nose.

There was no reply. Was he standing in the darkness watching her?

'Hello, are you there? I did what you asked.' She hoped he couldn't hear the nervous quiver she was trying to suppress in her voice.

She checked the phone again but there were no more instructions. Had she come to the right place? She glanced around. There was only one small park close by with swings and it was the one she waited at. She began tapping out a message.

Are you watching me?

No answer.

She heard rustling coming from the bushes. The cat scurried back past her and began to hiss at the trees. She took a step back, then another. Whatever was happening next, she didn't want it. She'd changed her mind.

Another cat pounced from between the trees and ran towards the hissing cat where they toiled in a fight. She turned and sprinted away from the swings and away from the park until she reached the other side of the road. Glancing back, all she could see were the two cats. No one else was there. Gasping, she bent over and took a few deep breaths. 'Macie, you idiot. It's cats, just fighting cats,' she mumbled under her breath.

Standing straight, she checked the phone again and he still hadn't replied. He had been watching her. He'd told her to cross the road which must have meant he was close. It was no good, she had to find out why he wasn't showing himself. She pressed the call button, but her call was immediately rejected. What was going on? He was playing a game with the police, but she thought she was different. She was the one he'd chosen to tell his story to and scaring her in this way wasn't a part of the deal.

A whooshing sound caught her ear as she turned to walk home, then a boy stopped and got off his scooter. Was he a boy or a man? Did he give her the phone earlier? She couldn't tell. It had been so dark but the more she looked, the more she thought it was.

The voice in her head told her to play it cool, ignore him and walk past. Although her knees were beginning to knock under her leggings as she stood, she couldn't allow him to see her fear. She parted her knees as she took a step. Phone in hand, she gripped it. Maybe filming him live and narrating at the same time would scare him into leaving her alone.

Swallowing, it dawned on her. The dumb phone was only for phone calls and texts. She couldn't livestream him and tell all her fans where she was. She didn't even have any numbers in the phone that would help. And there was no way she remembered any offhand.

She stepped off the kerb and cleared her throat as she went to walk away from him, reminding herself to not look scared and act cool.

'Stop,' he said in a gruff voice.

She did as he asked, not turning around to see if he'd moved.

'He said you passed.' There were two of them. Where was the other one?

'You're not him. Who are you?' He started the scooter. As he got closer, she let out a shriek and began to run as fast as she could, but she was no match for electric wheels, not in her stupid pinching boots. 'If I passed, leave me alone,' she cried out, but it was no good. He'd caught her up and the only thing she could do now was fight.

FORTY-EIGHT

Gina pulled up with Jacob outside the old nursery. As she drove, he'd been doing some online research. 'This place has been a few things before it was a nursery, guv.'

'Hit me with them.' She stepped out of the car and stared at the police cordon that was flapping in the breeze. After the bloodied towel had been found at the bottom of the back garden, and the scene and the house had been secured again, there had been no chance of having a permanent patrol outside, not with them being under resourced.

He walked over to the path and scrolled the webpage he was reading. 'It was a kids' nursery for several years, before that it opened up as a community centre, but it lacked funding and soon closed. Then it was vacant for a couple of years. Before that a company took over the building and tried to rent the individual rooms out as offices. This is interesting...' He scrunched his brow as he read on.

'What?'

'It was used as a hostel, temporary accommodation for the homeless for quite a few years.'

She lifted the cordon up and went onto the car park. 'The same as the Cleaver?'

'Basically.' He followed her onto the dark land.

'We need to contact the council first thing in the morning. Find out everything we can about this place. We have a connection. This used to be a hostel and Wesley Reid was killed in a hostel.' She bit a piece of skin from her bottom lip. Holding her arms up and allowing them to fall to her sides, she sighed. 'Where does Judith fit into this hostel scenario? I feel as though we're taking one step forward and two steps back. She lived in a nice house, had money in the bank and had a nice little job. How does she fit into this world?' She shook her head. 'Wrong question. How did she fit into this world? The killer led us here. There has to be something in her past.'

Gina stared up the road, noting that Hetty's bungalow was in darkness and all the curtains were closed. It pained her to know that Gracie was in there with that woman and so close to this horrible building. Her phone began to ring. It was Briggs. 'Sir?'

'Someone called in to report a car stuck in a verge. It looks like the car drove into it, narrowly missing a wall.'

'Okay. I gather it isn't a run-of-the-mill traffic accident.'

'You gather right. The car is registered to Sasha Kennedy, the homeless support officer who you interviewed at the Cleaver. Didn't she meet you at the old nursery too?'

'Yes. Is she okay?'

'That's what's strange. The officers at the scene have said that it looks like she must have crawled out of the passenger door, but she is nowhere to be seen. I've got them calling the hospitals as we speak.'

'Keep me posted. Where did this happen?'

'On Inglenook Lane. It's a single-track road and normally quiet but her sister lives a short way from there and we interviewed her this evening, Tanya Kennedy-Williams.'

'I'm coming back in.' Gina checked her watch. It was the middle of the night.

'No, go home, get a few hours' sleep. I know you have to be at Judith Morgan's for seven and I want you to be there. Let's see if this incident is relevant to the case first. We'll let uniform dig around. If they find her, I'll message you immediately. She probably got picked up by a passing motorist and taken home or to a hospital. Maybe she'd had a drink and fled the scene. This could be anything and I don't want you diverted from the case in hand. Catching this killer is our number one priority.'

'Of course, but I'm not ruling out that they could be linked. Any news, call me immediately.'

'Any sign of a link, I won't hesitate.' He ended the call.

'Was that about the homeless support officer?' Jacob asked.

She nodded. 'They found her car in a ditch and she's nowhere near it. I don't like it.' Gina tightened her ponytail. 'When I spoke to her, she mentioned that she was having trouble with a kid, her window had been smashed. What if she is the link to everything, the homeless support officer? She'd be heavily involved with people needing emergency accommodation, like Wesley.'

'But not Judith.'

Jacob was right. She stepped back under the cordon and gazed at the houses opposite, taking in the whole road. Curtains were closed everywhere and there wasn't a person to be seen. 'Inglenook Lane is in the middle of nowhere. Sasha would have been dazed and injured from a road accident. She's a part of all this. It's too much of a coincidence.'

'You don't know that for certain, guv.'

'When we were at the old nursery, and we went into that room with the red writing on the wall, she had to leave. It was a message for her. The killer went to the old nursery early the next morning after killing Wesley Reid. They left that bloodied towel there on purpose, knowing we'd track it. They led us there on purpose. They smashed the window, entered the building and left that message for her to see. She knew it was for her and she's been running scared since. Why did I not see it?'

FORTY-NINE

MACIE

She lay on the pavement, her leggings torn where she'd fallen in the road. She could have sworn the man on the scooter was going to attack her but all he'd done was chased her for a few seconds and then whizzed off. Limping along the back of the houses, she stood by her back gate and leaned against it, taking a few deep breaths. *He said you passed.* Those words whirled around her head as her short breaths turned into little laughs. She passed. He was never going to turn up at the park and tell her everything, just like that. He wanted to make sure she was the right person, so he set her up to see if she'd bottle out and tell the police. She thought she'd proven herself by being alone outside her back gate earlier, but maybe that wasn't enough. She'd not only passed once, but she'd also passed twice.

She licked her hand and wiped her scuffed knees, buffing them with the sleeve of her coat. Great, her dad was up and not only that, he was in the kitchen, making himself a drink. She waited and watched until he'd finished. As he turned the light off, she crept back into the garden and up the path until she reached the back door. She waited a little longer. He had to be back in bed by now. She glanced up and she saw two figures in her bedroom. It had to be her dad and Garth. The detective had left. Something had happened?

She opened the door, careful not to make a sound as she stepped into the dark kitchen, inhaling the smell of freshly made coffee. One foot after another, she walked across the tiled floor, trying her hardest not to make a noise. As her hand reached the living room door handle, her dad called out. Slowly she turned around and pasted a smile on her face. The last thing she needed was for him to worry. 'Where have you been? I was just about to come out looking.' He stood at the top of the stairs, coat zipped up and woollen hat pulled over his forehead.

Mouth suddenly dry, she went to speak but no words came out. She was hardly going to tell him that the murderer has messaged her, then sent some buffoon on a scooter to test her. She passed the test and was so close. He trusted her now, that was for sure, and his story was going to be watched by millions when she released it. Her dad or Garth could know nothing. At the end of the day, the buffoon hadn't hurt her, she'd fallen.

'Well?' He came down the stairs and looked down at her.

'I couldn't sleep.'

'So, you went out while a murderer is targeting you?'

'He doesn't want me, Dad. I just tell news online and I am eighteen, I'm allowed to leave the house. This is ridiculous. I don't even have my phone. No one can contact me. I went out the back to meet Becky at the park, that's all.'

'How did you meet Becky if you didn't have your phone?'

'She hangs around there with a couple of others most nights. It's just a hangout thing, Dad, you wouldn't understand.'

'Have you been drinking?'

She blew a breath in his direction. 'No, I was just telling her what's been going on, that's all. I went out the back. No one saw me.'

'Tomorrow, young lady, you're going to school. I'm taking

you there and I'm picking you up and you're not to leave the premises during the day. Got it?'

Her shoulders slumped. 'Got it.' She'd let him have that one if it made him feel better.

'Why are your leggings ripped?'

'That's how we wear them now.' Macie listened as Garth shouted a yes above them. 'What's happening?'

'You received an email. Something about you giving sage advice on one of your "safety while out at night" videos. I don't know what that has to do with anything, but Garth seemed excited about it. He was just calling it in when I took him a drink up.'

Macie crept upstairs and listened.

'Yes, sir. We have an IP address for the sender. Whoever sent that message didn't even try to hide it. It's the old nursery on Salbei Avenue.'

FIFTY

Gina pulled the shoe covers and latex gloves on before entering Judith's house. Worry had disturbed her sleep, keeping her up most of the night. Firstly, because Hannah was due home later and secondly, the horrible messages from Hetty were killing her and thirdly, no one had found Sasha. 'I'm really concerned for her.'

'Me too,' Jacob replied. 'She didn't go back home; she wasn't checked into any local hospitals and the indents and trails at the scene showed that she crawled up the bank on her hands and knees.'

Gina exhaled. 'She didn't go back to her sister's either. She's missing and we have no idea where she is.' She paused. 'On top of all that, Macie got a comment, and the sender didn't use a VPN. It led us back to the old nursery. We were there last night, and I didn't see anyone around. The place was locked up. We need to know how far someone needs to be from the building to get a Wi-Fi signal. I think tech are working on that. For now, maybe Judith's house will help us out. We're looking for anything that connects Judith and Wesley, and now Sasha. We don't know much about Judith's past either. Find out anything you can.' She beckoned the uniformed officers into the house.

'Shall I get the search downstairs started?' Jacob asked, his hair slightly ruffled. Gina noticed that he hadn't shaved. Like her, he'd probably got up after barely any rest and not ready to face another day.

She nodded. 'That sounds like a plan. I'll take upstairs with two officers.'

Jacob led the rest of the team into the living room to instruct them further.

Gina went up with the two officers who were joining her. Judith's house made her shiver. She'd come home the day before and walked up the same stairs. Had Judith known that there was someone up there or had she been ambling up to get ready for work? Gina imagined how happy and excited she would have been about her date, later that day. The officers awaited her instruction. 'I'll take the main bedroom. Could you take the spare bedroom, the cupboards and the family bathroom?' She smiled.

The officers nodded and went on their way. Gina nudged the door open. Yesterday, Judith's body had been laid out with a pound coin placed on her head. All that was left in her place was the mattress and bloodstains. It was time to delve a little deeper and see what they could find out about Judith. She thought of the horrible messages that Noel had sent to her and how upsetting that must have been.

As she opened and closed the drawers, her mind wandered to Sasha and Tanya. The two sisters looked alike in many ways. Same hair, eyes, face shape and mannerisms. Something struck her. Tanya had said that when Noel Logan introduced her to Wesley and Lydia over dinner, Wesley had been funny with her. Where was she going with this?

She rooted through Judith's clothes, her mind unable to stay off Sasha and her whereabouts. She sifted through the neatly folded jumpers, then the skirts. Her hand got caught in a tangled web of tights. Wrestling them off, she placed them down. She pulled out a pair of earrings from a jewellery box and placed them on the top of the drawers. Jacob peered around the door. 'The search downstairs is well underway. Thought I'd see if you were okay up here. What are those?'

'Two matching earrings.'

'Are you seeing something I'm not?'

'They're not quite the same. If you look at them from afar, yes, but closely, you can see that the some of the joins are slightly longer and the twists in the silver are tighter in the one on the left.'

'Handmade?'

'Yes.'

'What has this got to do with the case?' He raised his eyebrows.

'Nothing. It got me thinking, that's all.' She scrunched her brow. 'Wesley knew Sasha. When Noel introduced him to Tanya, he gave her funny looks because he thought she was Sasha. They look alike in a way that if you hadn't seen one for years, you might think they were the same person. I guess when Tanya showed no recognition of him at all, he dropped it but at that dinner, he recognised her, or should I say, he thought she was Sasha.'

'So, you're saying you think Wesley knew Sasha? Sasha said she hadn't met Wesley.'

'Recently she didn't, but in the past, maybe? One of her colleagues dealt with Wesley when he went to the council. It could be the link between Sasha and Wesley.'

'Why didn't she say if she knew him?'

Gina popped the earrings back into the jewellery box. 'Maybe she didn't know him by name.'

'If she recognised him after, why didn't she come to us?'

'I don't know.' She exhaled and slid the wardrobe open. She

pulled out three boxes and placed them on the dressing table. 'Great, lots of photos. Do you want to take a box?'

He nodded and took the lid off the box covered in kitten pictures. For several minutes, silence fell upon them, until Gina reached the last photo in a tiny album marked 2007. 'Look.'

'That's Judith.' Jacob pointed at the photo. 'The hair's a bit wild but it's her.'

'And that's Wesley. Granted he's changed a lot. Under that belly and long hair, you can see it's him and he has his arm around Judith here. They look so young.' The two murdered victims were lying on what looked like a single bed, both wearing jeans and jumpers. They were laughing as Judith held a bottle of beer up. In the framed picture of a sailing boat on calm water behind them, Gina could see the shape of a face holding a camera in its reflection, but the features were undistinguishable. 'That window. Do you recognise it?'

Jacob took the photo and held it under the light. 'It looks like the smaller sash window in that room at the far end of the building at the old nursery.'

'I know it's hard to be sure, but I'd bet on that too. If you look up, the cornice that divides the wall and ceiling is the same too. It's that room, the one that Sasha looked so uncomfortable in. I have a feeling she was there too. Maybe she took the photo. There's something else in that reflection. Look hard.'

He stared. 'I can't see anything, guv. Shame this photo is so grainy. It looks like it was taken in low light, and it's weathered.'

She pointed. 'There's a dark shadow on the back wall. You can just about see it, by the boat sail. It almost blends in but there is yet another person in that room. Wesley, Judith, maybe Sasha and an unknown.'

Jacob nodded. 'We could be looking at our murderer.'

'I have a feeling we might be.'

Gina's phone went. It was Briggs again. 'Sir.'

'Tanya Kennedy-Williams is at the station. She insists that

something is wrong with her sister. After the police turned up in the night to see if she'd seen Sasha, she'd tried to call her dad, but his phone had been turned off. She's just managed to get hold of him, and only then did he tell her that Sasha turned up to see her last night. He said she looked anxious, then left again. Sasha told him not to tell Tanya that she'd visited, saying it didn't matter and she didn't want to worry her. When Tanya got back, her dad was tired and left for home straight away, not thinking much of the visit. There was something else. When she left, he watched her pull off and another car followed. At first, he thought it was a coincidence but now, he's not so sure.'

She ended the call. 'Sasha was being followed. Someone has taken her. Injured people don't just vanish.' She stared at the photo again. 'Identifying the other two people in this photo are key to finding Sasha.' Gina bit the side of her mouth. 'Sasha wasn't left dead like the others and displayed with a pound coin on her head. There's a chance she's still alive. We must find her. She's next.'

FIFTY-ONE

Rushing through the station, straight to the incident room, Gina and Jacob entered to the hustle and bustle of the small team who were working the case. Wyre sat in the one corner, scrolling through the files. Briggs held his mobile in his hand and she heard Garth's name mentioned. Her phone beeped and it was yet another message from Hetty.

Hannah is so angry with you. She can't believe how you left little Gracie with strangers, dumped her on anyone who would look after her. I wouldn't trust you to look after my dog, let alone a child. We all know what you are, Gina. An evil bitch who only thinks about herself. Gracie deserves so much better. It's a good job she has me.

In any other circumstance, Gina would head straight over to that woman's house and have it out with her but right now, she was stuck. How dare that woman claim that she was unfit and insult her like that. Gracie deserves better than being with Hetty. She put her phone away and turned her attention to her team.

'I guess O'Connor has left for Judith's post-mortem?' she asked.

PC Kapoor nodded as she bit into a banana.

Gina hurried over to Wyre. 'Any more on that email from the perp?'

She shook her head. 'Garth hasn't managed to get anything else relevant but he's remaining at the Perrins' household for now. PC Smith swapped guard duty with another officer in the early hours. Garth did say that Macie's social media had blown up with comments and messages and the whole team are working through them. She's popular, that's for sure. We think the murderer might try to make contact again and when he does, hopefully he'll leave a trail that will help.'

Gina nodded. 'We're being played good and proper. Did you see the photo I uploaded to the system?'

Wyre nodded. 'Yes. I've tried to zoom in, but the image is so grainy. I don't think we'll be able to get it enhanced in all reality.'

'The original isn't any better. I've passed it to digital forensics to take a look.' Gina knew that would be the case. They could do a lot but working miracles wasn't one of those things. It wasn't like in films where police could just zoom in and the clarity would suddenly be perfect. 'Any updates on James Caid?'

'No. It's like he's vanished off the face of the earth. We've had officers patrolling the Hangar and the surrounding area, but no one has seen anyone on a scooter this morning. We're still looking and if I hear anything, I'll let you know straight away.'

'And Tanya, how is she?'

'Worried sick. Her dad has just arrived. I've left them in the family room for now. She wants to speak to you.'

Gina swallowed, knowing that a tough conversation would follow. 'Any news on Sasha?'

'I wish there was.'

'I best go and see them.'

Briggs finished his call and stood by the boards. 'We're treating Sasha's disappearance as highly suspicious. We have tried everywhere, and we haven't managed to locate her. Her phone is dead and the crime scene investigators at the site of her accident are now saying that there appears to be skid marks behind Sasha Kennedy's car. We know that her father watched someone pull off in the same direction when she left Tanya Kennedy-Williams's house. We also now know that there are no junctions or turnings off that road for another quarter of a mile. If they were behind her, they saw the accident. It's a single-track road so they couldn't have overtaken her before that.' He paused. 'This was left on the dashboard.' He pulled a sheet of paper from the printer and held up a photo of a pound coin next to an evidence marker. 'This leaves us with no doubt. Our killer has Sasha Kennedy, and her life is in imminent danger.'

FIFTY-TWO

Gina ran along the corridor to the family room and took a deep breath. The last thing she wanted to do was to alarm Tanya and her father any more than she needed to. 'Ms Kennedy-Williams, Mr Kennedy, thank you for waiting.'

Tanya gripped her phone and remained seated. Her father stood. 'Call me Dai. Have you found her?'

Gina shook her head.

'Dad saw her last night, not me. He said she wasn't herself, didn't you, Dad?'

'She was anxious.'

Gina sat opposite them and turned the fan heater on. 'I know you've already spoken to our officers but are you okay going through everything again, with me? I'd like to make sure we haven't missed anything.'

Dai Kennedy nodded.

'What did Sasha say?'

'Not much really. She came in and just checked her phone every few seconds like she was waiting for someone to call or checking something. I mean she's always scrolling through her phone, so I didn't think much of it. She asked me where Tanya was, and I told her that she'd just popped out and I was looking after the little one. Sasha was going to wait for Tanya to get back.' He scrunched his brow as he thought.

Gina knew where Tanya was, she was speaking to her outside Noel Logan's house before making a statement at the station, but Gina could see from Tanya's expression that she didn't want her dad to know. 'And did she say anything after that?'

'She didn't stay long but she seemed upset. Some kids had smashed one of her windows and a boy on a scooter had damaged her car. Is it the kids? Have they done something to her?'

Gina leaned forward and clasped her nervous fingers in her lap. The very mention of the boy on the scooter was now playing on her mind and James Caid was still out there. It had to be him. 'We don't know anything for certain yet. What else did she say?'

'Nothing, really. I was about to make her a cuppa and slice some cake and then she'd gone, just like that. Oh, she did tell me not to say anything to Tanya, didn't want her worrying for nothing and that it was just a window. She left because she got a message. She said something about a window repairman heading to her flat to fix the broken window. I watched her leave, and I could tell she was worried. As a father, it broke my heart. I don't know why people are so horrible. Sasha is such a caring woman who does so much for other people.' He shook his head and exhaled. 'I've paid her credit card a couple of times.'

Tanya turned to face him. 'You never said anything about this.'

'I didn't want to break her confidence, love. She'd helped a few people that she works with. You know, paying for them to stay in hotels when the hostels were full. She did it because she cares, Tanya, and I guessed I cared enough to help her. I kept telling her she'd end up destitute, but she didn't see any other way. It was killing her to send people back onto the streets because she couldn't help them. Anyway, it was nothing and it was only a couple of times. That has nothing to do with all this, so we'll talk about it later.' He sipped his drink. 'I saw a car pull off as Sasha left last night. I didn't think anything of it but...' He shook his head and Gina saw a wash of sadness spread across his face.

'What made you think something of it?'

'There are no more houses close by. Whoever was in the car can't have been visiting anyone. They'd parked in a pull-in-place, alongside the woods. I reasoned that they were stopping to talk on a phone or maybe they hadn't been well or stopped to pee. It happens.' He paused. 'When Sasha pulled off the drive, they started the engine up and followed in her direction. What did strike me as off was that the main beam lights were on. They literally dazzled me as they passed but then again, I've accidentally driven with mine on. Again, I didn't worry. It's not like they were revving the engine or beeping the horn.'

'Did you see the make of car?'

He shook his head. 'No, all I saw were those green and black blobs you see when you've stared at bright lights. The person in that car could have hurt Sasha. They could have taken her, and I didn't think anything of it at the time. She was in danger and I...' He put his head in his veiny hands.

Tanya placed an arm around him. 'You didn't know, Dad.'

'I knew she wasn't herself.'

'Tanya, how has Sasha seemed to you lately?'

Tanya shrugged. 'Fine. It looks like she hasn't been telling me much. We're sisters. I wish she'd told me how bad the kids had been to her. I could have helped.' Tanya looked at Gina with pleading eyes. 'Please, you have to find my sister.'

'Did Sasha ever mention Wesley Reid to you, before his murder?'

'No. I can't see how she'd have known him.'

'Did she ever mention the name Judith Morgan?'

Tanya shook her head. 'I do recognise that name though. I saw it on a Facebook community group. She's the woman who was murdered yesterday. I'm even more worried now.'

'Do you recognise that name?'

'No, never heard of her.'

Gina knew that Noel would never have mentioned going on a date with Judith while he was with Tanya and also with Lydia, but it was worth an ask. For a moment, Gina wondered if Tanya had ever looked at Noel's phone. Could she have known that he was cheating on her? If it wasn't for the fact Tanya was with her when Sasha was run off the road, she'd delve a little deeper.

Someone knocked at the door.

'Thank you for speaking with me. An officer will be in to update you soon. I'm going to do everything I can to find Sasha. You have my word.' Gina stood and followed Wyre away from the family room. 'Has something happened?'

Wyre nodded. 'You could say that. Kayleigh Blunt is in reception.'

'The woman who discovered Wesley Reid's body? Is she okay?'

'Yes. She wants to report that her brother, James Caid, is missing.'

FIFTY-THREE

MACIE

Macie prodded a cold pea on her plate and threw down her fork. She wasn't in the mood for her canteen favourite of cheese pie and chips. Her friends sat at another table, talking about all the parties and fun things they were planning. No one asked her to go out any more. She smiled at Becky, but Becky looked down at her food while she joined in with the others. Macie had turned down their invites too many times.

What she needed now was an invite from the killer. He had promised her the inside story and she needed it more than anything. Soon school, crappy canteens and the daily grind would be history. She'd make it up to Becky after.

She pulled the phone from her pocket and there had been no more messages or calls. She'd watched the news and a report of the other murdered woman was all over it. Judith Morgan, much-loved friend and librarian. Damn. She'd missed out on being at that scene because he'd landed her in the police station. Maybe she shouldn't have gone to the old nursery and got picked up, like he told her to, especially as he'd given her no more information in return.

'Nice phone,' one of the boys said as he burst into laughter.

'Shut up,' Becky said as she nudged him in the ribs. Becky still had her back.

'Mine's broken, dickwad.' She stuck two fingers up at him and shook her head. She stood and walked out of the canteen and along the corridor so that she could hear her thoughts.

The dumb phone beeped. She pressed open on the message.

Come out of school, go to the back of the field and there is a broken piece of fence. Go through it and wait by the large oak tree. I'm going to tell you everything, as promised.

Heart going like a jackhammer, she glanced around wondering if anyone could see how tense she was. Would he send the buffoon on the scooter again? She hoped not. In fact, if he did, their deal was off. She would hand the dumb phone into the police, and he was on his own.

Leaving through the PE block door, she headed across the damp field. Cold water began to seep through the edges of her boots as she squelched her way to the back of the field. As she reached the broken fence, she swallowed. She'd promised her dad she wouldn't leave the premises at all. He'd dropped her off and watched her walk down the school drive like she was a little kid. She'd never felt so embarrassed. Even Becky had noticed and asked if everything was okay. It didn't matter. Very soon now, the truth would be out there, and she would literally be their hero.

Prising the wiry fence apart, she fed her leg through first and followed that by her body. 'Damn.' Her mac had torn on a sharp bit and her black trousers were coated in thick mud along the hem. There would be no hiding the state she was in from the police and her dad when she got home. That's when her gaze fixed on the oak tree. Not a car passed by. 'Hello,' she called out, but there was no one around. She glanced up and down. There was a dark saloon car parked up but there was no one in it. There was no sign or sound of the scooter.

A few drops of icy rain began to fall. She shivered. None of this felt right. What was she doing? As she swallowed, it was as if her heart skipped a beat, then it began to pound like it was trying to burst through her chest. The wind began to whip as a downpour caught her face. He wasn't here so she was turning back. The phone beeped again. She wiped the rain from her face and read the message.

Stay exactly where you are. Do not turn around. Do not run.

Her hands and legs began to tremble. What had she done? What was she doing? It all sounded like a good idea at the time. A crackling branch followed by the sound of a heavy foot came right up behind her. 'Don't be scared,' he whispered, 'by the end of today, everyone will know your name.' His warm breath on the back of her neck made her shiver. The sound of a zip followed by his jacket ruffling as he stepped closer made her shaky legs leaden. She could run, she could scream but she wouldn't get far, and no one would hear her. It was just him and her.

'You won't hurt me, will you? All I want to do is help. I want to tell your story.'

His hands came over her head and he brought an eye mask over. Resting it against her eyes, he gently tied it at the back. Then he held her from behind, embracing her and nestling into her neck. She inhaled his pine-scented shower gel and a tear trickled down her face. She let out a sob.

'Don't cry, my love. It'll all be over soon. You don't know how long I waited for this moment and now I have you. I'm going to show you something special because you are special. So special.'

FIFTY-FOUR

Gina hurried to the interview room where the desk sergeant had left Kayleigh Blunt. 'Thank you for coming in.'

She wiped her mascara-stained eyes and pulled her puffer coat around her body. 'He said I had to.'

'Who did?'

'My brother, well half-brother, James Caid.'

'He sent you here?' Gina sat and Jacob entered, his pad already open. He pulled a pen from the inside pocket of his suit jacket and sunk into a bucket chair.

'Not exactly. He said if I didn't hear from him within the next hour, to call the police.'

'When was this?'

'I don't know exactly. I was half asleep when he came over. It was gone three in the morning. My daughter was asleep, and I didn't want to wake her, so I let him in. Sorry. I'm not meant to have visitors at the unit where I'm staying. I mean they're not meant to visit at night. Please don't tell anyone. I don't want to go back to the Cleaver.'

That was a promise Gina couldn't keep so continued with

the questioning. She might need to delve further into Caid's whereabouts. She would do her best for Kayleigh, though. 'Let me get this right. He turned up where you're staying in the early hours and told you to call us if you didn't hear from him within the hour.'

She nodded. 'I fell asleep.' She began to cry. 'It's not like I wasn't worried, I was just so exhausted with all that had happened over the past few nights. I couldn't stay awake. It's not the first time my brother's been in trouble. He's always up to something, mixing with the wrong people but he said things were going to be different, that he had something in the pipeline and all our problems would soon be over. I never know what to believe.'

'Why didn't you call us sooner if he told you to contact us?'

'I don't know. Because he was high, I wondered if he'd meant what he said but it played on my mind all morning and when I couldn't get hold of him, I knew something had happened. He always answers when I call him.'

'How did he seem when you saw him last?'

'Like I said, he was high. Jittery. I think he'd just taken something. His eyes were wide, and he was talking so fast I had to tell him to slow down.' She pulled her sleeves over her hands and hugged her body tighter.

'How did he get to yours?'

'He walked.'

'Are you sure?'

She nodded. 'He's been using an electric scooter, but he didn't have it when he came to me. I asked him where it was, and he said it was gone. I don't know what he meant by gone but he wouldn't say any more. I don't know if it was his, but he probably sold it for drugs.'

'Did he deal drugs?'

She shrugged. 'My brother has a lot of problems. That's all I'm saying.'

'Was he with anyone?'

She shook her head. 'No, but he kept saying he had to be somewhere, or he was going to be in trouble. I think he was meeting a man; someone he's mentioned a couple of times.'

'Can you tell me more about this man?' Gina held her breath as she and Jacob waited for the answer.

'He uses my brother. Gets him to do all kind of unpleasant jobs and my brother being my brother needs the money. He doesn't have a choice in it. He said the man had made him promises and for some reason, he no longer trusted him. I saw something in James, he was scared and anyone who knows him, knows that fear isn't something that normally affects James. He was into something. It was something bad and I don't know what's happened to him and I'm worried.'

'Has he ever worried you like this before?'

'He's never failed to check in when he's said he will. This is a first. There is something else. I overheard him on the phone to this man.'

'And what did he say?'

'He said that he didn't want to hurt the woman. I kept asking him what woman and he shrugged me off.'

'Think, Kayleigh, do you know where he might have gone? We can only help him if you can give us more. He could be anywhere.'

She exhaled and closed her eyes for a moment while she gathered her thoughts. 'He mentioned that this man had paid him to break into the old nursery on Salbei Avenue. He was told to graffiti a wall and to leave a bloodied towel on the grounds there, only a few hours after Wesley's murder. My brother didn't do it. He is a lot of things but he's not a murderer.' She shook her head, her damp dark hair sticking to one of her cheeks. 'There's something about the old nursery. He told me that something bad happened there and he had been hired to help put wrongs right. Something to do with a girl and her father. The old nursery, that is my only idea about where he might go. I know he'd squatted there, before he and a few of his friends at the Hangar were cleared out. That's where he said he met this man. He has to be there otherwise why would he have told me all that?'

Gina's mind was awhirl with thoughts. What man? Sid Payne, his friend at the Hangar? Her mind darted to Gareth Alderman, maybe he was capable of more than they thought. 'Think, Kayleigh. Did he say anything else when you saw him?'

'I don't know. It all happened so fast. Wait, he said the man mentioned a girl, his daughter. I think James was helping him with his daughter.' She bit the end of her sleeve. 'You have to check the old nursery. He must be there.'

The messenger had used the IP address for the old nursery and the planted evidence, and the graffiti tallied up with what they knew. She nodded for Jacob to follow her out of the room, and she closed the door so that Kayleigh couldn't hear. 'We need to check on Macie, now. Call the officer guarding her house, and call Mr Perrin.' Her thoughts threatened to sink her. What if James Caid was helping Mr Perrin with his daughter, Macie Perrin? The whole idea didn't make total sense, but she had to make sure Macie was okay.

She ran to the incident room and grabbed a phone while searching for the number of Cleevesford High. PC Smith had now arrived. He, Kapoor, and DC Wyre waited to hear what she had to say. Instead of speaking, Gina waited as the phone rang out and eventually a woman answered. 'Is Macie Perrin still at school?'

'Her father called about an hour ago to check and she was still here then. She was at lunch then and now she's in an English class.'

'Could you check again?'

A couple of minutes passed, and the woman spoke again. 'She's not here. No one has seen her since lunch.'

Gina felt as though her heart was about to stop as she ended the call. 'Macie is not at school. Smith, head over to Cleevesford High and see if there's CCTV. See if anyone saw Macie leave.' She quickly updated them with all that Kayleigh had said and they watched Jacob end his call. 'What did the officer say?' Gina asked.

'At around eight in the morning, Mr Perrin left with Macie and said he was going to work after he dropped her off at school.'

'Did you try calling him?'

'Yes, and there was no answer. His phone is turned off, so I called his workplace.'

'Was he there?'

Jacob frowned and shook his head. 'The man who answered said he rushed out a while back without saying a word. He grabbed his coat and left.'

Briggs had entered quietly, and Gina wondered how long he'd been in the room listening.

'Jhanvi, I need you to stay here. Call the council, call social services and look for any old news on the old nursery on Salbei Avenue. It was once a hostel and I'm hoping that the records are at hand. The hostels are a link. The killer wants us to delve deeper and find it. Find out everything you can and fast.' With O'Connor still attending Judith's post-mortem, she knew she had to rely on PC Kapoor to step up on the investigative side.

'I'll work on that with you.' Briggs smiled at the uniformed officer.

'We need an alert put out for Sasha and Macie. Someone has to have seen something. A woman and a girl don't just vanish.' She swallowed.

'I'll liaise with corporate communications, get the press informed.' Briggs sat next to PC Kapoor. 'Just go. We've got this.' He nodded and she knew her whole team were doing all they could.

O'Connor walked through the door eating a baguette.

'Great, you're back. You're coming with us,' Gina said to him as she grabbed her own coat and looked at Jacob. 'Let's head to the old nursery. We need backup. I don't know what we're about to walk into but it's not going to be good.'

FIFTY-FIVE

MACIE

'Where are you taking me?'

The man in the front seat of the car didn't reply. He'd bound her hands with a thin cord, not what she'd expected. In a situation like this, she'd always thought she'd be able to fight or yell but for the first time in her life, she knew what it felt like to be rendered so scared, she couldn't utter a word. She'd complied with his every instruction even though her head was telling her to run. She'd frozen and a part of her still felt frozen.

'Head down.'

'What?'

'Head down,' he yelled as he took a corner sharply. She fell to the side, unable to use her hands to stop her face from crashing into the car door. He spoke weirdly, like he was trying to disguise his voice. It was too deep, too gruff, unnatural in every way.

'I don't want to do this any more.' A tear trickled down her cheek. It wasn't meant to be like this. He was going to give her an honest account of why he was doing all this, and she was going to report it once he'd made his escape. After all, the people he was hurting were bad people. He'd promised her that they were. That's why she sympathised with him. Now, she wasn't so sure. She wasn't a bad person and look at how he was treating her. 'You're going to hurt me, aren't you?'

'Shut up. I need to concentrate.'

She swallowed. Maybe knowing where she was would help. She knew that he'd probably been watching her through the rear-view mirror but now, her head was nestled at the back of the car seat, right behind him. She lifted her bound hands up and slipped the eye mask off and it gathered under her chin. She squinted and pressed her eyes together a few times until her focus had improved but it was no good. She wondered what he'd done with her glasses. All she could make out were blurs of colour and one left her heart banging. She could just about make out a blob of brownish red. As she inhaled, the metallic smell made her stomach turn. It was unmistakably blood.

He stopped the car, and she heard the chugging sound of metal. It was a garage door opening. Nausea rose in her throat as the greyness of daylight vanished for pitch-black darkness. The roller shutter came back down. She began to fiddle with the binds, but they were too tight and knotty. 'Put the eye mask back on, Macie.'

With shaky hands, she did as she was told. The only thing she could do right now was cooperate and show him that she wasn't the enemy. He told her she was special. If he'd meant it, she was going to be okay. That didn't stop her knees from jittering. Who else had been in the back of his car and bled? She knew of two victims, and both had died at the scene as far as she was aware. There was someone else. He'd taken someone. This wasn't his way of working. He killed them at the scene. She'd convinced herself she was safe. That blood had proven that everything she thought she knew was wrong. Taking someone in his car wasn't what he did. His silence was suffocating. 'Is there a third victim? You said you'd tell me everything.'

'All in good time, Macie. We have all the time in the world. No one will ever find us here.'

She swallowed. He stepped out of the car and opened the back door. After helping her out, he flicked a light on which illuminated the edges of the eye mask. The darkness had gone. All she had to do was to reach up and pull off her mask, then she could see him. She could see the man who had taken her. But, if she did that, who knows what he might do. *Play it cool, Macie.* Maybe she was never meant to see his face.

The pipes began to clang through the walls.

'What's that noise?' she asked, a quiver in her voice.

'Evil. There's evil in the walls, there's evil everywhere and we need to deal with it. Are you going to help me banish the evil away, Macie? We'd make a great team.'

What had she got herself into? There was no way she could reason with someone who thought there was evil in the walls, if indeed he really did. She missed her room and she even missed school. She missed her dad too and the mangy fox that visited their home.

The engine ticked as it began to cool, and she recoiled at the scent of petrol.

'I'm going to lead you through the house. I know you can't see but you're going to have to trust me. Do you trust me, Macie?'

She nodded furiously.

'Take my hand.'

Without waiting for her to respond, he reached out and pulled her through the cold room. His hands were smoother than expected for a double murderer but what did she expect? Knives were smooth and he'd worn gloves to blindfold and bind her.

Warmth hit as he led her through a door. Her soaking feet scuffed on what felt like carpet. 'Keep walking.'

A key turned in a lock and, with a creak, the door opened.

The musty smell and cold air wafted up and out, the chill catching her bare neck. That's when she heard the banging pipes once again, coming from below. 'We are going down. Take one step at a time.'

No, she wasn't going into a cellar. If she went down those stairs, she was never coming back out. Never. He had her hands in his vice-like grip. All she had was her feet. She kicked out and hard. He yelped but managed to grab her foot, sending her painfully onto her bottom. 'I'm not going down there.'

Heart now banging away, she felt as if her world was spinning as she gasped for air. Her idea of trying to play it cool had gone out of the window. The cloying atmosphere filled with the stench of rust, petrol and human misery told her she had to fight.

He grabbed her foot and dragged her down and with each step her tailbone smashed onto stone. At the bottom, he lifted her off the ground using what felt like super-human strength to contain her limbs as his boots clopped across the stone floor.

'Let me go,' she cried. That's when she heard someone whimpering.

'It's no good.' The person sobbed loud and from the gut. 'No one comes... no one.'

All Macie wanted to do was go home but it was too late. She only had one option and that was to play him at his own game and win. She was better than being a whimpering mess of a girl. It wasn't a strategy that was working with him.

He dropped her onto a chair. She flinched as a cold blade trailed across her wrist. 'I wouldn't move if I were you,' he said.

She remained dead still as he snipped the cable. He yanked her arms behind her back and began to tie them to the chair with rope, ringing the length around her wrists several times.

Macie took a deep breath. 'I'm sorry. I didn't mean to kick you back there. I was scared.' She let out a small cry and hopefully he'd see that she was being sincere. 'I know you won't hurt me.'

'That's my girl.' He patted her on the head, like she was a dog.

'Can you remove the eye mask? Please?'

'Relax, Macie. All in good time. Besides, I have the biggest present for you. Sasha is going to confess, aren't you?'

'Nooo...' the woman yelled.

Macie had heard that name before but where from? How did she know Sasha?

Come on, Macie. Work it out or you're going to die? Why are you really here? What does he want from you? Work this out and you can find a way out?

Her body silently panicked but her exterior remained calm. She was Macie Perrin and Macie was going to find a way out of this situation and she would make the most of it. No guts, no glory. Now was her time to test that theory. She only hoped she wasn't about to pay with her life.

She could no longer hear her captor over the woman's crying, but she did catch the sound of something click, just once, and then the room went dark. He'd turned the light off. The woman fought for breath as he walked in her direction, then she held her breath save for the occasional whimper. His footsteps got nearer and nearer to Macie. Her own breaths sped up. She felt his cold fingers on her cheek as he pulled down the eye mask. 'Can I have my glasses?'

He pulled them out of his pocket and placed them on her face, then he was halfway up the stairs before she could focus properly.

She only needed to see his face for the second she had. She knew exactly who he was, but he wasn't hanging around to talk. Before she opened her mouth, he was up the stairs where only the thinnest shaft of light shone like a sword, with the point reaching her side. She caught a glimpse of the bleeding woman, the one she'd seen arriving at the Cleaver on the morning of Wesley Reid's murder. Taking a deep breath, she tried to quell the sick feeling inside as she glared at the woman's matted hair and the blood streaked across her face.

Glancing back up, she watched in frozen fear as he stood in the doorway, his frame almost filling it as he observed them from the top of the stairs. She wanted to beg him not to take what little bit of light they had and shut the door, but something told her he'd like that. All Sasha's banging and screaming had got her nowhere but that didn't stop her from kicking the metal pipe again. Macie needed to be cleverer about things.

'Sasha,' he said, 'we've spoken about this, haven't we? Tell Macie why you're here. They say confession is good for the soul and it's always best for the truth to come out before a person dies.'

'Let me go,' the woman yelled.

This was the story. Sasha was the story, and he was giving it to her straight from the horse's mouth, but once she knew the truth, would he ever let her go?

FIFTY-SIX

Uniform had already beaten Gina and Jacob to the old nursery and more officers were on their way. The police car was parked away from the main building as she'd requested. Caid couldn't see them coming or he'd flee again. She almost stumbled out of Jacob's car as he skidded to a halt. Phone pressed to her ear; she hoped that Wyre had some answers for her before she went in.

'Nanny.' Gracie waved at her and beamed her a gorgeous smile.

Gina turned to see Hetty loitering with a few bystanders, watching as the commotion unfolded. 'Just give me a moment.' She ran up to the woman and held her phone down. 'Hetty, I know we've had our differences, but you have to take Gracie back into your bungalow now.'

The woman stood; arms folded. 'I don't have to do anything you say.'

'Please, it's not safe.'

'Of course, it's safe. The woman who manages to save every day is standing right in front of me. Go save the day. Do what's important to you because she's not.' Hetty grinned and looked down at Gracie.

'What does Nanny Hetty mean?' Gracie looked up, her large eyes making Gina want to scoop her up and remove her from the situation.

'Nothing, chicken. I'll speak to you later.' She leaned down and hugged Gracie before looking back up at Hetty. 'Take her to yours now.'

The woman stared for a few seconds. 'You were always a bloody drama queen. Come on, kid.' She grabbed the little girl's hand.

'But I want to go with Nanny Gina.'

'Not now.'

Gina listened as Gracie's protests become louder but she was relieved that Hetty had taken her away from the situation. This was no place for a child.

Gina placed the phone against her ear again. 'What did the head teacher say?' she asked Wyre.

'Macie left after lunch. Some of the other students saw her leave out of the back, through the PE block door. She's also on their CCTV but we lose her halfway across the field. I'm walking that route now and it leads to a broken fence at the end of the school field. She must have left here. Damn.' Wyre paused.

'What is it?'

'There's a bit of torn jacket on the fence and an old mobile phone on the path by the road.' Gina bit her nails as she waited for more. 'It's the killer. He lured her here. He's been communicating with her on this phone.'

'We need Caid, and we need to find the person pulling the strings. We're at the old nursery now and we're going in. Got to go.'

'I'll be there as soon as I can, guv.'

Gina ended the call and popped her phone on silent. She didn't want to alert anyone to their presence, not yet. Stab vest in place, she stepped onto the kerb and hurried over to see what an officer was looking at. 'Caid was riding that scooter,' she said as she kept back, not wanting to disturb any evidence. The scooter had been dumped in the brambles along the side of the house. She peered through and could see a path running alongside the parted shrubbery. Maybe Caid had cut through, hoping to not get seen approaching from the front knowing that any officers driving by would miss him. 'The window on the side of the house has been smashed.' It was the opposite side to the boarded-up window.

Jacob hurried up to her, his phone pressed to his ear until he ended the call.

'Are the council on their way?' she said in a hushed tone. The last thing she wanted to do was to scare James Caid away if he was in the house. He might have Sasha or Macie and she had no idea what he was capable of.

'No, guv. No one can get here for at least half an hour.'

'Well, given that we believe a life might be in danger, we're going in. Do we have any more backup yet?'

He walked across the drive, back towards the road and nodded. Moments later O'Connor and six other officers were by her side, one of the officers holding a battering ram. She gathered them around. 'I don't want us to go in all guns blazing. Sasha and Macie's lives are in danger. Our perpetrator has already killed twice. I suggest we go in through the smashed window. Put the battering ram on hold for now and follow me.'

She peered through the broken window. Bunching her coat over the end of her hand, she knocked the final shards of glass out, that's when she spotted blood on the sill. She glanced at the officer furthest away. 'Make sure there's a paramedic on standby. Go back and tell them that we've found blood, so an injury is likely,' she whispered to him. She only hoped it was an injury and that Sasha and Macie were still okay.

Jacob threw his coat over the window ledge and Gina climbed in first, careful to step quietly onto the tiled floor. She shifted out the way and waited for the others to climb through, then she beckoned them to follow her. Listening intently for any sign of activity, she halted them by the door. Gently she pressed the handle and opened it out onto the main hall and front door, the one they'd entered through last time they came. She heard loud clanking coming from below. 'Guv, can you smell that?'

She nodded. 'Petrol. Make sure a fire engine is on its way.' She paused. 'I don't like this at all.'

He nodded and made a quiet call before rejoining the pack.

'This way.' She led them towards the back of the building. Sasha hadn't shown them this part when she'd been here last. Gina pushed the door at the back open and it led to a large industrial kitchen. Dust covered the stainless-steel countertops and pans hung from the ceiling. She trod quietly, following the clanking noise through another door that led to a storeroom. A large steel shutter dominated the far end. She knew that there had been a follow-up visit where officers had checked the whole building so nothing had been out of place then, apart from in the one room, but something was amiss now, like who was making that noise?

She stopped and listened. It sounded like pacing footsteps and then the banging started, like metal on metal. 'This way.' She followed the noise to a locked door. 'There's no way we can do this quietly. James Caid, please open the door. You have nowhere to go.'

The banging came again.

'Guv?' Jacob stared into a far corner of the room.

'What?'

'Caid isn't behind that door.'

She furrowed her brow and followed his line of sight. Beside a tower of stacked boxes, the glassy eyes of James Caid stared back at her, peering from under a dustsheet.

Jacob ran over and lifted it away, immediately pressing his

fingers to Caid's neck to check for a pulse. 'He's dead.'

'We need to get that door open now. Sasha, Macie,' Gina called out.

An officer hurried over with the battering ram.

'Stand away from the door. Officers are coming in. You're safe now.'

The banging stopped and the officer stood poised to knock the door open. After the second attempt it bounced off the back wall. Gina passed him and hurried down the very few steps that appeared to lead to another storeroom. She ran over and removed the gag from Mr Perrin's mouth, and he gasped for air. 'They're going to kill Macie. Find her.' His voice was a slur.

'Who are they?' Gina asked.

He wiped the blood from his head and frowned. 'I don't know,' he cried. 'I don't know. I heard him say he was watching all the time. He's here.'

'Was that James Caid, youngish, rides a scooter?'

'No, the other man killed him.'

'What does he look like?'

'I didn't see him. I heard it happen.'

'What did you hear?'

He squinted and looked like he might pass out.

'When?'

'A few minutes ago, I think.'

A paramedic entered. 'Step aside.'

Gina's phone buzzed as it rang away on silent. 'Sir. We're just at the old nursery. We've found Mr Perrin and Caid is dead. I don't know much more yet except that the perp is close by, but I can't even be sure of that.'

Briggs replied. 'Gina, we've got something. We're with digital forensics and relaying everything in real time so listen up. Garth called. He and the team have been literally going through millions of comments, likes, followers and messages. We've never had so many messages to go through. The Grim

Reaper messages lead back to the old nursery. This user has several profiles under lots of different names, but none that relate to the case. But he has constantly used the same IP address.'

'He's using the Wi-Fi here?'

'It looks that way. Wait. There's more coming in...'

'What?' Gina felt her hands shaking.

'He's just sent a message to Macie on Instagram but it's to us. He knows we're monitoring everything. He's saying that Mr Perrin doesn't deserve Macie and that he can't protect her. He says that he can, and he will, and that Mr Perrin has to live with that. He is also saying... he's glad to see so many police officers at the old nursery taking things seriously.'

'He's here now?'

'I think he is. He's toying with us.'

She ran out of the storeroom and through the building, throwing the front door open. She stood on the pavement and watched as a paramedic helped Mr Perrin out.

'Gina,' Briggs said.

'I'm still here.' A crowd had formed, and all Gina could see were faces everywhere and she wondered which face in the crowd he was. She spotted a bobble hat behind two taller people. She ran over and parted them only to reveal a boy amongst a sea of onlookers. 'Sorry, there are so many people here. He has to be one of them.'

'He's just messaged again. He said he'd never wear a bobble hat.'

She gripped her phone and stood in the middle of the road. He was so close, but no one was standing out. O'Connor caught her up. 'Mr Perrin is being checked over and then we can speak to him.'

'I don't want this crowd leaving. Get uniform to help you. Block the road off. We need to speak to everyone. The perp is right here, right now.'

'Get off me,' Mr Perrin shouted as he shook the paramedics away and ran into the middle of the road. He turned in a circle, staring at each of the people, then at the houses on the opposite side of the road.

'Mr Perrin, what is it?'

'I found this, in my pocket. I didn't put it there.' He handed the scrunched-up bit of paper to Gina.

She took it off him and read the article. It described an incident at the old nursery, back when it was a hostel.

'Macie published something about this incident. It's all about this. It has to be. It's this place.' He stepped away from her. 'Macie, Macie,' he shouted.

O'Connor caught up with the man and led him out of the road.

'Gina, what's happening?'

'Looks like our murderer left a clue in Mr Perrin's pocket. It's an article and it relates to something Macie had previously worked on. It's about the accidental death of a girl in a hostel. I know who it is, sir. I'm looking at his photo right now. They kept his daughter's name out of it but not his.' She continued reading the article. 'He's changed a lot but it's him.' She relayed the man's name. 'Find out anything you can about him, asap.'

'We have another message. He says his work here is done and now he must go.'

Gina held her phone by her side. No one had come, no one had left. She glanced up. He had to be watching from a building. *His work was done.* She hoped that didn't mean what she thought it did. Her stomach clenched with fear for the teenage girl and the woman.

She held her phone back to her ear. 'He lives in one of these houses. The Wi-Fi stretches from the old nursery to his house. That's how he's doing this. We need more officers, now. Get his address.' Shaking, she knew that it was game over for their perp but she hoped it wasn't game over for Macie and Sasha.

FIFTY-SEVEN

SASHA

Cold, she was so shivery her teeth kept chattering. This is what it felt like to die. The tearing pain from the wound was like nothing Sasha had ever felt before. Burning hot in the centre and radiating out in excruciating throbs. She tried to shuffle on her side but all she could do was let out a primal roar as the unbearable pain ripped through her.

A cry escaped her lips as she thought of her family again. She wanted to be surrounded by the warmth of Yasmin's cuddles and her sister's house, not here in a cellar facing her end. 'Macie,' she croaked with a cough. The girl now knew everything, but he wouldn't let her live.

There was no reply. As she fought her swimming head once again, she listened for a sign that the girl was okay but there was none. In darkness they lay, dying or... Sasha sobbed. Macie wasn't dying. A dying person made sounds. Macie had to be dead, and it all started with her and what she did.

However hard, she tried to banish thoughts of that night. Fifteen years ago, she'd met Wesley Reid in a pub, but she didn't know him as Wesley. When they met, he'd said his name was Reedsey. Reedsey had been drinking with Judith. Tears began to flow down her face as she relived that fateful night in her head.

While living and working in Birmingham, Sasha had come back to stay with Tanya for a couple of nights, but Tanya had to work. Sasha had entertained herself by seeing if any of her old friends still frequented the local pubs. Big mistake! If only she'd stayed in and watched TV, she wouldn't be here and about to die and the girl, that poor innocent girl, would still be alive.

She sobbed as she remembered Wes telling them back then that he'd been staying in a hostel close by. Drunk and merry, Sasha hadn't wanted the night to end. On arriving at the hostel, they got louder and louder until a gaunt man in a dressing gown shouted from the end of the dark corridor, telling them all to shut up as they'd wake his daughter. 'I'm so sorry,' she yelled into the dark cellar. If only she'd gone home at that point instead of being louder and drinking more.

Sasha would never act like that now. Shame burned through her. More tears slipped down her cheeks as she thought of that little girl who, a while later, came into the room and took the can of cider from Reedsey. If only she'd known what was going to happen next.

She roared so loud; her head began to pound. Each detail now haunted her every dying thought. A week later, she'd seen that article in the paper about the accidental death at the Salbei Avenue Hostel. She'd skim read it on the train, along with the rest of the local paper. Girl gets hold of cider and vodka, drinks too much and dies from organ failure after being on life support. Sasha had refused to believe it could be. Maybe if she'd paid closer attention to the article, she would have memorised the bereaved father's name or seen the photo of him in the paper, but she'd been drunk that night, so drunk and she wanted to forget, to imagine that it couldn't have been the same girl.

'I left before she died. I thought she'd be okay. She seemed fine.' Her huge choking sobs filled the cellar as she lay on the stone floor.

She heard a shuffle. 'Macie,' she said with a splutter. 'Please remember to tell them that I didn't mean for that poor girl to die. I left earlier that night.' She yelled as a pain seared through her arm, the wetness spreading. Although it was dark, the room was swaying like she was being cast out to sea.

'Macie's gone,' said the voice in the dark. She sobbed and choked as she felt his breath on her neck. 'I heard everything you said to Macie and I recorded everything we spoke about.' He paused and she flinched as he shouted. 'You could have stopped it. You could have helped her. She was twelve, for God's sake, and you left her drinking with them, her killers.'

He let out a cry.

'Trevor, I'm sorry. I am so sorry.' Tears spilled from her face. 'Please give me a chance to make it up to you.'

'You can never make it up to me, Sasha.'

'I thought we were friends. We've worked together for a year, and you said nothing.'

'We were never friends. I found you on Facebook and I knew what you did, and I knew you were from Cleevesford. I trained hard to get that job at the council, saying that my own stint as a homeless person made me want to help people. All I ever wanted to do was help people like me, to make sure that another child didn't suffer like my daughter at the hands of people like you.'

'Please, Trevor.'

'Don't you dare plead with me. I know exactly what you did and soon, the world will know.' He laughed manically. 'Where were we? Oh, yes, when your sister had your niece, you moved back to Cleevesford, and last year you ended up working with me of all people. I wanted to hurt you so badly then, but I couldn't. Slowly, I began to like you and even disbelieve in my own mind that someone so nice could have been so evil. There were a few times when I wanted to say something to you, but I couldn't. Instead, I kept watch on the other two while I silently seethed but I contained it, I really did.'

'What changed?' She had to know.

'The Salbei Avenue Hostel. How could they reopen that place?' Sasha flinched as he roared and kicked a chair. 'I didn't want them to publish that article and that photo of me. They blamed my little girl, but I knew better. When I found her dying the next morning, my world had ended. But I'd seen you all arrive. I'd listened to you talking. I knew your names but when I asked you to shut the hell up, you all laughed. You all told me to get lost and what match was I against you three?' She listened as he began to sob. 'I should have killed you all right there and then. You all killed her, and the police failed when her death was declared as not under suspicious circumstances. Just another kid who'd drank too much,' he yelled. 'She was not just another kid. She was mine and I failed to protect her from monsters like you, Wesley and Judith.'

'I'm sorry,' Sasha blubbed.

'Sorry, sorry, sorry. Everyone is sorry now. No one was sorry then.' He pressed his index finger to his lips. 'Not everyone is bad in all this. Not long ago, I spotted a YouTube video about my daughter's death at the hostel. No names were mentioned but then again, there was no coverage except for that one article. It was just a known fact in the area that a girl had died there. That's when I first saw Macie. She was talking about my daughter.' He paused. 'Someone else had given her a thought when the world had forgotten her.' He paused. 'And, when that disgusting man came in to collect the keys from me, he had no idea who I was, but I knew exactly who Reedsey was. Wesley Reid. I knew I had to stop him so that no other child could get hurt. You'd placed Kayleigh there and I kept thinking of her and her child.'

Sasha sobbed along with Trevor, knowing that all that time

of them being colleagues and friends, he'd known that she was party to his child's death. She couldn't hate herself more right now.

'I couldn't let him hurt anyone else like he hurt my child. That's why I killed him. Then I thought, why should you and Judith get off with what you did. Judith was easy to find. I'd seen her in the library. Once I'd taken Wesley out, I knew she had to go too and then there was you. Pathetic little no-life Sasha. You made it hard for me, Sash. Then I thought, your niece deserves better than someone who let my daughter die,' he spat.

She flinched as a chair flew across the room. Still in darkness, she lay there, half-drifting out of consciousness. 'I'm dying, Trevor. I didn't know what was going to happen when I left that night. The whole night was a drunken blur. That's no excuse.' She paused and coughed.

'Sasha, we've spoken about this. I know okay, so stop pretending.'

Her choking cries filled the room. 'I deserve this. You're doing the right thing. Please don't hurt Macie. She hasn't done anything wrong. Is she dead?'

'Yes, and that's your fault too.' He paused. 'Say my daughter's name.'

She didn't know her name.

'Say her name and I will get help for you. You could live if you got to a hospital right now.'

Tears spilled from her eyes. 'I don't know it. I'm sorry, Trevor. Please forgive me.'

She felt a cold hand on her arm. 'Goodbye, Sasha. I tried to be a better person and I tried to forgive you, but I couldn't. I think with you, Judith and Wesley gone, my work is done. I'm done.'

His hand left her arm, and he scurried up the stairs and closed the door. 'Trevor, I'm sorry,' she yelled, ready to accept her fate as her jumbled thoughts drifted. 'Macie, please forgive me too. I'm sorry this has happened to you. It's my fault.'

'Emilia, that was her name. I want her to be your last thought. I never was going to a wedding in London, and I don't have a niece, you robbed me of the family that I had. I have no one.'

As her eyes closed, she knew the fight was over. Sasha could feel herself drifting into death. The smoky smell in the air caught her attention. She gasped for a final breath as a tear rolled from the corner of her eye and then nothing. It was over. She whispered one last word, the name, Emilia.

FIFTY-EIGHT

Gina ran past the old nursery and stared at the house next door. Smoke began to escape from the open window. Briggs was phoning her again. She called over to O'Connor and pointed at the house. 'Hello,' she shouted over the commotion.

'Trevor Cage lives in the house right next door to the old nursery. That's how he's been using the Wi-Fi and he's had access to the building for his work. He would have been able to go in and get the Wi-Fi code.'

'His house is on fire, sir. I have to go.'

'Gina, don't do anything stupid. I need you to keep safe. I love you.'

With no time to lose, she placed her phone in her pocket. 'Get that door open now. We can't let the fire reach the old nursery. Get someone to make sure there is no one in the building. The place reeks of petrol.' She ran towards the house with an officer. Within seconds the battering ram had the door open. 'Sasha, Macie,' she called out, but there was no answer. The billowing smoke came from the kitchen at the back.

Sirens filled the street as a fire engine pulled up. Flames licked the kitchen units, then the wooden table. The cellar door was open. Holding her coat across her mouth, Gina stood at the top of the stone stairs.

'Guv, wait for them to put the fire out in there,' Jacob called her from the front door. The fire crackled and caught a mahogany sideboard in the hallway.

'I can't wait. If Macie and Sasha are here, I'm not leaving them to burn.' Another flame whooshed as it caught a strip of accelerant forcing Gina into the cellar. She slammed the door closed, hoping with all she had that the firefighters would get to it on time. All light gone, she pulled her phone from her pocket and shone the torch down the steps. 'Macie, Sasha.' Gina coughed as smoke began to tickle her throat. All she could hear were heavy boots charging above and then crash, something had caved in. The house was falling apart above her.

She saw a message pop up. It was Hannah.

I'm just on my way over to Hetty's to collect Gracie. We need to talk later.

She placed it back in her pocket and she thought of her own failings. Yes, she should have turned work down and stayed with her granddaughter as she'd promised Hannah she would. Swallowing, she reached the bottom step and shone her phone in the large, dank cellar as smoke seeping under the door began to cloud the atmosphere. She took a few steps forward and tripped over a mass on the floor, sending her phone crashing to the ground. Now she had no light.

Using her hands, she felt for that mass. A sticky warm liquid coated her fingers. Feeling along the body until she reached the neck, she felt for a pulse. It was faint. 'Help,' she yelled. 'Sasha, Macie.' She had no idea who it was, all she knew is that they had long hair. It wasn't Trevor.

Someone opened the door above, casting a ray of light into the cellar. She grabbed her phone and put it back in her pocket.

'Guv, you have to get out now.' She glanced down and saw Sasha covered in blood, a knife left beside her body.

A firefighter ran down the stairs and pulled Gina away from the woman.

'You have to save her. There's a pulse.'

The firefighter helped Gina up the stairs and as soon as she reached the front garden, a paramedic ran over and assisted her into the back of an ambulance. He placed an oxygen mask over her mouth, and she breathed in all that precious gas until she felt slightly better. 'I'm okay.' She pulled it from her mouth and went to step outside the ambulance. Wobbling slightly, she shook her head and exhaled. 'All good. You need to help her.'

As another firefighter gently placed Sasha on a gurney, Gina took several more breaths of air. Several onlookers held their phones up, recording every moment. She stood back, watching as James Caid was loaded onto another ambulance in a body bag.

Mr Perrin ran over. 'Where's Macie? You have to go back in there.' An officer grabbed him just as he was about to dart into the burning house. The upstairs had now caught, and another firefighter went in. Gina only hoped they'd come out with the girl.

FIFTY-NINE

'Guv,' Jacob called.

'What?'

'The two officers down at the back of the building, one said that the perp hit them both with a plank of wood. They tried to stop him, but he attacked them again. One is unconscious and the other has what looks like a broken nose and he staggered to the side of the building. There's blood everywhere. A small team are going in through the back but the building stinks of fuel, so they'll be approaching cautiously.'

Mr Perrin stood on the path outside Trevor Cage's house. He fell to his knees, screaming Macie's name.

'We have to go in there.' Gina pointed at the old nursery. 'He's in there.'

The upstairs sash window creaked as Trevor lifted it.

'Is that Macie's coat?'

Jacob nodded. 'It looks like it.'

Gina squinted to get a better look but all she could see was another flash of black and white. She caught sight of what looked like a skull print before it vanished from view. 'He has Macie.'

'Gracie, Gracie,' Hetty called out. Gina ran over to the woman who had squeezed her way through the crowd to get to the front.

'Where is she?'

'I don't know.' The woman shook her head. 'I told her to play in the back garden but when I checked on her, she'd gone out of the back gate. I thought she'd be here looking for you.'

'No, no.' Gina felt her stomach turning. If Gracie wasn't with Hetty, where was she? Gina ran towards the old nursery and stood underneath the window where she could just about make out Trevor's outline. 'Do you have a little girl with you? Please let the little girl go. Gracie, Gracie. Talk to me, Gracie.' She could hear the crackling of a radio then a quiet voice told her that the officers were at the bottom of the stairs. 'Tell them to hurry. I think he has my granddaughter too,' she said in a hushed tone to the officer. She couldn't hear or see Gracie, but it was best to assume the worst. Maybe he didn't have her. If he didn't, where was she? Her heart raced under her shirt, and she felt her vision swaying as anxiety took hold of her. She was trying not to panic but she needed to panic. Gracie was missing.

'You don't get to make any demands. You get to listen. If you come anywhere near me, one flick of this lighter and the whole place goes up.' Trevor held a lighter up to show them. 'This is where it all ends,' he yelled. The onlookers went silent as all their phones continued to record. 'Where were you all when Emilia needed you? Where were you?'

'Mr Cage, please come down and we can talk about this. No one else has to get hurt.' She tried to remember the details in the article but there hadn't been many to go on. She now knew his daughter had been called Emilia. *Remember, remember.* She tapped the side of her head, trying to recall everything. One wrong move and he could hurt Gracie. The huge lump in her throat threatened to choke her. *Please be okay, Gracie.* All she wanted to do was hold Gracie close and never let her go.

'Talking never got me anywhere. I'm done with talking.'

'Gracie,' Gina called. There was no answer. She paused in hope that she would hear her granddaughter's sweet voice calling her from a place of safety. Gina's hands trembled. She had to keep him calm and talking long enough for the team to get into position. 'Is Macie, okay?'

'Oh, she's just fine.' He flung Macie's coat out of the top window.

'Can we see her?'

'No.' He stared at her before continuing. 'Back then, I needed your help. I begged for your help, but no one listened. No one wanted to prosecute her killers. The press blamed my little girl. She was meant to be safe in that hostel, but they hurt her. Wesley, Judith and Sasha did this. All this, it's their fault.' He let out a loud roar and sob.

Gina stepped back and looked up, trying to get a better view but the window only opened as far as his nose. 'Gracie.' Once again, her granddaughter didn't answer her call. She glanced back and saw Hetty sobbing and another onlooker consoling her. That's when she heard a glugging sound as Trevor Cage poured petrol over his head.

'Please don't kill my daughter too,' Mr Perrin pleaded as he escaped the officers and ran over. 'From one father to another. I love Macie with all my heart. If you take her, I don't know what I'll do. Macie has never done anything to hurt you.'

Trevor Cage lifted the window further so they could all see his full face. He grabbed a lighter out. 'Macie is an angel, she deserves to be with the angels,' he said.

'No, let her go, you bastard,' Mr Perrin yelled. An officer came over and dragged him back.

'Mr Cage,' Gina called, hoping that the man wouldn't hurt Macie or her granddaughter. 'Trevor.'

He glanced down. Gina could see the sorrow and loss etched in the man's face. 'What happened to your daughter was tragic, it was unforgivable but please don't hurt yourself, Macie or little Gracie. It won't bring Emilia back. She wouldn't want you to hurt them.'

He half-sobbed and laughed. 'I don't want to bring her back. I want to be with her. This is where Emilia died, and this is where I've chosen to die too. I'm going to be with her forever. I bought that house so that I could be near her and at times, I'd wake up in the night and I heard her calling me. She wants me to be with her.'

'She wouldn't want you to die. She loved you. You were her father. She'd want you to live. She wouldn't want you to hurt the girls.'

Gina watched as Trevor gestured to someone who was just out of view. 'Nanny,' Gracie called as she peered out of the window next to Trevor, a worried look on the little girl's face. 'Nanny, I'm scared.'

'Please let her go,' Gina yelled as tears began to flow.

He pushed Gracie out of the way. Trevor stepped out of view for a few seconds then he came back, his bottom lip trembling. 'I don't want to live. You, all of you, you don't know how lucky you are. If you have children, go home now and tell them that you love them. Tell them that and mean it. Tell them like it's the last time you will ever see them because you never know if today will be their last.' He flicked the lighter and ignited the fuel sending flames whooshing all over his face and body.

Gina screamed out Gracie's name as the flames caught his face, then she ran towards the front door. Jacob followed close by. 'Gina, don't go in.'

She listened to officers shouting, followed by an order to leave the building. Trevor Cage had planned his end. He'd doused the room and the building in accelerant in readiness to burn it to the ground. Gracie was in there and unless Gina got her out, she'd die. Three officers burst past her and a firefighter ran towards them, helping them out. Gina called the firefighter back. 'There are two girls in there. Please help me save them.' Gina felt her breath shorten as she yelled Gracie's name over and over again. 'I'm going in.'

Water burst from the hoses as they tackled the spread. Gina ran along the smoke-filled hall, hoping it wasn't too late for her gentle granddaughter and the curious YouTuber. She went to run through the flames, screaming as she did, and a firefighter dragged her back onto the road. 'Let me go,' she yelled as she fought the man off her. 'My granddaughter is in there. I have to get her out. I am not leaving her to die.' Her sobs choked in her throat as she could only hope that they brought Gracie out alive. Her legs went and she fell to the tarmac and sobbed. Her granddaughter was dead because of her, and she knew how Trevor felt in that moment, the loss he'd suffered. It was over. Her life was over and all she wanted was to join Gracie in that burning house. She turned to see Mr Perrin crying wildly on the path, the reflection of the flames making his eyes glow orange as he stared at the horror in front of him.

'Gina,' Jacob called as he placed a hand on her arm. He pointed to Gracie being carried alongside the building by one of the officers.

'She ran out the back, guv. One of the officers found her. She's okay.'

Gina sprinted over to Gracie with all she had and grabbed her from the officer. She hugged her tightly and kissed her head. 'Are you hurt?'

'Nanny, I'm okay. I came to see you round the back and I thought you were in there. I was just talking to the man, that was all, then he told me to run away quickly, so I did. He said he was going to see his little girl, Emilia. Don't be sad, Nanny. He's going to be with her and I'm with you.'

As she hugged Gracie again, she watched as Mr Perrin screamed, knowing that it was too late for his daughter and Gina's heart went out to the man.

SIXTY

'Mum, what the hell is going on?' Hannah ran straight over and snatched Gracie out of Gina's arms. Hetty hurried over to join her.

'I...' Gina burst into tears. 'I thought...'

'How dare you get my daughter caught up in all this? How dare you?' Hannah spat before walking off with Gracie in her arms. Gina remained speechless as Hannah pushed through the crowd. Not once had Hetty mentioned that she hadn't been watching Gracie, that Gina had warned her to take Gracie and stay in. Her ex-mother-in-law had remained conveniently silent. Gina took a deep breath and acknowledged the sadness that remained. Macie had died in that building. Gina had been lucky. She ran over to the ambulance. A paramedic closed the back doors on Sasha. 'We're taking her straight to Cleevesford General.'

Brushing her tears away, Gina held a hand up. 'O'Connor?'

Her colleague left Mr Perrin and ran over. 'Yes, guv.'

'I want you to go with Sasha and keep me informed all the way. Liaise with the staff and let me know if she comes round. She's all we have. Be gentle with her and call her sister, too.'

'Will do. Are you okay? You should be with your family.'

'They don't need me, Harry.'

Gina watched on as firefighters forced everyone back even further as they tackled the spreading blaze. Gina glanced up. Her stomach dropped as she thought of Macie. Only once the firefighters had got into that room, could they confirm if Macie was there, but the whole building had been swamped with fire. There's no way a person could come out of that room unharmed. She listened as doors banged and more water pumped. Then she saw a firefighter emerge through the blaze in the room that Trevor had been in. Smoke billowed from the window as they fought with everything they had.

Jacob glanced at Gina. She watched his Adam's apple bob and his hands clench as they did the only thing they could do, which was to wait.

After what seemed like an eternity, a firefighter emerged from the main door. Gina ran over. 'Have you found Macie?'

He removed his protective hood. 'There is only one body. It belongs to the man.'

Gina exhaled. She stared up at the two smouldering buildings. Where was Macie? Had they missed her? That's when she turned around and saw the girl. A rope hanging from her wrists and a dazed look about her. Her bag crossed her body, and she clutched it tightly. Just as she was about to fall, Mr Perrin ran over and caught her. 'Macie.'

'Dad. He tied me up and left me in his car. I managed to undo the rope. What happened here?' The girl allowed him to hug her closely and she reached around his shoulder and hugged him back. Gina wiped a tiny tear from her eyes as the two were reunited.

SIXTY-ONE

MACIE

She lay in the hospital bed waiting for her father to come back. She'd begged him to go home and get her a laptop and, in his eagerness to make her happy and comfortable, he'd agreed to bring one back along with some fresh clothes.

The police had taken her statement, but DI Harte was on her way. Macie lay back on the crisp sheets and pulled the memory stick from her tangled hair, the only place she was able to hide it. The police could have it but only after she'd had time to read it first. She watched as the bald detective constable walked over to a police officer, leaving her door unattended. Where could she hide the stick? Glancing around, she saw the pack of fruity sweets her father had brought her. She slipped the stick into the bag and left it on the side table.

A nurse knocked and smiled. 'Hello, Macie. How are you feeling?' she asked.

Macie fumbled to straighten the hospital gown as she sat up a little higher. 'I'm fine now. I really want to go home. I think he just gave me a sedative or something to make me sleep. It's all out of me now,' she slurred.

'Well, we'd like to keep you a little longer, just to make sure.

We'll see what the doctor says later.' The nurse checked her blood pressure, made some notes on a chart and left.

The girl rolled her eyes. Didn't they know that she had important work to do? Her viewers were waiting for the full story. She'd been on a blackout for ages since the police had hijacked her tech and all her channels. Now, she had a real story to tell. One which she'd lived and breathed. One that had been worth all the sacrifice and danger. She'd turned down all the normal events people her age should be enjoying, and she'd lost friends over it but now, nothing mattered. Swallowing, she thought of Becky. She wished that she and Becky were still close. She also wished she had a working phone so that she could see what was going on in the world. Was everyone talking about today? They'd told her that Trevor Cage had died by suicide, but Macie already knew. He'd told her how he longed to be with his darling Emilia. Tears slipped down her cheeks. It was a sad story. She hoped they were together now.

He had kept his promise. He'd told her everything and he'd given her an exclusive. Sasha had blurted everything out, too. Yes, it had been scary but in return, she would tell the world what he went through.

'Macie, may we come in?'

DI Harte and DS Driscoll entered before she could answer. 'I guess you want to know everything.'

DI Harte sat in the chair on one side and DS Driscoll dragged a chair from the far end of the room and sat beside her. He pulled out a notepad. 'Yes. First, how are you feeling?'

She flung her head back onto the pillow. 'Everyone keeps asking me that.'

The detective tilted her head. 'We're all just concerned, that's all.'

She lifted her head back off the pillow. 'Well, I'm okay and I want to go home.'

'And I'm sure you'll be able to very soon. Can you tell us everything in your own words?'

She began by filling them in on how he'd contacted her, and she'd agreed to do what he asked in exchange for his full story. 'I'm sorry that I deceived you, but I knew I had to play along otherwise I'd never have known who he was. He'd already arranged to come to mine and meet me out the back, but it wasn't him, it was a young man who I saw later that night riding a scooter. He gave me a phone so that Trevor could contact me.'

'The one we found at the back of the school?'

She nodded. 'He said you'd find it and all that was on it. He also said it no longer mattered. After that, he blindfolded me and took me to a cellar which I now know was in his house, next door to the old nursery. I didn't know at the time as he drove me straight into his garage.' She swallowed. 'That's when he locked me in the cellar with Sasha. She told me everything.'

'What did she tell you?'

'That Trevor's daughter had died, and she could have saved her.' Macie went on to tell the detectives about the drunken night when they'd given the girl a drink. 'Sasha said she hadn't been feeling too good. Just before she left, they'd begun to play drinking games, but the girl didn't want to join in. Instead of helping her to get out of the situation, Sasha left her with her murderers. Trevor blamed Wesley Reid and Judith Morgan for killing Emilia, and Sasha for letting it happen.' Macie went on to tell them how Trevor had trained for his job to help people and that when Sasha had ended up working with him, he'd purposely befriended her to try and find out more. 'He bottled it though. Every time he had an opportunity to ask her about what happened, he didn't. He said that my haunted building video of the old nursery made him notice me. He said I reminded him of Emilia. He wanted to help me, and he thought Emilia would have wanted that too. That's why he chose me.' She stared into her lap. Yes, Trevor had scared her, but she understood him. She felt sorry for him. He was a victim in all this, too.

'Do you need a break?'

Macie shook her head. 'I got in your way at the old nursery under his instruction. Anyway, that's in the past now. Do you want to know about Caid?'

DI Harte nodded. 'Yes, please.'

'Trevor got that guy doing his donkey work and even gave him a scooter to get around on. He knew the man was selling drugs and Trevor told me that he didn't like him, but he needed his help. Caid had agreed to do anything for him as long as he made sure his sister Kayleigh got a council flat out of it. Trevor had promised that once it was all over, he'd make sure she was bumped up to the top of the list. He spoke fondly of Kayleigh, though. Said she deserved more and that he wanted to keep her safe. He said Wesley needed to die because he was also a threat to Kayleigh's daughter. Emilia had died at Wesley's hands, and he said he couldn't live with himself if anything happened to that little girl. He also paid Caid to scare Sasha and Judith. He said he wanted them to "feel the fear" just like Emilia had.' Tears began to flow down her face. However hard she tried to make them stop, she couldn't. She thought she was going to die at one point and when she was having a major panic attack in the cellar, it had been Sasha who had spoken to her in a soothing voice.

'Here.' DI Harte passed Macie a box of tissues. 'Can I get you anything?'

Macie shook her head. 'It might sound like I'm on Trevor's side. The truth is, I don't hate him or Sasha. I understand them. Sasha misread a situation when she was drunk and left a child drinking with Judith and Wesley. Yes, she was irresponsible, but she had no way of predicting what came next. Trevor, he lost his daughter, and I can't imagine how that feels. If something like that had happened to me, I know my dad would have felt the same. Even though I give him a hard time, I'm pretty sure he'd kill for me. I'm sad that Trevor is dead. Really sad.' More tears began to spill. 'Wow, my head is woozy.'

'You've been through a lot. Maybe you should get some rest and we'll speak again.'

Someone knocked at the door and then opened it. Her dad awkwardly stepped in, acknowledging the detectives as he did. He nodded to someone outside. 'It's okay to come in.'

'Who is it, Dad?'

Becky peered around the door, looking slightly sheepish. 'Hi, I bought you some brownies.'

'Becky.'

Her friend walked over and hugged her tightly. Macie had never been so glad to see anyone in her whole life. Today she would recover and tomorrow, she'd begin planning her future and it was a bright one, thanks to Trevor giving her the memory stick. She would always be grateful to him for choosing her. For now, she was going to enjoy a chocolate brownie with her friend and when everyone was gone, she was going to read what was on that stick.

SIXTY-TWO

Wednesday, 16 November

Gina and Jacob followed the intensive care nurse through to the bay where the monitor beeped and Sasha lay still, eyes stark as she stared out of the window.

'Hello, Sasha,' Gina said in a gentle voice. The woman had received emergency surgery for the stab wound. After speaking to Macie yesterday, Briggs had queried Sasha's position with the CPS. With no witnesses to the original crime and only what Macie had said while she and Sasha were being held against their will, the CPS had decided there was a lack of evidence to prosecute for child cruelty against Emilia.

Sasha didn't turn around to look at them. She remained still and blinked. 'Thank you for getting me out of that cellar,' she said, her voice almost a whisper.

Gina sat next to her and tried to get her attention. The woman's gaze met hers. 'I'm glad you're awake. It was touch and go. Have your family been to visit?'

'My sister and Dad came. They'll be back later.' She sobbed. 'You should have let me die. I deserved to die.'

'No one deserved to die, Sasha.'

'I left Emilia with them. We were so drunk. I could have protected her. I am to blame, and I will take my share of the blame. That's the least I can do. Will I be arrested?'

'No.' It didn't matter that Gina believed that a chunk of the blame lay with Sasha. Sasha had failed to take care of Emilia; she'd left the child in a high-risk situation and gone home. The child later died, and she went on with her life without even really noticing. 'Did you know back then that it was Emilia who had died at the hostel?'

Sasha sniffled and cried in pain as she wiped her nose. 'I wondered. Her name wasn't published but I saw that a child had died. Deep down, I thought it was her, but I chose not to believe it was. I blocked that night from my mind and when I saw that writing on the wall, "I will make you pay," it made me sick to the stomach. It was written in the same room that we'd all partied in, the same room that Emilia had died in.' She sobbed hard. 'I never knew that my friend and colleague had been her father. I was such a horrible person, so horrible.'

Gina passed the woman a tissue, but she threw it to the floor. She tore the cannula out of her arm and pulled the oxygen tube from under her nose, flinging it on the bed. 'Just let me die,' she yelled. 'How am I meant to live with this for the rest of my life? I could have saved her. It's all my fault.' Sasha went pale and began to cough hard.

The nurse ran back. 'You're going to have to leave.' Ushered out, Jacob and Gina headed back into the main corridor.

Shaken, Gina headed to the coffee machine and fed it a few coins. She passed the first one to Jacob and took the next one for herself. 'It's been a long week. We can't charge Trevor Cage as he's dead. Caid can't answer for his crime as Trevor murdered him. It really feels as though justice hasn't been served. We have Noel Logan on perverting the course of justice but that's it. I hate it.'

'I hate it too, guv, but Sasha is alive. You went down into that cellar, and you found her. Macie is alive, too.'

'Look on the bright side, hey.' She pressed her lips together in a forced smile.

'Did you call your daughter last night?'

'She didn't answer. She's ghosting me. I deserve it. I dumped Gracie on Mrs O when I should have been taking care of her, then I put her life in danger.'

'I wouldn't say dumped, guv. I think she wanted to look after Gracie so badly, she was glad a murder case came in, and as for what happened at the old nursery, you could never have predicted that Gracie would sneak out of Hetty's and come looking for you.'

'None of that mattered. My granddaughter ended up in the same room as a man who had rigged the building to burn. That was unforgivable. I don't think Hannah's ever going to speak to me again. I've blown it big time. I'm never going to be allowed to see Gracie again.'

Jacob smiled sympathetically. 'Never say never. Right, best get back and work through the shedload of paperwork that's piled up from this case. I hope you're buying the pizza because it's going to be a late one.'

SIXTY-THREE

MACIE

Wednesday, 23 November

Becky followed Macie up to her bedroom. She pushed the door open, grabbed a spare chair and popped it in front of her laptop.

'So, when are you going to tell me your big secret, Mace?'

'This is it.' She held the memory stick up.

'That, really? What's on it?'

Macie shrugged and smiled. 'It's not what's on it, it's what it's led to. Well, this and what happened.'

'You haven't told me much.'

'And I'm not going to tell you.'

Becky leaned back and folded her arms. 'What's the point of me being here then?'

'I need someone to celebrate with.' She popped the stick into her laptop and waited for it to open the files. She clicked on the first one and watched as a man and a woman sang happy birthday to the smiling toddler. 'This stick contains Trevor Cage's life. Every moment with his wife and daughter, then when his wife died, him and his daughter.' She omitted to mention that it also contained all the digital recordings of all that Sasha had said in the cellar, when she was alone, but she wasn't going to share those with Becky.

'Come on, I can't wait forever.'

'You know I've been in all the papers?'

'Yes.'

'A couple of days ago, I got approached by an agent.'

Becky rolled her eyes. 'Don't get fooled by a scam, Mace.'

'Not a scam. I checked her out and I checked the company out. I even emailed her back using the email on their website just to make sure and she replied. It's genuine.'

'OMG. And?' Becky rubbed her hands together.

'They only mentioned a book but when they found out about the footage, they said they wanted a series and guess what?'

'What?'

'The advance is insane. I'm going to be rich, Becky. I've made it. I sent the contract back immediately. I'm going to be famous!'

Becky screamed and hugged her friend. 'Now if you tell me we're not going out to celebrate, we definitely can't be friends. I mean it this time. I won't forgive you, Macie Perrin.'

'We are so going out.'

Macie smiled. Everything had fallen into place, just as Trevor had promised when he asked for her help. She glanced at the memory stick. She'd only removed one file and she felt it was the right thing to do. In Sasha's state of delirium, she'd cried like a deranged baby as she confessed all. At the end, she'd paused and a while later she'd started talking again. Sasha had admitted to buying the two bottles of vodka from the all-night garage while walking back to Wesley's room. Doing shots had been her idea. And she had poured out the first shot for Emilia, then another while urging her to drink it, then she left that poor child with Wesley and Judith. It was a small detail but oh-so relevant. The public would hate her for pressuring a child to drink to her death.

She'd thought about passing the confession to the police and using it for her story, but she saw a good side to Sasha in that cellar. When that cellar door had closed, Macie had never been so overwhelmed. She couldn't breathe and her throat had closed. For a moment, she thought she might die. It had been Sasha who spoke to her soothingly, Sasha who had cared and, despite what the woman had done, Sasha had to live with that knowledge forever and ultimately, she would pay the price until the day she died. She'd always wonder if Macie would tell but Macie had a plan. It wasn't all for the love of Sasha. If Sasha made any objections to her writing her book or making her series, that file would be leverage. However she felt about Sasha, she would use the file to get her own way. Trevor was dead, James Caid was dead. The story was ripe for telling now.

She smiled. The power was hers and it felt good to be powerful. Her new life was about to begin. Was she going to go back to school? No, never. She had toyed with the idea, but she was done with being told what to do by anyone. She was Macie Perrin, and she was moving up to the next level. Hello future!

EPILOGUE

Wednesday, 23 November

Gina sipped the cup of tea that Sasha had made her. There was no need to tell her that Frederick Bertram had been charged with possession for the drugs they found, or that he lost his job. There was no need to tell her that Lydia Gill had dumped Noel Logan after finding out that he'd been cheating on her and that he'd also been charged with perverting the course of justice. She wondered if Sasha knew that Gareth Alderman had been allocated a studio flat and that the mental health team were helping him. What Sasha did need to know was that Macie had a book and TV deal and at some point in the future, everyone would know everything, and they'd probably come for Sasha's side of the story.

Sasha stared blankly into her tea as she sat on the settee, her dressing gown pulled over her warm clothes as she digested that bit of information.

'I guess the whole world is going to know about what

happened?'

Gina nodded. 'Are you okay?'

The woman looked like she wanted to say something, but she cleared her throat and popped her drink on the coffee table instead. 'I guess. I'm in agony from the stab wound, I quit my job, I don't have next month's rent, the press is probably going to start hounding me soon, but I've gone past caring. I'm moving in with my dad for a bit, while I recover and work out what happens next for me.' Tears drizzled down Sasha's cheeks and she hiccupped a cry.

'Sasha, things just take time. It's good that your dad will be looking after you. He seemed lovely when I spoke to him.' Gina knew that her recovery would be tough.

'I'll always blame myself. That is the price I'm going to pay for the rest of my life. I could have done more for Emilia, and this would never have happened.' She stood. 'Right, I best pack a few things. My dad is expecting me. Is there anything else?'

Gina knew when she was being ushered out. 'No. Well, take care and if you need me, you have my number or you can call the station.'

Sasha nodded and stared at her feet. As she let Gina out, a man appeared at the door.

'Hello, neighbour,' Sasha said as she wiped her tears away.

'Hi, I popped up to see how you were a few days ago, your sister said she'd come to get some clothes for you because you were in hospital. Sorry, I don't know your name.' He passed her a box of chocolates. 'I thought these would help.'

As Gina left them to it, she hurried towards her car. A few flakes of snow came down. She got in and removed her thick gloves just as her phone rang. She trembled as she accepted Hannah's call. Before she had a chance to say hello, Hannah spoke.

'Mum, I want you to stop calling me and no more messages or I will report you for harassment.'

'I am so sorry, Hannah.' Tears began to slide down Gina's cheeks.

'You're always sorry. No more. I trusted you to look after Gracie and you did anything but. I will never trust you again. You put my child's life in danger, and that's unforgivable.'

'I told Hetty to take her to her bungalow and stay in. She let her go in the garden and didn't watch her. All she had to do was keep Gracie in for a short while.'

'Hetty said you'd try to blame her and what a surprise. She's done more for me and Gracie than you ever have, and you try to tell me it's her fault!' Hannah paused and Gina went to speak but a choking sob came out instead. 'Don't contact me again.' Hannah ended the call.

The drive home seemed long as she sobbed her heart out but as she pulled up on her drive, Briggs was waiting. Great, now he would see her mascara-streaked face and red eyes. He held up a takeaway and a bottle of wine. She stepped out of her car, tears streaming down her face, and she hugged him so close, she knew she was quite possibly hurting him but he didn't push her away. With his spare hand he reached up and stroked her hair as he pulled her head into his chest. There weren't many people she could talk to but Briggs was one of them. She couldn't lose him, not now, not ever.

'Gina what's happened?'

She had no words, she couldn't speak. Her heart ached for what she'd lost. Things were bad when she thought she'd lost Briggs but losing her daughter and granddaughter felt like her heart had been squeezed to death.

'Come on, let's get you inside.'

She had no idea what the future held but she knew right now, she wanted to be with Chris Briggs. There was no one else and she had no one else. Secrets create loneliness and she knew that was something she and Briggs had in common. All they really had was each other.

A LETTER FROM CARLA

Dear Reader,

I'd like to thank you massively for reading *Their Cold Hearts*.

If you enjoyed *Their Cold Hearts* and would like to keep up-to-date with all my latest releases, just sign up at the following link. Your email address will never be shared and you can unsubscribe at any time.

www.bookouture.com/carla-kovach

The hostel setting in this book is close to my heart. At eighteen, I spent almost twelve weeks living in one of these buildings and it was a scary time. Not scary because of the people, but scary because of the uncertainty of what could happen to me. Uncertainty of how I'd dig myself out of the hole I was in, and the prejudices I faced for being in a hostel. I was also worried about the other residents, but I didn't need to be. Yes, there were problems and some of those issues were with people, but the support outweighed those. There is always going to be conflict when so many people are living in close proximity to each other.

Most people I met there were lovely. There were Kayleighs, Gareths and Wesleys in abundance. There were families who'd had their homes repossessed, people with mental health and addiction issues, and young people who had just come out of the care system. It showed me that anyone can have a bad run in life and end up in that situation. I formed a bond with some of those people and they were the most beautiful souls. We helped each other through it. It was the only way to survive. They became my family for the duration.

I met a couple of them a few years later and it warmed my heart to see that their lives had improved. The girl who left care was training to be a social worker. The man with the two little girls had found another job and somewhere to live. They were happy. People need a chance in life and I think chances should always be available.

It upsets me to think that so many people live on the streets or are facing homelessness. If I could wave a magic wand, everyone would have somewhere safe and warm to live, but sadly I can't.

Whether you are a reader, tweeter, blogger, Facebooker, TikTok user or reviewer, I really am grateful of all that you do and as a writer, this is where I hope you'll leave me a review or say a few words about my book.

Again, thank you so much. I'm active on social media so please feel free to contact me on Twitter, Instagram or through my Facebook page.

Thank you, Carla Kovach

facebook.com/CarlaKovachAuthor

twitter.com/CKovachAuthor

instagram.com/carla_kovach

ACKNOWLEDGEMENTS

I'd like to say a massive thank you to everyone who has helped me to bring *Their Cold Hearts* to life. Writing a book takes a team. It needs editors, cover designers, people working in every aspect of publishing from admin to management. Team Bookouture are fabulous.

My editor, Helen Jenner, is absolutely amazing and I couldn't do all this without her. Her edits are second to none and I love working with her.

Huge thanks to Lisa Brewster for the cover design. I love it.

The Bookouture publicity team are fantastic. Noelle Holten, Kim Nash, Jess Readett and Sarah Hardy make publication days special. A big, fat thank you to all of them.

To all the bloggers and reviewers, you're so generous with your time and I'm always grateful that you chose to read my book.

Many thanks to the Fiction Café Book Club. They're hugely supportive of authors. I'm also grateful to be a member of the supportive Bookouture author family. Thank you to all of the other authors.

Beta readers, Derek Coleman, Su Biela, Brooke Venables, Anna Wallace and Vanessa Morgan, are all brilliant and I'm grateful that they read my early draft. Special gratitude to Brooke Venables who writes under the name Jamie-Lee Brooke, Julia Sutton and Phil Price, who are all authors. Our support group keeps me happy and motivated.

I'd like to say a super thanks to Stuart Gibbon of Gib

Consultancy for answering my policing questions and without his knowledge I'd most definitely be making a mess of things. Any inaccuracies are definitely my own.

Lastly, I'm grateful to my husband, Nigel Buckley, for all those lovely cups of coffee and all those words of encouragement. Thank you.

Printed in Great Britain
by Amazon